NIGHTINGALE & CO

Nightingale & Co is first published in English in the United Kingdom in 2025 by Corylus Books Ltd, and was originally published in German as *Die rätselhafte Klientin (Nachtigall & Co.)* in 2023 by dtv Verlag

Corylus Books Ltd
corylusbooks.com

ISBN: 978-1-7392989-8-2

Nightingale & Co

Charlotte Printz

Translated by Marina Sofia

Published by Corylus Books Ltd

1

'You're *where*? Brandenburg Gate?' Carla could barely get in a word for the torrent gushing from the other end of the line. 'You're on the film set again? You've got what? A rifle! Impossible!' She refrained from flinging the receiver into its cradle. She checked her diary and the clock on the wall above her desk. Could she rescue Lulu from all this palaver and still get back in time to meet her new client? Not likely.

'Please!' Her aunt sounded unusually scared and pathetic. 'You have to convince them, or else they'll cart me off to the police station!'

Lulu was a good actress.

'I beg you...' she whispered. There were indeed harsh masculine voices in the background and even a police siren.

'I'll come as quick as I can,' Carla promised. Of all the adventurous exploits that her aunt Lulu had been up to since the death of Carla's father, this sounded like the craziest one by a long margin.

Should she take the S-Bahn or a taxi? Carla hesitated as she grabbed her lace summer gloves, a final present from her father. It would work out just fine, she told herself with a smile, that had always been Father's motto. She missed him, not just because of the presents, which he always seemed to pull out of a hat. Her mother used to call him 'the Raisin Bomber of Charlottenburg', in a slightly jaded tone. But since his fatal car crash, there were no more raisins to be had – they had to watch every pfennig. Better take the S-Bahn then!

Carla checked to see if she had sufficient coins in her handbag, locked the door of the Nightingale Agency, ran up to the second floor and called out to her mother, 'I'll be right back!' then rushed back downstairs.

As she made her way down Grolmanstraße through the summer heat towards Savigny Station, she congratulated herself for having had the foresight to wear her sensible shoes as well as the new faux-Chanel bouclé suit. It would almost certainly be a great help to look older and more earnest, if her crazy aunt had really got into trouble with the police.

Carla was breathless by the time she got onto the platform, but her reward was that the train drew in just then. Three rattling carriages with an oily smell.

The deadly combination of sweat, smoke and eau de cologne hit her like a wall once she was inside the carriage. She tried to take only shallow breaths, but everything started swimming out of focus. She grabbed a strap just before the train set off.

She'd started having these dizzy spells since last year, right after the accident which killed her father but which she'd survived. Carla hated this fuzzy loss of focus, although the doctors kept saying there was no need to worry, that she was lucky she'd overcome her head injury so well. She considered herself anything but lucky.

She clung fast to her strap, until the dizziness subsided a little. Then she squeezed past a couple of men who didn't even look up from their newspapers, muttering her apologies as she sat down.

She closed her eyes in relief for a moment and touched the die on her lucky charm to collect herself. Not a good idea, it just made her feel worse. Better do some spotting, like in dancing. She opened her eyes to stare out of the window, but it was moving too fast.

Her eyes fell on the newspaper opposite, magnetically attracted to the large picture of Kennedy. Her heartbeat quickened, not because of JFK himself, but because he reminded her of Richard. Kennedy could have been his brother, they both had that tall, rangy look, a fine head of hair, as well as that unusual, electrifying glow. The slightest side glance from Richard turned her insides to liquid syrup. She dreamt of embracing him and breathing him in. After four semesters she'd finally worked up the courage to approach him. He'd looked at her and she'd gone up to him... but was then unable to do anything except stand there, not saying a single word. Carla looked down at her lace gloves. She should've dropped one of the gloves, he'd have picked it up and then... What would it have felt like, to ruffle his elegant quiff? Her fingertips started to tingle. His hair must be so silky, with a strong smell of brilliantine, moss and freshly-cut wood.

She sighed. She'd been studying law, but after Father's death, she and her mother were left without a pfennig, so she had to take on the Nightingale & Co. Agency to earn some money for the two of them.

She tried not to think of all that and focused instead on the headline below the Kennedy picture in the *Berliner Morgenpost*. It had to do with the press conference the other day, on the 10th of August, where he'd spoken about the Berlin problem. Kennedy was quoted word for word: 'There has been a tremendous passage from East to West which, of course, I know is a matter of concern to the Communists.' Surely every single person living in Berlin knew that. Carla squinted a little to see the next sentence: '...because this tremendous speed-up of people leaving the Communist system to come to the West and freedom, of course, is rather illuminating evidence of the comparative values of the free life in an open society, and those in a closed society under a Communist system.'

Why on earth was Kennedy using all those indirect

allusions, instead of simply stating that the Allies would do their best to preserve freedom in the West?

Father thought JFK was nothing more than an idle talker. 'A politician who won't wear a hat so as not to damage his quiff has no respect for anyone,' was his opinion after a couple of glasses of Berliner Luft peppermint liqueur. Father must be turning in his grave knowing that the hatless Kennedy had been sworn in as the American President in January.

The S-Bahn stopped with a squeal of wheels. The doors opened, letting in more of the sticky-hot summer air, but at least the seat opposite was now free. Three more stops and then she'd have to change at Friedrichstraße. Heavens, the timing was tight! What on earth was Lulu thinking, carrying an air rifle close to the border with the Eastern sector?

A small, plump woman with a hat decorated with oversized flowers sat down opposite her. She took out a roll of sour gumdrops and popped one in her mouth. Carla couldn't look away: the woman and the hat reminded her of her aunt.

The woman noticed Carla staring at her and offered her a gumdrop with a twinkle in her eyes. That was exactly what Lulu would have done, although she might have embellished things with a dramatic 'I always have some on me for any kissing scenes in the film. Did you know that Walter Giller is the best kisser of them all?'

Carla shook her head. 'Thanks anyway,' she said and smiled in as friendly a manner as she could. It really wasn't nice to stare at somebody and then turn down their sweets. This was all because of the film *Emil and the Detectives* – after seeing that, she had nightmares and never accepted anything from strangers ever again.

'Please yourself!' the woman shrugged indifferently, put away her gums and took out a *Constanze* magazine from her enormous handbag. She took off her gloves, licked two fingers and started leafing through the magazine, as if she were at home on the sofa. Carla observed her greedily devouring a richly illustrated article about Farah Diba and the Shah of Persia. That was exactly the kind of thing Mother would read too – she adored royal beauties.

Oh no! She blushed as she realised she'd forgotten to buy Mother's favourite magazine. Naturally, her mother had not uttered a single word about this omission, and she never would. She was so proud of the fact that she never complained. She preferred to suffer in silence.

When Carla finally arrived at the Brandenburg Gate, she could already hear the screech of the autograph hunters long before she even set eyes on them. 'Horst, Horst, Horst!' Great, so the film set must be close by. She walked hurriedly towards the barriers designed to keep the fans away from the actual filming.

Scores of young women were waiting with their autograph books for the stars of the film *One, Two, Three*. Carla could understand all too well why Lulu was so keen to get a part in this Billy Wilder comedy. The main stars were James Cagney, Liselotte Pulver and of course the one whom all the girls had come to see: Horst Buchholz.

It broke Lulu's heart when, after two casting calls, they opted instead for the Austrian actress Rose Renee Roth, who in one fell swoop became Lulu's arch-nemesis. Since shooting started, Lulu kept hanging around the film set, hoping against all hope to secure a role.

But what on earth was she planning to do with the air rifle? Shoot her arch-rival? Could you even kill someone with that? Probably not. Then what? Shoot the hat off a border guard to get her name in the papers? Yes, that sounded more like her.

Just behind the film set there was the crossing to the Soviet zone, which was teeming with even more border guards than usual. Ulbricht must have been worried that comrades might be tempted to flee to the West – after all, the film was about one of the most seductive drugs of American capitalism: Coca Cola.

As Carla approached the set, she noticed lots of shrivelled balloons lying on the street, which reminded her of a complicated but well-remunerated case she'd solved with her father. They had to secure used condoms for evidence. They'd been able to solve the case, but the memory of it made her hair stand on end. She shook her head to get rid of the unwelcome images and tried to search for Lulu instead.

She was good at observing details, on the streets, inside buildings, she could recall everything in great detail even hours later. More than that, she could even picture things she'd not actually seen in a particular place but that should have been there, or things that had happened there. Carla found this somewhat disconcerting, but her father was far more pragmatic about it and explained it was the collective unconscious. It was neither strange nor magical, it was simply a useful skill and he encouraged her to develop it further, particularly when he noticed that it helped them move an investigation forward.

No sign of either Lulu or any policemen anywhere. She'd have been easy to spot with her extravagant hat in this sea of young autograph seekers in their capris or petticoats. There were guards in uniform every fifty metres. The artistes' entrance had no less than three guards in front of it.

You couldn't make out much beyond the barriers, other than the Brandenburg Gate. Some tracks had been laid and a mounted camera was being pushed backward and forward slowly by two young men, until someone with a megaphone yelled 'Cut!' which made the camera trolley and a few extras come to a standstill.

Not a trace of Lulu. As she turned to check in the other direction, a wonderful aroma of freshly brewed coffee wafted towards her. She could do with a coffee now, but she couldn't figure out where the smell was coming from, nor where Lulu could possibly be. Had she somehow strayed beyond the barriers? She'd said on the phone that the police had arrested her, but there was no sign of police anywhere, just the private security on set and the border guards at the Brandenburg Gate, who looked grey and frozen like tin soldiers.

'Horst! There he is, Horst!' cried one of the autograph hunters, pointing somewhere beyond the barriers, running towards it and trying to climb over. The others followed, shrieking. Carla shielded her eyes with her hand and watched them.

Indeed, it was Horst Buchholz heading towards one of two stalls, which Carla had not hitherto spotted. Liselotte Pulver was standing in front of one of them, taking a cup from a woman in a white apron. There was a snack stall right next to the coffee stall, and she became aware of the appetising aroma of grilled sausages and chips. Carla's stomach started to rumble. Her cheese sandwich was still at the office, and she wouldn't have much time to eat when she got back.

Where was this aunt of hers?

She claimed she'd be carted away by the police if Carla didn't come to back her up in the great fib she'd told them. But there were no police around. Or did she mean the border guards? That would make sense, because surely it was a grave error to wander so close to the border with an air rifle. What if Lulu had been taken to Hohenschönhausen Prison, because she'd been rude to them?

Goodness, the smell of those sausages! She couldn't help but look at the food stalls, where Liselotte Pulver was being escorted by a man. She was nodding and laughing her famous big laugh, which reminded Carla of the time she'd queued for hours to get tickets for Father for the premiere of *A Glass of Water* at Zoo Palace Cinema. But then the accident happened and when she found the tickets months later in her drawer, she burst into tears. They'd never do anything together again. Instead, she had to look after Mother and grab hold of his crazy sister as soon as possible and head back home. She couldn't risk having the new client turn up to find the door locked. After all, there were many rival detective agencies in Berlin.

Carla walked up to one of the guards standing at the cordoned-off entrance to the film set. She was confident that, dressed as she was in her sober little suit, she did not resemble any of the autograph hunters.

'Excuse me, have you seen any police officers around here?' she asked. He shook his head and pointed at one of his colleagues who was standing closer to the Brandenburg Gate. She went up to him and asked again.

'Whaddaya want with them?' This guard was obviously bored and looked forward to a bit of disruption to his routine. He tapped his burly chest, grinning; his chest looked particularly fine in the dark blue uniform. 'Ain't I ace enough for ya?'

'No, no, none as ace as you!' Carla wasn't even lying, for the man was very attractive, his eyes full of mischief. 'But they've got something you don't have!'

'Impossible!' He scrutinised her more closely and raised an approving eyebrow.

'Yes, they pulled in my grandma,' she said. Most people loved their grandmothers; aunts were decidedly less popular.

'A wee little thing, covered in jewels and armed to the teeth with a hat and a gun?'

Carla nodded, stunned.

'Nah, sorry!' The guard laughed out loud. He must be teasing her. How else would he have known to mention the hat and, above all, the gun?

'I'll be in trouble if I don't bring Grandma back soon...' Carla wished she could squeeze out a few tears, but the only actress in the family was Lulu. Maybe she'd be more successful with a little tip.

'All right then, don't wanna spoil your day. It's all good.'
He pointed towards the food stall. 'They took...' he
hesitated a moment, '*Grandma* over there and are now
having a fine ole time.'

Carla looked where he was pointing, but all she could see
was Horst Buchholz raising his bottle of beer with James
Cagney.

'Behind the food stall are the cheap seats for the crew,'
he explained.

'And how do I get in there?'

'Got a smoke by any chance?'

Of course she had. First rule of detecting: always have
some cigarettes on you. Carla opened her bag and took out
a pack of Lucky Strikes.

'It's all yours!'

'Look at that, will ya!' He pocketed the cigarettes, waved
and called to his colleague, 'Off for a quick break.'

Then he pushed the barriers to one side and politely
gestured to Carla that she should go through. She was
pleased that she'd be spared the death stares of all the
female autograph hunters.

The closer she got to the film set, the more alluring the
smell of coffee and fries. There were people bustling
around between the cardboard backdrops, tables full of
tools and clothes trolleys. On their left, a workman was
connecting a sidecar to a black motorbike bespattered with
mud. The guard sighed.

'Would love to have one of those!'

'A dirty motorbike?'

'Nah, got one already. I meant the sidecar, so I could
cruise through Berlin with pretty girls and their
grandmas!' He looked at her admiringly. Was he always so
ready to turn on the charm?

A couple of steps further, two women were blowing up
balloons with a hand-held pump. When the balloons
reached their full size, Carla saw what was written on them

and had to laugh. The first lot said *Russki go home,* the other *Ami go home.*

'Be swell if they both got the hell outta Berlin!' the guard commented with a broad grin. They ducked behind a plywood model of a tall building and finally reached the back of the food stall.

And there she was! Carla was struck dumb at the scene unfolding before her eyes.

Aunt Lulu was sitting at a table, giggling with two uniformed policemen. One of them must have told an incredibly funny joke, because they were all bent over with laughter. One of the men was smacking the table with his hand as he laughed, making the now-empty currywurst containers jump, while the gun leaning on the table right next to Lulu rattled.

Carla didn't know whether to laugh or to cry. Aunt Lulu had once again managed to rescue herself.

It was late. Too late, she could tell without even looking at her watch. She'd have to get a taxi to be back in time. And even so, she'd need to have the traffic lights all going her way.

Before Carla could say anything to Lulu, the guard stepped forward and picked up the pellet gun. The two policemen instantly snapped to attention and Lulu's eyes bulged when she finally noticed Carla.

'Careful!' said one of the policemen, the table-thumper.

'Just a pre-war Diana 25,' said the guard, holding the gun in shooting position and pointing it skywards, 'I know it. A harmless toy.'

'Depends,' said the other policeman, getting up and standing to attention. 'If one of these things hits you...'

Straight in your heart would be nice, thought Carla, looking daggers at her aunt, who was making gestures of appeasement.

'Child! How nice to see you here *at last!*'

Carla took a deep breath and started counting backwards

from 777, so as not to lose her composure. Seven was her lucky number and she really could do with some luck right now.

'Just imagine,' continued Lulu unabashedly, 'While I was waiting for you – for so long – I managed to sort things out with these nice gentlemen. Sit down, my child, and Trudi will make you a nice portion of fries.'

What was she on about and who on earth was Trudi? Aunt Lulu always assumed people knew whom she was talking about. Lilo, Billy, and now this Trudi person.

'I don't have time for that, unfortunately,' said Carla, trying to ignore the rumbling in her stomach. 'As I told you on the phone, I have an appointment.'

'But, child, your father would hate to see you all skin and bones! And Trudi...'

'So that's poor, poor Grandma?' said the guard, shaking his head.

'I see you've got it all in hand!' said Carla, turning round and rushing towards the barriers. That was it, done, over!

'Wait a minute!' called Lulu after her, 'I can explain.'

But I don't want to hear it, thought Carla, speeding up. She bumped into something soft. A man had suddenly appeared out of nowhere and they collided. His peaked cap flew through the air and landed on the floor.

'Watch out, will you?' she said.

Then she looked up. Oh, no, it couldn't be... it was Billy Wilder. Lulu had shown her hundreds of pictures of him and of his films. His glasses hung lopsided, and it was all her fault.

'I'm so sorry,' she said and wished she were four metres behind the Brandenburg Gate. She bent to pick up the cap, desperately wracking her brains for more English vocabulary, but drawing an absolute blank. 'So, so sorry,' she said as she handed him the cap.

'Isn't the saying "More haste, less speed"?' he said in German with a slightly rattling voice. He took the cap, slapped it against his thighs a couple of times and put it back on his head.

Of course, he was from Vienna and Berlin. 'You're right. I should have looked where I was going.'

'According to Lubitsch, whom I admire greatly, even the most dignified person makes a fool of himself at least twice a day,' the Hollywood director continued, adjusting his glasses back and forth until he was satisfied. 'This was merely the first time today!'

'Please accept my apologies.'

Billy Wilder winked at her. 'Take it easy, you know that nobody's perfect!' Then he headed off to the coffee stall.

A heavy hand grabbed Carla's shoulder. She was ready for anything by now. Getting arrested, thrown out, sued. She superstitiously touched the lucky die on her necklace.

'I'll take you out this way, there's a taxi stand here.'

To her relief, it was the guard who'd helped her before. 'Seems like you're in a hurry.'

'Thank you, that's kind of you.'

He handed her the rifle. 'I confiscated that, just in case.'

Carla stared at the rifle, then at the guard and then, over his shoulder, at Billy Wilder helping himself to a coffee. Had she really just experienced all of that? Now she'd have to rush through the city with a gun to complement her fake Chanel suit. She'd almost certainly be too late for the meeting even if she shot her way through the crowds.

The guard must have realised that she was about to keel over, because he smiled encouragingly.

'By the way, my name's Bruno,' he said as he shyly handed her a note, 'Here's the phone number from the place where I sub-let. Just in case you feel like havin' a coffee some time.'

'A taxi to start with, perhaps?' said Carla, stuffing the note in her handbag.

'No taxi required,' said Aunt Lulu, all out of breath. She still had the two policemen in her wake.

That was all she needed! How had her aunt moved so fast, when she hated any form of sport other than dancing? At least she hadn't witnessed the collision with Billy Wilder, otherwise she'd have tried to make a lifelong friend of the film director.

Lulu dramatically handed Carla a portion of chips, as if she were presenting her with the Oscar for best film rather than a greasy paper bag. 'For you!' she said.

'I've got my hands full.' Carla waved her handbag and the rifle. 'Besides, I don't have the time.'

'I've solved the problem. These charming gentlemen will drive us to Charlottenburg. I've explained to them how important it is for you to get to your meeting with the mayor's spokesman in time.'

All three men looked respectfully at Carla. She tried to keep an earnest face and cleared her throat. What had Lulu just invented?

'Thank you,' she said at last, unable to bear Bruno's amazed glance. 'This shows a great spirit of citizenship on your part, I'm sure the mayor will appreciate it.' No need to be too honest, she was sure there would be no police escort for a meeting with her actual client.

Soon after, Carla was sitting next to Lulu on the back seat of the black police Volkswagen Beetle, eating her chips to the accompaniment of the howling siren.

'Can you please explain what you were doing with an air rifle on set?' Carla whispered, looking anxiously at the two policemen. 'And what about the call? There was no one arresting you, obviously!'

Aunt Lulu handed her an embroidered handkerchief. 'You're going to get your suit dirty. Not much of a loss, though, this horrible colour would insult even blind people. I wouldn't use it even as a coat for my little Fritzi to go walkies.'

Carla bit her tongue and instead took the last three chips out of the newspaper. She could read the titles clearly through the grease, and now she understood where Lulu had got her idea about the mayor's spokesperson.

Adenauer warns that Willy Brandt is sowing panic. It bodes ill for peace if the Mayor of Berlin claims that its inhabitants are afraid that the Iron Curtain will be cemented there.

Carla crumpled up the newspaper, leaned back against the seat and closed her eyes. Her aunt's soft hand squeezed hers. 'Well, child, we got out of that alive. Tomorrow I'll pay my debt by taking you out to lunch at Café Kranzler and tell you all about it. My treat, of course.'

As always, Carla was unable to say no to that.

2

Just five minutes left!

Carla managed to freshen herself up in haste in the toilet, then flung open all the windows and prepared a fresh folder for her new client. She didn't write the name on it, simply the number 120861/A. That was the filing system for the Nightingale Agency, date and the client order for the day. Her father had impressed upon her that it was important to store the client files by number rather than names, to keep them fully confidential.

Three years ago, a furious husband had tried to steal compromising pictures of himself and his mistress from the agency. He couldn't find the file – which was a good thing. The bad thing was that he'd been so angry that he destroyed the entire agency décor. Mother had been horrified: what if the man had come upstairs to their living quarters? Father promised to install new, vastly better locks, but he never got around to it, and her mother of course didn't complain about it, because the Raisin Bomber of Charlottenburg had more important things to do.

Carla shook the flowery cushion on the rattan chair positioned in front of her desk. She'd not made any improvements since the death of her father, it would have felt like an insult to him. Besides, she loved his black swivel chair. She knew how much he'd saved to acquire this leather monster that was his pride and joy. In the long term, however, she had to admit that she might have to exchange it for something more suitable, it was far too big for her, and she looked like a child pretending to be the boss in it.

Maybe the clients would appreciate the ficus plant by the window or the atmospheric paintings on the wall, which were perfect for filling awkward silences. Sunrise at Wannsee, a copperplate engraving of Charlottenburg Palace or Aunt Lulu as a witch. She very nearly laughed, but then her eyes rested on the two bell-shaped bottles on the sideboard. Father's was half-full with rather dusty pfennig coins, while hers was nearly full. Her father told their clients that he was collecting coins for Carla's wedding shoes. It was his less-than-subtle way of letting her know that he'd have liked to see her settling down. But she'd seen enough marital strife on the job, so she pretended not to hear him.

The truth was, those pfennigs were the result of a bet between the two of them.

Father had got the idea when he installed a phone in Grolmanstraße. Clients started to call beforehand to arrange an appointment. He decided it was a good opportunity to develop their Sherlock Holmes skills, so he added a loudspeaker to the system, so that Carla could listen in. They both tried to guess things about the person purely from the sound of their voice. Could they draw any conclusions about their looks, their education, job or hobbies?

Whenever one of them was right about something, a pfennig would be added to the bottle. At first Father easily outclassed her, but by the time of the accident her bottle was starting to overtake his, even though she was spending less time in the agency because of her studies.

Ingrid Niemöller, the client she was seeing today, had sounded a little out of breath; perhaps she was slightly overweight or not very active. Asthma or simply overexcited? Or she might have been speaking so quickly because she was afraid that she'd change her mind. However, she'd not had any awkward pauses or fillers such as 'erm-hum'. She obviously knew what she wanted and was probably used to speaking to strangers. Carla hadn't been able to detect a single filler word: those pesky 'actually', 'so to speak', 'really', 'quite', and not even any 'would', 'could', 'should'. It was all 'I want', 'I need'. Perhaps Frau Niemöller worked in retail or was an executive assistant?

Three minutes left.

Enough fresh air. Carla was in such a rush to close the window, that she nearly missed Katrin waving at her from the house opposite. She waved back and signalled a W with the thumb and index finger on both hands. This meant that Carla had to work. A Y meant that yes, Katrin could come over. The two letters could be easily spotted from across the street, and Katrin loved all those codes. She'd instantly learnt the full finger alphabet. Half a year ago, Carla had rescued Katrin's beloved toy tortoise from the clutches of Fritzi, Aunt Lulu's black poodle, and ever since then the little girl had wanted to become Miss Sherlock Holmes. She abandoned her dolls, because they didn't fit in with her career plans. Carla was sure she'd succeed; she was not only a bright girl but, at just ten years old, she already had more oomph than Carla. A natural talent.

Carla turned away from the window and quickly brewed a coffee in the tiny kitchenette. The smell of fresh coffee was always good for relaxing, especially with tense women clients. Many appreciated having a cup to hold on to. It was funny that women seemed to find admitting having a problem harder than having one in the first place. Conversely, men preferred to speak about their problems very quickly, get it out of the way at once.

The phone rang. She hoped it wasn't Frau Niemöller changing her mind, which often happened in divorce cases. The man came home with a bouquet and the world seemed a better place. If Carla had known that, she wouldn't have been in such a rush. She picked up the receiver and was relieved to hear that it was Alma Hochbrück, not the new client.

They knew each other from the charity work they did for the Berlin Fledglings Orphanage. This time, however, Alma sounded very sniffly and was whispering, as if she was afraid someone might overhear her. Maybe she'd been crying. Alma asked if she could come to the agency the following day, although it was a Sunday, because it was the only day she could make it and it was extremely important. She wanted Carla to reassure her that anything they discussed would be 100% confidential. Carla promised her that confidentiality was of utmost importance in her agency. She liked Alma a lot and was rather sad that she'd have to interrupt her call because of Frau Niemöller's arrival.

'Of course,' Carla said warmly, 'You can come whenever you want, I'll be delighted to help.' She hung up and wrote down the appointment for tomorrow at 17:00. Despite Alma's unhappiness, she couldn't help feeling relieved to have another client, because she was down to her last reserves, just enough to keep them going for another couple of weeks. August was always a quiet month.

Why did Alma want to see her? The Hochbrücks always struck her as a perfectly happy couple. Both good-looking and intelligent, and he had a good sense of humour. Did the professor have a mistress? Or maybe he visited prostitutes and had brought back some disease? This sort of thing seemed to happen more frequently than one might expect.

The doorbell roused her from her reverie. It was exactly 16:00! A huge point in Frau Niemöller's favour. She liked punctual clients.

Carla reached out her hand to greet the client and had to look up to catch the eye of the tall, slender woman in front of her. No pfennig for appearances then! As self-assured as a model, Frau Niemöller strode forward into Carla's office in a black-and-white suit in the Chanel style. She was clearly used to being listened to carefully. The client took possession of the rattan chair, pushed the cushion away with a mocking smile, straightened her skirt and sat down. She looked around for something on Carla's desk.

Ashtray, Carla realised, and brought out the orange-brown Murano monstrosity out of the middle drawer. She'd always hated it, because it reminded her of that terrible day with her mother, but of course she couldn't tell her father that. *I'll replace it next week with a modern steel ashtray with a lid*, she told herself.

The client bent to take her cigarettes out of her handbag, and a haze of Shalimar spread through the room, a mix of vanilla, citrus and roses that Carla really liked. The perfume gave an unexpected edge to the classic suit and underlined the more feminine aspects of her attire. Carla noticed the double pearl necklace and the silk blouse. Could the suit be a genuine Chanel?

'Clothes are the windows into a human soul' was Father's mantra. For some, those windows were opened wide and you could look straight in, while others used clothes to shut themselves off. Frau Niemöller's suit looked custom-made, but the black-and-white bouclé did not really suit her. Carla suppressed a smile, because it struck her that the woman opposite her was also trying to appear more serious and older than she was. Her skin was smooth and even, she must be at the most in her late twenties. She had the same hairstyle as Carla, her dark hair tied back into a perfect low chignon.

What could have brought this woman here? She didn't seem distraught enough for a divorce or a cheating spouse. Besides, Carla couldn't spot any wedding ring, merely a plastic ring of white and pink flowers – the kind that Katrin had made recently at a children's birthday party. The ring didn't match the rest of her appearance. Was Frau Niemöller a businesswoman or a lawyer? Was it a case of industrial espionage?

Carla offered her coffee and asked how she could help. Frau Niemöller declined, then lit her cigarette with a gold lighter and breathed in deeply. Marlboro – not exactly a woman's cigarette.

'Do you work alone?' asked Frau Niemöller instead of answering, and inhaled deeply once more.

'I have excellent associates whom I can call upon as and when required. But if you wish for utter discretion, I can of course handle everything personally. What is this about?'

'I'm looking for a man,' said Frau Niemöller earnestly.

'I see.' Carla was curious where this was leading.

'But first I'd like to know how much this is going to cost me.'

'Hard for me to say, without knowing any details. Our daily rate...' Carla hesitated. She still found it difficult to talk about money, but then again, Shalimar was expensive, and the suit was probably Chanel.

'Our daily rate is 40 marks, plus expenses,' she continued, 'We have a three-day minimum booking, which needs to be paid in advance.'

Frau Niemöller nodded. 'That's fine.' She took a deep breath and stubbed out the half-smoked cigarette. Carla knew at once she should've asked for more.

'It happened at the German–American Folk Fair...'

Oh no, not another such story! Carla did her best to conceal her disappointment. A GI had got her pregnant? They had had to search for so many missing fathers, and the US Army was not very helpful, despite the contacts Father had cultivated.

But the German–American Folk Fair? That had taken place this year for the first time. She knew that because Aunt Lulu had been determined to celebrate her birthday there. It had been on the 29th of July – so no chance of detecting a pregnancy on the 12th of August. What else could it be? Rape? A bit too late to take this to the police. Maybe a theft?

'It sounds a bit...' Frau Niemöller grabbed the pearl necklace around her neck and let it slip through her fingers pearl by pearl, as if it were a rosary. 'I think I do want a coffee, after all.'

'Of course.' Carla was unsettled. By now she'd normally have an inkling what it was all about. She stood up and poured coffee into the Blue Onion porcelain cup. 'Milk, sugar?'

'Under no circumstances.' The woman nevertheless used the spoon to stir her coffee, then set the spoon to one side and took a sip.

'Do you believe in love at first sight?'

Carla almost choked and thought of Richard. Of course she did, but in the end it was nothing but youthful fantasies, and would soon pass, like a cold. She'd had feverish dreams about him every day at university, yet by now she really only thought about him very occasionally.

'What do you mean, Frau Niemöller?'

'I mean exactly what I said, love at first sight!' Frau Niemöller began to smile and this time the smile conjured up a pink shimmer on her cheeks, as if her skin was being dusted by mother-of-pearl powder. The client now looked weightless, as if on a cloud, and not a day older than twenty.

'By the way, please call me Niki, I prefer that.'

'Niki?' Not exactly the short form for Ingrid.

'That's the name I'd have picked for myself if I had the choice. Don't you think it's unfair that all our lives we have to bear a name that someone else burdened us with?'

Carla nodded. Nobody had bothered to find a suitable name for her; on her ID card she was Karla, after Karl-Otto. Nobody had searched for a girl's name. Nobody wanted a girl. Nobody had wanted her.

'There's a crazy activist painter Niki de Saint Phalle, who paintballs figures made out of plaster.'

'Interesting,' muttered Carla, realising that Niki

Niemöller seemed to have wide-ranging interests, from German-American folk festivals to activist painters. Still avoiding the matter in hand. 'So, Niki, what can I...?'

'I put myself forward for the Queen of the Folk Fair contest and I even won third place.' The woman sat up straighter and smiled more broadly.

'Wonderful,' said Carla, hoping that she wasn't conveying her disapproval of beauty contests, unless they were for dogs or cats. 'And?'

'You can only take part if you give out your name and address, but I had to remain incognito, so I not only wore a blonde Marilyn wig like the one in *Some Like It Hot*, but I also gave a false name and address.'

'Yes?' Carla studied Ingrid more closely – was this a Jekyll and Hyde problem?

Frau Niemöller shuffled in the chair. 'This kind of behaviour is not really compatible with my job.'

'Giving false details?'

Ingrid shook her head emphatically. 'No, having any kind of fun. My behaviour has to be beyond reproach at all times, beyond any ethical doubts. That's in my contract. If they find out, I'll get fired. And Jack, the man I lied to, must think I'm a monster.'

'Jack what?'

'He told me his surname, but I didn't quite get it and it seemed so irrelevant at that moment in time.'

Carla had experienced over and over again that GIs gave a false first name and a deliberately unclear surname. At least this seemed par for the course.

'Did he say where he was from?'

Ingrid smiled. 'Yes, I definitely remember that, because at first I thought he meant Atlas. I must have looked confused, because he repeated that he was Jack from Atlanta, Georgia.'

'So why this masquerade? These lies? Are you working for the Church?'

Ingrid gave a wicked grin. 'On the contrary. If they knew about my job, they'd excommunicate me.'

'Sounds mysterious.'

'I'm a sales representative for a pharmaceutical company for women's diseases.'

'Do women's diseases require such high ethical standards?'

'I sell Anovlar!' Ingrid made this proclamation as if she was handling gold.

What on earth was Anovlar? Carla wracked her brains for any residual information, but she hadn't come across it before.

'It's a tablet, well, a pill, that you take to avoid getting pregnant. Isn't that wonderful?' This was clearly a rhetorical question, because Ingrid continued without any pause. 'But it's a delicate matter. Many doctors believe that if they prescribe such a pill, they're supporting wanton behaviour among women. They'd rather see birth control remain the domain of the men. You know, coitus interruptus...' Ingrid mimed something with her hands.

Carla blushed deeply, and got even more flustered, because she knew her cheeks now looked as if they'd been slapped. Ingrid wasn't to know that thus far her knowledge of men was purely theoretical. There was nothing wrong with that, of course, it was just Lulu who went on and on about it, as if it was a disaster on par with the *Titanic*.

'...and condoms,' Ingrid continued unperturbed. 'Women are not allowed to have any control over their bodies, because that could lead to Sodom and Gomorrah, the pill would make women behave like crazed sex-maniacs. So if I want to hit the sales targets – which is what my company expects of me – I have to have a spotless reputation and visit each doctor's surgery looking as earnest as a nun with a headache. I have to make it clear that this pill is intended for married women, who shouldn't be bearing any more children for health reasons.

Naturally, that's a lie, but we don't discuss that. Do you see my dilemma?'

'Not quite,' said Carla. If this pill had existed when her mother was young, then she probably wouldn't be alive now, because she and Father wouldn't have had to get married. And if he hadn't married into the Nachtigall family, then what job would he have chosen? He'd wanted to become a journalist, or maybe a cook or a singer – or everything at once, Karl-Otto Koslowsky, the singing journalist-cook.

'Are you listening to me?' asked Ingrid Niemöller, cocking her eyebrow.

'Of course, I understand,' Carla lied. If she had such a well-paid job, then she wouldn't bother to enter any beauty contests. 'It was impossible for you to give Jack your real name and we should find him for you?'

'Yes. I've already been to the venue, but no one gave me any information.'

Of course not, the American Army always suspected that any woman asking about a GI was likely to produce a pregnancy and other such complications. It was quite ironic that it was the opposite in this case. Carla suppressed a smile and asked, 'Do you have a picture of the two of you from that evening?'

Ingrid finished her coffee, leaned back in her chair, visibly more relaxed than before, and played with her pearls again.

'Unfortunately, I don't have a picture.'

'Can you describe him at least?'

Her eyes were shining. 'A tall man – taller than me, with broad shoulders and dark-blond hair, cut short, of course. Thick blond eyebrows above grey-blue eyes, his mouth rather too big, the upper lip almost thicker than the lower lip, and of course lovely American teeth – so white.' She sighed wistfully.

'Any special marks?'

'He had a little burn mark on the inside of his wrist.'

'How old do you think he was?'

'A little older than me, early thirties perhaps.'

Jack from Atlanta in his thirties with grey-blue eyes – not enough to go on. 'Do you remember anything else about him, even if it didn't seem important at the time?'

'He said his name was Jack, but his mates called him Bobbs, not all of them, some called him Jackov.'

'You mean Jacob, with a b?'

Ingrid shook her head. 'No, it was a V for sure – Jackov.'

Could that really be a version of Jacob, or a play on possible Russian roots? She had had a case where a British captain of Italian origin who was known as Dussolini by everyone in his company. Still, that had been easier to crack.

'But others called him Bobbs. Everyone seemed really pleased to see him, which I rather liked.'

'Bob like Robert?' Unusual to have two nicknames.

'No, it sounded a bit different, really more like Bobbs. But no matter what they called him, they seemed to treat him with respect.'

'What rank was he?'

'No idea, but I don't think it was just because of his rank, he seemed very approachable.'

Approachable was a word that she hadn't heard in a while. 'May I ask what makes you think that he felt the same way about you?'

Ingrid laughed. 'Until now I always thought people who came with such a story were mad. I never expected to experience anything like it. Your eyes wander through a room full of people and suddenly come across the eyes of this person, and you feel like drowning in them. Your heart warms up, everything expands inside you, you're ready to burst!' She pointed towards her chest. 'Everything feels different, the organs inside don't know what they're doing, your pulse is racing, you're trembling, you can barely stand straight, you're hot and cold all at once. Then the other person approaches and you can almost sense his aura, time stands still, everything falls silent, there's nothing else in the world...' She nodded, almost to herself, then took another cigarette from her bag and lit it.

'Those are physical reactions,' Carla let slip, thinking of Richard and wanting to somehow warn Ingrid. 'These bodily sensations wear off after a while, you cannot rely on them or build a future on them.' She was quite the expert on not building a future, for sure.

Ingrid examined Carla. 'I understand what you're saying – it's exactly what I'd have said before it happened to me.' She pointed at the pink-and-white plastic ring. 'Jack made this for me at a children's toy stall. Our engagement ring. "We are made for each other, it's God's will", that's what he said.'

Far out, thought Carla, but it wasn't the first time she'd come across soldiers who spun any old yarn to the German Fräuleins, all the while with a family back home in the States.

'What else did you do? Did he have any special preferences? Of the friends that you mentioned, was there anyone who had any particular traits, or any names that Jack might have used?'

'No, I was so absorbed by Jack, that it felt like we existed in our own little bubble. I remember we stood by the shooting gallery at some point, but he refused to shoot, because he said it wouldn't be fair, since that was his job. He was so straitlaced in a way, as if it was really important to him to do the right thing at all times. Although he was devouring me with his eyes, he kept his distance and treated me as respectfully as if I were a queen.'

Approachable and respectful, a strange description, more suited to a priest perhaps.

'He was charming and helped me to position the gun and I managed to shoot a Berlin Bear for him.'

'One of those big cuddly toys?' This would appear on a camera somewhere.

'No, just a keyring. Then we...' Ingrid looked around the room, trying to remember. 'Yes, then he wanted to eat chips. I didn't, of course.' She ran her hands down her slim body. 'My body is my asset – most gynaecologists are men. But he insisted, said they were the best in Berlin. He literally fed me, we shared every last one.' She sighed. 'Please help me find him. I have to at least explain why I lied to him.'

'We'll find him, but I couldn't tell you how long it might take.'

'Thank you.' Ingrid took a wallet out of her bag and threw 120 marks on the table. 'Can you start right away?'

Carla stared at the money in surprise. Nobody had ever paid so carelessly before. This pill must be a money-maker. She should've asked for 50 marks per day. 'Any additional expenses will be on top of that, of course.'

Ingrid nodded and stubbed out her half-smoked cigarette.

I'll get started on Monday, Carla told herself. Bobbs, Jackov or Jack, she'd crack the case. The Nightingale & Co. Agency had always solved every case. Not always to the satisfaction of the clients, which is why they asked for payment in advance.

She took the grey book from the second drawer and wrote a receipt. Ingrid took it, stuffed it in her handbag and got up.

'I'm sure it's just a small job for you, but for me, it's life and death to see Jack again.'

'You can count on me.' Carla got up and accompanied her client to the door.

'You can reach me on the phone in the morning between eight and nine, after that I'm on the road. Please find him as soon as possible!' And with that she flew down the stairs.

Wasn't that always the case? Once they decided to use an agency, they wanted results immediately. But the results were not always what the client had been hoping for.

3

'You're late again!' Wallie stood up with a groan and handed her bald colleague the sexy sequinned corset that everyone had to wear behind the bar at Eden. 'Everything is being chilled, refilled with ice cubes, the two new beer barrels have been connected. I'm a bit fed up that this is the third time this week that you've left me to prepare the bar all on my own.' She tried to sound severe, but the more she looked at Edgar, the harder it was to be harsh with him. His usually calm grey eyes were sparkling with enthusiasm. There had to be a serious reason for him being late.

'What happened this time? Let me guess. The Shah of Persia tried to arrive incognito and you had to prepare two suites for him at the Kempinski? You could still wipe down the bar occasionally!'

The bar was made of dark wood, and traces of hundreds of glasses had left their marks on it, which always made her think of soap bubbles. On her first day working as Nelly at the Eden, her boss had asked her to scrub away the marks, and she only realised that she'd been set an impossible task when she saw Edgar, Irina and Jutta laughing at her.

'Nelly, you'll never guess who's coming here tonight!' Edgar took a new wig out of the cellophane wrapper, long red locks, supposed to resemble the singer Milva. He held it under his chin like a beard and began to hum a Christmas carol.

'Idiot!' Wallie tried not to laugh, she was still cross with him.

'I've told the entire film crew to come here, told them they had to see the Eden Bar if they wanted to experience the real Berlin, and I promised them a place right at the front, of course. This is my chance! Your Lucky Angel is about to make it big!'

'You bet! Hollywood's calling!' Wallie rolled her eyes. Edgar was ready to believe anything when it came to his appearance as an angel. He was usually as stiff and serious as a tax inspector from North Rhine-Westphalia, but when he transformed into Lucky Angel at the Eden, he was ready for anything and truly believed in his future career as a singer. Quite schizophrenic, right? But weren't they all? There were two conflicting souls fighting within her too. She stifled a deep sigh, after all, she liked proper Edgar just as much as the naïve angel.

'Even if Gregory Peck were to show up with Audrey Hepburn here tonight, who's gonna mix the drinks while you are performing?' She pointed both thumbs towards herself and gave a dramatic groan. 'Saturday, of all nights! Does the boss know about it?' The boss loved slobbering all over celebrities, that might have been the reason he'd given Edgar this job, so that he could send all the guests from the Kempinski to his club. It certainly wasn't Edgar's vocal talents.

'Don't be like that, I know you love my performances. Especially my legs. You said they were better than Marlene's, remember?' He danced around her and finished with a deep bow. 'I beg you to help me. I have it on good authority that the boss'll be meeting with some award-winning architect and the head of planning tonight. For the building of the New Eden.' He sat upright and was instantly transformed into the wary concierge who noticed everything. 'There's something going on in the city, eh? Can't you feel a certain nervous tension?'

'You on your period or what?' joked Wallie, as she started fine-slicing a lemon. 'The only thing making me nervous is the thought of all the customers about to descend on us in five minutes.'

'I tell you, there's something about to kick off. Billy Wilder told me that today, at the Brandenburg Gate, someone was shooting the balloons they needed for the motorbike scene.'

'Pranksters.'

'Don't think so. The balloons had writing on them: *Ami go home* and *Russki go home*. Besides, it was a woman who shot them down.'

'Some maniac who's still in love with Hitler.'

'No, I tell you, something's going on. Everyone in Berlin is on tenterhooks.'

'Sure! The Kempinski staff are better than any secret service.'

'Kempinski might not know anything, but the head concierge does,' Edgar nodded sagely.

'What would happen if your colleagues snitched on you?'

He tapped his forehead. 'Silly question! Nothing! My boss there knows about this.' With a taunting smile, he put the wig on his bald head, stopped and made a kissing moue with his lips. 'But his wife would be devastated, of course, for if her husband could see me now, he'd instantly leave her for me.'

'You big show-off!' Wallie threw a damp dishcloth in his direction. 'So, who's the VIP coming tonight?'

''Careful, this is an expensive wig!' Edgar picked up the dishcloth and folded it. 'Billy Wilder and his whole *One, Two, Three* crew.'

'A lot of them have been here already. Remember that crazy evening with Horst? How's that going to help you?'

'Those were the actors. It's the string-pullers that I need. And who could be more suitable than the producer of *Some Like It Hot*? Tony Curtis and Jack Lemmon dressed up as women musicians – I bet you anything that Wilder likes that sort of stuff!'

'That film was finished long ago. And Wilder is married, in any case.'

'So what! I repeat, so what? Maybe it will inspire him to write another masterpiece. What's wrong with you? You're not usually so miserable. Have you had a fight with James? Lighten up! Maybe Wilder will discover you!'

'As what? I'm not a fan of acting!' She managed to say that without a single flutter of her eyelids. Not bad.

'Who needs talent? You, my beautiful Nelly, are fairer by far than Marilyn Monroe...'

'Nonsense! Better get ready. It's getting busy outside.'

Edgar drew his hand to his head, saluting, then flung his red locks over his shoulder and disappeared into the tiny staffroom behind the bar.

Wallie went to the entrance. Without even realising it, that idiot had hit the bull's-eye. James wouldn't show up today, maybe never again. That jealous dolt could not leave off spying on her. Simply because she didn't want to spend every evening with him, he was sure that she had other lovers. Although it was James who wet himself with fear whenever she sneaked into his apartment behind his landlady's back, James who was always on call for the BBC and only had time for her when it suited him.... and yet he still acted like the jealous guy. In spite of all that, she missed him – he was a good kisser, and instinctively knew what Wallie wanted, often before she realised it herself.

She peeked through the spyhole to watch out for James. Yes, she had ended things with him, but she didn't expect a true Scotsman to give up so easily. But no, she spotted Paunchy-Andy and Baldy-Holger and all those students who were not her favourite kind of customers. Most of them left no tips, but at least they were better behaved than Baldy-Holger. His friend Paunchy-Andy wasn't quite as bad, but they both kept trying to chat up Angel, asking her if she was a ginger down below as well. If they ever realised that Angel wasn't a woman, they'd have waited outside to beat up Edgar. Because their boob jokes came second only to their jokes about homos, the enemies of any male friendship. And from male friendship they would switch to the unfairness of having to compensate the victims of the Second World War. 'And who's gonna compensate us for all we had to endure on the front?'

Working here could be really unpleasant at times. She adjusted her sequin top, pulled back her shoulders and opened the door.

***

For the past three hours, every single seat, every millimetre of space at the smoky, sweaty bar was full. Some were singing 'Hello Mary Lou', others were dancing between the barstools and the tables, and others were hammering their glasses on the bar in time to the rhythm.

Drops of sweat were trickling into her eyes, and occasionally into the cocktails she was mixing. She was glad of any order that didn't involve extra work. She needed Angel around. He'd gone back to the staff room to repair his make-up but what for? Billy Wilder wasn't going to show up anymore.

Jutta, one of the topless waitresses, made her way up to Wallie and tried to say something, but it was impossible to hear over the chants of 'Hit the Road, Jack!' Jutta cast a pleading glance towards the staff room. Wallie dried her hands and followed her.

Angel was standing in front of a spotted mirror, powdering her nose. The music was less loud here, but the bass beats were still pounding through Wallie's body.

'Angel, please go out there,' said Wallie. 'Do some work for a change!'

'What's up?' Angel looked at Jutta.

'Someone has to tend the bar, and you've left me there on my own for hours, so go!' Wallie nodded towards the door. Angel rolled his eyes, but under Wallie's stern stare, he finally left the room.

'Everyone's gone crazy today,' moaned Jutta, holding her breasts. 'Every time I have to go past Baldy-Holger, he squeezes them as if they were his property. I've told him to keep his hands to himself, but he won't listen. I bet he'd behave differently if the boss were here.'

Wallie nodded. Rolf Eden would have crumpled him up and turfed him out. 'His girls' were taboo. Eden was a man of honour, who was proud of the fact that his very young bar girls were willing to play horizontal games with him. When Wallie had turned him down – he always tried it on with blondes with big tits – he couldn't believe it.

'Looky here...' he'd said to her, as if he were talking to a very slow child. 'I'm Rolf from the Eden!'

'And I'm Waltraud from Tilling – nice to meet you,' she'd said, looking him straight in the eye. He stared at her in disbelief for a whole second, then he burst out laughing. She expected him to kick her out and find a more accommodating girl, but that hadn't happened.

'We can't kick Holger out, or else Paunchy-Andy will fetch all his mates and there'll be a riot. Just put on one of my sequin tops.'

'I will, but then he'll just pick on Irina, even though he usually complains that he doesn't like "them gypsy types". He's totally out of order today!'

'Then Irina has to wear something as well.'

'One more thing,' Jutta swallowed nervously, 'Baldy-Holger said he'd be waiting for me outside.'

'Can't your boyfriend come to pick you up?'

'At five in the morning?'

The door opened. 'Come on, girls, we need you!' yelled Angel and slammed the door shut again.

Wallie went to the metal locker that wouldn't shut

properly anymore and was covered in graffiti such as *Fuck you, Maria I love you, Peter's dick is a lazy slob*. She took out one of her tops for Jutta. 'This should have gone in the wash, but it's still better than having Baldy-Holger's hands all over you.'

The door opened once more. 'Come on!' yelled Irina, 'they'll be getting antsy if we don't deliver more drinks. And we have to get rid of Baldy-Holger – he's off his rocker tonight!'

'What did I tell you?' Jutta had done up the zipper but held up the top. 'Damn, it's too big for me!'

'Then stuff something up your chest. As for Holger, don't worry, I'll deal with him.'

The customers were hammering in staccato blows on the bar outside.

Wallie took the dirty towel from the washbasin and gave it to Jutta. 'Take this!'

She ran to her trench coat, which hung on a peg next to the broom because it was a safer spot than the locker. She turned her back to Jutta, took out a little tube from the inside pocket and handed it to her friend.

'Got this from a mate. Bye-bye, Holger!'

'Drugs?' asked Jutta, 'You know we're not...'

'No, it's something completely new. Just a couple of drops and he's out of it.' Wallie congratulated herself on killing two birds with one stone. She could try out the new formula, all while helping Jutta. Naturally, she had no idea what to expect, but she knew for sure that something would happen. A tiny quantity would be enough to put an average-sized man out of action, she'd been told.

She adjusted the towel underneath Jutta's top and then winked at her. 'We'll get through this!' She opened the door and they were immediately engulfed with noise, smoke, heat. Wallie's heart started to drum to the bass rhythm.

Just a regular Saturday night in Eden, she thought to herself, little realising how wrong she was.

4

The following morning, Carla spotted her aunt from a distance, dressed all in black, sitting in her favourite outdoor corner seat at the Café Kranzler, nibbling on something green. Strange... why was she the only person sitting outside at the Kranzler on a Sunday? It wasn't that warm yet, but that didn't scare off Berliners.

Something wasn't right. Lulu was never punctual, because she always wanted to make a grand entrance and invent extravagant excuses for her delays. She only wore black at funerals, because she was convinced the colour did her no favours. As for that incredible black hat, she only wore it for special occasions, because it had been created by the legendary Madame Berthe, who, since the war, produced the most expensive hats in Berlin on the corner above the Astor Cinema.

That green thing in Lulu's hand – could that possibly be a stalk of celery? Carla squeezed her eyes to make sure she could see better. Then the red stuff in the cocktail glass in front of her must be a Bloody Mary. Surely not a vulgar Bloody Mary? Lulu was even less likely to have a Bloody Mary than Carla was likely to wander naked around Ku'damm. Unbelievable! Carla broke into a run. When she got to the table, she saw her aunt was in tears.

'What's happened?' she asked, alarmed. Lulu's tears were leaving traces on her make-up, so they must be genuine.

'My child, what dark hole have you emerged from? Haven't you heard the news on the radio?'

Carla blushed. 'I was on my course for elegant ladies, like every Sunday, and there's no radio allowed there.'

Her aunt got up with a groan, hugged her, clinging to her chest.

'Child, they've only gone and done it!' she sobbed.

'Done what?' asked Carla, wondering if they were talking about *One, Two, Three* again. But that wouldn't explain why no one else was there. It must be something more serious.

'They're building a wall,' said Lulu. The words were like a punch to her stomach. Carla felt faint. Ulbricht had lied to them. That was why there were so many guards at the Brandenburg Gate yesterday. How naïve of them to believe that it was merely for the film set. Ulbricht had declared in June 'No one has the intention to build a wall here' when in fact he'd already been shipping tonnes of cement.

'Right through Berlin.' Lulu began to bawl, which shook Carla to the core. Her aunt hadn't cried that hard even at Father's funeral.

'That's impossible,' said Carla, trying to comfort her by stroking her back gently, 'It can't be done. I mean, think of the U-Bahn and S-Bahn! And so many people live in the eastern zone but work in the west.'

She was just talking nonsense, who cared what Berliners wanted. They were still being punished here, while in the rest of West Germany, they were all living a normal life once more. Meanwhile, Berliners were being pushed back and forth like pawns by the Great Powers. But why a wall, that surely would result in a checkmate for both sides? Or no, it dawned on her that in this case, neither side had to sacrifice their king or lose face: it was a draw rather than a checkmate.

'I'm sure the Americans won't stand for this insult! They'll demolish the wall at once.'

Her aunt pushed her away. 'Not on your life! They won't

risk getting into another war over it. We're on our own!'
She blew her nose so dramatically that her black straw hat
fell to the floor. 'You should be aware of that, given that
you're a snoop!' She threw a meaningful look at her hat
and sat down.

Carla bent down to pick it up. The hat changed into a
whirlpool in front of her very eyes, everything was heaving
as if she were on a ship. She clung to the table and focused
on her feet, as she tried to get up again. She hoped her aunt
wouldn't notice, so that she wouldn't send her to endless
appointments with snake-oil merchants and spiritual
healers. Carla laid the hat on the table, and Lulu carelessly
plonked it on her head.

'Why are you just standing there, child? You look a bit
peaky, sit down. Not much we can do about the situation!'
Lulu drank the rest of the cocktail in one slurp and looked
around for the waiter. 'I don't think I'll ever be able to eat
again, given the shock, but I have to drink urgently!' Lulu
wiped her tears. 'I went this morning to the film set – and
what did I find? Nothing but barbed wire. No Billy Wilder,
no Buchholz, nobody. That's the worst. Where are they
going to film now?'

Carla bit her lips. Not surprising that Lulu's first thought,
despite the shocking news, was to worry about the filming.
But then, she wasn't much better herself. She hadn't
thought for a minute about her mother, who was probably
glued to the radio right now, unable to understand what
was going on. After all she'd been through!

'I should look after Mother,' she said.

'Nonsense, Ida will be fine!' declared Lulu, who'd never
liked her mother. 'I'm far more miserable.' She did indeed
look very woebegone. The wrinkles around her nose and
mouth had deepened, her lips had lost their plumpness, and
despite being overweight, she suddenly seemed to be quite
gaunt, as if fear had hollowed her out. Carla was unsure if
those were deep feelings, or merely great acting talent.

'Ida is lucky, I don't have a treasure like you in my house! I only have Fritzi! So please have a drink with me, you wouldn't leave me all alone now, would you?' She looked around. 'Have they walled up the staff here as well?'

'I can imagine where they are.' Carla stood up, trying to breathe through her dizziness, and went inside. A bunch of waiters, men and women, were standing in front of the bar listening to the radio.

No chance of ordering anything. She joined the waiters and thought of all the people who had relatives in East Berlin. The newsreader on RIAS Berlin sounded like he himself could not quite believe what he was saying.

In the early hours of this morning, the border police and members of the Factory Combat Groups started to deploy barbed wire and fences. 69 of 81 checkpoints have been closed. Inhabitants of the German Democratic Republic and East Berlin can only pass through the remaining ones with special permission. The S-Bahn traffic will be halted.

Fearful mutters and whispers were heard all around the room. 'No way, how will that work? This Ulbricht is *meshugge*. And where's Kennedy? Why Kennedy? What about Adenauer? You crazy or what, Adenauer, he couldn't give a monkey's about us. Maybe if Willy comes along...'

They searched for other radio stations and indeed the Free Berlin station crackled and then they all heard the voice of... not Willy Brandt, but Adenauer.

Carla felt a hand of her shoulder. 'Anything new?' It was Lulu who'd joined the congregation.

An older waiter noticed her aunt and dutifully brought out an armchair. 'For you,' he said, with a little bow. Lulu sat down gratefully. 'Thank you.'

'Quiet!' called out one of the female waiters. 'Can't turn this up any louder!'

Carla would have liked to sit down as well. She still felt wobbly whenever she moved her head. She remembered when she got stuck in the air raid bunker all by herself, aged five. When the Coal Cellar Monster had sat on her chest in the dark and laughed at her. She swallowed a couple of times. This was something entirely different, she told herself, *it's bright daylight, no one is being buried under collapsing walls.* It was merely a wall being built.

Lulu squeezed her hand, while Carla tried to focus on what Adenauer was saying:

I am fully aware that the stubbornness of the Pankow regime has led to this serious situation. Together with our allies, we will take all necessary measures.'

'You don't believe that yourself,' muttered Lulu and shifted uncomfortably in her chair.

The Federal Government asks all Germans to trust in the measures we will take. It is imperative that we should respond with firmness but also calmness to the provocation from the East and not undertake anything that might worsen the situation instead of improving it.

'Of course not,' cried out Lulu indignantly, 'He's the champion of not lifting a finger for Berliners, this Chancellor!' A couple of the waiters nodded in agreement, while others shushed her.

We continue to feel strong bonds with all Germans in the Soviet Zone and East Berlin, they remain our brothers and sisters.

'Such idiocy, I can't bear to listen anymore!' Aunt Lulu shook her head in disapproval and stood up. She looked around for the waiter who had brought her the chair, and gave him a tenner. 'This is for the Bloody Mary and keep the change!' she said, feeling visibly generous, nodding at Carla. They left Café Kranzler together.

'This is not the way I imagined our lunch together,' she said as she took out a handkerchief and wiped the tear-tracks on her face. 'But we've survived worse, it would be a joke if we didn't survive this!'

'I'll go to Mother, but I'll take you to your car first. Where did you park it?'

'Took a taxi.' Lulu was avoiding her eyes. 'I gave the car to Trudi today to thank her for yesterday, with the police.'

'Fine,' Carla interrupted her aunt and kissed her hastily on both cheeks. She was tired of all these tales; besides, what had happened this morning in Berlin trumped any crazy story that Lulu might tell her. And she really didn't like the thought of Mother being all on her own.

'I'll call you tomorrow,' Carla promised, with a slightly guilt-ridden conscience, because Lulu really did seem to be overcome with emotion. The simplest solution would have been to take her home, but Lulu and Ida had never got on, so strike that idea. While Father was still alive, they'd made a bit of an effort, but now they could give full rein to their disdain for each other.

'Take care,' said Carla, setting off at a trot for Savigny Square. Lulu was always out and about and had plenty of friends and acquaintances, while Mother didn't. She hoped that running would dissipate her dizziness. She looked out for a newspaper kiosk. She wanted to read as much as she could. How was it supposed to work? Would West Berlin be cut off like an island? It would require a lot of support. She couldn't help remembering the days of the Berlin blockade and what happened to Mother at the time. She'd been living on a kind of island for many years now, not deliberately. Since Father's death Mother had only left the house once – to go to his funeral. She refused to wear her prosthetic limb. In the apartment she managed to move around on her narrow wheelchair but of course she couldn't go down the stairs. There was no lift, although Father had asked the landlord over and over to introduce at least a paternoster lift. The staircase of the building was large enough. The landlord's answer had been very clear: if they didn't like it, the Koslowsky family and their agency could move out. There was still a housing shortage in Berlin, so Father had carried Mother up and down the stairs whenever she needed it. He'd been strong as a bear, but Carla was much smaller and weaker. And even if she'd been able to help her, Mother wasn't keen to accept any aid.

She hoped that Frau Pallutzke would be there at least. The two widows had a strange love-hate relationship. Whenever they met, they would at first gossip with gusto about the other tenants. But then the little barbs started appearing, such as 'Well, had one glass too many last night?' or 'Put on a bit of weight lately?' And the harmless conversation would go downhill from there, until it became too much for the two of them and they wouldn't speak to each other for a while. No one knew how long the offended silence would last.

Didn't the Pallutzke woman have family in Lichtenberg? In the East? Oh, and Helga! The only person whose visits Mother looked forward to. She lived in the East in Weißensee.

Carla accelerated, her dizziness entirely gone by now. The kiosk in Savigny Square was drowning in people, all eager to read the special edition of the *Berliner Morning Post. Brandt demands a strong response from the Western powers.* Carla grabbed one and was about to put down the coins, when she remembered a copy of Constanze. She thought it might distract her mother, so she asked about it, and was met with disbelief. 'Holdin' ya all up!' the vendor said, throwing the magazine at her after a brief search. He took her money with a sneer, as if it were a handout.

As she turned away, she looked at the cover of *Constanze*: *The Shah of Persia and His Beautiful Wife.* Absurd! Would this really distract Mother from the misery of Berlin? Was there anything that would work as a distraction?

Unless... she still had a bottle of Berliner Luft in her office. From the last client, who'd not only paid her rather high bill promptly but had even brought Carla the peppermint liqueur and chocolates. Carla might not be a fan, but the shared passion for that liqueur was one of the few things that her parents had still had in common during those last few years.

Carla entered the building, which seemed sheltered from the tumult outside. There was a smell of floor wax and furniture polish. The yellow wall tiles might be old, but there wasn't even the tiniest hint of a spiderweb on them. The brass knobs on the wooden doors gleamed with fresh polish and there wasn't a single dry leaf in the purple bouquets in the hallway windows.

As she entered the agency to get the liqueur, she remembered Alma's strange phone call yesterday. Alma had asked her if she could make an appointment for Sunday, but now it felt like yesterday was from another life. From now on, she'd probably divide her life into the time before and after the Wall. Would Alma show up in spite of everything going on today? It had sounded pretty urgent.

Carla took the liqueur out of the filing cabinet, then locked up and went up a flight of stairs. A combination of stale air, Elnett hairspray and soggy wool hit her nostrils as she went in. She refrained from opening all the windows, it would only irritate her mother.

'I'm back!' Carla called out, hoping to hear the shrill 'Hello' of Frau Pallutzke. There was only silence. So Mother was on her own.

Carla hung up her light summer trench coat on a hanger. Then she went into the adapted bathroom to wash her hands. Her mother had always insisted on that, even before the war, and even with Father. Carla looked at herself in the spotty mirror above the washbasin and was surprised how matter-of-fact she looked, as if the world hadn't just ended in Berlin.

No wisp of hair had escaped from her low bun. Mascara and eyeliner were still in place around her brown eyes, and her Revlon lipstick was still full of Plum Happiness. She gave a nod – now she could appear in front of her mother. She'd be sure to appreciate those little things that were so important to her: cleanliness, tidiness, poise, duty.

Carla dried her hands, picking up the papers and the liqueur as she made her way across to the living room, where she put everything down next to the piano.

Her mother was sitting slumped in her favourite blue armchair listening to the radio with her eyes closed. Willy Brandt was giving a speech. Tears were streaming down her face. On the side table next to her there was an almost empty box of Ritter pralines.

Carla made a mental note to get more of those. 'Mother,' she said quietly.

'Sssh!' her mother said, without opening her eyes.

Carla pushed the empty wheelchair to one side, pulled the second armchair closer to the radio and sat down, hoping that her mere presence would alleviate her mother's pain.

A clique that calls itself a government is trying to lock in its own citizens. The concrete pillars, barbed war, dead zone, watchtowers and machine guns all bear the signs of a concentration camp.

Mother twitched. Carla knew this was not because she'd lost someone in the concentration camps, but because she'd idolised Hitler and had refused to believe in the camps. After finding out the truth, she'd been shocked at her own naivety and terribly ashamed. Carla was mystified at the extent to which her mother had blocked out her own family history. The Nachtigalls had arrived in Prussia two centuries ago, because they were Jews and had hoped for a better life here. This only came about when they converted to the Lutheran Church.

Brandt's voice got louder, forcing Carla to pay attention.

Their strategy won't work. In future, we will bring more people than ever to Berlin, from all over the world, so that they can see the naked, brutal reality of a regime that has promised people heaven on earth.

There was frenetic applause at the end of the speech. Carla would have liked to clap as well, but she contained herself. Mother stretched out her hand with its finely manicured nails and switched off the radio.

All you could hear now was the tick-tock of the grandfather clock, which made the silence seem even more unbearable.

While Carla wracked her brains to find a comforting word, she glanced at her mother, who was dressed in her Sunday best and looked even more doll-like than usual. The white hair was in a teased up-do, her face entirely free of make-up, but with extremely plucked eyebrows, which gave her a look of permanent reproach even when she didn't say a word. Her navy-blue floral dress with white collar was, as always, neatly pressed and fastened with a broad belt to emphasise the waist. The wide skirt was draped artistically to cover the missing leg. Carla tried to never look further down, where you might notice that the pretty doll was broken. Because it was all her fault.

Her mother finally took out a handkerchief from the sleeve of her dress and wiped her eyes dry, before sitting up and addressing Carla.

'The food is ready in the kitchen.'

'We decided that I was going to do that today,' said Carla with a barely supressed sigh. Mother liked to eat at precisely six in the evening and disliked any changes to her schedule. But of course she never admitted it, because she didn't want to inconvenience anyone. Since Carla had an appointment with Alma later, she was planning to eat around four. But did the meal have to be ready before three o'clock? It was just one more way in which Mother could put her in the wrong. Nothing Carla did was ever good enough.

'I've brought you some papers and some Berliner Luft.' Carla gestured towards the piano.

'You shouldn't have.'

She brought the papers, clearing the now-empty chocolate box, and put the copy of *Constanze* on the side table near her mother's armchair. Then she went to the sideboard, which was made of dark oak, just like the grandfather clock, opened one of the glass doors and took out two light green liqueur glasses. She poured the liquid into the glasses and handed one to her mother.

'Maybe a little later,' she said, shaking her head, 'I need to eat something first.'

Carla managed to avoid mentioning the chocolates and took a large sip instead. The sweet peppermint taste burnt her throat. Tears rose into her eyes.

'What would Father have said about it all?' she wondered, and her hand automatically touched the lucky necklace that he had given her in high school. A single silver die with quartz pips – light brown like her eyes.

'He'd think the world had gone mad!'

Carla had to laugh as her mother shook her head in disapproval.

'The Pallutzke woman was here. A courier left something for the agency, apparently. I left it in the kitchen on your plate. She just wanted an excuse to talk to someone.'

'You mean, she hand-delivered the mail herself?'

'You don't get it, do you? She takes every opportunity to spy on me.'

Carla finished the liqueur and went to the kitchen to check what it was. The table was already laid with the brocade tablecloth and the Sunday dinner service with the golden edging. The freshly laundered Sunday cloth napkins were in their silver rings marked with her mother's initials. The envelope lay on Carla's plate like a surreal starter. All that was missing was a sprinkling of parsley.

The letter was from Alma Hochbrück, to reassure her that she was definitely still showing up today, even if there were tanks in the streets. The matter she wanted to discuss was vital and could not be delayed.

Vital. Right, thought Carla, ever more curious, but also slightly relieved, because it showed that there still would be clients, no matter what.

'So, what is so urgent?' asked Mother, who'd rolled up in her chair.

'I have to go to work soon.'

'Just as well that dinner is ready, then.' Mother moved her chair triumphantly to the head of the table, where Father used to sit. 'The blanquette of chicken and the rice need to be warmed up, the beetroot salad is all ready in the fridge.'

Sunday evening they had a hot meal, while during the week it was always cold cuts. This tradition stemmed from the time when Mother was still walking around on two legs and busy with volunteering at the church on Sunday, so the main meal of the day was in the evening.

Carla finished all the preparations, Mother said grace and then they sat in silence once more. Carla couldn't tell her she'd met Aunt Lulu, nor that she'd been to see Achim's friend in the pathology lab. The first one would anger her, the second was still secret and anyway no fit subject for the dinner table.

She forced herself to eat the beetroot salad. Mother was a good cook but she didn't care what other people liked to eat. You had to be grateful and eat whatever was laid in front of you. *I could actually refuse to buy things that I don't like*, thought Carla, trying to wash down the earthy taste of the beetroot with a long sip of water, but deciding the menu was one of the few joys her mother still had left, so how could she be so cruel as to take it away from her?

She had no trouble getting stuck into the chicken, and was surprised to discover how hungry she was. She salted it a little more, but she knew it wasn't a good idea. *Three, two, one*, she started counting and, sure enough, it all kicked off at two.

'Salt makes women ugly. Water retention.'

Carla nodded and added more salt.

'I just want to help. It wouldn't hurt you to show a little more restraint in your eating habits. Obesity runs in your father's side of the family,' Mother touched the wide belt as if by accident. 'If you don't watch out, you'll end up a cannonball like Lulu.'

'Hmm,' said Carla noncommittally, trying to avoid a quarrel.

'No man wants a fatty in his house.'

Carla silently held out the rice bowl, but her mother refused it daintily, so Carla got another portion for herself. She knew that if she reacted to these little darts, it could all escalate and become catastrophic. Better to suffer in silence.

'Portion control is not part of your course for elegant ladies?'

'Ummm...'

'And clearly neither are conversational skills...'

Carla would have loved to burst out with news of what she'd been doing that morning, but she knew she shouldn't, because Achim had smuggled her into the lab. She could imagine her mother's reaction if she were to tell her, 'Just imagine, I learnt how to dissect a cadaver. It smells awful, but at least we all wash our hands.'

'We learnt how to go up and down the stairs without stumbling.'

'Can't say I noticed any improvement to your galumphing.'

'It takes time.' Carla swallowed everything she'd been about to say, dabbed her mouth with her napkin, folded it neatly and then stood up.

'Thank you, Mother, that was delicious, but duty calls. We have bills to pay...'

She took her handbag and left the apartment, running down the stairs to the first floor. If she could have done it, she'd have liked to run far, far away from her life.

5

When she got to the agency, Carla opened all the windows and bustled to and fro in an attempt to calm down. She had to get used to all of this, because she'd promised Father that she'd never let Mother down. She'd rather die than break her promise to him.

But maybe a cigarette wouldn't hurt. Carla reached for the carved ivory cigarette case that she kept handy for her clients. Mother never tired of telling her that women who smoked were sluts. Precisely. If Ulbricht could build a wall in the middle of Berlin, then surely everyone had the right to get drunk and to smoke. She couldn't get drunk until after she'd met the client, if at all. So she opened the lid engraved with an elephant head and took out a Lucky Strike. If only she could find the matches now...

While searching for them on the desk, she realized that she needed to replace the Lucky Strikes that she'd given to the guard. She opened the bottom drawer at the side of her desk – only five packets left. She made a mental note of that and flung one packet in her handbag. It made a rustling noise.

She frowned. Had she forgotten to throw away her box of tissues? When she looked inside the bag, she found the note that the friendly guard had given her yesterday. It seemed like light years away.

Nevertheless, she stopped frowning and realized that Bruno had managed to brighten her day even at a distance.

He had such sparkling eyes – were they brown or blue?

Carla took out the note, put the cigarette back in the case and smoothed the paper out with both hands. She smiled as she remembered how Bruno had made a lunge for the air rifle, whereupon the two policemen had jumped up. Speaking of which, she still hadn't found out what Lulu had planned to do with the rifle, but she'd ask her.

Would love to see you again, he'd written. Then there was his number and beneath it his name. Bruno Eisenberg.

Should she give him a call? But what was the point? Yes, he had flirted with her, but she didn't have time for amorous encounters. She threw the note in the bin.

A squall of wind slammed the window shut. She jumped up, and only then noticed that the clouds had started gathering. She closed the other windows, just as the first drops started splashing the dusty pavements on Grolmanstraße. She could see Katrin in her red Sunday dress running back indoors with her plaits in the wind.

It was just before five. Carla went back to the desk, took out a new folder, laid it down next to her notebook and then went to the kitchen to prepare tea. She knew from their meetings at the Berlin Fledglings that Alma preferred tea. While the water was coming to a boil, she couldn't help wondering how such an attractive woman like Alma could have problems. Yes, of course, beauty did not protect you from trouble, but things did get considerably easier if you were attractive. Anyone who'd survived the schoolyears knew that. In secret she'd given Alma the nickname Nessa, the name of a Celtic goddess, which was exactly what Alma looked like, with her red-golden curls and pale face. Her violet eyes looked a little sad, as if she'd experienced thousands of years of sorrow, which Carla found oddly comforting. She was not surprised that all the children from the orphanage loved Alma. And all the men were filled with desire, although she was anything but a vamp. On the contrary, her figure had something childish and androgynous about it, which looked nevertheless very feminine in the black shift dresses she liked to wear.

Alma's husband, Alexander, had been awarded an innovation prize for the design of a building. He was a professor of architecture at the Technical University. He was usually the one doing the talking, but not long ago Alma had unexpectedly spoken up. She'd suggested that it might be helpful for the children in the orphanage to do art therapy. Carla had never heard of this previously and wanted to find out more, but when Alma wanted to launch into details about light and darkness and colour methods, the professor seemed in a rush to get away, as if he was ashamed of his wife.

Probably there was no big mystery behind Alma's problem, merely a standard divorce request. Otherwise, why would she have whispered on the phone? Carla took the teabag out of the pot, put a cosy over it, then laid the cups on the tray, alongside a selection of Bahlsen biscuits, picking up the only chocolate-covered one as she carried the tray over to the coffee table.

If Alma was sensitive to the arts, then she'd probably notice the lack of flowers and valuable paintings. And wasn't she born a von Stellmark? So money wouldn't be an issue, she hoped.

Ten past five. Carla took another biscuit and then another one with sugar on top. She took the notebook that she'd placed so carefully next to the new folder and started scribbling in it, to quell her impatience. She drew one brick on top of another. She had to laugh – yes, a wall, what else could she draw. She kept on going, until it became clear that she was attempting to draw the barriers around the Brandenburg Gate. She remembered clearly the strange little piles on the street, which had reminded her of the condom case. When she tried to draw them, however, the pencil in her hand seemed to develop a mind of its own – something her father had always encouraged. It drew little circles which then changed into balloons, like the ones she and Bruno had seen on the film set: *Russki go home, Ami go home.*

The pencil went into overdrive once more and the figure of a woman appeared on the paper, someone who looked a little like Virginia Peng, the love interest in the Nick Knatterton comic strip. She was carrying a rifle – and suddenly Carla remembered all the deflated balloons and realized how Lulu had used the rifle. No wonder the police had showed up. Was her aunt trying to scare someone to death, in the hope that this would garner her a part in the movie? This could only make sense in Lulu's crazy world.

She laid down the pencil, crumpled the paper and threw it into the bin. She sipped some tea, which had got cold despite the tea cosy.

Quarter to six. Alma had said it was a matter of life or death.

A short sharp shower outside, as if the gods themselves were displeased with Ulbricht's exploit.

Carla's gaze fell on the bin, where she'd thrown Bruno's note. Maybe it had been a mistake to do so. She bent down to fish it out, smoothed it out again and put it in a folder marked *Misc.* At some point, she might require a bodyguard for a client.

Six. Her client would most likely not show up. Carla decided not to wait any longer. She switched the radio on and started tidying up. She almost didn't hear the bell. She ran to the door to open it.

'Miss Koslowsky, thank you so much for waiting.' Alma looked embarrassed. 'I'm so sorry!'

'Not to worry. You told me you were coming, and today everything is a little strange in Berlin.'

The client stretched her hand out carefully to greet her. Carla invited her in. As Alma took off her wet headscarf, Carla tried not to stare at her, but she had never seen her with such wet and shiny wild locks. Nessa was clearly not of this world, a faerie queen!

Alma sat down so carefully, as if every single move caused her pain. Muscle ache? Then she pulled the coat tighter around her, as if she were cold.

'Tea?' asked Carla.

'Just water, thank you.'

Carla brought a glass and a jug and sat down next to her.

'You're probably wondering... I am so...' Alma spoke so quietly that Carla could hardly hear her.

'Take your time, catch your breath.'

Alma drank the water in one go, then poured herself another glass, which she also downed in one. A procrastination technique, as Carla knew well.

'Everything we discuss here is strictly confidential. You can be sure of it.'

'Please forgive me. I'm an hour late so I should get straight to the point. Alexander mustn't find out I was here, because of the children.'

'Of course.'

'You know him, so you can imagine what it's like to be married to him.'

He was dominant, successful, very full of himself. This seemed attractive to some women, so he probably had affairs. Carla nodded.

'I'd like a divorce,' Alma said loud and clear now. 'And custody of Mathilda and Gregor.'

'How old are your children exactly?' asked Carla, who'd met Mathilda on a trip with the orphanage but had difficulty gauging children's ages.

'Mathilda will turn nine and Gregor is twelve. Is that important?'

'I'm simply asking because of child maintenance. But for that, he would have to be at fault,' explained Carla, trying to remember the exact terminology. 'If you are the one to blame for the breakdown of the marriage, or if it's a debatable breakup of the marriage, then he can ask for the marriage to continue.' That was all far too cold and factual, she sounded like a robot. 'Does he have a lover?'

'No, but he is still at fault for the breakup of the marriage. He...' Alma groaned, then gave herself a push. 'He is violent with me.'

So that's why she was moving so slowly.

'I'm afraid that's no motive for divorce. A man who beats his wife is regarded by the courts as quick-tempered and they usually advise the wife not to annoy him.'

She tried to nod, to make the matter more palatable to Alma. Should she take her hand? But Alma was not waiting to be comforted – she didn't want pity, she needed help.

'He also forces me...' Alma blushed.

'In front of the children?' Not the most sensitive of questions, but there was a glimmer of possibility there.

Alma's violet eyes were wide open in shock. 'Of course not, he's got a little bit of decency left.'

Shame. It was cynical, but those were the legal principles. 'Legally speaking, he can demand his conjugal rights by force, but not in front of the children, because that would constitute indecent sexual acts in front of minors.'

'You sound like a lawyer!' Alma stood up indignantly, then winced in pain and hunched back down.

'I'm so sorry. Is he having an affair with his secretary or, even better, with one of his students?'

'No.'

'Does he like men?'

Alma shook her head.

'Any sign of mental illness? In that case, marriages can be dissolved.'

'Is he completely sane if he beats his wife?'

'Probably not, but that isn't enough. If he were an alcoholic or addicted to drugs or gambling, you'd have a better chance.' Carla paused. 'If you're set upon a divorce, then you don't really need my services. I'd advise you to find a lawyer as soon as possible. Because the beatings generally get worse.'

'You're so funny.' Alma's laugh was full of bitterness, 'Alexander's not only a Freemason, he's also connected with all the top brass of Berlin via their various construction projects. No matter what lawyer I go to, none of them will help me, instead they'll let Alexander know as soon as I walk out of their office.'

'I could recommend a lawyer in West Germany, who specializes in family law.'

'That's not the kind of help I need from you.'

'I'm not sure what I can do to help you. Of course, if you have a suspicion about him...'

'I was hoping you could take pictures of his attacks.'

'These pictures can only be taken by your doctor, in evidence, and he has to have another witness present with him. Just like rape, physical abuse is very hard to prove. And the only way it can be used as a reason for divorce is if you can prove that your life is in imminent danger.'

'So he has to kill me first, is that it? Will that be enough proof that he's dangerous? And what about my children? They need to be protected from him.' Alma's voice was ready to break. 'This will mess them up so badly!'

'I'm really sorry. I wish I could tell you something different...'

Alma turned ashen. 'I hoped you'd provide me with some support, since we know each other from the orphanage. All the men who know Alexander will help him, of course, if only to ask him later for a favour in return. But we women don't do that sort of thing, do we? Each woman has to fight on her own!' She jumped up so abruptly that the table clattered, and her long hair whipped through the air.

Carla drew back, annoyed. Alma winced again and sank back down.

'There must be something I can do?'

Dammit, thought Carla, *there must be something*. 'I will call a doctor friend, she might have some ideas how to protect yourself in case of immediate danger. How are you set up financially?'

Alma drew her fingers through her damp red hair and dried them on her skirt.

'What do you think? Right after the wedding my dowry ended up in his account. I don't have my own account, because he forbade it, after which he had one of those fits of anger. He wants to have full control over everything. That's why I save every pfennig I can from the household money and hide it in an old cigarette case. I hide it between my period pads and girdle, he'll never look there. But I only have 117 marks and 20 pfennigs, that won't go far.'

Carla tried to imagine living like that, and suddenly her own life didn't seem so bad. She had her own bank account, a job and no man to make her life an utter hell.

'I have inherited some valuable jewellery from my grandmother,' said Alma, pointing at her pearl necklace. 'I could sell those, leave him and disappear somewhere with Mathilda and Gregor. Could you help me do that? I can't take these myself to a pawnshop.'

Cara shook her head. 'That wouldn't be a good idea. You'd be accused of depriving the children of their father...'

'But that would be the best for all of us.'

'No, it would be a catastrophe, punishable in court, and it would mean you lose your children forever. I cannot help you with that, we have to find a legal way to do it. I'll speak to the doctor and the lawyer that I know and tell them that you need an urgent solution.'

Alma looked straight into Carla's eyes, deeply disappointed, piercing Carla's heart.

'I was really expecting more of Nightingale & Co.'

'I'm sorry you feel that way, but I promise that I'll try to find a solution as soon as possible. What is the best way to keep in touch?'

'I'll get in touch in three days' time. Whatever you do, please don't call me at home. If Alexander does notice anything in spite of my attempts at concealment, then please tell him that we spoke about art therapy for the Berlin Fledglings, yes?'

Carla nodded. 'Yes, I remember, light and dark...'

Glancing at her watch, Alma stood up, her eyes filled with tears. She asked in a small voice, 'Do you believe in evil?'

Carla could feel Alma's pain, but she wasn't sure what to tell her. She couldn't think of anything better than the Einstein quote her father used to like. 'The world is a dangerous place, not because of those who do evil, but because of those who look on and do nothing.' No sooner had she uttered that, than she felt like biting her tongue.

Alma picked up her bag. 'Is that really what you think? Especially given what happened today in Berlin? So we've all looked on and done nothing?'

'I'm sorry, that was inappropriate,' stammered Carla.

'Inappropriate? It was the stupidest thing I've heard in a long time. The people who infringe on human rights are the evildoers, not the victims who didn't yell stop in time.'

'That's not what I meant...'

'I don't care what you meant. But just so that we're clear, I can't sit and do nothing. Never! I'll free myself from the evil in my life, no matter what it might cost me!' She stormed out of the door, but without slamming it, simply closing it with a light click. Carla was stunned at the superhuman level of self-control.

Something was not quite right about Alma's story, but Carla could not find any concrete proof. Besides, why would Alma lie to her?

6

'Don't mind me!' Wallie said sarcastically to the red-haired woman storming out of the building, nearly knocking her off her feet. The woman didn't show the slightest sign of remorse, just ran away. Wallie hadn't been able to avoid her, she slipped in her court shoes on the wet cobblestones and nearly lost her balance. She managed to avoid falling heavily, but she dropped her heavy leather suitcase.

'Nothing but idiots in this damn city!' OK, so the woman had been crying, but that was no reason to be so rude. After all, everyone in Berlin felt like crying today.

Wallie bent down to pick up the suitcase, grunting as she lifted it. It was filled to bursting, her whole life seemed to be inside it, or at least everything that still belonged to her. At least it hadn't fallen in the puddle just in front of the house. She was lucky after all. Her lips twisted into an ironic smile. Then she remembered the other occupant of the house on Tucholskystraße, who was now locked in behind the Wall. She really was lucky, just like her mother had always said. 'My Wallie was born under a lucky star and will always land on her feet.'

Mamushka's grave was in Pankow, and the border was drawn right through the graveyard, so who knew if she'd ever be able to see it again. In any case, Mushka would be overjoyed that she fled over here, even though Rosa Luxemburg had been her great idol.

Wallie had been to Grolmanstraße before, two years ago. She'd been curious to see how her father lived when he wasn't with them. Then, when both her parents died, she'd wanted to become acquainted with her half-sister. But both times she just stood there and couldn't move. Even if it was some semblance of family. She'd been too cowardly, hadn't even made it as far as the doorbell, and just went straight back to Tucholskystraße.

Things were different now though. Since this morning, she no longer had a home. Without Jutta's help, she'd have been stuck in an overfilled refugee camp in Marienfelde. She'd never have made it here on her own and she certainly didn't want to ask James for help. Oh, he'd have loved to see her crawling back to him, begging for his help. Fat chance!

The lights were still on at the Nightingale Agency. The little Carla was a real worker bee, so diligent and clever and tidy, as Dad always used to say.

Wallie pulled herself together, opened the entrance door and pressed the light switch. The lights were so bright, she had to close her eyes. The gleaming wooden staircase was covered with a spotless red carpet, fastened to every step with brass stair rods. She looked around in wonder. If it was so luxurious here, what would upstairs be like? Her house in Tucholskystraße was all grey with dust, the lightbulbs in the staircase were constantly burnt out. She was sure some of her neighbours would be glad to see the back of her. To work in the West and live in the East to save money, that was a real thorn in their side. The only person who wasn't like that was Frieda on the fifth floor. Who would take care of her friend now? She was ill and couldn't leave the house. The tenants' council looked down on her, but that never bothered Frieda at all.

Wallie panted as she dragged the suitcase up the stairs. She stopped on the landing to catch her breath.

'Well, I never!' She gave an admiring whistle. 'Usambara

violets in the corridor!' She grinned as she imagined herself plucking one to take to Frieda. But no, she was now on the other side. Anyway, it was a stupid idea. Endless ideas, as Mum used to say: 'My Wallie is a dear, but full of hare-brained ideas!' Wonder what she'd think of Wallie's idea to come here?

Wallie didn't think it was crazy. It would be lovely to have a sister land in her lap, all grown up and out of nappies. She hated being an only child. It made her brain work in overdrive. She would have had such fun with a little sister – they could've played all sorts of pranks on people, invented a secret language with silly rules. They could've crept into the same bed at night to gossip about boys. They could've plaited each other's hair and talked about their dreams. Who knew what her half-sister might dream about?

Wallie shook her head. It was too late for pranks and a secret language, they were both twenty-two years old now, but there was still plenty of time left for other things.

But what if Carla didn't want a sister at all?

Wallie swallowed hard. There was no way she could turn back now. She had to make it over here. The only people she knew in West Berlin were Irina and Jutta, and they shared a sublet room and were scrimping and saving every pfennig to start a new life in West Germany. Edgar was saving for his sister Adele. And even if James had still been her boyfriend, he was not allowed to bring anyone into his apartment, according to the clause the landlady had made him sign.

The sounds of keys jangling brought her back. A short flight up a door was being locked. That must be the agency. She ran up the steps and looked around the corner.

Was that small, dark-haired creature really her half-sister? She looked like Audrey Hepburn in photos, but in real life she seemed smaller and frailer.

'Hello-o-o!' she cried out.

'Yes?'

'Can I talk to you?'

'Are you looking for Nightingale & Co.?' asked Carla with a smile.

'Yes!'

Carla examined her, then took a step back when she saw the suitcase behind her.

'It's Sunday, it's quite late...' she said in a more dismissive tone.

'It's urgent though, you're the only one who can help me.'

'We don't have any rooms for rent.'

'Sure thing. It's a tricky matter. Achim sent me,' said Wallie, hoping that she too might know Dad's old friend.

Carla's face lit up. She did look a lot like Dad, thought Wallie, but with those clothes she looked about as sexy as a governess with dysentery.

'Achim? Why didn't you say so at once?' She unlocked the door again. 'Do you need any help with the suitcase, or can you manage on your own?'

'Thanks, I'll manage.' Wallie followed her into the office, curious to see what the place she'd heard so much about looked like in real life. It looked a bit like a waiting room – the entrance hall downstairs was decidedly cosier. And what on earth was with those two funny bottles full of pfennig coins? Did detectives get tips?

'Would you like to drink something?' asked Carla.

A large stiff drink would probably be good for both of them. Not that horrible, sweet peppermint mix that Dad always slurped.

'May I smoke?' she asked instead.

'Of course. Do sit down.' Carla handed her the cigarette case with the carved elephants. That was the exact same one they'd had at home, until Wallie had to pawn it after Mum's death. Dad had clearly liked to get his two-for-one deals.

Wallie lit her cigarette and inhaled deeply. She wasn't quite sure how to start. It was like trying to make her way across a frozen lake, unsure of how thick the ice was.

Carla looked tired and fragile. It probably wasn't easy for her to look after her mother. But at least she had an apartment, a home. So come on, spit it out!

Carla handed her the ashtray, smoothed out her governess skirt and sat down. She remained as upright as if she were the Queen and smiled elegantly. Wallie got goose bumps. Her smile was exactly like Dad's, or at least a miniature version of it.

'So, what brings you here?'

From the mouth of this queen, the question sounded somewhat condescending. Carla seemed so pure. An impeccable problem-solver for the dirty affairs of her clients.

She suddenly felt grubby. But that wasn't her fault, neither of them was to blame for either of the crises – the family and the Wall.

'I'm not quite sure where to start.'

'Most people feel like that.'

'It's a little different with me.' Wallie stubbed her cigarette and looked at Carla firmly. 'You won't like what I have to tell you.'

'Let that be my problem.' Carla straightened the bow of her navy-blue blouse. 'Go ahead.'

'Fine then, I'll be blunt.' Wallie took a deep breath, knowing that it would destroy Carla. 'We're sisters. Your father is also my father. My mother was his lover for many years. I'm here because I can't go back to my apartment because of the damn Wall, and I don't know where else to turn.'

Carla's face froze and she held her hand in front of her mouth, making a sound as if she was about to throw up. She jumped up and ran between the windows, unsteady, as if she were on a ship's deck. Then she stopped in front of Wallie, her eyes slicing through her like a sword.

'Get out right now!'

'Calm down, I've got proof.'

'Shameless liar!' Carla was as pale as drifted snow and shaking, but she managed to grab hold of Wallie's suitcase, although she was unable to fully lift it. She dragged it to the door and kicked it down the stairs, where it tumbled down to the landing.

'Out!' she said in a hoarse whisper.

Wallie tried to remain calm. The best strategy was to wait. She felt sorry for Carla, but she'd realise sooner or later that she was telling the truth.

'Out!' repeated Carla, louder this time and pointing at the door.

'Anything else?' asked Wallie very calmly. After all, she was bigger and stronger than Carla.

'Is everything alright there, Miss Koslowsky?' came a shrill, unpleasant voice from the entrance hall.

Carla froze again, then hurried into the hallway and bent over the bannisters. 'All fine, Frau Pallutzke!'

So that was the voice of the caretaker, whom Dad used to imitate often. Wallie followed Carla into the hallway and discovered that the suitcase had burst open and there were clothes scattered all over the stairs. Visibly disgusted, her half-sister was trying to stuff the blouses, skirts, sequin tops and girdles back into the suitcase. For a moment, she wanted to help her, but then she realized it was probably a trick to get her out of the agency, so she remained in the doorway.

Carla slammed the suitcase shut and came back upstairs.

'You've missed something!' Wallie repressed a giggle, pointing at the Usambara violets, on which two pairs of her red knickers had landed, looking like tiny doll's hats.

Carla pushed the suitcase with her foot into the agency, then went down to get the knickers and threw them into Wallie's face. Wallie picked them up and folded them neatly.

'I don't believe a word you're saying,' snorted Carla, 'I just didn't want to cause a scandal with the Pallutzke woman. If you continue to harass me, I'll call the police.'

Could she not feel that Wallie was telling the truth? Or did she simply not want it to be true?

Wallie rolled up the sleeve of her jacket and showed her the man's watch she had on her right wrist. She took it off, turned it round so that Carla could read the engraved words and held it in front of her. Carla's eyebrows rose, but she didn't touch the watch.

'A Rolex Oyster in red-gold from the 1920s. Your grandfather, Dad's father-in-law, gave it to him when he became a partner at the Nightingale & Co. Agency. For Karl-Otto Koslowsky.'

'The watch was buried with him!' Carla was swaying, as if she'd been punched. She was holding on to the table for balance.

'I'm sorry but he made other plans with Achim and his lawyer, so that I'd get at least something from him.'

Carla shook her head ever more violently, as if to give herself courage. 'The undertaker must have stolen it and sold it.' She stopped shaking her head, but her tone was icy. 'It's a rare and valuable object. And you are a con artist.'

She grabbed the watch and examined it.

Wallie let her be. It distressed her to see how hard it seemed to hit her sister. Small wonder, actually. After all, she'd always known about Carla, while Carla had never known about her. Naturally, it was a shock. Dad had behaved like a coward.

Carla weighed the watch in her hands, as if it were a baby. Then she held it against her cheek, trying to blink away her tears. Wallie could see them. She felt sorry for her, but only a little bit. At least Carla had had a father all those years, while she had to put up with a never-ending parade of uncles.

'This watch belongs to my family.' Carla put the Rolex in her drawer. 'And now, beat it!'

Wallie felt her ire rise. Enough! What did Carla think she was after? A con artist would have picked a family that had more to give than that.

'I've got lots of pictures. My mother was an artist and a photographer.'

'That doesn't prove anything.' Carla was not to be reasoned with.

'Letters too.'

'Fake.' Tears were pouring down Carla's cheeks, but her face seemed made of stone.

'Why on earth would I do this?'

'No idea. Maybe you're crazy?'

Wallie took a small document case out of her handbag, placing a set of photographs in front of Carla. She took out her favourite picture. It wasn't nice of her, but Carla had forced her to do it. The picture had been taken during a summer excursion on a hot summer day on Lake Müritz. The three of them were sitting in their swimsuits on a picnic blanket, their happy smiling faces smeared with chocolate.

'That's enough.' Carla pushed the picture off the table. Wallie bent down to pick it up. She could see Carla's legs trembling under the table.

Carla had to clear her throat a couple of times until she recovered her voice. 'What exactly do you want?'

'A place for the night.'

'Impossible. Even if you were my sister a hundred times over, I don't want you here.' She wiped away her tears with the sleeve of her blouse, smearing the eyeliner and mascara, looking as if someone had died.

'Have you forgotten what happened today?'

'Of course not.'

'Then you've got to help me.' Wallie refrained from adding that Dad would have asked her to help, although that was of course true. 'Please.'

Carla shook her head violently.

'Then I have no choice. Although I admit I'd rather not show these pictures to your mother, her life is hard enough as it is.'

'You wouldn't dare!'

'I would do anything it takes. Or, you know what, I could show them to the Pallutzke woman!'

Carla blanched and clung to the table once again.

'You'll sleep here in the office, in the broom closet.'

'Great, I love police cells,' muttered Wallie.

'We'll tell Mother that you're a distant cousin of Father's from Lichterfelde and that you fled over here as a temporary solution. If you breathe a single word to her or to Pallutzke, then you're out of here. I'll get the inflatable mattress and bedsheets from upstairs.' Carla stood up and went to the door.

'Do you want to go up to your mother like that...?' Wallie drew a circle in front of her face.

'What?' Carla looked annoyed, but then she realized and disappeared into the toilet. Two minutes later, she came out, having taken all her make-up off. She was still pale, with dark rings under her eyes.

'I'll tell Mother I got caught in the rain.'

'You know what? I'll take off my make-up too and come upstairs with you, and you can say you picked me up. Besides, I'm hungry and thirsty.'

'Hungry?' Carla rolled her eyes. 'Sure, bet it gives you an appetite, destroying other people's lives.'

'I didn't want it to be this way.' Which was not quite true.

'No, you're just greedy.' Carla examined her from top to toe, with a particularly disdainful glance at Wallie's bountiful bosom. 'At least, given how cheap you look, nobody would think we're sisters, not even Pallutzke.'

'Just because Audrey Hepburn and Marilyn Monroe aren't sisters, doesn't mean that we can't be.' Wallie tried to lighten the atmosphere with a joke. Carla could stop being so insulting now.

'Sisters? Never! You've destroyed the last good thing I had in my life. You've taken away even my memories.'

'Nonsense, you've got an office, a home, even a mother!'

Carla stopped. 'That isn't worth a thing. Nothing at all!'

She suddenly seemed to come to life. She rushed to the windows and tried to open them up, but one of them was stuck. What on earth was she up to? Wallie's heart began to hammer. Surely not, could her sister be as emotionally fragile as all that? Dad hadn't mentioned that. All he kept repeating was what a clever girl little Carla was.

'Please don't!' she begged, as Carla was rattling the window. 'No worries, I won't tell anyone anything, I'll leave tomorrow and never come back again.'

Too late, the window had opened now. Wallie flung herself upon Carla.

'Carla, please don't do this! This isn't a solution!'

'Oh yes it is!' Carla turned around and pushed her away with surprising strength. Wallie was winded and took a step back. Carla used the opportunity to pick up one of bottles with the coins. She ran to the window with it, leaned over and let it drop.

Wallie heard the sound of glass shattering and coins rolling all over the cobblestones. Carla was completely, utterly mad!

'There, feeling better now?'

'No,' said Carla, 'Not at all.'

7

Carla finally fell asleep shortly before dawn. When her alarm rang, she felt as if she'd been wading through treacle, and as nauseous as if she'd drunk a litre of Berliner Luft and eaten a sizeable portion of bad mussels. She dragged herself out of bed with some difficulty and tried not to think of her father. Instead, she focused on what she had to do: have a shower, get dressed. She was still heavy as lead when she went into the kitchen.

She heard voices – a disgustingly cheerful Wallie, and Mother's voice, which sounded remarkably different. Chirruping, almost like a nightingale. Oh, she should have sent this swindler packing yesterday!

She stopped in the doorway, surprised. The good dinner service, the one with the golden edging. When the two women noticed her, they fell silent, as if they were already keeping secrets from her. They stared at her as if she were the stranger.

'Good morning,' Carla managed to say.

'You look tired,' said Wallie, who was sitting in Carla's place.

Mother nodded and looked somehow triumphant. Carla looked at her more carefully and noticed that she'd changed her hair, it looked a bit less like concrete, freer somehow.

'New hairstyle? From *Constanze*?' she asked, ignoring Wallie.

'Coffee?' asked Wallie, standing up and manoeuvring her big body around the tiny kitchen, as if it were her natural environment. She'd tied Carla's favourite flowery apron around her waist, although she wasn't slender enough to tie a double bow with the apron-strings, Carla was pleased to note.

Wallie didn't wait for an answer and poured out some coffee into the third cup that was on the table. For the first time since Father's death, Carla took his seat.

'The hairstyle isn't from *Constanze*,' said Mother cheerfully, 'Cousin Wallie took pity on me.'

Pity. Carla nearly choked on her coffee and tried to regain her composure. She had offered to help Mother with her hair hundreds of times, but she kept saying that Carla didn't have the right kind of hands for a hairstylist, which was obvious from the way she did her own hair.

'Looks good on you.' It was true, but Carla felt she was choking on the words.

'Wallie was a hairdresser, before she got discovered as a singer.'

Incredible what an accomplished liar Wallie was. Hairdresser? Singer? She hadn't mentioned a word of that last night. And how had she managed to convince Mother, who hated all diminutives, to call her Wallie? Anyway, all that so-called evidence could have been garnered from who knows where. In the daylight, it seemed even less likely that Father could have betrayed them like that. Wallie was a natural blonde and so much bigger and curvier than her. Wallie had blue eyes, while her own were brown.

Carla took a roll. Had Wallie been to the bakery already? She'd obviously spent a great night on the inflatable mattress. Even though she'd ostensibly lost her home yesterday and destroyed Carla's life in the process. Yet her so-called half-sister didn't look like a victim of unjust world politics, on the contrary, she seemed to be blooming.

'She says my hair is very delicate,' Mother nodded in a self-satisfied manner, glad that someone had recognized her problem at last.

Yes, as delicate as your heart, thought Carla. She pressed her lips tightly, so as not to let anything slip, ignoring Wallie's winks as she cut her roll. She spread butter and plum jam on it but could not bite into it. The brown stuff suddenly looked disgusting.

'I'm so sorry, I need to go down into the office, I have lots of things to do today,' she said, pushing the plate away.

'So you could use Wallie's help.'

'Cousin Wallie would rather keep you company. I'm sure she has many more ideas for your delicate hair. I'm sure she's more of an expert in that than in investigations.' Carla smiled straight up at Wallie's face. Wallie nodded with an admiring grin.

'It'd be an honour,' she said. 'I can't imagine anything better than having a heart-to-heart with Auntie Ida.'

Was that a threatening tone? Would Waltraud tell Mother everything? But that meant she'd get kicked out instantly, so it was surely not in her interest.

'Cousin Wallie is talking nonsense.' Her mother glowed with joy, sitting up straighter in her wheelchair. 'It's not very inspiring to sit and chat with an old woman like me who never leaves the house.'

I need to get out of here, Carla thought. *Or I'll go crazy.* She took her cup and stood up. 'I'm late,' she mumbled and rushed out of the apartment.

***

One flight down, Katrin was sitting in the doorway of the agency in a checked dress with a lace collar, holding her gym bag on her lap. She was chewing the end of one of her thick plaits; the more she chewed, the more preoccupied she seemed. She looked upset. Grateful for the chance to forget about her own worries for a moment, Carla hunched down next to Katrin to find out why she was waiting there for her.

'What happened?' Carla asked, taking a sip of her coffee before it got completely cold, 'Why aren't you in school?'

'Mum didn't want me to go because of the circumstances.'

'What circumstances?'

Katrin stared at Carla as if she'd gone mad and tapped her finger to her head. 'The Wall? The crisis?'

Of course, the whole city was in a state of emergency, not just the Koslowsky family. Not that it made the sudden appearance of Wallie any more palatable.

'So there is no school today?'

'No, but Mum is a worrywart.'

'Well, you can't stay with me today, I have too much to do. Would you like a biscuit?'

'No, I got summat for you for a change.'

Katrin stood up and held out her gym bag, smiling with pride. Her skinny arm was trembling, so it must be something heavy.

Carla was moved and picked up the bag with her free hand, but it was so heavy that her arm gave way and she nearly spilled her coffee.

'Yesterday I went out for a sec after our chat.' Katrin searched Carla's face. 'And suddenly it was tinklin' all round me with gold, as if by magic. Or as if that guy up there,' Katrin looked up at the ceiling, 'wanted to comfort Berlin for all it's goin' through.'

Carla broke into a sweat. In her angry outburst yesterday, she hadn't thought for a minute that the bottle or the coins could fall on someone's head. She wasn't sure what to say.

'But...' continued Katrin, throwing her dark blonde plaits over her shoulder and sticking out her chest, 'Sherlock Holmes doesn't believe in miracles, so I switched on my brain and realized that it wasn't a gold rain, but the coins from your bottle.'

Whenever Katrin switched to proper German, it was clear she wanted to impress Carla.

'So I collected them all. And now you have to make me your assistant!'

Carla gave the bag back to Katrin. 'That was very kind of you,' she said, somewhat hoarsely, 'Please keep the money.'

Katrin stamped her foot. 'I thought you'd be jazzed about it! You said these coins meant summat to you, because of your daddy!'

Carla swallowed hard. She didn't want to lie to Katrin, but she couldn't tell her the truth either.

The phone in the office started to ring. She stole a quick glance at her watch – it was just after eight, so it could be something urgent. The watch reminded her again of Wallie, her father and Achim. She would call the latter right away and ask him if he'd known about this all these years.

Katrin was still standing in front of her, looking as if her world was about to crumble.

'I'm sorry, I didn't express myself correctly. You've done a very good job and I'm grateful. Please consider that money the first salary for being my new assistant. Come here.'

'Really?' Katrin still looked doubtful.

This poor child had picked up all those coins from the dirty Berlin cobblestones. Carla set the coffee cup down on the stairs and held her arms wide open.

Katrin hesitated for a second, then went in for a hug. The smell of Fa soap mixed with unwashed hair and wet wool brought a lump to Carla's throat. She couldn't remember the last time someone had done something so nice for her. She mustn't be harsh with this little girl, her life was no bed of roses either.

'How did you manage to keep the money hidden from your brothers overnight?' she asked as she let Katrin go and looked into her thin face.

The girl laughed, 'Got a secret hidey-hole that the

Abominables don't know about.'

'Excellent. As my assistant, you definitely need a place where you can hide important documents,' said Carla.

Katrin beamed. Just then, the phone started ringing again. Maybe it was just Aunt Lulu, she could be as stubborn as herpes, but it might also be a new client.

'One condition, before I have to go to work.' Carla tried to sound severe while hoping she'd be able to reach the phone in time.

'Anything!'

'Any assistant of mine does not chew her plaits.'

Katrin stood up straight and saluted as if Carla were a colonel; 'Aye, aye, ma'am.'

'Dismissed!' said Carla, unlocking the door and then bending over to pick up her coffee cup. 'See you later.'

Katrin's shoulders sank, and Carla was afraid there'd be another big debate, but then the phone started ringing again, so the girl gave up, waved at her, hoisted the heavy bag on her shoulder and ran downstairs.

Carla rushed to the desk, stumbling over the mattress, which was not in the broom cupboard but in the middle of the room. The cup fell and smashed into smithereens, and she nearly lost her balance, then ran to the phone. Too late! Again!

'Damn!' She ran back to gather the shards and wipe up the coffee stains. She picked up the blanket lying on top of the mattress and folded it neatly, laying it on the tiny sofa near the entrance, next to the wardrobe. The whole office stank of the spilled coffee, yet there was a bit of Wallie's smell clinging to the blanket. Musky, somehow indecent, which made Carla even angrier. She had to get rid of that woman, and quickly.

She let the air out of the mattress. That was exactly what she should do to Wallie, let the air out before she had the chance to say anything more and destroy Carla's life with her presence.

After she'd stowed everything away in the broom cupboard next to Wallie's suitcase, she switched on the desk lamp and put on some fresh water for coffee. She opened a window but the air outside was already warm.

Speaking of Wallie's suitcase...that she'd kicked down the stairs the previous day... What else might be in there, other than those vulgar panties? None of her business.

On the contrary. Anything to do with Wallie was her business, after all she was the one who'd shown up here and forced her to see her whole office with fresh eyes. She'd never noticed before that the place had become a shrine to her father. She had to get rid of it all, especially that ridiculous leather chair. That and the monstrous ashtray, so as not to be reminded of his betrayal.

She went into the broom cupboard and opened Wallie's suitcase. A strong smell arose from it. She searched through Wallie's stuff: underwear, some of it quite decent from Triumph, nylon stockings, some of them still in their original wrapping, a toiletry bag with the usual stuff, a lot of lipsticks, a wig. She shook the hair on the wig – short grey hair. Perhaps it had belonged to her mother? A sentimental souvenir? After all, it seemed hardly possible that Wallie would wear it. It had to be significant, somehow, after all this suitcase must contain the most important things from her half-sister's life. She continued her search. Three skirts, a petticoat, capri trousers in a pink Vichy check pattern, tops, jumpers, no photos, no diary, nothing, only a pencil case with some pens. She must have left a lot behind in her apartment. Carla wondered what she might take under such circumstances.

The phone rang again. She closed the suitcase hastily and ran to the phone, grabbing her pen and notebook on the way. She was ready to take notes. 'Nightingale & Co.,' she answered.

Someone hung up.

The day could only get better. She remembered the water

– yes, it had long since boiled, while she was rummaging through the suitcase. She put some fresh water in the kettle and went to tidy away the suitcase, next to the air mattress.

While waiting for the kettle to boil again, she tried to distract herself from thinking too much about the good-for-nothing Wallie by making a list of all she had to do that day. First, call Achim and ask about Wallie. Then, get in touch with her army contacts. She had let that slip a little since Father's death, which might pose a problem now. If she'd met up regularly for a casual lunch with Dave and Mike, it would've been easier to ask for a favour. The only person she had continued to meet with was Sally, they'd gone to watch *Gone with the Wind* together because it was Sally's favourite film. But Sally was only responsible for the army night clubs, Dave was the one who had access to all the personnel files. How on earth could she find this Jack, also known as Jackov or Bobbs?

Almost against her better judgement, she found herself envying Ingrid. How could one be so certain that one's feelings were reciprocated? How unfair that Cupid shot his arrows at whim, and only in the rarest of cases did they spark a flame in both people at the same time. The more common situation was that one was in love, while the other suffered. She used to think that Father must have loved Ida once upon a time, after all, he had all those unusual nicknames for her: 'Little Roach', when she came back from swimming with red eyes. As a child, she thought her father must be a saint because he was so gentle and loving with Mother. Only a saint could love such a merciless woman. Well, not quite such a saint, as it turned out.

The water boiled and Carla made coffee. The aroma reminded her of the four lumps of sugar that Father put in his coffee when he got home after his experiences as a POW during the war. 'There are only a few short, sweet moments in life.' He must have known quite a few of those in his life. Wallie and she were nearly the same age. How did that happen with Wallie's mother? How long did it last? Not long, probably. Love is the fire that burns out all too quickly, nothing you can rely upon. Obviously, you couldn't rely on the family either, as she'd just found out. It might be best for each one of us to build a wall around ourselves, to keep us safe from all this madness.

She sat down next to the phone and searched for the number to Achim's office.

Ringing again, but this time it was the doorbell.

Alma was standing in front of her, but she was barely recognizable. Her left arm was in plaster, there was a blue-green bruise under her right eye. She was trembling, although she was wearing two thick knitted jumpers.

'For heaven's sake!' Carla cried out, helping Alma to the rattan chair and bringing a couple of cushions to make her more comfortable.

'I'm sorry, I didn't know where else to go.'

'Were you the one calling earlier?'

Alma nodded, but the movement seemed to cause her some pain.

Carla brought cups, coffee and biscuits, even offered some alcohol, but Alma turned that down.

She regretted once more not being a lawyer, so she could advise Alma in more detail.

'Thank you,' whispered Alma, picking up her cap and clasping it with both hands, as if eager to have a little warmth in her life. 'I know you told me yesterday that you can't do anything, but I had to try again. I don't trust anyone else, they all adore my husband.'

Loud knocking at the door made Alma cower.

'Are you expecting anyone? No one must see me here.'

'Carla, it's me, Wallie, let me in! Or should I get the keys from Pallutzke?'

Was that a threat? Wallie hammered on the door and Alma cringed at every sound, looking around for a place to hide.

'Please excuse me for a moment.' Carla stood up and flung the door open, pushing Wallie back into the corridor.

'What's this about? I'm working now. You go and cosy up to Mother. Do her hair or go for a walk, just leave me alone.'

'I could help.'

'In my agency, it's all about delicate cases, not delicate hair.'

'Two heads are better than one.' Was Wallie aware that she was quoting Father?

'I've got plenty of ideas myself,' hissed Carla.

'As you wish,' Wallie shrugged. 'Then please bring me my coat, which I left in the wardrobe.'

Carla turned round in silence and set off for the wardrobe. That seemed to be what Wallie was after, for she stormed into the office, stopped short upon seeing Alma and then crouched down beside her.

'You must have been through something terrible!'

Alma looked towards Carla in fright. 'Who is this?'

A con artist, was what Carla would have liked to say, but of course that wouldn't have been helpful. 'Please don't worry, this is Waltraud von Tilling, a distant cousin who occasionally works for the agency.' *As a cleaner*, was what she'd have liked to add, but she refrained from doing so.

Alma seemed relieved.

Wallie stood, went to the kitchen as if she owned the place, brought her own cup of coffee and pushed a chair right next to Alma.

'Waltraud is of course as discreet as I am,' said Carla, throwing her a crushing look. 'Alma, I think we should contact the lawyer in the West who specializes in tricky divorce cases. I will write down the number for Dr Elisabeth Adler, she can help you far better than I can.'

'But I thought... I mean, you know me and so...'

'Alma, like I said yesterday, there isn't much we can do if Alexander isn't having any extramarital affairs.'

'I'm of a different opinion there, if you don't mind, cousin dearest...'

Cousin dearest? Carla felt a flush of anger mounting up to her face. *I'd like to wring her neck*, she thought, but tried not to let it show.

'We could do quite a bit for Alma.'

Alma sat up and looked more hopefully at the two of them. 'Yes?'

'My cousin is not aware of the situation...' Carla intervened, praying that Wallie would hold her tongue.

'Not true,' said Wallie, 'I'm fully informed. You are Alma Hochbrück, your husband is award-winning architect Professor Alexander Hochbrück, and he thrashes you... sorry, I meant to say he beats you, clearly. You need a reason for a divorce and I think we can provide one.'

'Really?' Relief flooded over Alma's face like sunrise on a summer's day.

It was dishonest to give Alma false hope. And how did Wallie know all this? Was it possible that Carla had been so upset last night, that she hadn't locked away the client folders properly?

'Yes, really.' Wallie gave an indecently broad grin. 'Don't worry, that is my speciality.'

'How do you...?'

'Let that be our concern, the less you know about it, the better.'

'Thank you.' Alma gave a deep sigh of relief. 'You're a lifesaver.'

Wallie nodded. 'I can believe that.' She pointed at Alma's bruise. 'You'd better get that looked at.'

'It's fine.' Alma inadvertently touched her face and shuddered. 'How are we going to keep in touch? You mustn't come to my house, by any means. If the neighbours see you, or the children, and Alexander finds out, then I'm in trouble. If it's urgent, can Carla please call and say it's about the orphanage?' Alma stood up. 'He thinks I'm out shopping now and must not get suspicious. Will you be coming to the gala dinner for the orphanage, Carla?'

Carla nodded.

'Please don't mention anything about seeing me to him.' Alma shuddered again in pain. She looked from Wallie to Carla. 'Can I rely on the two of you?'

'Of course,' said Wallie, with such a warm, concerned and firm voice, that Carla felt she would trust her with anything.

'It shouldn't take long. I – I mean we...' Wallie demonstratively included Carla, 'We are known for prompt results.'

Carla stood up and accompanied Alma to the door, to end this charade as quickly as possible. When she returned, Wallie was standing right in front of her.

'Don't say anything!' Wallie stuck out her ample bosom like a Viking warrior, 'I really think I can seduce her husband.'

'Overestimating yourself a little there? Hochbrück doesn't have a mistress or any other vices you can use.'

'Nonsense, everyone has some secret vice, and I could make him kiss me even if he were a homo. All we need is someone to take a picture at the right moment and we're all sorted. If you don't want to do it, I can get a friend of mine.'

'That's very naïve of you. For a divorce, you need more than a photo of a kiss.'

'Then I will swear that this creep broke his marriage vows with me.'

'You would lie under oath?' Carla had to sit down. Wallie obviously had no scruples. 'Under oath for a client? And why do you think you can simply inveigle your way to working here?'

'Maybe Dad wanted it this way?' Wallie cleared away the cups on the tray and started munching on the biscuits.

'Yummy, especially the chocolate ones.' She sounded a bit muffled with her mouth full. 'You have to teach bastards like him a lesson, don't you?'

'Of course, but by legal means.'

'But can you do it legally? Is it legal to rape your wife and beat her?' She took the last biscuit and carried the tray into the kitchen.

'If you want to change the law, you should study it first.'

'I don't want to change the law, I merely want justice.' Wallie came back and sank down into the rattan chair. The corner of her mouth was smeared with chocolate, which made her seem more vulnerable. Carla wished she wouldn't look like that, she wanted to hate her.

'And who decides what justice is?' she asked, in a sharper tone than she had originally intended.

'Well, good old common sense, what else?'

Carla rolled her eyes. 'Good old common sense brought Hitler into power, good old common sense blamed the Jews for everything, good old common sense burnt books and more! Stop telling me about good old common sense!'

'Finished your ridiculous little speech?' Wallie's lips curled sceptically. 'If each one of us had had a bit more courage to follow their good old common sense, then we wouldn't all have followed the Führer like lemmings...'

'Would've, could've – all speculation. I forbid you to get involved in Alma's case and do something illegal. The agency has to be above suspicion at all times. If I get my permit revoked, then Mother and I are out on the streets. We're not allowed to engage in any criminal activity, any illegal act will turn on us.' *And how,* Carla completed the sentence in her head. After all, that was why Father was dead.

Her words did not seem to penetrate Wallie's skull, because she was smiling at her almost with pity.

'It must be nice to be so sure of what is right and wrong. I promise I won't do anything to compromise you. And now I'm off to do something decent, because your mum asked me to buy a few things for her.' She took her trench coat out of the wardrobe, started whistling a perky little tune and left the office.

Of course. Her poor mother had no one else to look after her.

Speaking of which. She finally sat down and called Achim's law firm, hoping to hear that Wallie was nothing but a nasty swindler taking advantage of the wall-building situation. But Achim was away at a conference on inheritance law in Vienna and was hard to reach. In case of emergency, they could leave a message for him at the hotel. For Heaven's sake! Carla thanked them but said she would rather speak to him personally. She felt quite dazed, not surprising in the heat. It wasn't just the heat, she knew that. She walked slowly towards the window, opened it and held her head out, as if to clear it. But the sultry summer air made her feel as sticky as she'd felt inside the office filled with false promises.

8

So this was where the swine worked! Wallie got off Carla's bicycle and leant it against one of the linden trees that had clearly survived the war better than the buildings of the Technical University. A quick glance at the watch she'd inherited from her dad and reclaimed from Carla's drawer told her that she'd make it in time, despite the furious crowds demonstrating in front of the town hall, which had paralysed half of West Berlin that day. Wallie had to make a detour to avoid them, but she still managed to hear their useless shouting: 'Berlin wants more than words! Berlin wants action!' She always felt an itch to run away when she saw mass demonstrations. What sort of action did they want? Hadn't they learnt anything from the past? It wasn't enough to just stand there and repeat slogans. Everyone had to contribute.

It was a good job that she'd 'borrowed' Carla's bike to hear all of that though, because if she'd taken the U-Bahn she wouldn't have heard it and someone like her needed to be well informed. Besides, she couldn't help feeling a little thrill of pleasure at the thought of her sister's face when she saw the empty bicycle stand. That silly little lock had been embarrassingly easy to pick.

Suddenly all the doors opened and students poured out in little groups, breaking up and re-forming, heading towards the canteen. Wallie joined the flow. She didn't get the feeling that the students were any too anxious about the Wall being built, there was no moaning or muttering about it, no shaking of heads. They were studying and going to eat, like good little citizens. Just not quite so smartly dressed. They seemed to study in more casual clothes over here, good job she'd prepared for that. The capris and the jumper were a bit tighter on her than what the other girls were wearing, but it fitted in with their style. In fact, there weren't that many female students. In the East, there were far more.

She thought of Erika and her wild student friends, who lived on the first floor of the Tucholskystraße building, and who were just as much of a thorn in the neighbours' side as Frieda on the fifth and of course Wallie herself. On the 8th of March, Erika had thrown a party, because Humboldt University had set up a programme of support for women in science, the first university in Germany to do so. Wallie had been far more interested in the men who came to the party. She liked Heinrich, a bear of a man, and started flirting with him. He seemed to like it and they'd ended up expressing their passion in the broom cupboard, where Erika stumbled upon them and burst into tears. Wallie had been filled with consternation, firstly, because she'd never thought that the somewhat brash Erika could cry, secondly because she'd never mentioned a boyfriend. The reason she'd been embarrassed to admit to the boyfriend was that Heinrich was studying medicine in the West, at the Free University.

Wallie looked at the students here and thought they were lucky. Because of course Heinrich would have had to stop his studies now. Those East Berliners studying in the West had been whisked off to drive lorries or tractors or to work in agricultural cooperatives. They had to prove that they weren't an enemy of the people. She wondered whether he and Erika still kept in touch. At the time, she'd run away from Erika's tears and found comfort with Frieda and a few glasses of Blaue Würger Kristall vodka.

Wallie remembered Frieda's deep, warm voice and how she'd preface every drink with 'Hop and hoes, and down it goes!' and then laugh her smoky, sensual laugh. 'Babes, Erika should stop wailing – men think with their eyes and one floor below. All of 'em. Especially those who study, though they don't think so themselves. It's dumb to reproach them for it. Our bodies are still stuck in the Stone Age, there's no point denying it. We women just have to be smart and take advantage.'

Erika, who joined them later, thought Frieda's way of thinking was naïve. Men weren't hormonally challenged Neanderthals, they were in control. They held all the strings, supported each other, kept women down, oppressed them in all sorts of ways. Manipulating them by wiggling your bottom, that wasn't equality, it was prostitution.

Wallie squared her shoulders and entered the canteen. She had a job to do. The past was the past, what counted now was the present. She might be able to find something out about Alma's husband here among the students. When so many people get together, there'll always be some gossip.

She grabbed one of the grey plastic trays and queued for mashed potatoes with sauce. Didn't smell too bad. She began to salivate, even though she'd had a leisurely breakfast with Carla's mum for the past two days. A good chance to find out more about the family. *Careful now,* she warned herself, *curves are fine, but no rolls of fat, please.* Even though she personally agreed with Erika, Frieda's advice was just as good. Men were easier to charm when you were curvy, and you had to use what weapons you'd been given.

Her curves, however, did nothing for the cashier, who looked at her with disdain and demanded her student card. Wallie said she'd forgotten it, but the woman was stubborn as a mule. Just when Wallie was about to give up, a student behind her tapped her on the shoulder and gave her his card, which the cashier accepted without a murmur, much to her surprise.

Wallie thanked the young man but turned down his invitation to join him at his table. His student card said Mechanical Engineering and she was looking for architecture students. But the student refused to let her go, behaving as though he'd purchased Wallie's company by giving her his card.

'No,' she said a little louder. People turned round, but that didn't seem to bother the student.

A shorter man appeared next to them.

'This lady is joining me,' he said, waving the student away.

She had to look down at him, so the first thing she noticed about him was his flowing, somewhat too long chestnut locks. When he looked up at her, she nearly spluttered. He was incredibly good-looking, could have passed for James Dean's brother – and it was clear he was aware of it.

'We know each other,' said James Dean Junior. When he opened his mouth, his bad teeth ruined his appearance. She looked at him more closely: he did look familiar, but where from?

'Really? With that chat-up line you couldn't have turned a monkey's head a hundred years ago!' Wallie searched her brain, surely she'd have remembered a pretty face like that?

'But I do know you, you're Nelly!'

From Eden, of course, that was why he'd gone straight into using informal language with her, that was how you addressed bar staff.

'Yes,' she replied snottily, 'And during the day I study here, if you don't mind. Any other questions?'

'Of course, I'm sorry, I didn't mean it like that. Would you like to join us?' He pointed to a table. The other guys sitting there seemed a bit older, like him.

'Fine,' Wallie resigned herself. After all, she had to start somewhere.

James Dean II headed towards the table, then turned around and said to her; 'Apologies, I haven't introduced myself. My name is Klaus. Architecture.'

Bull's-eye! Wallie tried not to grin. The fun was about to start.

'I would have loved to do architecture,' said Wallie, 'But my marks were too bad, so now I'm studying...' What else was there? 'German.'

'But you have the canteen in the Silberlaube?'

'Yes, but yours is nicer!' *Silberlaube? Not a clue*, thought Wallie, but tried to brush over the awkward moment with a laugh. 'I prefer it here, still dreaming of architecture. Bauhaus and whatnot.' She really should have prepared more thoroughly for this.

'Naturally, this is where all the good folks are!' They reached the table. The other students looked at her with interest, and a couple of them winked meaningfully at Klaus, holding up their thumbs as if Wallie was a trophy that he had brought back after a tournament.

'Klaus goes and does it again!' said one of them, who wore thick horn-rimmed glasses.

'Always gets the best-looking ones,' said another, who looked older than Klaus, in fact quite grey and ill.

'I have to apologise for this horde,' said Klaus, shaking his head, although Wallie was sure he was secretly proud. 'I'm an assistant lecturer here and look after these apes. This here is Nelly. Imagine that, she'd like to study architecture!'

'Of course, with those curves,' said Glasses, winking at her. 'Tuck in.' He nodded and dug his knife into a meatball.

Wallie sat down and took a spoonful of mashed potato. The smell might have been fine, but it tasted of wallpaper paste and wet tissues, liberally salted.

'If this is better than the Silberlaube, I'll eat a

broomstick!' whispered Klaus.

Wallie swallowed it down bravely, wiped her mouth with a napkin and smiled at him. She'd have loved to bring Hochbrück into the conversation right away, but she reminded herself to be patient.

'So, Klaus, let's continue the game, it's your turn,' said Glasses, with his mouth full.

What sort of game would that be?

'So, Klaus, if Willy Brandt were a building in Berlin, which one would he be?'

Really, that was the kind of game they played? They had nothing better to do? But she had to keep up with them. Watch and learn.

'The Congress Hall,' said Klaus immediately.

'Why?' asked the ill-looking one.

'That floating roof, that flowing shape...' Klaus demonstrated with a wide hand movement that nearly took the glasses off his friend's nose. Glasses drew back and rolled his eyes.

'Besides,' said Wallie, 'That roof is exactly like Brandt's rolling Rs!'

Everyone stopped eating and stared at her in surprise. Good move.

'Not bad! Want to join in?' said Klaus.

'With pleasure.'

'Let's see,' began Klaus, but Glasses interrupted him with a wicked grin, 'So which building would Adenauer be?'

'Adenauer? Let's see...' she repeated, to gain time, but all the buildings she could think of were too beautiful for that stubborn old Catholic man, who couldn't give a shit about Berlin. She tried to remember anything she might have learnt from her mother about architecture.

'I know! The Ullstein House!' she said at last, pleased with herself.

They stared at her, waiting for an explanation.

'It's almost neo-gothic, looks a bit like a cathedral. A giant with a skeleton of steel.'

Glasses whistled. 'Not bad!'

'Do you play games like that with your professors?' asked Wallie, eager to weave Hochbrück into the conversation at last.

'Nah, they've all actually built stuff, Eiermann, Scharoun...'

'I heard that Professor Hochbrück is the best?' asked Wallie.

They all smirked as they turned to look at Klaus.

'Ask him, he's the teacher's pet,' said Glasses with a tone that Wallie couldn't quite pin down. Was it envy or contempt? In any case, it was a good move. They were getting to the human side of things.

'I'm his assistant, not the teacher's pet. He appreciates my work and my ideas.'

'Of course he does,' the ill-looking man intervened, with an extravagant hand movement that spilled some sauce over his shirt, not that it bothered him. 'The Professor is the pet of all sorts of important people, or how might you explain the scandal surrounding the project in the Fasanen Street?'

'What scandal, you haven't got a clue what you're talking about!' Klaus rolled his eyes.

Wallie wondered if he was having an affair with Alma's husband. She thought not, or there'd have been a much clearer edge to the conversation.

'Hochbrück's design was simply more realistic. He's so experienced,' said Klaus, full of admiration. 'At least he's not an opportunist like the Kressmann-Zschach woman.'

They all groaned, Wallie had no idea what they were talking about, and raised an eyebrow at Klaus.

'Zschach is an architect and she married her second husband, Mayor Kressmann, so the boss of Kressmannsdorf...'

'Kressmannsdorf?'

'Kreuzberg, I mean. She only married him so that she'd be the first to know about planning permission in the city,' said Klaus impatiently, as if he was having to explain the basic principles of an alphabet to someone illiterate. 'You can have the best ideas as an architect, but if you don't have the connections, it simply won't work!'

'Give me a break! That arrogant bastard Hochbrück!' said Glasses.

Klaus put his hand on the other's arm and interrupted him. 'Watch out, you're going too far.'

Unimpressed by Klaus's warning, Glasses continued, all the while mopping up the sauce with a bit of bread and then placing his cutlery on the plate. 'He never had a proper idea in his life! I remember all too well, when he invited us to his chic glass attic studio in his super-villa in Dahlem. With a custom-made staircase. How nice of him. Supposedly, so that we could be more creative in our thinking. When in fact he was just shamelessly using us.'

'You should be flattered that you were part of his team!' said Klaus, tapping on his forehead. 'When was the last time you had a genius of an idea, that was fully worked out and on time?'

Glasses ignored him and continued talking to Wallie, as if Klaus hadn't said a word. 'I'm puzzled why this man keeps on getting all those awards for his rather mediocre work. He's been shortlisted once again for the LaGuardia Competition.'

Klaus grinned, for no discernible reason. Wallie had been expecting him to argue further, but he didn't. The discussion was going off-track, time to dig a bit deeper.

'An acquaintance of mine told me that Hochbrück gives preferential treatment to some of his female students. As his assistant, surely you can tell me if that's true or not?'

They all stared at Wallie indignantly, as if she'd said something embarrassing, then started to laugh.

'Good joke!' gasped Klaus, showing far too much of his

teeth. 'Alexander is Catholic, and SO married that you shouldn't waste any hopes on him.'

'And Klaus should know,' said the man with the dirty shirt.

They probably thought she was keen to get to study architecture by stealth. No problem, this wouldn't bother Nelly from Eden in any case. She laughed cheekily and shrugged her shoulders, so that her deep décolletage became even more visible.

'You could try with Müller in Statics, he's supposed to like blondes,' said Glasses.

'Couldn't care less about Statics,' Wallie began, but couldn't continue because the sickly-looking man started gasping with laughter. He drew the shape of giant tits in the air and said, 'Not interested in being static!'

The others all began to laugh too. Obviously, she wasn't going to get much more out of this.

'Thank you for your company. I have to go now.' Wallie stood up and made her way to the conveyor belt for the dirty trays, wiggling her bottom as she went. She could feel them all staring after her. She bent over as she placed the tray on the belt and turned round suddenly – indeed, she hadn't lost a single one of the men. So at least her attractions remained undiminished. But she hadn't got a lot out of it. She waved at the students and went to get Carla's bike.

So Hochbrück had a loyal assistant, didn't play around with his female students, probably wasn't gay either, possibly a committed Christian, faithful till death do us part. Wallie shuddered: what a horrible idea. Eternal love and fidelity were worse than chronic illness. At least with the latter, you had some surprises every now and then.

The Professor would be a tough nut to crack. Well, if the worst came to the worst, she'd put something in his drink. It had certainly worked with Baldy-Holger. She wanted to get this picture for Alma and her kids. And to annoy Carla a little, she had to admit.

No sign of the damn bike.

Whatever the case may be, Hochbrück was still human, and humans were always prone to vanity. She'd learnt that not from Frieda, but from Tucholsky, her mother's favourite author. 'People are always keen to hear promises, flattery, praise and compliments. When it comes to flattery, it's always better to go three sizes bigger than you expect.'

But for that, she'd have to find a way to get close to the man. Maybe that gala dinner for the orphanage at the Kempinski?

Where the hell was that bike? Nowhere to be found. To annoy Carla by borrowing the bike was one thing, but to return home without it would be a disaster.

First things first, though. She'd go on foot to the Kempinski and check to see if Edgar was on duty.

She saw him as soon as she went through the golden revolving door at the Kempinski. Goodness, he looked so serious – bald head, no lipstick. But he looked pale, somehow not quite himself.

He was standing next to Reception, behind the slightly taller lectern of the Chief Concierge, watching over everything like a spider contemplating his web. A single frown would be enough to sow panic among the bellboys.

As Wallie drew near, he looked up in surprise and stopped dead.

'Edgar,' she began.

'Nelly, are you crazy? Not here!' he hissed, looking all around him.

'I need your help urgently,' Wallie pleaded.

Fine drops of sweat appeared on his forehead. 'I've got a break in half an hour. We can meet outside the currywurst stand at Bahnhof Zoo. Go now! And next time you come to the only five-star establishment in West Berlin, please wear something decent.' He shook his head as he examined her from head to toe. 'I have to accompany you outside, otherwise I'll get into trouble. We don't tolerate horizontal business here.'

He came out from behind his lectern, took hold of her elbow and dragged her towards the revolving door.

'Nonsense!' Her capris were a bit tight, but surely not indecent. No need to make such a fuss. But she swallowed her indignation and smiled, as if he'd paid her a compliment. After all, she needed his help.

'See you later.' He nodded and pushed her so hard towards the revolving door, that she stumbled even in her ballet flats. What sort of Angel was that? She'd show him the next time he came to Eden and wanted something from her.

***

Half an hour later, they were indeed standing in front of Gerda's currywurst stand. Wallie waited patiently without saying a word, until Edgar had gobbled his currywurst and 'red-white' fries with ketchup and mayo. He apologized to her with his mouth full.

'Sorry about earlier. But the director had just been showing his very fussy wife around the redecorated rooms. You know she hates women wearing trousers and thinks all women without a wedding ring are sluts. If I was rough with you, I'm really sorry. I'm not quite myself, I'm worried about Adele.'

'Why?' Half a year earlier, with Wallie's help, he'd been able to find a place for his sister Adele in a good mental health clinic. But of course – the Wall! The clinic was outside West Berlin, in Brandenburg. Wallie realized the implications.

'How can I pay her a visit? What can I do? Can I bring her over here? What will happen to her?'

The reason Edgar was working at the Eden was to make extra money for Adele. He'd thought it would do her good to be in the East, because she'd grown up there and it helped her troubled psyche. He really had been a lucky angel for his sister and spent every spare moment with her.

'I'm so sorry,' said Wallie, 'Is there anything I can do to help?'

'I'm still in shock, apologies. What did you want to discuss so urgently?'

Although she really did feel sorry for him and Adele, Wallie knew that the quickest way to reach her goal would be to attack his weak points.

She made up a story designed to appeal to him. It didn't take too long to win Edgar over, despite his own problems. Shocking what this lousy Hochbrück was doing to her sister, incredible how depressed poor Carla had become, so much so that she struggled to leave her bed. Of course Edgar would help her to teach this man a lesson. He'd get hold of a room for Nelly and speak to the housekeeper at the Kempinski to allow her to work as a waitress during the gala dinner for the benefit of the orphanage, a waitress at the table of Professor Hochbrück.

He went back to the Kempinski full of energy. Don't you just love do-gooders?

9

'By no means!' Carla looked at Lulu's poodle and shook her head. 'Fritzi will not be staying here, over my dead body!' Bad enough that Wallie had been driving her mad for the past few days, she didn't need a dog who barked for no reason, filling the office with the nasty smell of damp fur.

Aunt Lulu fell into her ingénue role, full of suffering innocence. She sank into a heap and wiped a non-existent tear from her eyes. 'No one on earth cares to help me,' she whispered, a little out of breath as she bent over Fritzi. 'Heartless and cold, but a little bit of love would warm up this poor creature here...'

Carla rolled her eyes. 'Love is something else, not smooching a drooly snout or taking a flea-carpet to bed.'

'You, Maid of Steel, have no idea what you're talking about!' Lulu stood up again with a slight whimper. 'You have no idea what passion means. I have to go to Munich! They're going to continue filming there and Fritzi would just get in the way.'

Carla remembered bumping into Billy Wilder at the Brandenburg Gate. It felt like years ago, not a mere five days. All the troubles since: the building of the Wall, the reaction of the Allied Forces, Wallie showing up.

'I have it on good authority that this time Billy has a part for me.' Lulu handed her the dog leash decorated with gold studs, as if she were giving her the Holy Grail. These cheap tricks made it hard for Carla to take her seriously.

'Of course, but I think you should fly there instead of driving,' she said. 'You have to hurry! You're the only one who can save the film!'

Lulu looked stunned. Carla continued with her exaggeratedly anguished face. 'Lulu, the main part is waiting for you! Haven't you heard? I have it from an even more reliable source, one of my top informers, that Liselotte Pulver has fallen ill.'

'Oh?' Lulu seemed simultaneously sceptical and delighted.

'Yes, quite tragic. After a lengthy breakfast of Bavarian sausage this morning, Lilo Pulver exploded today in the food market in Munich.'

Lulu snapped indignantly, but then the corners of her mouth started to tremble, and she burst out laughing. Her little round body swayed from side to side, until she finally punched Carla's side. 'Stop, you should respect your aunt! That's not on!'

Loud hammering at the door startled them.

'Clients?' asked her aunt, wiping away her tears of laughter.

Carla shook her head. Clients tended to use the doorbell and Frau Pallutzke would yell, '*Helloooo*,' every time she heard a knock. It must be Wallie.

'What is it, child? You look as if you're expecting death warmed over,' said her aunt, deep in thought. 'It must be a man.'

Carla opened the door without answering.

'Finally!' Wallie entered the agency laden with bags, but with a cheerful smile.

'No need to tell you to make yourself at home,' said Carla behind her.

Wallie put her bags on the little sofa by the entrance, then turned to face Carla and Lulu and started taking off her gloves.

'It wasn't easy to find those little pralines that Ida likes so much,' she said.

Aunt Lulu stared at the two of them, with one eyebrow raised.

'Aunt Lulu, may I introduce you to my half-sister Waltraud von Tilling?' She pointed at her aunt. 'This is Lulu Kollo – that's her stage name. In fact, she is Father's sister, so your aunt as well, so of course her real name is the same as *our* father's,' for a moment there she had a lump in her throat when she said *our*, 'so Marie Luise Koslowsky.' Lulu had once upon a time been married to a von Bergendorf but had long since dropped that name.

'Who did you say?' Lulu stretched her neck, as if peering through a lorgnette to see Wallie better. 'Who?' she said in a real tragic voice, at least a Medea.

Wallie finished taking off her gloves, stepped forward and held out her hand. 'Delighted to make your acquaintance, Dad told me so much about you.'

Lulu sank into the black leather seat behind the desk without saying a word. Carla had never seen her so speechless, and even Fritzi seemed surprised by this state of affairs, for he started rubbing his head on her knees and whining.

'I'll get some water,' Carla said, going to the kitchen. It was some comfort that her aunt obviously had no idea of Father's love life in the eastern part of the city. So he hadn't even told his sister. She was curious to see how she'd digest that information.

'Such a cute dog.' Wallie tried to break the ice and knelt down beside Fritzi, but he started growling at her, a low but nevertheless menacing growl.

'Karl-Otto's daughter?' Lulu looked in alarm at Carla, completely ignoring Wallie. 'Which hole did she crawl out of? You let a swindler like that come and go as she pleases?'

'She's got proof,' Carla justified herself.

'Poppycock! Proof is cheap. After the war, everyone managed to find proof of just how white and untarnished they'd been, every one of them had only joined the Nazi party to save their Jewish friends.'

Carla knew what Lulu had been up to during the war, so she could sympathise with her indignation.

'I completely understand,' Wallie said, 'I never wanted to upset anyone from Dad's family, but I had no choice once the Wall went up. There was no way I was going to stay behind in the East. I've always worked in the West.'

Lulu jumped up, hands on her hips. Fritzi got out of her way just in time. 'Couldn't care less! What sort of proof do you have?'

Wallie took the Rolex off and handed it to her, together with the photo.

'Humph,' said Lulu, pushing the picture aside with such force that it fell to the floor. 'Sure, that's my brother, sitting on a blanket by the lake. But God alone knows if you're the little girl in that picture.'

Carla instinctively bent down to pick up the picture. She looked at the pleasant summer scene. Something suspicious about it, but what exactly?

She screwed up her eyes and examined the girl on the picnic blanket a little closer. Lovely blonde hair. She couldn't help wondering if her mother would have loved her more if she'd looked like a little blonde, blue-eyed angel. But that wasn't what troubled her. If the girl had been a stranger, then Carla would have considered her not only pretty, but actually quite irresistible, because she seemed so open and happy, as if she could always find a reason to have a laugh. Then she suddenly realized what it was.

Wallie's necklace. It was the exact same one she had. She touched the little die that hung, as always, at her throat.

'The necklace,' she said in a colourless voice, holding out the picture.

'What about it?' asked Wallie. 'Father gave me the gold necklace when I was nine or ten.'

Carla's was silver.

'Gold like my hair, and the dots were made of blue sapphires, to match my eyes. Supposed to bring luck. Ah well...'

He had told Carla it was to remind her that luck was fickle. She felt like ripping the necklace off her neck and throwing it in the toilet.

'And where is this necklace now?' asked Lulu, who could feel that Carla wasn't able to ask anything further.

Wallie shrugged. 'Pawnshop.'

Lulu and Carla groaned at the same time, just as Wallie added, 'I had to pay for Mum's funeral. She wanted a real big party, with a live band. That was in 1959. I'd only just started working at the Eden. Before that I was working as a salesgirl at the Import–Export group. Earned 280 marks. We sold relays, signal boosters and even brightly coloured phones to the capitalist markets.'

'Brightly coloured phones? No way.' Lulu glared.

'The plastic mix wasn't quite there yet, so they had a little crack just behind the receiver.' Wallie kept grinning, as if all this was incredibly funny.

Carla wondered if this was before or after her career as a hairdresser and a singer. And wouldn't Father have helped her out financially?

Nobody joined in Wallie's laughter, so she stopped suddenly and continued talking. 'Money was tight, so I started working at the Eden, but hadn't saved enough yet. But the necklace didn't fetch much, because it had my date of birth engraved in it. And besides, they weren't sapphires, just glass, and the chain was just gilded silver.'

Bad luck, thought Carla, mine are certainly gems, smoky quartz like my eyes. Her necklace also had her date of birth. This was so typical of her father, the Raisin Bomber, presents were cheaper when bought in bulk.

'Are we supposed to be moved to tears by this hard-up story about the funeral?' Lulu remained sceptical. 'Without the actual necklace, I can't believe a word of it.'

'The pawnshop is in the East,' said Wallie gently but firmly, as if Lulu was being a difficult child. 'Bit difficult to go there now.'

'How convenient!' Lulu shook her head and scratched Fritzi's back. There was another awkward silence.

The date of birth engraved on the necklace had managed to convince Carla. And the fact that he had bought the exact same type of jewellery for the two of them.

The phone ringing rescued them. She pushed Lulu away from the leather chair, picked up the receiver and hoped it would be a new client.

Instead, it was Ingrid Niemöller, who wanted to know if there was any news for her. Damn. Carla hated lying, especially in front of Lulu and Wallie, but she couldn't tell her the truth either. Namely, that she still had no idea who this Bobbs or Jackov was. She had spoken to several of the organisers of the folk festival, but with little success. She took out a folder from the drawer and pretended to read from it, all the while telling Frau Niemöller that the agency was examining several promising threads. The client wanted to come at once to the agency to pay for additional days, but Carla looked at the clock. It was nearly seven and the gala dinner would start at eight. She needed to freshen up and get changed, so she told Ingrid to come the next day, and hung up.

Wallie was standing by the window, while Lulu was shooting poisoned darts at her with her eyes.

'Sorry, you two, but I need to get ready for the dinner.' Carla stood up and hoped that would be the sign for all of them to get moving. She took the folders from her desk and locked them up in the filing cabinet.

'And you, miss,' said Lulu, 'should saddle up your cannonball...'

Carla and Wallie looked at Lulu without understanding. 'To prepare for the next Baron Munchhausen tall tale!' Lulu tapped her forehead again.

Carla suppressed a chuckle. It was so nice to not have to bear this sudden additional family member all on her own, to see that even someone like Lulu was struggling to accept it.

How could a swindler know, though, that Father tended to buy the same present for everyone? No, although it was painful to admit it, she had to draw the conclusion that Wallie was probably telling the truth.

'Where's the receipt from the pawnshop?' Lulu asked suddenly.

Wallie shrugged. 'Somewhere with my stuff.'

'I'd like to see that.'

'You don't have to treat me like a traitor to one's people. I left the East so that I could feel like a human once more.' For the first time, Wallie sounded a bit rattled, and Carla had to admit she found it not unpleasant.

'I'll take you downstairs,' she said to Lulu, checking once again that all the folders were safely in the filing cabinet and that it was locked. Then she nodded towards Wallie. 'See you tomorrow.'

In the hallway, Lulu handed the leash to Carla so that she could carry the giant poodle downstairs, because he could no longer cope with the stairs on his own. She sighed, picked up the heavy dog and tried not to inhale. The wet fur and meaty dog-food smell made her sneeze in spite of her precautions.

'She's lying,' said Lulu, lifting both arms in the air, like a mournful Cassandra. 'I can feel it in my bunions. You're mad to believe a single word she says, and to leave her on her own in Karl-Otto's office.'

'She's sleeping there for the time being, and Mum quite likes her,' said Carla, still panting after carrying the dog.

'Ida has always been a bit weak in the head. She loves anyone who flatters her. Or did you tell Ida that her husband had a mistress in the East?'

'Of course not,' Carla coughed. 'We said Wallie was a distant cousin.'

'It stinks to high heaven!'

Carla set Fritzi down in front of the entrance and tried to brush the dog hairs out of her suit.

'What are you gonna do now?' asked Lulu.

'I'll...' But before Carla could say anything else, Lulu interrupted.

'I know what I need to do! Billy Wilder can forget about me. I'm not going to Munich, I'm clearly needed here much more urgently.' She kissed her niece enthusiastically on both cheeks and patted her on the back. Carla wasn't sure if this was good news or bad news.

10

Carla walked through the revolving door at the Kempinski, took the elevator and went up to the freshly renovated loft space. She checked her black evening dress in the mirrored walls of the elevator. She'd had it made the day before at Uli Richter's fashion house. She caught the bellboy's admiring look. He instantly looked away, but Carla had noticed, and it made her smile. The dress really brought out her slender figure. She was almost tempted to believe Lulu when she said her niece looked like Audrey Hepburn.

Her throat felt bare, because for the first time in years she'd left behind her lucky charm necklace. It was like leaving her armour behind. Even the big brash rhinestone earrings that sparkled with every move she made couldn't stop her from feeling naked.

She wondered whether she'd be sitting at the same table as the Hochbrücks and was cross that Achim hadn't returned from Vienna, otherwise she'd have been accompanied by him.

Her mother had been desperate to find someone to accompany her, so she'd been vehement about insisting she didn't need anyone. Which wasn't quite true and anyway didn't stop her mother from phoning everyone she knew asking about the availability of their sons. Yes, it would have been nice to walk into the room on the arm of a gentleman, and for a brief moment she allowed herself to think of Richard. Then suddenly she remembered the nice young bodyguard, Bruno Eisenberg. That's whom she should have called.

She kept an eye out for Alma but couldn't spot her anywhere. She gratefully took a glass of champagne from one of the waitresses and searched for her table. Every seat cost 100 marks, of which 99 would go to the Berlin Fledglings. For that symbolic 1 mark per person, the Kempinski had given them the room and the dinner, including the waiting staff, while the drinks were supplied by the KaDeWe.

Father had founded the private orphanage together with two friends right after the war. While searching for little Therese Mützler, he'd experienced how overburdened the public services were, and it shamed him to discover that there were so many children living on the streets in Berlin, and the things they had to do to survive. The orphanage was now sixteen years old, and it filled Carla with pride when young people came to the Nightingale agency to speak to her father and thank him.

Professor Hochbrück and Alma had only joined the committee three years ago, when they'd discussed modernizing the building in Schaper Street and adding a new wing to it. Since then, the Hochbrücks had been active members, accompanying the children in leisure activities or trips.

There was a constant stream of people stopping to talk to Carla, drink with her, telling her how much they missed her father. Every time she heard that, she instinctively reached for her neck to touch her necklace. She had to stop doing that.

She finally found a card with her name on the table with committee members closest to the stage. She looked around for a waiter, because she wanted to get rid of her champagne glass. She saw Professor Hochbrück coming towards her. A shorter man, who reminded her of someone, was trying to keep up with him.

When Hochbrück reached Carla, he gallantly kissed her hand and introduced the man next to him, who looked a bit like an American film actor. Gregory Peck? No, he was taller and darker. Steve McQueen? Then the man smiled and Carla noticed his rotten teeth, and realized there was no way he was American.

'Do you know Alma's brother, Klaus von Stellmark?' asked Hochbrück. Ah, so that's why he looked familiar. There was a subtle likeness to Alma around his eyes, his gestures. The auburn hair was much straighter and darker than hers, like roasted chestnuts.

'I didn't want to waste Alma's place and come here on my own. After all, every mark helps, right?' said Hochbrück.

'Why couldn't Alma come?' asked Carla, who, after all, officially didn't know anything.

Hochbrück frowned. 'She wasn't feeling well, unfortunately.' He looked slightly annoyed. 'Women's troubles, you know...'

Of course, women's troubles! How cold-hearted this man could be.

'So Alma's brother stood in for her.'

'Very sorry about Alma, but pleased to meet you.' Carla wondered what Klaus knew about the whole matter.

'My sister has a... delicate constitution,' said Klaus with slight condescension.

'Well, I appreciate Alma's delicate nature!' Carla couldn't resist throwing in, although she felt herself getting hot under the collar when she thought of Alma's black eye and broken arm.

A gong signalled the official start of the event. They all took their places and Carla found herself sitting between Alexander and Alma's brother.

The president of the committee, Dr Lederlein, came out in front of the red curtain and thanked everyone for coming, despite the tense situation in Berlin. Still, life had to go on, and he gestured towards the donation boxes scattered all around the room, mentioned the names of Professor Hochbrück and Karl-Otto Koslowsky and then announced the choir of the orphanage.

The curtain opened on ten little bowing boys and girls, dressed in blue. The choir mistress stepped forward. Carla had hired her over a year ago. With her white face and long black hair, Carla mentally compared her to Snow White. Paula Becker was not only beautiful, she was also remarkably good at what she did, and energetic. The choir had made great progress and had even been invited to a festival. She'd hired Paula against the wishes of Vera Hubermann, which had led to some tensions within the committee. Vera was a child psychologist who worked as an honorary consultant for the orphanage, and she threatened to leave. Carla had had to use all her persuasive skills to stop her from going. Still, it had been worth it.

Paula nodded at Carla, then turned to the choir and tapped her baton for the first song.

After a few minutes, Carla was discreetly wiping the tears from the corner of her eyes. Father had always laughed at her for being so prone to tears, especially when it came to Schubert, whom he didn't like. According to him, Schubert was responsible for Mother's misery, and he'd quote a verse. Carla tried to remember how it went, instinctively grasping for the necklace again, but she remembered it even without her lucky die.

Do you want to ask about the nightingales
Who, with soulful melody,
Delighted you in the days of spring?
As long as they loved, they existed.

Only after the funeral did Aunt Lulu explain what her father was hinting at. When Carla's mother was sixteen, she'd fallen in love with her piano teacher and got pregnant, whereupon you couldn't see the man's heels for dust as he made a quick exit. Father had married her nevertheless, because, according to Lulu, he had really loved her, and he became the & Co. in the Nightingale agency. Ida was grateful that he saved her from a scandal, but she never got over the pianist. Then the child, a little boy, died at birth, and something in her broke. So much bitterness came out of that wound, that it was impossible for her to recover, no matter how much Father tried.

Polite applause brought Carla back to the here and now. Professor Hochbrück handed the choir mistress a large bouquet of red lilies and kissed her on the cheeks. Paula appeared to freeze and move a little away from him. Carla became more alert. Indeed, Paula was keeping him at arm's length, holding the flowers in front of her as if they were a shield. Suspicions raced through her mind. Had the two of them been having an affair? Did Paula know something about the brutal attacks on Alma? After all, Alma had done some art therapy in the orphanage. Maybe Wallie was right and there was a way to prove what kind of person Hochbrück was? He'd just finished his impromptu speech, wished them all 'Guten Appetit' and came back to the table.

While the others were still clapping, the food started coming out. Carla pretended to listen to one of Klaus's long-winded anecdotes, but in fact she was studying Alexander. On the other side of him sat Gina Gorzelany, this year's German fashion ambassador, who seemed to have succumbed to his charm. Hochbrück's friendly smile seemed open and warm, there was not a trace of brutality to be seen. Hard to believe that this man could beat his wife – Carla could see Alma's dilemma. But why hadn't she told her brother? He clearly didn't know anything about it. How else would he be able to regard Alexander with such admiration? Maybe Alma was too proud to share her pain with him, or the relationship between the siblings was strained?

Siblings. Carla sighed. And to think she used to wish for one.

'Your starter, madam,' said a voice behind Carla and a white coupe bowl with golden rim was set in front of her.

'Watercress soup with asparagus,' the voice explained, as Carla's heart stopped. Surely she must be hallucinating, because she'd just been thinking of siblings? She turned around suddenly and saw Wallie taking the next plate of soup from a tray and setting it in front of Alexander Hochbrück. She was bending far further forward than necessary and touching him lightly on the shoulder. When she saw Carla looking at her, she winked at her, as if they'd planned it together.

The champagne rose back up Carla's throat, and she had to press her napkin to her mouth. What was Wallie doing here? She was probably still after getting that odious picture, the bitch!

'Hello, Nelly,' said Klaus, gripping Wallie's arm and turning her towards him. Wallie, who'd only seen him from the back, turned pale. Ah, thought Carla, so that wasn't part of the plan. Nelly?

Wallie pulled her arm away, breathed deeply, then bent forward and whispered something in his ear, which made Klaus raise his shoulders. He seemed disappointed, while Wallie looked relieved.

When Wallie finished serving and headed back to the kitchen, Carla stood up, excused herself and followed her. She grabbed hold of her half-sister just before she disappeared into the kitchen, holding her tight by her apron strings. Wallie continued walking, while the little lace apron fell to the floor. Then she stopped.

'You crazy?' Wallie bent down to pick up her apron and tied it up again.

'That's what I wanted to ask you,' seethed Carla. 'What the hell are you doing here? You said you were working at the Eden!'

'None of your beeswax! Unlike you, I'm doing the right thing!'

'And Klaus is your helper's helper?'

Wallie avoided her eyes. 'Not quite. On the contrary, I wasn't expecting him here tonight, so I could do with your help.'

'How on earth do you know Alma's brother? Was he the one who put you up to this?'

'That's Alma's brother?'

Carla enjoyed seeing Wallie's surprise. 'Exactly!'

'Come and get your damn plates, before they get cold,' someone yelled from the kitchen.

'I have to go. Will you help me, please?'

'What are you planning, anyway?' Carla's curiosity was greater than her anger.

One of the chefs came out of the kitchen bearing a tray with more soups for Wallie. 'Stop chatting and go!'

Wallie went back to the banquet hall. Carla followed suit and sat back down. Klaus and Hochbrück briefly raised their eyes in silent questioning. 'All good,' she told them.

While they were busy eating, she asked Klaus where he knew the waitress from. This time she listened carefully to his story. He knew Nelly from the Eden Bar, where she was the bartender. So imagine his surprise to discover that she was actually a student who was interested in architecture. With a boyish charm, he admitted to Carla that he felt ashamed that he'd underestimated Nelly. This confession made him seem even more sympathetic, and Carla was all the more puzzled why Alma had not confided in him. Yes, he obviously admired Alexander tremendously, but had he never wondered where those bruises came from? Then she remembered that she too had known Alma for a while and had never previously suspected a thing. Even though she considered herself an observant person.

Wallie was now serving the main course. Tournedos Rossini – filet of beef with duck's liver pâté and duchesse potatoes. Kempinski had pulled out all the stops. As Wallie bent over to put the plate in front of Carla, she whispered, 'We'll cope, dontcha worry.'

Klaus turned towards them in surprise.

'Thank you,' said Carla loudly, hoping he hadn't heard.

Wallie's strategy was not bad in and of itself. Going undercover at the university was solid research work. Getting a job here couldn't have been easy. But what Carla failed to understand was how Wallie was hoping to have a picture of herself and Hochbrück, without anyone to help them. Especially one of them kissing passionately, and where there were no doubts about identifying Hochbrück in the photo.

It wasn't a problem to hide a camera on your body. Carla had done it herself when it came to industrial espionage. But the little sound of the Minox shutter could not be disguised even with passionate moans. And Houdini himself would have trouble taking a picture where both of them came out clearly, without the other person noticing. Wallie's plan was ridiculous and doomed to failure, in spite of her half-decent prep work. There would be no pictures, no lying under oath.

Relieved, Carla sawed at one slice of her Tournedos Rossini. 'Delicious!' she exclaimed, even though no one was listening.

11

Wallie was singing happily as she climbed the stairs to Nightingale & Co. the next day. Carla would be amazed at how she'd managed to trick Hochbrück and resolve the situation. Alma's ordeal would soon come to an end. She no longer had to be the victim and could send her husband into the wilderness instead. To be able to act, to have power over another, that's what made life worth living! Powerlessness was worse than death. Unfortunately, any one of us could end up in a situation where we were at the mercy of someone else. And to think there were people who always blamed the victim. Pure fascism. You had to fight against that.

She hammered on the door.

No answer.

Wallie sighed. Why did it always take so long? Had Carla gone out for lunch? She paused indecisively in front of the door. Maybe she was upstairs with Ida?

The door opened, but only a tiny gap. Carla peeked out as if there was a danger of bombs going off in the hallway.

'At last,' cried Wallie, 'This will knock your socks off!' She waved the A4-sized envelope enthusiastically. 'I did it! Alma's saved! Stunning pics!'

She stepped forward but her sister refused to let her in.

'What is this?'

Carla gestured with her head towards the door, put her finger to her mouth and her eyes begged Wallie to disappear. Mortified, Wallie pressed even harder against the door.

'Why are you doing this?' Carla raised her voice. 'What do you want?'

'Hangover?' asked Wallie. 'Too much fun last night?' She stopped short, then shook her head. 'No, I can't imagine anyone taking such a spoilsport home...'

'We had an agreement. You can sleep in the office, but during the day it's all mine.'

Carla was suddenly extremely pale, as if she might faint any minute now.

'It's OK, I just wanted you to be the first to see the pictures. I thought we had the same goal, to rescue Alma.'

A woman appeared behind Carla. Not bad, she seemed classy, and beautiful with it. But she too looked a bit annoyed. Was she a friend or a client? Wallie shoved her half-sister to one side and held out her hand to greet her.

The beauty was still eyeing Wallie indignantly, but she looked attractive even with frowning eyebrows. Why was someone as elegant as her here?

'Please forgive me for bursting in on you like this,' chirruped Wallie, 'I work for Nightingale & Co. and needed some personal instructions from the boss, y'know, things that can't be handled over the phone.'

Carla tightened her shoulders and gave a brave smile, which looked a bit ghostly with her pale face. Wallie wondered if the client noticed how much it cost her sister to look professional.

'Frau Niemöller, may I present one of my collaborators, Waltraud von Tilling?'

Wallie held out her hand once more, and this time the woman took it, still somewhat hesitant despite Carla's explanation. Yet the grip of her manicured hand, with perfect cherry-red nails, was unexpectedly firm.

'Have you brought in this collaborator to solve my case more rapidly?' she asked.

'Exactly,' Carla nodded. 'That was exactly what I wanted to tell you. Which means that the daily rate will double, unfortunately.'

Respect! Pale but on the ball! She'd never have expected such improv talents from her sister.

Wallie felt the disbelieving eyes of the client sweeping up and down her body, and realized the possible reason why Carla didn't want to let her in. She was no doubt looking rather dishevelled, after all she'd been working all night. From the Kempinski room where she'd entrapped Hochbrück, straight to James's darkroom and then straight here.

'Please forgive her appearance,' said Carla, sure enough, 'The poor girl had to shadow a suspect all night in the zoo.'

The zoo? How on earth did she come up with that? Wallie wondered if she maybe smelled bad as well, given the developing fluid and stuffy cellar.

'The zoo?' Frau Niemöller seemed to thaw a little at that.

Carla shook her head sorrowfully. 'Yes, hard to believe. There are zookeepers who sell the exotic offspring and then tell the directors that the animals died.'

Muskrats and crocodiles, Wallie was about to add, but contented herself with merely handing over the envelope. 'And here is the evidence! Caught in flagrante!'

'Excellent,' said Carla, snatching the envelope. 'Another case resolved. Now Frau von Tilling can focus on finding Bobbs.'

Bobbs? Was that a dachshund or a poodle? Was that why Carla thought of a zoo connection?

'Wonderful.' Frau Niemöller was now looking gratefully at Wallie. 'Miss Koslowsky might have told you already that I also need to play a role in my day-to-day job.' She took her wallet out of the bag and asked Carla, 'So how much more is it going to cost?'

'I need to wash my hands,' said Wallie, leaving the two of them to it. She couldn't help hearing though that Carla was asking for an additional 120 marks from the client. Well, at least she had some business sense.

When she looked at herself in the mirror, Wallie had to laugh. Her up-do resembled a bird's nest, the mascara had run so badly that she looked like a panda. Perfect for the zoo. She splashed water over her face and tried to rescue her hairstyle, but without success. She'd have to wait until the client left.

Niemöller, Niemöller... she hadn't come across the name yet. The locks in Dad's filing cabinet were ridiculously easy to open, but it was a good idea to file the clients by number rather than name. She hadn't been able to crack the code.

When she heard the front door closing, she returned from the toilet and sat down in front of Carla's desk, on the rattan chair.

'Zoo?' she asked.

'Pictures?' Carla retorted.

Wallie pointed at the envelope lying on Carla's desk. She'd been robbed of her spectacular triumphant entrance.

'Just look at them!'

Carla opened the envelope and took out three pictures, examining each one of them. Her eyes opened wider and wider, her pupils dilating and constricting in rapid succession. 'Bit of alright, eh? That should be enough to get him, right?'

Carla had to clear her throat a couple of times, 'How... how on earth did you do this?'

'I seduced him, of course!' Better not to tell Carla the whole truth.

'Ah, really? Till he lost consciousness?' Carla pointed at the picture where Wallie, with a facial expression depicting perfect passion, or so she thought, was sitting with her breasts bared on Professor Hochbrück's naked body.

Maybe her sister was not quite so easy to deceive as she'd thought. 'Maybe you haven't experienced what we see here in the picture. Hochbrück is recovering here from his second orgasm. Do you know what an orgasm is?'

Carla's cheeks blazed red. Like someone had scrubbed them with a steel brush. Bull's-eye, then!

'How did you get him in this position?'

'First of all, I'm mighty sexy. Secondly – although that should be first – I'm also clever.'

'Clever? Didn't you feel like a prostitute?' Carla clutched her throat, seemingly ready to throw up.

'Did you ever consider that sex might be fun?'

'Sex with a wife-beater?' Carla's X-ray gaze penetrated her. 'A bit risky, don't you think?'

Wallie wasn't prepared to take that lying down. But how much should she confide in Carla?

'OK, I always try to be 100% certain. I sometimes help things along with a few knockout drops, y'know?'

'Knockout drops? What are those?'

'Something new. Gamma-something with butyric-acid something. I'm no chemist, but it works and disarms people.'

'And where did you get that from? James Bond?'

'Very funny!' She had to admit that Carla was good at questioning. 'Not at all. One of the bartenders at the Eden gave it to me, just in case one of the customers got pesky.'

'And you don't think it's disgusting to knock someone unconscious?'

'Not as disgusting as what that swine does to his wife at home.'

'And who took the pictures? Can't have been you.'

'Oy, my secret!' Wallie put her finger in front of her lips.

Carla shook her head. 'Don't tell me there's a witness to all your illegal activities! That's dangerous! The Nightingale Agency cannot take such a hit. If it all comes out, how am I going to support Mother?'

'Nothin'll happen, count on me,' said Wallie, tapping her nose. 'Besides, how d'you define illegal? The end justifies the means in capitalism, doesn't it?'

'Machiavelli died a long time ago,' Carla grimaced. 'No one here thinks like that. But you've obviously been brainwashed in the East. They all say over there that we in the West are fascist pigs without a conscience. Although we have a good, thorough constitution.'

Carla's naïve speeches were becoming unbearable. 'Really? Ask the wives of such monsters how well protected they feel by your good constitution.'

Carla shuddered and fell silent. After a while, she took a cigarette and a lighter out of the engraved ivory case. Had Wallie's question actually made her think?

'I could use one too.' Wallie took a cigarette and searched for the ashtray. Just then, Carla pressed the lighter and a big flame emerged. She grabbed the photos and held them to the flame. 'So that you don't do any real damage.'

Damn! Wallie jumped up and pushed the lighter out of Carla's hand with one hand while grabbing the photos with the other. She inspected the damage, panting a little. Luckily, only one of the photos had been singed.

'Jeez! What's all this in aid of? I've got the negatives.' Wallie brushed the burnt corner, watching in fury as the charred pieces fell to the floor.

'Know what? I give up. No point sitting here, talking to you. The sooner Alma gets rid of this monster, the better. I wanted to collaborate, but if you don't like it, fine, whatever! I'll take her the pictures myself and deliver her from evil. Why d'you want to withhold my material from her?' She stuffed the pictures, even the singed one, back into the envelope and went to the door.

Carla ran after her and held on to her arm.

'Wait, please don't! Remember, Alma asked us not to pay her a visit,' she begged. 'Hochbrück will suspect something, and we don't want to risk that. I'll call her and...'

'You saw how injured she was, the sooner she gets outta there, the better. I'll drive there, she can show him the pictures herself. Then he knows the game's up and he's gotta let her go. The way I look right now, I can pretend to be a cleaner. After all, Alma's still allowed to talk to a cleaner, isn't she?'

But Carla wouldn't release her. She seemed much stronger than she looked. Wallie had to shake her off quite vehemently. Carla stumbled to the floor and let out a cry.

Wallie hadn't meant to do that. 'I'm sorry,' she murmured, hesitating. Carla was standing up, luckily. A little bump like that was nothing compared to what Alma had suffered. Time to act!

Wallie stormed out of the office, ran down the stairs, took the bike that she'd picked up at Bahnhof Zoo in exchange for Carla's missing one and pedalled in the direction of Dahlem.

Why was her half-sister so stubborn? So inhibited and overcautious? Surely solidarity between women should look different to this? Surely Wallie hadn't put in all that work to help Alma and have a satisfied client, only to watch it all torn down? Her sister just didn't understand how the world worked. Alma would be delighted to be able to give that swine his marching orders. With such evidence in front of him, he wouldn't dare to beat her up.

Good job she'd remembered Hochbrück's address from the taxi ride last night. The taxi driver had helped her to dump the professor in front of his door, although he did so with a squeamish expression.

'These guys are the worst,' he said, looking at the imposing appointed villa behind the iron fence, 'Front all dolled up, back all sleazed up.'

You can say that again, thought Wallie as she pedalled faster.

12

'Here we are!' said Carla, opening her purse as the taxi came to a stop in front of the Villa Hochbrück. While Carla was paying, Wallie appeared on the driveway. Carla got out hurriedly and glared at her half-sister, who jumped off her bike, simply letting it fall on its side, and raced up the marble steps to ring the doorbell.

Carla was furious as she ran after her. She suppressed a groan and tried to ignore the pain in her left knee. Her weakness in front of Wallie, and the humiliation of falling to her knees, had hurt her more than the shove and the minor bruises. She had to protect Alma from Wallie's madness. Incredible how childish and unprofessional Wallie's behaviour was. She simply hadn't thought through all the consequences. She surely couldn't believe that those pictures would be enough to stop someone like Hochbrück.

Besides, Alma must have had a good reason to get them to promise not to show up here. It was crystal-clear what would happen if someone as aggressive as Hochbrück felt he was being cornered. Of course he'd vent his anger on Alma!

Carla limped up the steps, reaching the top just as a ginger-haired, doll-sized version of Alma opened the door. She'd last seen Mathilda in spring on a trip with the Berlin Fledglings. Nowadays, she seemed taller but even more fragile. Nessaluna, the moon daughter of the Celtic faerie princess. Carla's throat constricted as she tried to imagine what effect Hochbrück's brutality might be having on Mathilda. Such a sensitive child must no doubt be aware something wasn't right in that house. And because no one was discussing her mother's injuries with her, Mathilda might have been feeling a diffuse sense of guilt and trying to do everything to please Alma. The poor child probably had to behave like a little adult all the time. No doubt her brother Gregor could also sense more than was good for him.

Carla swallowed hard. Maybe Wallie was right? Maybe it was not only permissible but even urgently necessary to fight here with any means at one's disposal?

'Is your father at home?' asked Wallie, and Carla prayed that he might still be at the university.

Mathilda raised her pale, somewhat confused face and stared at Wallie in surprise, as if it was unbelievable that there was someone in the world who didn't know her father's whereabouts. She simply shook her head wordlessly.

Thank goodness for small mercies!

'Never mind,' said Wallie, her voice much gentler, bending her knees a little to look directly into Mathilda's velvety green eyes. 'We'd much rather speak to your mother anyway.' She reached out her hand. 'My name is Wallie, and yours?'

Carla couldn't hear the answer, because Alma's voice could be heard from inside, complaining bitterly.

'Mathilda! How many times have I told you that you shouldn't open the door to strangers?'

Wallie straightened up and threw Carla a triumphant look.

'I didn't, Mama,' said Mathilda, 'I looked through the keyhole and could tell it wasn't a stranger, but the lady who was on the Wannsee trip with us in spring.'

Just at that moment, Alma stepped out behind Mathilda,

holding her daughter with both hands, then looked up at the visitors.

Carla gasped. Wallie let out a disbelieving 'Huh?' Was this really Alma or did she have a twin sister? How else to explain her appearance?

A little rustling sound made Carla look towards Wallie. The controversial envelope had fallen from her hands, and she was swaying slightly, as though trying to recover from a heavy blow.

'I forbade you to come here,' spat Alma, 'Leave the premises at once, or else I'll call the police!'

'But why, Mama?' Mathilda looked astonished. 'Are these bad ladies? All they did was ring the bell.'

'No, they broke their promise. I don't want to see either of you ever again!' She pulled Mathilda inside and gave Carla such a harsh look it made her shiver. Then Alma closed the door as gently as if it was made of cardboard, a stage prop for a play.

Carla and Wallie remained outside, thunderstruck.

'But...' whispered Wallie, half to herself and half to Carla, 'How is that possible?' Then she ran back down the steps to her bike.

Carla tried to control her dizziness as she bent down to pick up the envelope. 'Wait!' she called and limped after Wallie. But the other woman had already mounted her bike and was pedalling away, as if chased by demons.

She probably wanted to escape an 'I told you so'. Yet there was no hint of gloating in Carla's veins. On the contrary, she could barely breathe, she felt so mortified. Why had Alma put on make-up before to appear to be a victim and misled them so badly?

Carla hobbled away, hoping to find a bus stop. It would be a minor miracle to find a taxi in this posh neighbourhood. She'd once been invited for dinner at the Villa Hochbrück with her father, but that was a long time ago and she couldn't remember the surroundings well.

Father! She instinctively felt for her throat, and once again it was unadorned. What would he have said about Alma's lies? She'd been completely unharmed when she came to the door, no black eye or plaster cast.

No wonder Alexander had mentioned women's problems last night. Alma must have used that excuse so that she didn't have to come to the dinner. That was why Klaus had to accompany him. Not because Alma was too badly hurt, but because she wasn't hurt at all. The fairy-tale about her brutal husband would have been discovered.

But why would Alma do such a thing? Was she perhaps being mistreated by him mentally and so she decided to make her inner injuries clearer by means of this masquerade?

How much further until this darn bus stop or U-Bahn? Her tights were laddered and wrinkling down by her ankles, while her knee was slightly swollen. No sign of a tree or a bench that she might lean on, only high fences protecting expensive villas.

Maybe Alma was mentally ill, the kind of woman craving attention, unwilling to live in her husband's shadow. Yes, Dr Freud, maybe you should open a clinic on the Ku'damm. Light and shade therapy à la Nachtigall.

The sound of a car engine stopped her from overthinking things. She hoped for a taxi. Unfortunately, it was just a blue-grey Porsche Cabrio overtaking her at rather too high a speed. The Porsche braked so suddenly that it skidded a little and smoke came out of its exhaust. The car then backed all the way to where she stood. She looked suspiciously at the car: what was going on?

The Cabrio came to a stop with a squeal of tyres right next to her, and Hochbrück got out, wearing a hat and sunglasses. Although his light blue shirt and black suit seemed impeccable, he looked a bit crumpled and hungover.

Porsche? Since when? Must have been bought with Alma's money. She had to restrain herself from visibly hiding the envelope behind her back. The envelope was too big to fit into her handbag, but he didn't know a thing, he was in the dark about it all.

'I'm sorry, I only recognised you in the mirror,' he apologised in a friendly voice. 'Have you had an accident?' He pointed towards her knee. 'That doesn't look good. Do you want me to take you to the doctor's?'

'That would be wonderful!' she said, clutching the envelope to her chest. She had to make him talk, find out more about this marriage and make sure that he wasn't going to see Alma immediately. Carla said her doctor was in Grolmanstraße.

'Of course, we'll be there in ten minutes,' he said, opening the passenger door for her.

'That was a successful evening last night. Do you know how much money was raised?' she asked as she carefully eased her way into the low, hard seat.

'Sadly not. To be honest, I am missing a considerable portion of the evening. It's all a haze somehow.' He smiled weakly. With his hat and sunglasses on, she couldn't see much of his face. 'I must be getting old. What are you doing in our neighbourhood?'

'Work. You know, it's all confidential.'

'Isn't this detective business a bit dangerous for a delicate woman like you? Your knee was not injured yesterday.'

Was there a threatening undertone in his voice, or was she just being paranoid?

'Although no doubt it's better,' he continued immediately, 'than sitting around moping on your own all day. Listen, I didn't want to mention it in front of Alma's brother, but couldn't you give my wife a little extra work to do in the orphanage? She has a tendency to brood and gets all sorts of strange ideas.'

He sounded so warm and loving and concerned, just the sort of husband one might wish for.

'What sort of strange ideas?'

'For Alma's sake, this has to stay between us.'

'Of course,' Carla nodded but crossed her fingers in secret.

'She spies on me,' he said, twisting his lips, 'She imagines all sorts of things about me and is even jealous of the good relationship I have with her brother.'

'What sorts of things?' This sounded more and more mysterious.

'I can't tell you, because it'll put Alma in a very bad light, you might even try to avoid seeing her. She's destroyed a lot of friendships this way. Even Paula has been upset by her flights of fantasy.'

The choir mistress who'd tried to maintain an exaggerated distance from Hochbrück yesterday. What on earth was going on in this marriage? Or was he manipulating her because he'd heard that Alma had paid her a visit? Was it pure coincidence that he'd just got home, or did he rush home because some neighbourhood spy had told him there were visitors for his wife and he was trying to do some damage limitation?

'I'm sorry to hear of your marital difficulties,' Carla said and then ventured further, 'Are you thinking of getting divorced?'

He braked suddenly and slammed the steering wheel to underscore every word. 'Over. My. Dead. Body!'

Carla winced at each hammering and had to check to see if the envelope was still in her grasp.

'Sorry, I didn't mean to shout,' he said, patting her arm, 'But I find it so irresponsible that nowadays everybody gets divorced for the slightest thing. A marriage has highs and lows, and you have to navigate them. For me the wedding is the gold link on a chain that starts with one look and ends with eternity.'

'An admirable point of view,' said Carla, somewhat anxious about Alma.

'Oh, those are not my words, but the words of Khalil Gibran. My father thought I was an incurable romantic. That old misery-guts preferred Schopenhauer.' Hochbrück laughed while casually driving through a red light. 'Marriage means halving your rights and doubling your duties.'

'Schopenhauer clearly understood the plight of married women in Germany very well,' Carla said.

'Miss Koslowsky, I know you're an old spinster, but it's such a shame that you've become one of those terrible feminists. Women should consider themselves lucky to get married. After all, compared to us, their bloom is over far too quickly. May I ask how old you are?'

No, thought Carla, but then mumbled, 'Twenty-two.'

'Oh!' He examined her a little too thoroughly. 'I'm sorry, I didn't mean to offend you. I merely thought you were a good deal older.'

'Here we are,' she said, pointing to a random corner house, 'My doctor is just over there.'

'Of course, my pleasure.' Hochbrück braked abruptly yet again, smoothly got out of the Cabrio and ran to the passenger side to open the door for her.

'Thank you,' said Carla, clinging on for dear life to her envelope. She got out and steeled herself. After sitting in the low-slung car, her knee hurt more than ever before.

'I thank you,' he said with a gallant little bow, 'So you'll think of a little task for poor Alma, won't you? We'll see each other at the committee meeting next week.'

'See you then,' said Carla somewhat uncertainly. She watched the Cabrio speed away. What on earth was going on with the Hochbrücks? Who was lying, who was cheating, who was playing tricks on whom here?

13

When Carla returned to the apartment a couple of hours later, she was bombarded by the aroma of freshly fried potato cakes and – could it be? – goulash. This combination brought a lump to her throat. Since Father's death, Mother hadn't once cooked her famous Nachtigall goulash with potato cakes. And to do it now, on a weekday, which usually meant a cold dinner? How did she get all the ingredients?

Carla omitted washing her hands and limped straight into the kitchen, where Wallie, freshly made up and wearing Carla's apron over an airy summer dress, was humming and washing up a chopping board.

'What's going on here?' Carla had assumed that Wallie had crawled away somewhere to lick her wounds. She'd not shown her face in the office while Carla was bandaging her knee and engaging in some research about Bobbs.

'Wallie seemed so sad,' said Mother.

Wallie? Sad? A joke a minute right there. Carla could not only not imagine Wallie being sad, she couldn't imagine Mother noticing anybody else's sadness. She'd certainly never noticed when Carla was upset. There'd not been a single word or gesture of sympathy even after Father's death. A flush of anger spread through her body and settled in her stomach like a lump of glowing coal.

'Today's the anniversary of Wallie's mother's death,' said Mother, almost triumphantly. 'See how well we get along? You think I'm a cripple, but I still have a social life!'

Carla was at once convinced that Wallie's mother had died on some other day. She remembered the story about the oh-so-expensive funeral party.

'So of course I asked Cousin Wallie if there was anything I could do for her, what her favourite dish was. Imagine, she said goulash, just like your dad.'

'Amazing!' mumbled Carla. She was ready to bet her mother didn't know *her* favourite dish. She stared hard at the kitchen clock, trying to master her dizziness. *Stop being bitter, there's no point*!

'You're a lucky girl,' she said to Wallie, 'Mother's Nachtigall goulash with potato cakes is a famous recipe.'

'It smells heavenly, so that alone...' Wallie noticed the thick bandage on Carla's knee. 'I'm so sorry.'

'About what?' asked Carla. She hesitated a moment, she didn't like talking shop in front of Mother, but then she burst out, 'You're sorry about storming away after you made such a mess of things? You're sorry about hurting me? Or you're sorry about doing exactly what our client...' Had she really just said 'our' client? 'What *my* client didn't want us to do and so set off who knows what?'

Wallie cleared away the chopping board. 'I've laid the table,' she said to Carla's mother.

'Thank you for that.' Mother patted Wallie's arm. 'The potato cakes are ready and we can start, after Carla has washed her hands, of course.'

'I'm not six years old,' she began, but the other two left for the dining room. She groaned and went to the bathroom.

Better not look in the mirror. She bent over the washbasin and splashed plenty of cold water over her face. Once she'd calmed down, she raised her eyes and watched the silvery drops of water sliding down her pale cheeks. 'This is a challenge to test you and make you grow,' her father used to say, but she couldn't trust anything he'd said anymore. Which brought her back to Alma. What was she so afraid of, why had she had put on such a show for them? Hochbrück had warned her about Alma's strange fantasies, but why had Paula shrunk away from him? She had to talk to her.

By the time she dried her hands and brushed her hair, the other two women were already at the table, laid out once more with the best dinner service. A fancy meal and the Sunday crockery – clearly Wallie had a strange influence on Mother's unshakable rules.

'It's past six. How often have we talked about this?' Mother's reproachful look drilled into Carla's chest.

'But we're all here now,' Wallie said in an appeasing tone, 'Shall I serve?'

'Please.'

Wallie took Mother's plate and poured a ladle of goulash in it. Carla rejoiced inwardly, for this was a serious blunder. You were supposed to take three of the potato-cakes and lay them on the plate and put the goulash on top of the middle one. She could the see the conflict of emotions on her mother's face, and finally she laid a hand on Wallie's arm to stop her. Then she explained her rules on how to serve the special meal.

Wallie smiled and nodded, 'Thank you, Auntie Ida, I understand, and will do better next time.' She took the failed plate for herself and then prepared the other two plates according to Ida's instructions and wished them *Guten Appetit*. For a while, all that could be heard was the grandfather clock in the living room and the chewing and swallowing in the dining room.

'You didn't answer my question earlier,' Carla said at last, unable to bear the silence.

'You know I don't like any talk about work here.' Mother looked at Wallie apologetically. 'This detecting business can be so disturbing.'

Maybe she should show Mother the pictures of a naked

Wallie lying on top of Hochbrück, if she wanted to see something truly disturbing.

'Why don't you tell us instead about the gala dinner last night? Did you have nice company at the dinner table?'

A student whom Wallie knew from her work at the Eden Bar, Carla was tempted to say, but managed to keep her composure.

'Cousin Carla looked very pretty in any case!' said Wallie.

'The whole point of the dinner was to raise money for the orphanage, not to look pretty.' Carla could hear how grumpy she sounded, but instead of banging her fist on the table and putting an end to this farce, she struggled to swallow a piece of meat.

'And how much money did you raise?'

'Almost a hundred thousand marks.' Would this lie get a rise out of Mother?

Just then the downstairs doorbell rang repeatedly

'Lulu!' Mother frowned and wiped her mouth delicately. She explained to Wallie that her crazy sister-in-law was the only person in the world who rang as aggressively as that. 'I'm sorry that she's disturbing our nice meal.'

She wasn't sorry at all, judging from the combative gleam in her eyes, which always appeared when she was about to have a loud argument that she was fairly confident of winning.

Carla went to press the button for the front door, but Lulu had already climbed up to their floor.

'Pallutzke let me in,' she panted. 'Let's go downstairs, child, we've got to talk.'

'How nice of you to come!' said Mother, rolling up in her wheelchair. 'Sit down and eat with us. It's Karl's favourite meal.'

Lulu stared at Ida. 'What, you're cooking your world-renowned goulash on an ordinary Friday?' She sniffed and made a face. 'With potato cakes too?'

Mother nodded and Carla could see her aunt's face full

of conflicting emotions.

'Well, of all things! I can't believe it! It must be fate.' She gave Carla her plum-coloured pea coat and went to wash her hands.

Carla went to fetch another plate, wondering what could have brought Lulu here.

'Oh, I see you have visitors,' said Lulu, sitting down opposite Wallie and looking disapprovingly at her plate.

'Very pleased to see you,' said Wallie.

Carla's mother came out of the kitchen with additional potato cakes and put them on the table. 'Help yourself, Lulu. There's plenty here for everyone.'

Lulu helped herself but looked at Carla as if to say, *what is all this about. Has Ida gone mad?*

'Ida.' Lulu heaped the goulash on top of her potatoes. 'Ida, it seems our cousin,' she couldn't help emphasizing the word 'cousin', as if Wallie was a quack pretending to be a doctor, 'Our cousin has won your heart in no time. You never cook this for me, not even on my birthday. I had to drown my sorrows at the German-American Folk Fair.'

'You're certainly good at drinking,' said Ida.

'Speaking of which, don't you think it's rather dry here?'

'Since Karl's death, we don't drink any alcohol on a weekday.'

'That's dumb,' grumbled Lulu, taking a contemptuous sip of cold fruit tea. Carla didn't like that stale, sour taste either. Father used to water the rubber plants with it surreptitiously – they seemed to like it and thrive.

'Auntie Ida just wanted to cheer me up, because of the Wall, and losing my apartment, and the anniversary of my mother's death.' Wallie stood up. 'It was delicious, but sadly I have to go to my appointment now.'

'Already?' Mother looked disappointed. Was she hoping for a ding-dong between Wallie and Lulu?

'Where do you have to go so urgently, that you cannot enjoy the festive meal made in your honour?' asked Carla, curious to see how Wallie would wriggle out of this one. After all, she just had to go to her job as a barmaid at the Eden.

'I'm afraid I can't stay any longer. My boyfriend...'

Lulu raised an eyebrow. 'Boyfriend? Only one? Why don't you stay with him?'

Wallie giggled with such affectation that Carla wanted to kick her shins.

'My boyfriend, Sir James Cunningham...'

'God save the Queen,' muttered Lulu. 'Sounds like a romance novel by Hedwig Courths–Maler.'

'He is Scottish and sublets. He's not allowed any women visitors.'

'Nice to see there's some decency left in the world,' said Carla's mother.

Decency? What a laugh! A barmaid with questionable morals. Carla bent over her plate and wished that Wallie would vanish into thin air. Which was of course as hopeless as wishing that the Wall would just disappear.

Wallie picked up her plate and took it to the kitchen. Carla couldn't stand it, she had to follow her there.

'Have you completely lost it? You can't just play fate, make a mess of things and then run away, leaving me standing there. Then show up here, as if everything is hunky-dory? Did you know that Hochbrück came tearing home right after you turned the corner? And what do you imagine happened next? Don't you think that maybe Alma had a reason for lying to us?'

'Too many questions in one go,' said Wallie, leaving her plate in the sink. 'OK, so I got it wrong, but I still think we were right to trick Hochbrück. We couldn't possibly know that Alma's story was bull. Based on the premise, we behaved correctly. What did we learn? That we can't trust anyone.' She gave a bitter smile. 'Not even people who ask for help.'

'You didn't behave correctly, I did.' Carla wanted to

shake Wallie as she stood there so calmly, as if she was some wise guru. Something about her attitude reminded her of Father, which made her even angrier. 'You're talking nonsense. It's precisely the people who need our help most who don't always tell us the whole truth. Some are too ashamed and try to make themselves sound better, others are afraid they won't be believed so they exaggerate. As a detective, you have to find out the kernel of truth in each story, and then help only within the legal framework. Otherwise, it's not help, but playing God, which is patronising.'

'Are you done? I don't care about Alma anymore. She lied to us. End of story.'

'Just because you made a fool of yourself with that little orgasm photo.'

'Oh, that sounds like a far more interesting discussion than the one in the dining room about the best laundry service in Charlottenburg,' said Lulu as she burst into the kitchen. 'Orgasm photo, you say?'

Wallie gulped, then burst out laughing, as if it were all a great joke. It was a real belly laugh, very contagious, and after a while even Lulu started giggling. Carla started to feel something loosening in her chest.

'I see that I always miss out on the best stories.' Mother's voice whipped any trace of laughter away. 'But I'm used to being left on my own.'

'So sorry,' said Wallie, pulling a handkerchief out of her corset and wiping her eyes. 'My fault.'

'I doubt it. I know who lacks any decency around here,' Mother threw an accusing look at Lulu and Carla.

Wallie apologised for not being able to help with the washing up and said goodbye. The remaining three sat back down at the table, and Lulu had another generous portion of goulash.

'Tell me, Ida, why are you spoiling this brat, whom nobody knows anything about?' she asked with a full mouth. Carla was sure she was doing it on purpose to annoy Ida, because normally she had good table manners.

'Wallie is Karl's cousin, so a cousin of yours too.' Mother looked bewildered. 'Isn't that what you told me?'

'That may be the case, but I've never met her before.'

'Karl always helped everyone.' Mother looked up at the ceiling with a long-suffering expression, as if her husband was up there.

'That's true. He had a generous heart.' Lulu took the last potato cake. 'But why did you warm to her so quickly?'

'Did I?'

'As far as you're able to, yes.' Lulu winked at Carla. 'I actually came to discuss something important with Carla, about my... will.'

'I thought all your worldly goods would go to your poodle?' Ida carefully rolled her napkin and put it in the silver ring.

'Very funny, Ida. Might I remind you that after Karl's death, I offered to convert the lower floor of the villa for you, but you turned me down.'

'Where is Fritzi anyway?' asked Carla.

'Oh, my goodness!' Lulu slapped her palm to her forehead, like a silent film heroine who has received horrendous news. 'I'd forgotten about her! Too much goulash. I must go down and free the poor creature from the car. Carla, come with me!'

They raced down the stairs to Lulu's turquoise Beetle, which was parked as usual on a double yellow line. But there was no Fritzi in it.

'I wanted to leave her in the car, but little Katrin came by and offered to take her for a walk. Besides, I wanted to speak to you in private.'

Carla gave a resigned nod.

'This Wallie is a swindler, I'm sure of it. I've set heaven and earth in motion and managed to reach Achim in his hotel in Vienna. He didn't have a lot of time, unfortunately, but he confirmed that my brother had a daughter with a mistress. He's been paying child maintenance since 1939, even after she carted herself and the child off to Switzerland.'

'So that's the proof...'

'No way! First of all, how do we know that it was Karl-Otto's child? And secondly, this mistress, Luise von Tilling, died three years ago from lung cancer.'

Maybe today really was the anniversary of Wallie's mother's death. Just then, they saw Katrin running happily towards them with Fritzi, and waved.

'How do we know that this woman is the daughter of this Tilling person? Fine, so she was living in the apartment in Tucholskystraße that Karl bought for Luise, but that doesn't mean anything. Why doesn't she have any friends? And if she is making so much out of the family relationship, why didn't she come to Karl's funeral? If you ask me, there's something not quite kosher about it all.'

'What does not-kosher mean?' asked Katrin rather breathlessly, as she handed Fritzi back to Lulu.

'That means that something stinks,' Lulu explained. She tried to calm down the clearly overjoyed Fritzi. Then she turned to Katrin, searching her pockets for a coin. 'Buy yourself an ice cream.'

Katrin blushed. 'No, ta, was my pleasure!' She shook her head till her plaits, which were braided together that day, nearly came loose.

'I apologise,' said Lulu. 'That is very kind of you.'

'It was fun, I showed Fritzi my secret hidey-hole.'

'That's wise, she's hardly going to tell anyone, is she?' Lulu laughed and turned to Carla. 'Let's have lunch tomorrow and discuss what we do with this case.'

Katrin's eyes widened. 'Case?' I'm Carla's assistant, you know.'

'That was our secret,' protested Carla.

'OK then,' interrupted Lulu. 'Let's see just how good

your observational skills are. Katrin, have you noticed the blonde lady who's living with Carla now?'

Katrin nodded. 'I'm not blind, am I?'

'And have you noticed anything about her?'

Katrin nodded and rattled down her observations: 'Her body and her hair are a bit like Marilyn Monroe's but her face looks different. She has thinner cheeks.' She sucked in her own cheeks to emphasise this. 'Her eyes are blue and her eyebrows are quite light-coloured, so she's probably a real blonde. And she speaks English.'

Carla and Lulu looked at each other in amazement.

'OK, here's your mission.' Lulu lowered her voice to share an important secret. Carla cringed, but Katrin was fully caught up in it.

'Keep an eye on all her comings and goings and report back to Carla,' Lulu said. 'We'll talk tomorrow, I'm sure we'll find out more, no sweat!' She trotted with Fritzi back to the car, winked at Carla and Katrin and drove off with a sharp squeal of tyres.

14

Well, hello there, thought Wallie as she approached the Eden Bar on Sunday night. Why was Edgar already waiting at the entrance? He never normally got there before her. To be honest, she'd been counting on Edgar not being there at all tonight. Lyndon B. Johnson was in town with a lot of troops, being warmly welcomed by the Berliners. The West Berliners, of course. The Kempinski must be swarming with bigwigs. Or maybe Edgar was expecting some VIPs from the entertainment industry at the Eden, so he needed her help.

The closer she got, the more she could see that he was deeply upset, his face all stony, his eyes dark with fear. Could it be about his sister?

'Edgar, what's happened...' but before she could finish her sentence, he grabbed her arm and pulled her away from the doorway, round the corner, looking all around in panic.

'Why are you acting like James Bond?' She tried to hide her anxiety with a joke.

'Stop kidding around, no time for that! We're in a mess – no, worse, we're in deep shit! And it's all your fault!'

Edgar using bad language? That had never happened before.

'What the hell are you talking about?'

'Hochbrück is dead,' Edgar came closer and whispered in her ear. 'I've got it from a primary source. And rumour has it he was murdered.'

'What?!'

He examined her as if he were an Eastern border guard and she was someone without the right documents. She must be coming out in hives. 'Dead? Hochbrück?'

Could it have been the stuff she'd slipped into his last coffee? A delayed reaction like with the green death cap mushroom? No, that couldn't be true. The gala dinner had taken place a few days ago. Still, the pictures... She broke out in a cold sweat. No need to panic, the only person who'd seen the pictures was Carla. After all, she wasn't stupid enough to leave traces in James's darkroom. She was only too aware of his jealousy. *Calm down, breathe...*

There was nothing to connect her to Hochbrück. Still, his face and naked torso suddenly came to mind and took her back to Thursday night. His face had been so relaxed, his body seemed vulnerable almost, without his shell – his suit with shoulder pads, his belly already running to fat. He felt cool, soft and somewhat leathery to the touch, with a bit of a tangy smell about him. When she placed him into position for the pictures, it almost felt like she was handling giant chicken legs for cooking. Yet she couldn't forget even for one moment the brutality hidden in that mound of flesh. She enjoyed exposing the brute. Now he was dead. And maybe he'd never been a brute after all, merely a victim of Alma's lies.

Her gullible sister really fell for every trick. What nonsense, that people who need help might be lying! In fact, the opposite was true. The people who most needed help were the ones that were victims of other people's lies. Alma had deceived them all, so she had her husband on her conscience. This delicate, apparently helpless woman would probably hoodwink the police too. To think that she'd put in so much effort to take the perfect pictures for that woman! To be fair, she'd also done it to impress Carla.

'So how exactly did Hochbrück die?'

'Weren't you listening? He was probably murdered.'

Edgar kept stroking his bald head. 'Mur-der-ed.'

'Gotcha, but how exactly?'

'Doesn't matter.'

It mattered a great deal. Who else could it have been but his lying wife? Everyone else who knew him, well, OK, maybe not everyone, but his students at least, had spoken admiringly of him.

'Don't you realise what this means for us?' Edgar was speaking so fast that Wallie could barely understand him. 'The police will investigate what he was doing in the last few days. And you spent half the night in the Kempinski with him, in a room that I procured for you.'

'Calm down, no one knows that.'

'Wrong! The housekeeper Elsa knows that you wanted to serve at his table. As do the cook and the waitress who was removed from the evening's schedule because of you. And so on and so forth. A hotel is a gossip factory. At least I was smart enough to make the room reservation in the name of Müllerheim, who doesn't exist, of course. But what happens if they rake all this up? What on earth did you want from him? What happened in that room? Is it true that he hurt your sister? Are you both involved? Did you kill him? You know how much I need my job.'

'Edgar, it's...'

'Sshh!' Edgar interrupted, pointing behind her. She spun round and saw Irina and Jutta walking up towards them, waving US flags.

'Why you both out here? A conspiracy?' asked Irina, starting to laugh.

'Or even worse,' added Jutta, 'A joint music show?' They both giggled. Everyone knew that Wallie was tone deaf.

'You caught us, please don't tell anyone,' said Edgar, going around the corner with them and holding the door open like a gentleman. 'We'll be right behind you,' he added as they walked in, then turned again to Wallie.

'Relax, Edgar. I've nothing on my conscience. Hochbrück

was alive and kicking when I dropped him off at his house on Thursday.' She remembered her half-sister had seen him the following day, so she really had nothing with which to reproach herself. 'It must have been his wife.'

'And how would you know that?'

'It's just my intuition... or maybe the Professor squirreled away some money from the orphanage committee, that sorta thing happens all the time.'

'If it's murder, the police will follow every line of inquiry.'

'What, you're not even sure it's murder and you're gettin' that het up about it?'

'I'll lose my job if they find out about the room.'

'Lemme stop you right there. We've done nothing wrong.' Of course, she had no wish for the police to start sniffing around in her private life. Should she call Carla to warn her? They'd be sure to find out that Alma was planning to get divorced. According to Agatha Christie's Hercule Poirot, the suspects were always those closest to the victim.

The staff door opened. 'Hey, you two, we need you!' called Irina. 'Boss says there'll be lots of Americans coming, maybe even General Clay and Lyndon B. Johnson.'

'That's all we need!' muttered Edgar. He raised his hand and waved at Irina. 'Coming!'

'Hurry!'

'There's zilch we can do,' Wallie told him. What a shame she'd broken up with James. He'd almost certainly know what was going on. The BBC was interested mainly in politics, but the murder of a well-known figure like Hochbrück, who had a finger in every pie, would no doubt have some political implications too.

'You know what, let me call James.'

Edgar seemed relieved, his facial traits softened all of a sudden. 'I thought it was over between you two?'

'I'd do anything for you,' said Wallie, patting him on the

arm reassuringly. 'Maybe James is on shift today, with the American delegation being here this weekend.'

Edgar took out a fistful of ten-pfennig coins from his pocket. 'Here you go, hurry!'

She took the coins and ran to the nearest phone booth in the direction of Ku'damm. She threw two coins in, not sure what she was going to say exactly. But she was certainly not the shy type.

'Hello, darling.' Wallie heard a sharp intake of breath when he recognised her. 'Where you been? Where you live now? I was in... angst.'

Bet you were, so much so that you came to look for me every evening!

'I miss you,' she said, trying to sound throaty and sexy.

He gave a sigh of relief. 'Me too!' He didn't seem too eager to find out any details about her but continued instead in his broken German. 'I will do the better. Very promised!'

Wallie had to smile, in spite of everything. He was trying so hard. James was the only member of the BBC crew who could understand and read German, but he wasn't that great at speaking it.

'OK, I believe you. Let's give it another go!'

'Wondersome! I'm so happy. When we meet?'

'Pick me up and take me home after work, please, there's been a terrible murder...'

'Sorry, darling, what? A murder? We've been so busy with Lyndon B. Johnson and his speech about brave Berlin. And those troops coming today. But no reason to be fear. I will bring you home... not in the East?'

She had to get more details about the murder before meeting him.

'No, I live in the West now.'

'Thank God!'

Was that really all he had to say to his lover who had had to leave her home, her whole world behind? A mere, thank God? How compassionate!

'Have you really not heard about this murder? My colleagues are scared too. I'd like to reassure them if possible.'

'I can drive all of them!' He laughed.

Wallie joined in the laughter, while wracking her brain as to how get more information out of him.

'They say there's a killer on the loose in Berlin...'

'Lots of killers still living in Berlin.' James was getting started on his favourite topic: the Nazi killers who had got away with it.

If she asked him directly about Hochbrück, he'd get suspicious and possibly jealous once more. Then an idea took root in her head; she couldn't believe how simple it all was. All she had to do was be honest for once. 'The woman where I live is my half-sister and she too is worried about this murderer...'

'What is half a sister?'

'Same father, different mothers,' she explained rapidly, biting down her impatience.

'You never spoke about a sister.'

'Wasn't necessary till the Wall was built.' Let James believe that he knew her, when in fact he hardly had a clue about her life. Not that it seemed to interest him all that much. Thank God.

'I see what I can do, OK?'

'OK!' She hung up and took the remaining coin, which had fallen with a muffled tinkle. Little useful information, except for the fact that it could hardly have been some spectacular murder. Maybe Edgar was wrong and it wasn't a murder at all. She looked at the coin. Should she call Carla? Maybe she'd already heard the news and had more information than James?

She walked back to the Eden, which had opened in the meantime. She changed hurriedly and was for once glad to see that their boss was right: the influx of Americans meant she had no time to think for the next few hours.

15

Shortly before the bus reached the Ullstein house, it started bucketing down. Great! Carla made a dash for it, handbag over her head, pleased that the swelling in her knee had gone down and she was almost pain-free. The Ullstein house looked even more sombre in the pouring rain. She'd been here often with Father, who loved this building, the symbol of good journalism for him. When the house was returned to its rightful owners in 1952, shortly before her thirteenth birthday, her father had celebrated so extensively that he needed three days to recover. They even forgot her birthday that year, although Lulu did bring a present a few days later. A new-fangled bra from Hollywood, and nylons, which Mother had instantly confiscated. 'Flat as you are, my child, you wouldn't be able to use this indecent stuff anyway!'

Father wanted to make it up to her, so he took her with him to the offices of the *Berliner Morgenpost*, where his friend Nepomuk was working in the photo archives. She knew Muki already from his visits to their home. He'd lost his right leg in the war and an eye in a Russian gulag, and Father helped him, because he was livid at how little the authorities seemed to care. Father had felt guilty, because he'd been in an American POW camp in Italy, where the conditions had been slightly better than in Vorkuta.

At one of the many lunches in the canteen at Ullstein, he told Muki how much he'd have liked to become a journalist. When he saw how crestfallen his daughter looked, he shook with laughter. 'Don't look so gobsmacked, Carla *Liebchen*, being with the Nachtigalls is still a bit of alright! My father-in-law – your grandad – said to me: "Karl-Otto, a detective and a journalist do much the same thing. They hunt out the truth. The only difference is that the detective doesn't twist the truth, even if the client doesn't like it." Although he did change the name of the agency to the English word for Nachtigall, to appeal to foreign clients too. Still, that was no fluff, I tell ya, it's the honest truth!' Muki nodded. He nodded no matter what Father said.

The truth. No fluff... Carla felt a bitter taste in her mouth. All these grandiose words that Father liked to spout, when in fact his whole life was one big lie.

At the entrance, Muki was waiting for her, leaning on his crutches. Just like Mother, he'd never got used to his prosthetic leg, so he hobbled along on crutches. During those lunches, the two men had often joked that Karl-Otto had helped his friend obtain everything but a wife. Father would then ask her in jest if she might marry Muki later. This caused Carla a lot of guilt at the time, because of course she didn't want to marry an old, injured war veteran, she'd much rather have a handsome boy with green eyes... Or if an oldie, then at least someone like Gregory Peck. But because she cared so much for Father and Muki and didn't want to hurt them, she always used to whisper obediently, 'Yes,' ashamed of her lie. The two of them then laughed so hard, that she felt they were punishing her. They only stopped joking about this when Carla embarked upon her university studies. After Father's death, Muki had continued the friendship with her seamlessly, without ever proposing.

'Karl-Otto would be so proud of you!' Nepomuk was saying just then, going ahead. The sight of his carefully pinned, empty trouser leg swinging back and forth reminded Carla how creepy she'd found it when she was younger. Yet she always said yes to the so-called marriage proposal. Funny how a child's mind works. She wondered about Mathilda.

Nepomuk stopped suddenly and examined her carefully. 'You OK? You look a bit peaky.'

'All good. Thanks for your help.'

'For nowt. Let's go downstairs, I've collected all the stuff we have. You know Gerda already?'

Carla shook her head.

'Our new photographer. She does good work, is a lot keener than old Schober. In fact, she sometimes uses up too much film. But that's a blessing for you today.'

They took the lift to the basement, where the archives were.

'And how is your mama?' Nepomuk struggled to open the heavy iron fire door to his realm. Carla held back, not helping him, because she knew how important this was for him. 'I'm a cripple, not dead yet!' he'd roared at her when she tried to open a door for him after Father's death. Father had been the only person allowed to help him.

He always asked about Ida, because, just like Father, he never noticed how much Ida disdained him. Father kept bringing him over for dinner, in the hope that the common loss of limbs would bring them closer together. Something they could discuss over a nice goulash à la Nachtigall. How little he knew his wife!

Nepomuk was clearly expecting an answer though. She cleared her throat.

'Mother is still grieving.' She was surprised to discover that it might be true.

'I miss him even more,' groused Nepomuk. 'At least Ida has a daughter. Give me your coat, you're completely soaked. I'll hang it up and bring a coffee with cream.' Nepomuk hesitated for a second, then said with genuine regret in his voice, 'But only two pieces of sugar, right?'

Father always put four pieces of sugar in his cup. 'Better sweet now than soon enough dead!' he'd say to anyone who ventured to say something about his health. She suddenly missed him so much that she began to sway. She wished he were here, she'd throw herself into his arms, in spite of everything. 'Tain't true!' he'd say and chase Wallie away, and she would believe him.

'Yes, only two pieces,' she muttered, 'I'll get started, I've an errand to run for Mother afterwards.' She sat down at the desk with the lighting console that he'd reserved for her and tried to collect herself.

She was trying to get a breakthrough in the Niemöller case. She'd peppered all three contacts at Army HQ with questions but had been unable to get the list of names of the GIs who had come that evening to the folk festival or had helped out with the Queen of the Folk Fair competition. So she needed more pictures of the event.

The only picture that had actually been published in the paper was the picture of the three winners, but she knew that the on-site reporters took many more. So Nepomuk had put at her disposal all the negatives of the German-American Folk Fair. She took out her notebook, switched on the console, picked up the magnifying glass and started scanning.

Gerda had indeed captured the atmosphere of the festival perfectly. Carla could feel the good mood, almost hear the music from the merry-go-rounds. There seemed to be such a desire to have fun. Happy little girls with faces smeared with candyfloss. Boys jumping up and down at the shooting galleries. Men toasting each other with beer. Stalls full of souvenirs and currywurst and chips. Lots of American flags. It was all in black and white, but the pictures were bursting with life and colour. She hoped to find a picture of Ingrid and 'her' Jack. It was hopeless to try to identify Jack on his own. There were far too many tall, blond soldiers. The pictures were largely taken from a distance, so it was hard to distinguish the faces clearly.

When she got to the picture of the three winners, she did a double take. She almost didn't recognise Ingrid Niemöller. The blonde wig and make-up completely transformed her, she seemed a full-blooded vamp. Compared to her, the other two winners were nothing but pale imitations of Doris Day in *Pillow Talk*. How come Ingrid hadn't won? Were the men in the jury scared of this tall, attractive woman? Jack hadn't been scared off, though, but where was he? She looked at the pictures of the winners with the organisers, before and after the show. Gerda had taken lots of them. Of course, because it was full of celebrities. The flowers were given to them by Marlene Schmidt, the current Miss Germany and Miss Universe. As luck would have it, she'd fled from the GDR to the West somewhere near Stuttgart, so this picture would probably appear in all of the West German press, maybe even in the American papers. But no one would be interested in Franz Amrehn, the rather unassuming acting mayor standing next to Marlene Schmidt.

Carla examined the public and the GIs with the magnifying glass. They were all staring at Ingrid. Maybe Ingrid would recognise him if she got copies of each picture of the young GIs. She took the last roll of film and continued searching, just in case there was a picture of just Ingrid and one soldier.

She stopped suddenly. She looked at the last picture once again, more closely, through the magnifying glass. Her lips began to twitch.

There was no magical clue about Jack, but it was a picture of Aunt Lulu standing in front of a hot dog stand, surrounded by her friends the Shakefield Girls. This is what she called them in a humorous reference to the Ziegfield Girls of the 1920s. The older her friends got, the better the name suited them. They'd been friends since before Lulu became an actress, because she had first tried to become a showgirl, but was far too short for it. She'd drowned her sorrows in the Delphi Dance Bar, where she met these women, who were also trying to earn money as dancers.

Carla tidied the films away, thanked Nepomuk and asked for the copies she needed.

'That'll be expensive,' he muttered, 'Tomorrow OK?'

'Money is not an issue, for once,' said Carla. 'Call me when they're ready to be picked up. Thank you.' She gave him two packs of Lucky Strike, which he put at once in his jacket pocket.

'Here, look, this is the evening edition for tonight.' He handed her the freshly printed *Berliner Morgenpost*, opened it up and pointed to a picture of Hochbrück. 'Isn't this the architect fella that Karl-Otto never much liked, because he was such a show-off?'

Carla grabbed the paper. 'Mysterious death' screamed the headline next to the picture of Hochbrück. 'Found dead by his wife in their villa in Dahlem. Could it be murder? Police are investigating.'

'You're so pale, shall I get you some water?' A loud swooshing noise flooded her ears. Hochbrück dead? Oh, God, Wallie – the pictures she'd taken would endanger the agency. She had to get back home at once and talk to Wallie. Make sure that all the negatives had been destroyed. Was it possible that frail Alma had solved her problem in such a brutal manner? That furious look when she'd slammed the door in their faces. Besides, hadn't Alma herself said that she'd make sure she'd banish evil from her life, no matter what it may cost? Was the fairy princess now a banshee?

She remembered Hochbrück banging on the steering wheel in his car, saying that Alma was making his life difficult with her lies. And that he'd only get divorced over his dead body.

Would the police come to the agency? Only if Alma told

them that she'd been there. Maybe their visit to Dahlem had escalated the conflict? Of course, they might also question her, simply because they knew each other from the orphanage committee and had sat next to each other at dinner.

She had to speak to Wallie urgently, but she hadn't spent that night in the office. Carla assumed she'd been with her Scottish admirer. But what if that wasn't true? What if Wallie had been arrested, because they thought she might be Hochbrück's jealous mistress? And what if Wallie had boasted about her illegal activities at the Eden and now Nightingale & Co. would be associated with it?

She thanked Muki, who'd just brought her a glass of water, gulped it down and stormed off without any explanation. When she stepped out of the gloomy building, she had to blink several times, because the sun was now out and the azure sky was blinding her.

16

Carla fell into Pallutzke's web as she was heading up the stairs to the agency. The caretaker was standing at the far end of the staircase and wiping between the spindles of the bannister with a leather cloth. As soon as she spotted Carla, she posted herself squarely in the middle of the stairs and marked her territory with her unmistakable scent of wet floor-cloth, dog food and Elnett hairspray.

'A man came to see you at noon today.'

'I'm afraid I was out, did he leave anything for me?' asked Carla.

'He just rang once and then went away.'

So more likely a client than the police. She'd have liked to know what the man looked like, but she wouldn't give Frau Pallutzke the satisfaction.

'Nice to see family solidarity, isn't it?' said Frau Pallutzke, nodding and smiling.

'Yes.' Carla tried to pass by the portly caretaker, but she wasn't budging. It was like running up against a wall.

'I mean your cousin from the East.'

'Yes?'

'Nice to see Ida finally having someone to talk to.'

'Excuse me, I'm expecting an urgent...' Carla waved vaguely towards the upper floor.

'But what about the rent? I have to tell the new landlord that there are now three of you in the apartment.'

'We were three with my father, and the rent did not go

down when he died. Anyway, this is none of your business...'

'I didn't mean it like that...' Her unpleasant voice was getting shrill. Luckily, the phone ringing on the first floor came to her rescue.

'Sorry,' said Carla, 'Got to work to pay the rent!'

'Of course, work comes first,' said Frau Pallutzke, still not budging. Carla held her sleeve in front of her nose and squeezed herself past the blue-green polyester cleaner's tunic.

'Don't mind me, give my regards to dear Ida!' Pallutzke screeched after her.

Carla got to the phone just in time.

A somewhat uncertain male voice introduced himself as Otto Stratmann. He was a lawyer and had been appointed as the on-duty legal counsel for Alma. He explained that the police no longer thought that the death was an accident but murder. They'd arrested Alma and were holding her in custody at Lehrterstraße prison.

That prison of all places! Carla had been there once with Father to pick up Lulu. The cells, which at the turn of the century had seemed state of the art, appeared tiny to her. There was a horrible smell everywhere, because there were no toilets in the cells, merely buckets.

Lulu had gone to the papers afterwards to report on the scandalous conditions there. Not only the sanitary ones, but the fact that the cells were less than seven square metres, while any dog in the Federal Republic was allowed between six and ten square metres by law. There was an uproar for a time, but then nothing changed – apparently because of lack of funding. If Carla's memory was correct, the whole place was as dark as a coal cellar. She couldn't help thinking about Alma's enthusiasm for light and shade and art therapy. Would she ever be able to escape those shadows?

Stratmann said that Alma wanted to speak to her urgently. She hadn't told him why, but he would be grateful if she could go, because Alma did not want to speak to him.

Why would Alma ask for her? If her silly charade came to light, this would count even more against her. She might then be accused of premeditation or malice. Didn't she have any friends she could call, or relatives?

'What about her brother?'

'He doesn't want to see her, he's completely broken down. Looks like he was a close friend of her husband.'

'Is he at least looking after the children?'

'No, that's not allowed. Social services have taken them, there are no grandparents left.'

There was a knock on the door. Judging by the sound, not Pallutzke, not Lulu and not Wallie. Could it be Frau Niemöller?

'Just a second,' she called towards the door and then whispered on the phone. 'Please leave me your number and I'll call you back. I have to check my diary.' But she already knew she was going to go.

She jotted down the number, hung up, and on the way to the door checked her hair in the small pocket mirror she fished out of her handbag. She powdered her nose quickly too. Then she opened the door.

'You?'

Wallie smiled charmingly. 'I thought I'd surprise you by behaving like a lady for once.'

'They've arrested Alma.'

'Makes sense.'

Wallie seemed unbearably calm. She must have known already, but where from? The arrest had not made it onto the news yet. Had she heard this from her Scotsman – had she spent the night with him?

'But why would Alma kill her husband?' she asked.

'To get rid of him once and for all and inherit.'

'This just goes to show how little you know her! She'd never risk losing her children.'

'She's very crafty. She's been planning it for a while, tried to get you involved. We nearly fell for her lies, then we'd have been witnesses to how he abused her.' Wallie laughed triumphantly. 'But that didn't work, because we didn't fall for it!'

Yes, of course, you saw through her right away, thought Carla sardonically. In her mind's eye the compromising pictures Wallie had taken flickered like an expressionist silent movie, black-and-white shadows fornicating. She tried to scrub those images off her retina by focusing on the clock.

What did she in fact know about those pictures and Wallie's relationship with Hochbrück? Were there other pictures still to uncover? Why did Wallie insist on taking them? And how come she was so calm and unconcerned, surely she must be somewhat nervous now? After all, the man she'd drugged was now dead.

'I think our visit to Alma's house led to an escalation. She begged us not to come and minutes later there was Hochbrück with his tyres squealing.'

'But he was still very much alive then. So it can't be our fault, since he was only killed last night.'

'I think I want to speak to Alma.'

'What's the point? Give me one good reason.'

'Because she asked for my help.'

'See, I don't understand. You already refused to help her, which, looking back now, was quite sharp-witted of you. You were passing her on to a lawyer in the West.'

'Because it was the right thing to do, she was the only one who could help her.'

'I hate to admit it, but obviously you really are more experienced than me and so you probably caught on that she was lying to us.'

'As I said, people lie in an emergency. And I have the feeling there is something here that stinks to high heaven. I think Alma is the victim here.'

'A feeling?' Wallie rolled her eyes till all Carla could see were the whites. 'Stop talking to me about *feeeeelings*! If you ask me, I think Alma's been playing the victim all her life.'

'I don't believe that, and Father told me to rely on my gut instinct.'

'Yes of course, I didn't have the privilege of so many in-depth discussions with Dad.' Wallie sounded genuinely offended. 'And what does your gut instinct tell you about me?'

Carla was convinced by now that Wallie was indeed her half-sister, but there was something more to it. Had she changed a few details – but why and which ones? She instinctively reached out to her neck to stroke the silver die, but of course it was no longer there.

'We can talk about this later, now I have to call Alma's lawyer.'

'You should stay out of it. That's what my mum would've advised. And she was often smarter than our dad.'

Carla reached out for the phone without a word. But just as she was about to pick up the receiver, it rang. This time it was Lulu, who wanted to be the first to tell her about Hochbrück's murder and Alma's arrest. Carla didn't even get a chance to tell her she already aware of that, because Lulu was chattering away nonstop. Lulu liked Alma, because she'd got her the first job with the production company of Atze Brauner a couple of years ago. So she asked Carla if she should get in touch with her police contacts, maybe arrange a meeting with the interim chief of police?

Carla tried to stem the tide of Lulu's words, but she got distracted when she glanced at Wallie. Wallie had lit a cigarette and gone to the window. Something was different about her, she seemed to droop a little, there was less brashness about her.

What if there was another angle to the story? What if

Wallie had shown up at that moment in time because she was Hochbrück's lover, and knew that Alma was going to come to the agency? The photos might even be real, because Wallie was hoping that Hochbrück would finally get a divorce. Nonsense, that was a complete red herring. Or maybe Wallie had some help taking the pictures, and that someone was now blackmailing her? Where had she developed them anyway? And where'd she got that drug from, how exactly did it work, could it have been a delayed effect? Did Wallie even work at the Eden Bar? Carla had really not done her homework at all. She had to find out more about Wallie, even if – or maybe because – she was her half-sister. She had to change tack, win her trust and see where that would take her.

Wallie stubbed the cigarette out on the windowsill and threw the butt out of the window. She turned round and saw Carla staring at her.

Carla looked away at once, and tried to focus on what Lulu was telling her. She was asking if the murder would present any problems for the orphanage. Carla hoped not. Lulu was about to say goodbye, when Carla remembered the German-American Folk Fair. She was really losing it! She asked her aunt if one of her Shakefield Girls had taken any pictures at the festival and was very disappointed to hear that was not the case. Only Trudi had taken a couple.

Trudi? That rang a bell, but before she could explore it any further, Lulu was asking why, given all that was going on, Carla was suddenly interested in a folk festival. She was trying to find a plausible explanation when there was another knock at the door.

Wallie opened it and showed Ingrid Niemöller in. Carla said a hasty goodbye and hung up to greet her client, who had dark rings under her eyes. She looked tired and older. Little wisps of hair had fallen out of her tight bun, and her lavender suit looked creased. She didn't have an appointment, so something must have happened. Had someone found out about her behaviour and fired her? If so, good job that she'd paid in cash in advance.

Wallie offered the woman a coffee and disappeared into the kitchen to prepare it. Very efficient, almost as if they really were a team.

Carla asked her client to sit down and handed her the cigarette case. Frau Niemöller lit one and inhaled greedily.

'Have you found my Jack at last?'

'Not yet, but we've made good progress.'

Wallie, who was bringing in a tray with coffee from the kitchen, raised her eyebrows and looked daggers at Carla. She set down the tray with condensed milk, sugar and biscuits, then sat down next to Carla, as if she were the boss. Carla felt the urge to jump up.

'I was in Little America and spoke to any number of soldiers there,' said Wallie.

'Heavens, your task was not to make my search public knowledge!' Frau Niemöller angrily stubbed the cigarette in the ashtray.

The kettle started whistling and Wallie went to the kitchen, murmuring, 'Coffee,' and leaving Carla to calm down their client.

'We are very discreet, I can assure you, there's nothing connecting you.'

'I dream of him every night, I can't bear it.' Frau Niemöller leaned back in her chair, closing her eyes. 'I shouldn't have told so many lies. This is all coming back to haunt me now...'

Wallie appeared with the coffee pot and was about to say something as she sat down, but Carla got there before her.

'There's something else worrying you, isn't there?'

Ingrid opened her eyes, throwing Carla a grateful look, and slid to the edge of her chair. While Wallie poured the coffee, she explained that her new boss wanted to meet her husband. She had of course pretended to be married, because otherwise you couldn't work as an Anovlar representative. So far she'd managed to get away with it because she said that her husband was a travelling salesman for doorknobs and screws, who was away from home a lot and wouldn't mind her doing the job while she still didn't have any children. But now her department had a new boss, who insisted upon meeting her husband over dinner.

'No sweat,' said Wallie, 'We could find a suitable guy for you.'

Carla flashed her an angry look. 'What Miss von Tilling means is that we are under even more pressure to find Jack in time, so that you can go there with him.'

'But what will he say when he discovers that I lied to him and to the jury, that I'm neither a real blonde, nor a Lufthansa stewardess, but a brunette pharma saleswoman?'

'If it's a genuine sentiment, then that won't matter,' Carla said, trying to convince herself. 'You said that your meeting felt truly special. If I remember correctly, he even said that he felt you were destined to be together?'

Ingrid nodded and showed the plastic ring on her finger. The colour had peeled off in several places by now.

'That's exactly how I felt too. Do you have anything for me at all?'

While Carla hesitated, trying to find a synonym for 'No', Wallie intervened once more.

'You must be patient just for two more days, then we'll know more. Our work, just like that of the Allies...'

What admirable parallels she was capable of drawing.

'... has not been made any easier by the building of the Wall. During the visit of the Vice-President, there's been heightened security for the American forces, so we haven't been able to gather information as effectively.' Wallie sounded so convincing, that Carla almost believed her.

Frau Niemöller's face lit up. 'I can postpone the dinner for a couple of days, on the pretext that my husband has some important appointments in the West.' She rearranged her stray wisps of hair and took her wallet out of her handbag. 'I'm sure you've had expenses.' She handed Carla two fifty-mark notes. 'No need to write a receipt, I'm sure you're sometimes out of pocket in your investigations.' She stood up. 'But the day after tomorrow I'll be back at 17:00 and expect results.'

Carla could not help glancing at Wallie, who was struggling to control a broad grin. She stood up hurriedly to let Ingrid out.

'Why hello there, what a boss!' Wallie had taken the banknotes and was waving them in the air. 'Do you always milk your clients to this extent?'

'The Nightingale Agency doesn't milk anyone, we take our work very seriously.'

'Daddy never seemed to me to be so pompous.'

Daddy? Carla had never dared call him anything else but Father. 'Yet he was always decent.'

'So why did this Niemöller woman lie so much to Jack?'

She clearly wanted to change the subject, and Carla had nothing against it. So she explained.

'No kidding, there are tablets that stop you from getting pregnant? I could make a killing with those in the Eden. The boss would set up a dispenser in the women's toilets.'

'They're not chewing gum, they're medicine.'

'No, they're more than that, they're ultimate freedom.' Wallie was unstoppable now. 'With that we now have a barrier against sperm, but one that cannot be seen. Now you can decide for yourself, no more condoms, no more interruptus. Did Ingrid leave you some samples by any chance?'

'Of course not. We don't take payment in kind here, certainly not with such things.'

Wallie groaned loudly. 'Hard to believe we've the same father. Daddy would never have been such a boring party pooper. I'll go see if I can catch Niemöller.' She rushed to the window to look out, then ran to the door. 'We're in luck, she was stopped by Pallutzke!' Wallie grabbed her bag and stormed out.

Carla felt as though Wallie had sucked her dry of all her energy when she left. A voice inside her was saying 'Run after her!' while another voice was telling her to just sleep it off and wait for it all to be resolved. The Niemöller case, the murder of Hochbrück, her problems with her half-sister, her mother, the orphanage, the rent, love... But since she'd caused Mother's accident at the age of ten, she'd known that there was no higher power in this world that could make things better. One single unforgivable mistake had been enough to turn her life – the whole family's life – into hell. She wasn't allowed to make any more mistakes.

Carla stood up and wandered to the window. Wallie had just managed to extract Ingrid from Pallutzke's web of intrigue, much to the latter's dismay. Further behind, she spotted Katrin, hiding behind an advertising pillar, examining Wallie and writing something down in a notebook. Carla had to smile. Meanwhile, her client was heading for a small blue cabrio, parked between two freshly planted linden trees. She took a small box out of the boot and gave it to Wallie. Wallie looked extremely upbeat once more. She shook hands quite earnestly with their client and seemed to make a solemn promise.

Of course, promises and lies, she was really good at that. Wallie clearly took more after their father.

'The door was open!' panted a little voice behind Carla. She turned round in surprise and found Katrin puffing there. 'You were downstairs just now?'

'Yes, but I thought that if Miss von Tilling is down there, that means you're here alone, and I wanted to give you my report about her.'

Carla remembered the mission Lulu had entrusted her with.

'I noticed this chap, he dropped by a few times. He spoke to Frau Pallutzke, asked about you, but didn't go inside. And just the other evening, he smoked a cigarette just by the advertising pillar, and looked up to your window.'

Carla found it hard to keep a straight face. It must be a client, who wasn't sure if he really wanted to know what his wife was up to when he wasn't at home. 'And what did this man look like?'

'He was tall. Dark hair.'

'Anything else you noticed about him?'

'Could have been from the army. He had that posture and no beer belly.'

'An American?'

'No way!' That sounded very convinced.

'Poor, rich?'

Katrin shrugged. 'Average, I guess. But the soles of his shoes were a bit worn out.'

'You saw that in the dark?'

'No!' Katrin sounded almost offended by Carla's stupidity. 'I'd seen him before, in daylight.'

'And what did you find out about Miss von Tilling?'

Katrin grinned mischievously. 'I'm still on the case.'

'OK, thanks. You've done very well. And now I have to go back to work.'

'Sure. I'll be on my way then!' And Katrin ran off, her plaits whipping through the air. Carla wasn't sure if she should put a stop to all this nonsense. Of course it was exciting for Katrin, but wouldn't it be better for her to focus on school and do something with her life? It was twice as hard for girls. Girls... Suddenly she saw Mathilda in her mind's eye, who was only a tiny bit younger than Katrin, yet so different. She was so fragile, while this one was full of beans. Would Wallie have resembled Katrin at that age? Hmmm, not sure she wanted to make such a comparison. Finally, Carla picked up the phone and called Alma's lawyer.

17

The consultation room for meeting those held in custody was much brighter than Carla remembered, so bright and flickering in fact that the neon lights themselves seemed to be protesting at the indignity of being held captive. Thank goodness it also smelled different, more like coal, spilled ersatz coffee and floor polish, rather than human excrement.

Carla and the tanned lawyer, Otto Stratmann, had been waiting for ten minutes for Alma. He'd spent all that time leafing ceaselessly through the few pages in his dossier, which looked like a toy in his big hands. His head seemed two sizes too small for his broad shoulders, perhaps because his very light-coloured, very short hair blurred the contours of his head. The dark grey suit threatened to rip apart at the seams over his shoulders, and the trouser legs were too short, which made Carla wonder if he'd borrowed it from someone.

When their glances met he immediately looked away, back to the big clock hanging over the door, ticking loudly. Reminding everyone locked in here that they'd never get that time back again, as Carla thought after yet another torturous quarter of an hour. She was not in the mood for wasting any more time.

'Isn't it nice that Adenauer is finally coming to Berlin?' she asked.

'Hmm.' Stratmann didn't even look up.

'Shouldn't you be informing me of what exactly happened?' she finally asked directly.

'Not much to say,' he replied, still looking down at his dossier. 'Mrs Hochbrück said on the phone that she found her husband dead on the stairs when she came home. After the police officers arrived at the scene, she changed her story and said it was self-defence. I can't tell you anything more.'

If it was self-defence, why didn't Alma say so at once? It didn't look good, changing a statement like that, but on the other hand, it spoke for her being innocent. Criminals tended to stick to their version of events, the version that exculpated them.

Silence fell once again. Tick. Tick. Tick.

'Do you ski?' she attempted another question.

He did look up at that, his barely visible eyebrows certainly raised. 'Are you clairvoyant?' Then he shook his head. 'Ah, of course, you've made enquiries about me.'

Actually, she hadn't. There'd been no time for it, because the previous evening she'd met up with Paula to find out more about Hochbrück. Paula had greeted her warmly, thinking it had something to do with the choir at the orphanage. But when Carla asked her about Hochbrück, she turned extremely pale and her face became an impassive mask. Everything between her and Hochbrück had been absolutely fine, she wouldn't start ruining his reputation after his death. Then she practically pushed Carla out of her apartment.

'I wish I were a clairvoyant,' she now told Stratmann, 'An ideal quality for a detective. However,' she drew a circle in the air around his eyes, 'That particular shade of brown must come from the mountains and those marks are made by ski goggles.'

Stratmann smiled for the first time. 'Skiing is my thing. I almost made it to the Olympics at Cortina d'Ampezzo. But shortly before that I broke my ankle doing a slalom on the icy piste. End of a dream!'

'Is this your first case?'

Stratmann blushed under his tan.

'You never forget your first case, and you do your best to win. So Alma is lucky to have you,' she said encouragingly. At the same time, she remembered how unsure of herself she'd been during her first solo case after her father's death. Industrial espionage in a tool factory.

Before Stratmann could reply, the door opened and a uniformed guard brought Alma in.

The moment Carla saw her, she wished she could magic her away from there. The Celtic faerie princess now looked like a homeless person. Her beautiful red locks were stuck to her scalp, the white suit was grimy and stained. Her tights were laddered, her ballet flats covered in a grey film. But worst of all was the utter despair in her eyes.

'Thank goodness you're here,' she mumbled and sat down. 'Mr Stratmann, I'd like to speak to Miss Koslowsky alone, if I may?'

Stratmann looked somewhat helplessly at Carla, who nodded. 'Yes, please give us ten minutes.'

The lawyer stood up, unsure whether he should take the dossier with him, hesitated, started to say something, then stopped and finally left the consultation room in silence.

'What happened, Alma?'

'Alexander fell down the stairs in the house. You know, the narrow metal staircase leading up to his studio. It was self-defence, it was an accident.'

'I'm really sorry about that, but why did you want to speak to me?'

'It would help if you could confirm that he was being violent. Not just for my sake, but also for my children.'

'Then I'd have to lie, because everything you told us at the agency was a complete fantasy.'

'I was afraid that no one would believe me. But he really did do all those things I told you about.'

'What happened that evening? Please tell me in chronological order, and as detailed as you can.'

'I had to take Gregor to the hospital. He'd been playing in the garden with some boys from his hockey team. We have a lot of space and the boys always train in our garden before a match.' Alma sprang up and started pacing. 'There was an accident, Gregor had an open gash in his forehead. It bled so profusely that they all started to panic. I did too. I sent the boys home and decided not to wait for Mathilda, who was at her ballet class. I drove straightaway to the hospital.'

One of the neon lights flickered up, buzzed and then went out completely. A corner of the room got darker, but the table remained fully lit. Alma sat back down. She seemed eager to talk about everything.

'At the hospital, they did an X-ray and stitched Gregor's cut. Luckily, there was no concussion, but they advised him to stay there overnight for observation. Plus, I had to go back for Mathilda.'

'So you went home on your own. What happened then?'

Alma hesitated a moment, seeming to dread her memories. 'When I got home, Alexander was beside himself. His son is his darling. At first, he just yelled at me, demanding to know why I hadn't called him so that he could come to the hospital. He'd got home, nobody was there, all he could see were kitchen towels covered in blood. Mad with anxiety, he had to ask the neighbours what had happened, which he found humiliating. And of course he didn't know which hospital we'd gone to. So Alexander grabbed the hockey stick and started...'

Carla didn't want to imagine what happened next. Alma began sobbing. 'At first I thought he was justified, that I deserved to be punished, but he just got more and more brutal. I just couldn't bear it anymore and snapped. I can't remember exactly what happened next, but I must have tried to defend myself, pushed, he lost his balance and fell down the stairs. That staircase doesn't have a bannister.'

She was breathing heavily. 'Thank goodness Mathilda wasn't home at the time. I swear, it was self-defence. I can't go to prison. What would happen to my children?' Alma clasped Carla's hand. 'Your father would've helped me!'

The sudden switch to the informal 'you' shook Carla.

'What can I do?'

'You can testify on my behalf.'

'I'm not the only one who knows about the story you told us, so does Miss von Tilling.'

Alma groaned. 'He always hit me where it wouldn't be visible.' She pulled up her twinset and showed her ribs covered in bruises.' 'Please help.'

Carla found it difficult to switch to the informal 'you' with Alma, but she didn't want to offend her. 'Can't your doctor testify? Surely his expertise is more valuable in court.'

Alma shook her head. 'Dr Schollwitz is an old friend of Alexander's. Whenever I was badly injured, he'd come to the house. Alex paid him cash so that no one in the surgery would ask any awkward questions. He reprimanded Alex a couple of times, but he wouldn't say anything in public, certainly not now, when it might ruin his reputation and Alex's.'

'What about your gynaecologist?'

'I was only allowed to see her during my pregnancies, and during those he didn't hit me. She'd been recommended to him by Dr Schollwitz, but I guess he was worried I would get friendly with her, or try to prevent future pregnancies. So immediately after the birth, it was back to Dr Schollwitz. Alexander was keen to have lots of children, because he'd been an only child.'

'I can't commit perjury, but what happened between your husband and Paula Becker? Would her testimony be more helpful to you?'

Alma turned so pale, that Carla thought she might faint.

'We mustn't get Paula involved in this, leave her out of it. She has psychological problems, it wouldn't be right. I can only count on you and your impeccable reputation.'

But perjury would spell the end of this impeccable reputation. Would Father have committed perjury for Alma? Not sure about that, though he'd certainly have tried to help. But for that, Alma had to be completely honest. No more kid-glove treatment.

'Why was Alexander in his office when you came home? If he was that worried about Gregor, would he not have come running downstairs when he heard the car?'

'Please think of my children,' Alma begged, not even bothering to reply, 'Where would they go if I get locked up?'

'They have a very nice uncle.' Carla was getting fed up with Alma's avoidance tactics.

Alma's eyes filled with tears right on cue. 'My brother hates me!' she said angrily, wiping her face with her dirty sleeves, 'He's quite disturbed.'

It was remarkable how many people in Alma's vicinity seemed to be psychologically disturbed: Paula, the brother, the husband. Maybe it was Alma who had something wrong with her. Just like Hochbrück had hinted in the car. 'So why does your brother hate you so much?'

Just at that moment, Stratmann came back in and sat down.

'We need to use the remainder of the time to discuss a possible defence strategy,' he said. 'Miss Koslowsky, I'd like you to leave now.'

'She can stay, I don't need any defence, it was an accident, self-defence. Please!'

Alma's panicked eyes dug deep into Carla's heart. She seemed genuinely stricken. But why was she hiding something from Carla? Did she have a lover, maybe? That was something she should've considered earlier. What if someone was passionately in love with her and helped her to get rid of Hochbrück?

'Why do the police think it was murder? What evidence do they have?' Carla asked Stratmann.

'The position of the body at the foot of the stairs. The hockey stick had been wiped clean. Fibres from Alma's clothing on his clothing.'

'They lived together as a couple, of course there was transfer of fibres. Was Hochbrück tested for blood alcohol levels?'

Stratmann nodded and searched through his dossier. 'He had a BAC of 2.5 b.'

'2.5?' Carla started to feel hopeful. 'That's wonderful!'

Alma looked questioningly at her.

'That means that he was well over the moderate intoxication threshold, which lies between 1 and 2 blood alcohol. 2.5 means he was severely impaired, and that means lack of balance. Those architect's steps are a trip hazard even when you are sober, so it really does look like an accident. Why had he drunk so much that evening?'

'He always had a couple of glasses before dinner.'

'But Mrs Hochbrück is the sole heir,' Stratmann intervened.

'Like most wives,' Carla said. 'Is there much to inherit?'

Stratmann looked concerned. 'Cash, properties – the prosecutor's office has indicated that money could be a motive.'

'Everything was bought from my dowry,' Alma laughed cynically, 'The Stellmark money.'

'If that's true and the prosecutor thinks greed might be the motive, better not mention the visit to Nightingale & Co.'

'Greed?' Alma seemed stunned. 'But why greed?'

'If your marriage can be considered exemplary, and Stratmann can bring witnesses to testify to that, then the prosecution would struggle to make money the motive, because why would you kill the golden goose? However, if it's clear that you wanted a divorce and he didn't, then you'd have had severe financial penalties, and therefore a strong motive to want him dead.'

'Is that true?' Alma asked the lawyer. Stratmann nodded.

'You should get other experts involved,' Carla insisted. She was beginning to wonder if this Stratmann fellow had even studied law. 'If Hochbrück was so drunk, then, in all that excitement, he could have easily fallen all by himself.'

'You mean I don't need to plead self-defence?' Alma asked in astonishment.

'Does anyone else know about your marital problems?'

'I don't think so.'

'Except for Paula. How long had she been his lover?' Carla decided to catch her out.

Alma's eyes widened and she seemed about to say something, but then paused, afraid she might make a mistake. She shrugged. 'No idea.'

She was still hiding something – a lover?

'And what does your brother know about your marriage?'

'He hates me, but he admired Alexander and would never do anything to harm him. I'm sure he'll testify what a devoted husband he was and how wonderful our marriage was.'

'Is there a lover in the picture?' Carla lowered her voice, as if that would make things any better.

Red spots appeared on Alma's neck. 'I've always been a decent woman,' she snorted with rage and visible disappointment. 'I've had enough of men!'

Carla could believe that. But of course she'd also believed in her injuries, the way the woman had moved and talked back then. Maybe she was a very skilled actress.

'I'm no lawyer,' Carla said at last, 'But the evidence for murder seems remarkably thin on the ground. Have you checked out the timeline for that evening?'

Stratmann blushed again, but Carla was all out of pity for him. Even if Alma was lying in one respect, there was no doubt that she loved her children dearly and their future depended on this.

'That alcohol level indicates more than just a couple of drinks before dinner. What father would get drunk while his injured favourite child is in hospital? I think you need to investigate that. How long had he been in the house when Alma arrived? Had he been on his own, or was he drinking with someone?'

'Yes, we'll look into all that, and now please leave.' Stratmann stood up to shake her hand and almost shoved Carla out the door.

'Please don't go!' begged Alma, but Stratmann, still quite red in the face, was not to be persuaded this time. 'I'll call you as soon as we have any news,' he said, closing the door firmly behind Carla.

18

'Thank you.' Wallie picked up the rain-damp envelope from the courier's hands and closed the office door. She put the A4 envelope on Carla's desk, then sat down on the leather chair and looked at it. From its smell, she could tell it came straight from a photo lab. Her whole childhood had been bathed in Mamushka's perfume, a mix of darkroom and Mouson's lily of the valley.

What photos could they be? Had Carla found the negatives of her and Hochbrück? How had she got hold of them? Was she trying to get her into trouble with the police to get rid of her? There was no point in sitting there and overthinking it. She had to open the envelope. But that would upset Carla.

Mum had told her to respect other people's privacy, but she was dead now, far too early. Lung cancer. Best doctors, all in vain. Suddenly, Wallie had had enough of her cigarette. She stubbed it out on the windowsill and threw it out the window. Then she opened the envelope.

As expected, there were photos in the rustling paper. Her heartbeat quickened. She was surprised to feel that the idea of Carla's betrayal hurt her more than she expected. She pulled out the photos.

'Well, I'll be darned!' she exclaimed in relief. They were pictures of the German-American Folk Fair, and some of them had been blown up. Not so dumb, her sister. She barely recognised the Niemöller woman. Amazing, how much a person could change with a wig and some make-up. She put the pictures back into the envelope.

'Might I ask what you're doing?' came the sharp question from the doorway.

Wallie started. How had she not heard Carla coming? She was usually good at spotting things like that.

'I'm helping you with your inquiries.' She noticed that Carla really had snuck in on tiptoe, holding her shoes in her hands. So that's why she hadn't heard her!

'You're breaking the law of postal secrecy.'

'Not quite,' said Wallie, trying to joke, 'It came by courier, not post.'

Carla rolled her eyes. 'You're acting without any human decency, as usual.' She came up to the leather chair, shooing her off with her handbag. When Wallie resisted, she shoved her with her elbows until she stood up. Then Carla took off her gloves and picked up the photos.

'Honestly, how dare you open my mail?'

'I figure this isn't the way to find Jack.' Wallie sat down on the rattan chair opposite her.

'Really? And you've got a better idea?' Carla was skimming one picture after another, but she looked tired and unfocused. Where on earth had she been?

'We should focus on the unusual nickname,' Wallie suggested.

'You don't say? Thank you for the genius idea, would never have thought of that on my own...'

'Who's been pissin' in your beer?'

'I don't think you realise.' Carla's voice got louder as she laid the pictures out on the table. 'Jackov's nickname was not Boobs, so it's not about these...' She circled her own tiny breasts with her hands. 'They called him something like Bobbs.'

'Actually, my English is quite good. I don't understand why you behave as if you're so superior and look down upon me. Do you think I chose to be in this situation? I'm as much of a victim here as you.' She could have left out that last sentence, it was a bit much.

Carla merely closed her eyes and breathed in and out loudly, her shoulders sagging suddenly, as if her puppeteer had suddenly let go of the strings. She looked even tinier than usual.

'I think we both need some coffee,' Wallie said.

'Umm.' Carla's voice was barely audible.

'And then you have to tell me what happened.'

When she came back with the coffee, Carla was still sitting motionless at her desk, but at least she'd opened her eyes now. Wallie put the steaming cup in front of her, picked up her own and waited for Carla to have a sip.

'So?'

'I ask myself what our father would've done,' Carla said, looking straight at her.

Our father – that sounded like a peace offering; it was the first time she'd relented.

'The answer is simple. In difficult times like this, our dad wouldn't have said anything, not before he'd had a glass of Berliner Luft – or two.'

The corners of Carla's mouth very slowly turned up into something resembling a smile. 'Berliner Luft – Berliner Air. I wonder whether the air in the west or the east agreed more with him.' She started laughing out loud. It sounded a bit rusty, like someone who'd not had much to laugh about in her life.

Wallie was relieved and joined in. Carla had regained a tiny bit of colour in her cheeks. It was surprising how pleased she was to see that, but it was probably unwise to become too attached to Carla.

Her sister got up, went to the filing cabinet and opened it up. 'I've got something better than Berliner Luft, or do you like that sickly stuff?'

Wallie refrained from replying with an enthusiastic 'yes'. As so often in life, there were more important things than the truth.

Carla took out a half-empty bottle of Asbach Uralt cognac and two glasses, while telling Wallie about the depressing visit with Alma at the police station. Three glasses later, she ended by saying that she had to help Alma no matter what.

'But why? She tricked us. I know that kinda woman, pretends to be a victim and manipulates everybody, so she can control everything.'

'This is not about a certain kind of woman, but about Alma.'

'You didn't wanna help her either at first.'

'Because a good lawyer would've been more useful. But now she's got a complete dolt as a lawyer, who doesn't know a thing about anything!'

Wallie wanted to shout, *this is not our problem, we should stay out of it, no way are we getting involved*. But now she felt she'd got a little closer to her half-sister and she didn't want to risk it all immediately. 'What do you think we should do now?'

'We have to establish the facts, the timelines – something stinks here. I'll check with Lulu's contacts in the police. We have to talk to the neighbours, the hospital, the brother, Paula.' Carla seemed to warm up to the idea of collaboration, and perhaps this wasn't just because of the cognac.

Wallie agreed to all of that in principle, but the investigations would prove what a lying bitch that Alma was.

'I'll help you with the neighbours,' she said at last, 'And I think Klaus has a soft spot for me. But he hasn't been in the Eden the last two nights, I'd have noticed him. Where does this Paula live or work?'

'She lives in Zehlendorf, I'll give you her address. I'm not sure where Klaus lives.'

'We can find that out, but first I wanna talk to Alma's

neighbours. They might've seen something. And then I wanna take care of Paula. Eden is starting later tonight, 'cos there's a private party till eleven, the half-climb party for the Barbara Valentin film.' Wallie tried to suppress a grin, but Carla noticed it.

'What's so funny about that? And what is a half-climb party?'

'A half-climb party is what you have when you've finished half of the film and actually there's nothing funny about it.' Carla didn't need to know that the boss had been making a fool of himself drooling over the blonde lead actress over the past few months. Nor would she find it particularly funny that the staff at Eden had been placing bets as to whether the boss would get laid.

'Thank you for your support, in any case.' Carla jumped up and walked to the window as energetically as if Wallie had given her a happy pill. 'Let's go and get this woman out of prison!'

Wallie could feel her conscience beginning to prick her.

'As for the Jack investigation,' Carla picked up the photos, 'You're right. We'll show Ingrid these blow-ups and try to figure out what this funny nickname, Bobbs, might mean.' She clapped her hands. 'Go, go, go, no time to lose! The sooner we get Alma out of there, the better for her kids!'

19

Wallie grimaced as the fourth housekeeper slammed the door in her face, as if she were no more than a street hawker selling dirty dishcloths. The socialists were right in that respect: property creates barriers. Back home in the Tucholskystraße, they'd have received her with open arms and gossiped about the neighbours. They'd have happily provided information, maybe even exaggerated a little bit, but this was worse.

So it was with diminished hope that she rang at the door of the neighbours opposite Alma. An elderly man in a baggy yet elegant suit, shirt and tie opened up. No housekeeper!

He looked at her expectantly. At last, she could introduce herself somewhat pompously as an employee of the Justice Department. She asked for help in an important matter and waved the wholesale trade permit that she used for shopping for the Eden Bar. The bigger the lies, the more effective.

He seemed delighted and invited her in, because he had indeed noticed something that he'd like to share. He led her through a dark, narrow hallway into a living room with an attached conservatory full of rubber plants. He invited her to take a seat in the woven bamboo seating area, then excused himself profusely.

Wallie could not believe her luck. The large bay window had a prime view over the entrance, the garage and the façade of the Hochbrück residence. Finally, a step forward.

The man returned with a tray with coffee and cake, setting them up on the glass table as if it were someone's birthday, including even a vase with yellow roses. Wallie had to curb her impatience until she'd tried the coffee – freshly ground, of course – and the cake – home-made, of course. Only then was he prepared to tell her what he'd witnessed on that particular evening. He sounded quite excited but didn't strike Wallie as a timewaster. He'd felt sorry for the little girl, because when Mathilda arrived home, she'd rung the doorbell several times to no avail. Nobody opened the door. Finally, the girl had to take the spare key which was – he winked at Wallie – as always in the wooden birdhouse. Not a great hiding place, the neighbour said, expecting Wallie to agree with him.

Wallie nodded and her heart rejoiced. At last, a promising trail! This was only the first of Alma's lies, because she claimed that Mathilda had been at ballet class and only got home after her father died.

She asked the neighbour what else he'd noticed that evening, and even took out a nice new notebook that she'd borrowed from Carla's office, in an effort to look more professional.

The neighbour poured a second cup of coffee and continued his unadorned but detailed description of events. After Mathilda had opened the door, he'd spotted the... erm, gardener from the neighbours on the other side. She had to forgive him, but one couldn't expect anything else from such a menial. The old man stopped to breathe in sharply, as if he wasn't sure if he could continue with such a sorry tale.

Wallie winced when he said lower species, but she refrained from making any comment, simply nodded encouragingly. The neighbour gave a sigh of relief and told her about the shocking habit of the gardener had of relieving himself on the Hochbrücks' compost heap.

Luckily, just then a silver UFO had landed on the roof of the garage and six SS troopers had marched out. They didn't arrest the gardener, but they rounded up all the red-haired gypsies living in the Hochbrücks' garage and dumped them in their UFO. Wallie must know that the heroes of the Third Reich had fled to one of the moons of the planet Walhalla, where Hitler was currently in cryogenic suspension, kept young for his return. He hoped he'd live to see that day.

Did she want another slice of cake?

Wallie's appetite disappeared. When the neighbour then told her under oath of secrecy that the building of the Wall had been organised remotely by the planet Walhalla, she had to admit that he was useless as a witness. She let it slip that she was on a secret mission on behalf of Walhalla but now she had to go.

As she walked through light drizzle in this neighbourhood that seemed so untouched by the war, she realised she still had a lot to learn. It had been a mistake to search for proof of something that she wanted to believe with all her soul. It made her blind. If that man hadn't completely lost the plot, she'd have believed everything he said, because she wanted to prove that Alma was lying. She had to change tack and instead look for proof of Alma's innocence. If she remained open-minded and examined everything carefully, she'd find the truth, regardless of what either she or Carla wanted to believe.

The road to Paula's apartment led past the Waldfriede Hospital. A good way to kill two birds with one stone and to check the timeline of events that evening. When had Alma arrived there and when had she left?

At the hospital she once again claimed to be an employee in the Justice Department, and was instantly allowed to check the visitor logbook. She made a note of the times, but they seemed to fit with everything Alma had told Carla. She also asked who'd been on duty that evening and managed to catch the nurse in question in the parking lot outside the clinic. She'd just come off her shift and was tired, not in the mood for chatting. Wallie reminded herself of Tucholsky's advice to exaggerate the flattery and told the nurse how vitally important her statement would be for a murder case. Finally, she gave in.

'It was bad,' she said, in a self-satisfied manner 'The boy was covered in blood. I personally think that witch murdered her son.'

'No!' Wallie hadn't expected such a monstrous accusation.

'She wasn't a real mother, that Frau Professor! She could have stayed overnight with the poor little fellow. We allow that nowadays, even if it's more work for us.'

'Maybe Mrs Hochbrück wanted to go home quickly to kill the man who'd hurt her son so badly? Maybe it was no hockey injury?' Wallie suggested. Better have it right out in the open and try to find a justification for Alma's behaviour.

The nurse looked at Wallie suspiciously. 'Who are you working for? The prosecutor, or the defence? Nobody here believes such a thing, not a soul. Mrs Hochbrück thinks she's above us, there's something strange about her, with all that red hair and all, like an evil goblin, and she behaved like one too, that's what we all think.'

'Something strange?' Wallie prompted her.

'Yes, something strange.' The nurse nodded vigorously. 'You weren't there, but I'm telling you. And I'll tell the court too. That she's an ice-cold killer, through and through.'

On her way to Paula, who lived just ten minutes from the hospital, Wallie wondered why the nurse was so hostile towards Alma. Was it even true that they'd offered to let her stay the night? Or maybe they didn't bother because it meant extra work for them? Maybe the nurse was in trouble with her boss for not mentioning the possibility of an overnight stay. Maybe it was her guilty conscience that had transformed Alma into a goblin. Or had Alma lied, because she wanted to head home and kill her husband? Unbelievable how easy it was to find multiple interpretations of the facts, each one leading to a different conclusion.

She hoped to get a clearer picture from Paula. She was looking forward to speaking with her. Carla had shown her a picture of the choir mistress: she looked like a bad-tempered Snow White, long legs and waist-length shiny black hair. She'd missed the performance of the choir at the gala dinner, because she'd been busy preparing for service. She was glad that Carla had shown her the picture, because she'd imagined a little grey mouse, like the music teacher she'd had in Switzerland, small and plump, with a permanent smile etched to her face even when she was punishing Wallie with a ruler for a harmless prank. Yet again proof how much you judge things based on your own experience.

Wallie slipped into the new apartment block where Paula lived, next to a woman with a pram. She rang the doorbell on the third floor.

Nobody answered. Carla had told her there were no rehearsals today, so Wallie rang again, with more gusto. She wanted a result.

Finally, a neighbour opened her door. The elderly lady in a pink satin dressing-gown was livid and threatened to call the police if she didn't stop that at once. Wallie waved her permit once more and explained how important it was to talk to Paula for the sake of the investigation. The neighbour seemed to thaw a little, and said she'd just missed Paula, who'd gone off to a rehearsal. She offered to pass on a message.

Wallie said there was no need, thanked her and went back down the stairs. The orphanage choir had rehearsals on Mondays and Wednesdays in Charlottenburg. But maybe she was working with other choirs also? Or maybe there were additional rehearsals? In Tucholskystraße the neighbours would've been fully informed. Where to now? She should pass by the university to get Klaus's home address, but it was too late, the secretariat would be closed. Nothing for it, back to Grolmanstraße.

Wallie could see from a distance that there were crowds of people waiting at the bus stop. Several buses had been cancelled. Since that terrible Sunday, nothing seemed to go according to the timetable in West Berlin.

She hated waiting, so she headed for the U Bahn. She set off at a clip, until she spotted a phone box at the end of the road, which gave her a better idea. Enough work for the day. She'd call James and with a little bit of luck, he'd pick her up and take her out for dinner. Food! In spite of the delicious cake that the Walhalla-fanatic had served, she was still hungry. Must be all that running around. Maybe an Italian restaurant? Did she have sufficient coins to phone? She took the purse out of her bag, but just then she realised she'd missed a trick. She should have checked at the bus stop to see if she could spot Paula, who might still be waiting there. She turned around and hurried back.

When she was about two hundred metres away from the stop, two buses turned up, one after the other. She started to run and just managed to catch the second of them. Breathless, she looked around for Paula, then made her way to the upper deck. But she was nowhere to be found. So she must either have taken the bus in front, or else she hadn't been there at the bus stop at all. Maybe she hated waiting, like Wallie, and had gone to take the underground.

Wallie found a strategic spot from where she could check at every stop if Paula was among the passengers getting off. But she was not.

The bus reached its final destination, in the Tauentzienstraße. Wallie got out, disappointed, and decided to do something about her empty stomach. She looked around for a currywurst stand, but no, she'd have to cross over and go to Ku'damm. Then she stopped suddenly.

Her eyes alighted on a young man who smiled at her. Wallie smiled back but then took a closer look. This was no young man! Unbelievable – no Snow White at all, she'd almost missed Paula! Hard to recognise her in that navy blue men's suit, her long hair hidden under a peaked cap. Was she going to a fancy-dress ball? Was she rehearsing with a carnival choir?

But then Wallie remembered Edgar explaining to her that you had to really enter the mind-set of the being you wanted to become. Paula was obviously not in the mind-set of Snow White at that moment. She was walking like a man, moving her hands like a man. Curiosity overcame her hunger – she couldn't let Paula slip through her fingers.

Wouldn't it be crazy if Paula went to the Eden Bar just around the corner, today of all days? But no, she turned off on Marburger Street. She stopped in front of Chez Nous and looked around. Wallie was forced to continue walking past her, so as not to break her cover. She went a few houses further and then slipped into the entrance porch of an apartment building from where she could observe what happened next.

After a few minutes, a blonde woman came out of Chez Nous and ran up to Paula. They hugged each other and then the blonde woman pulled Paula into another entranceway and kissed her passionately.

So that was that. But what did this have to do with Alma and Hochbrück? Had Alma had an affair with her and that was the reason why she wanted a divorce? Had Hochbrück found out about it and forced Paula to end the affair?

Would it be helpful to approach Paula now? Not really. But the day had been so unproductive that it couldn't get any worse. She approached the couple and cleared her throat ostentatiously.

'Can I join in?' she asked.

The two of them broke off so suddenly that Paula's cap fell to the floor. She stared at Wallie with red cheeks. Wallie bent down and picked up the cap.

'We're rehearsing for a new play,' said the blonde woman.

'Sure, a Greek classic, by the looks of it.' Wallie inched closer to Paula. 'Do the Berlin Fledglings know about your passion for classical drama from Lesbos?' She handed her the cap.

'Don't know what business it is of theirs. What do you want?' Paula took the cap but didn't put it back on.

'Are you a reporter?' asked the blonde woman. 'Or do you just like being a voyeur and intimidating people?'

Paula put a hand on her companion's arm.

Wallie took out her permit, waved it around and gave the whole spiel about being from the Justice Department. Then she asked Paula directly if Hochbrück had been blackmailing her about her 'dramatic' activities.

Paula put her cap on without a word, took the hand of her blonde companion and walked away.

They weren't getting rid of her that easily. Wallie quickened her pace and continued following them.

'We women have to stick together!' she called out.

Paula stopped so abruptly that her friend bumped into her.

'Whaddaya mean?'

'Alma Hochbrück is accused of murdering her husband.'

'Murder?' The blonde stared in disbelief at Paula.

'I'm sorry for Alma, but I'm not going to waste a tear on that bastard.'

'Why not?'

'I can't discuss it, I promised Alma.'

'Alma is in prison right now.'

'That's terrible, but I promised her.'

'Carla thinks that Alma is innocent.'

'Which Carla?'

'Carla Koslowsky, you know the one, from Nightingale & Co. She's helping Alma and would like to tell you that Alma has released you from your promise.' Wallie had no qualms about lying. 'It's murder after all.'

'And who are you anyway?'

'Carla's sister, we're working together to help Alma.'

'And Alma wants me to talk to you?'

'Of course! You might even be able to save her.' Wallie didn't hesitate for a minute there.

And that's how Paula ended up explaining what had happened between her and Hochbrück. It didn't take long. After a few minutes, Wallie rushed back in shock to Grolmanstraße, to tell Carla everything. But her sister was not at home.

20

'Child, that's sheer nonsense,' said Lulu, gunning her car's engine as if she was about to drive on the Avus circuit. 'Not a soul believes that Alma killed her husband. Never heard such nonsense in my life! Even more idiotic than the whole affair with Wallie, your so-called half-sister!' Lulu struck a dramatic Lady Macbeth tone. 'And believe me, that one will show the shite beneath the gold soon too!'

Lulu accelerated, honking her horn and overtaking a lorry. Carla was thrown to the left and barely managed to grab on to the glove compartment in the Beetle before lurching to the right. Her lunch was starting to bubble up in her stomach, and she wondered if Ricci's beef stroganoff might have gone off. She stuck her nose out of the window and breathed in the damp air. Then again, maybe it was the conversation with the interim police chief that had made her nauseous. Lulu had managed to wrangle a meeting with him. The two of them had been classmates and Grieser had even played on the same football team as Father.

'Nobody really believes that Alma killed her husband, yes, but this foul Grieser guy was very clear that they'd still accuse her of it,' Carla replied.

'Coward! Hannes is hungry for a quick sentencing, because Hochbrück is up to get an Order of Merit next month.'

'But he's dead?'

Lulu laughed, 'You can get this Order of Merit even as a corpse, it can be awarded posthumously.' She shook her fist at the driver of a Mercedes in front of her. 'You'll be a corpse yourself soon enough, Sunday driver!'

'And you'll get arrested if you keep on driving so fast.'

Carla bent over to pick up her handbag, which had fallen to the floor during Lulu's previous manoeuvres, but just then there was a sharp brake and she bumped her head against the dashboard.

'Ouch!' She rubbed her forehead.

'Idiot!' yelled Lulu through the open window, then turned to Carla. 'Sorry, sweetie, but we're too late. Why did that lousy Grieser guy have to drink two glasses of schnapps? I didn't think civil servants would lunch until five in the afternoon. We're cutting it fine and you know I can't be late.'

'No, it's a matter of life and death.' Carla smirked, because the appointment was with Alberto, Fritzi's groomer. If you were late picking up your canine friend, there'd be no further appointments for you. That was Alberto's hard and fast rule and not even Lulu dared to fall foul of that.

'You know how hard it is to handle Fritzi's curls and, besides, she adores Alberto.'

'Then let me take a taxi to Klaus.'

'No, no, we'll be fine. A promise is a promise. I'll take you to Alma's brother. After all that Grieser said about him, I completely understand that you have to talk to him, the sooner the better. Typical Berlin, that a drunk like Grieser has made it to such a senior position.'

'Surely you don't think it's any different in Bavaria or someplace else, do you? Father always stressed the importance of going out drinking with the right people. And it also helps that Grieser probably knows lots of the war secrets of important people, or so Father and Muki always said.'

Lulu nodded so hard that the peacock feathers on the hat she was wearing scraped against the roof of the car. 'Your father was always good with people. You have to continue his legacy. It was so obvious that you couldn't stand that Grieser fellow. But that's a dumb strategy, you have to play nicely, like me.'

Yes, but it wasn't Lulu's thigh that was being kneaded for over an hour by Grieser's sticky paw. It was one thing to sit drinking with people eye to eye, and quite another to be manhandled in a demeaning way. And for what? The police had no real evidence, other than the hockey stick. The investigation revealed that it had been wiped clean, but nevertheless there were some of Alma's fingerprints on it. They interpreted that as Alma trying to get rid of the prints. There were also a few fibres and a forensic interpretation of the fall down the stairs. But Alma's declaration that her husband had been so furious that he'd asked the neighbours about her whereabouts had not been confirmed by anybody. This worried Carla: why would Alma lie about this fact, of all things? The interviews with Alma's doctors hadn't brought anything new to the table either. And then Grieser had let drop that Alma's brother had said something, which according to him provided an ample motive for the murder.

Lulu turned into a side street off Kösliner Street, tyres squealing. 'What house number is Alma's brother?'

'37.'

'I don't like this area. Trudi told me that in one of these crummy backyards there's a crazy Catholic sect doing monstrous things. You sure you don't want me to come with you?'

'No, drive away!'

'Please make sure you get away quickly, OK? I'll call you straight after.'

'No, that will scare Mother.'

'OK, then see you tomorrow.'

Carla got out and slammed the car door.

Lulu bent over the passenger seat and called out of the window, 'And don't let yourself be played for a fool. If it's true what Grieser said, then he must've had a reason for betraying his sister. I had lots of spats with your dad, but would never have dobbed him in.'

Carla waved, then turned and made her way through the drizzle to number 37. The former tenement block still showed signs of war damage on its façade: bullet holes, cracks, broken stucco. Klaus lived in the undecorated building in the backyard, on the fifth floor. The collapsed roof had not been rebuilt. She rang the bell on the front door, then walked past the open gate through to the unpaved, muddy courtyard, which looked like a field recently dug up by wild boars. Wet bedsheets, which had long since lost their battle with whiteness, were hanging on a clothesline. In front of the bricked-up windows of the annexe someone had planted a dahlia in a rusty sardine tin. In the murky evening light it shone bright scarlet, a lonely beacon of hope in this sea of grey.

Grieser claimed that Klaus had been broken by the news of Hochbrück's death, unlike the wife. That's why Carla hoped he might be at home rather than in some bar.

But why would a von Stellmark live in such a shithole? Alma had told her the family was well off and the only reason she had no money was because Alexander had spent it all after their wedding. At the gala dinner, Klaus in his black-tie suit had appeared comfortably well off. And why would the siblings be at daggers drawn?

Carla climbed up the grimy staircase, feeling more and more overcome by filth with every floor she passed. The only decorations were the ceramic notices on every other floor. Stamping feet announced the arrival of a group of youngsters kicking a football down the stairs. They looked at Carla curiously but didn't dare to say anything. When she finally got to the fifth floor, there were only two doors.

The one with a glass inset seemed to lead to the attic with the collapsed roof, so the other one must be Klaus's apartment. She knocked on the door, which had obviously not been cleaned in years, softly at first, then louder. There was no answer. The rain had stopped at last. Two pigeons settled on the ruins of the roof, scratching and cleaning their claws on the iron bars covered in bird shit, cooing all the while.

Carla started feeling itchy all over. She knocked again but there was nothing to be heard other than the pigeons. She shrugged – fine, she'd have to leave him a message, ask him to get in touch. But where was her fighting spirit? She had to find out more about him, if she was really to help Alma.

She examined the door more closely. It was a simple lock, no big deal. She pulled the little Dietrich lock-picking set out of her bag, knocked once more on the door, just to be on the safe side, and called out his name. She suddenly remembered how she'd forbidden Wallie to do anything illegal on behalf of Nightingale & Co. But she was only going to take a look, it wasn't like she was going to steal anything or drug somebody. She had to be quick though, make sure nobody saw her.

For this lock, it was sufficient to use the simplest lock pick, which Father had made out of a repurposed wire hanger. She pulled up her tight skirt a little, crouched down in front of the door and pushed the Dietrich into the lock. She was a bit out of practice and didn't quite get the right catch instantly, so it took a bit longer than she'd hoped.

At last the door was open.

She went inside, putting the Dietrich away and taking out her Minox camera. She was surprised to see how light and tidy everything was in here, after the grubby staircase. Maybe Klaus, who was an architect after all, had put in those two skylights himself.

The small apartment was as neat as a monk's cell. There

wasn't a single item of clothing lying around. Everything was in its place, almost compulsively so. In the darkest corner there was an elegant metal bed, next to it two baroque chairs with silk fabric. Under the windows she discovered an antique cherrywood sideboard, with the initials KvS in gold on the front of the drawers. There were also two large Eiermann desks with construction models on them. She went up to the desks and started taking pictures. On the left side it must be the model for the gigantic project on Breitscheid Square, the ugliest eyesore in West Berlin – an American type of tower block. On the other desk she thought she recognised Olivaer Square, but something wasn't quite right, it looked smaller than Carla remembered it. There were no buildings yet, just streets and trees. She took pictures of both desks.

A sound startled her. She stopped, but it must have been the pigeons or a door down in the courtyard. Still, she should hurry. There was no kitchen or bathroom, not even a water tap. That must be why Klaus had stowed so many water bottles next to his bed.

On his bedside table was the book *The Train Was on Time* by Heinrich Böll. Next to it was a well-thumbed notebook. A brief look wouldn't hurt. *For Alma's sake*, she told herself, *just think of Alma and the children.*

She sat on the bed and leafed through the notebook. It was a mix of diary entries and sketchbook. The texts were not dated, sometimes just words and phrases, quotes, strange sentences, but sometimes clear extracts, as well as accurate designs for buildings, detailed sketches of door handles and even a flattering caricature of Hochbrück. She skimmed the pages, hoping that the word Alma would jump out at her, she was usually good at spotting such word patterns.

Sure enough, she found some references: at the start, there was 'devil Alma should go to hell', in the middle 'she's punishing him, she can't help it, castrates all who love her'. Carla put the notebook back and wished she could wash her hands. When she stood up, her heels struck something metallic. She bent down to look under the bed. A big, partly rusty metal box. Something useful at last?

Lots of medicine. Aspirin, Grippex, quinine, Pervitin... Wait a second! Wasn't that the so-called 'tank chocolate', or Göring pills? She remembered those from Nepomuk's tales about the war. The Wehrmacht drug, a cocktail of addictive substances, including amphetamine. She took a picture.

Nepomuk had become addicted to those pills after he was wounded, and Father had helped him kick his addiction. Many soldiers had struggled with that, including Heinrich Böll, who'd begged for Pervitin in his letters from the front. Was that why Klaus was reading a book by him? Father had said that many men were still taking those pills, and even Adenauer was only able to keep on going as Chancellor with the help of Pervitin. The drug kept you awake, took away your fear and pain, and made you ready to risk anything. It could also lead to hallucinations and panic attacks. And it was very addictive, which was why it was only available on prescription nowadays. Now she understood why Klaus had such bad teeth! She put the lid back on and shoved the box back under the bed.

Alma's brother was at most in his early to mid-thirties, so he must have been of the generation of young boys conscripted into Hitler's army in desperation in 1944. Very sad that he'd become dependent on the drug, but this was good news for Alma. The testimony of a drug addict could not really be reliable.

She didn't find anything incriminating in the wardrobe. The two suits and three shirts were from Gerhinger & Glupp on the Kurfürstendamm corner with Uhland Street. The socks and underwear were also of good quality. There was a laundry bag from the Wegers Laundrette in the Stülpnagelstraße, which according to Mother was the best laundrette not just in Charlottenburg but in the whole of Berlin.

Another sound made her stop.

Steps coming up the stairs. She held her breath.

The footsteps were getting closer. Carla put the camera away and hastened to the door. Too late, the key was already in the lock. Sweat broke out on her forehead, she couldn't afford to get caught. She looked around for a place to hide. Under the bed? Too low. The wardrobe? Too small. There was nothing for it. She'd have to improvise. Which wasn't her strength. Her heart was racing, she'd never encountered such a crazy situation before. She reached for her neck, but of course her lucky die wasn't there. She stepped behind the door and hoped she could make a dash for it. He was bound to discover her as soon as he closed the door.

At that moment, the door banged open. Klaus staggered in and stumbled towards the bed, groaning. He was so drunk, he didn't even bother to close the door behind him.

He fell onto the bed, without taking off his shoes.

He might fall asleep right away, then she could make her way across the room and... But no! He stood up and stormed in her direction, with a strange look on his face. Her pulse raced.

Why wasn't he saying anything?

He ran to the table on the right and with one swipe pushed the entire model of the Breitscheid Square off the table. Some pieces went flying across the room. Then he jumped on them, stamping on the trees, the constructions, the people, like a man possessed. Then he stopped suddenly, covered his face with his hands, let out a moan and started crying.

Out of here, quickly, said a stern voice in Carla's head.

She ran backwards, to keep an eye on him. She very nearly made it through the doorway, when something crunched loudly under her foot. She froze.

He took his hands from his face and stared at her with dismay.

'No, no, no!' he stammered, lifting up an arm and brandishing it, as if trying to get rid of a wasp. 'Go away!'

She was stunned. Did he think she was a ghost? A hallucination? He came closer. His handsome face was all sunken in, he looked much older than at the gala dinner. Grieser had been right about that: Klaus seemed to have taken Hochbrück's death much harder than Alma. He was standing quite close to her now, with dilated pupils in red-rimmed, glassy eyes.

Completely unpredictable.

What if he noticed she was real after all? She ran down the stairs as if she'd heard a bomb alert, stormed through the courtyard where the boys were playing football and straight out onto the street. Only there did she allow herself to stop and wait for her heartbeat to calm down again, her mind full of questions.

21

Just as Carla was about to enter the building in the Grolmanstraße, somebody called out to her. She turned to see Katrin running up to her full of verve.

''Bout that blonde...' she cried, then stopped mid-sentence and looked conspiratorially at her.

Carla tried hard not to laugh. 'Dear Katrin,' she began, but at that moment Frau Pallutzke opened the window to her concierge quarters and beckoned Carla sternly. 'Miss Koslowsky, a word, please!'

The choice between Scylla and Charybdis was child's play compared to this.

'Katrin, can you let me speak to Frau Pallutzke for a moment?' Carla ran up the three steps to the concierge apartment. All children were scared of the Pallutzke woman, because she blamed them for everything that was wrong about Berlin and the world in general, from fly-tipping in the front garden to dog poo on the pavement, probably the building of the Wall and Communism too.

'Miss Koslowsky, this ain't fair and square at all,' she said now, looking disapprovingly at Carla. But when she got closer, there was a surprising smile erupting on her face like lava. 'But I'll make an exception in your case,' she continued, so close now that Carla was almost entirely enveloped in her aroma. The housekeeper raised her eyes dramatically towards the ceiling, 'And of course for poor Ida's sake.'

'Is something the matter with Mother?' Carla's head was now full of catastrophic scenarios: her mother fainting, falling, bleeding...

'No, all good with Ida. Upstairs there's a... young man waiting for you. He hung around a good deal outside until I told him he could come in and wait in front of the door to the office.'

'Very kind of you.' Was the man a magician? Or simply very good at offering bribes? But even that didn't always work on Pallutzke. Some clients who'd hoped to wait inside for the office to open on a rainy day had found that out to their cost. Depending on her mood on the day, Frau Pallutzke could be indignant, offended or gracious.

Carla thanked her once more and hurried upstairs. On the landing Katrin was waiting to tug at her sleeve. She'd nearly forgotten about her. 'Can you give me just one more minute?' she asked Katrin, just as they both noticed someone approaching from further up the stairs.

'I'd almost given up,' the strapping young man said, bathing her in his warm gaze. 'You must be a very busy...' then, noticing Katrin peering out from behind Carla, he corrected himself, 'You must *both* be very busy young ladies.'

Katrin chuckled with pleasure, while Carla tried to remember where she knew the young man from. He was neither a client nor one of Father's acquaintances. Something about him reminded her of Lulu and a weapon... Ah, yes, of course, the attractive guard, Bruno, who'd given her his number.

He was barely recognisable without a uniform. With jeans and leather jacket he looked about three times more attractive and dangerous than Horst Buchholz in *Teenage Wolfpack*. But how did he know her name and address? And what was he doing here?

'Thank you for waiting, I'm back now,' she muttered, slightly overcome. She turned to Katrin. 'Can we talk later?'

'But I...' Katrin stamped her foot so hard that the staircase creaked.

Carla shook her head. 'Katrinchen, I'm really sorry, but work has to come first, you know that, don't you?'

'But this is work,' Katrin grumbled, her head lowering submissively. She started going down the stairs as if facing her own execution. Carla's conscience pricked her – what had Lulu started?

'I'll see you soon...' she said, but then, looking at her watch, she called after her. 'Better still, see you tomorrow before school, yes?' Then she ran up the final few steps to open the door as she nodded at Bruno.

For a brief moment, she expected Wallie to be parading around in a corset while getting changed for Eden, or that the mattress might be lying in the middle of the office, but it was all quiet and clean. There was a mere hint of Wallie's perfume in the air.

Carla took off her gloves, sat down at the desk and put her handbag on it. Then she noticed a sheet of paper on which had been written: 'News about Alma! Have to talk! Urgent! W'. *What horrible handwriting*, she thought. And why be so mysterious about it, she could have written down the information if she was bothering to write anything in the first place.

Carla offered Bruno a drink and then sat down.

'Groovy office,' said Bruno, then apologised profusely for disturbing her.

'What's this about?' she interrupted him.

'May I be perfectly honest?'

'Discretion is our specialty.'

'I just wanted to see you again.'

She searched Bruno's face for signs of duplicity, but his eyes met hers without flinching. In fact, he seemed to be gobbling her up with his eyes. It was Carla who had to look away first.

'I was gonna pretend I needed a job, 'cos there's no more

film-set-guarding for me, they're not filming in Berlin anymore, but...' he paused to smile at her, full of candour, 'that wouldn't be honest. I now drive a taxi, which fits better with my studies anyway. So why not tell you the truth? Won't take a shine off anyone's chandelier, will it?' He was smiling so emphatically during this confession that he was well-nigh irresistible.

This must have been the charm that had cut through Pallutzke's armour. She'd be sure to report to Mother what an incredibly nice young man was waiting for her daughter. It would be the topic for many a conversation.

'How did you find me?'

He winked at her. 'Good detective myself, ain't I?'

'Well...' This was all a little too smooth, too neat for Carla's taste.

Bruno then explained that he'd been chatting to the film catering woman at the chip stand, who obviously knew Carla's 'Grandma' – he grinned at this – very well. After all, it had been Trudi who'd let Lulu and her policemen onto the film set. At first the woman had refused to give away a single thing. 'Who knows what kind of thug I might be?' he winked again, 'A spurned lover of Grandma's or a Mafia enforcer?' But he hadn't given up and kept stuffing himself with chips. At this point, he tapped his non-existent beer belly, so that Carla's eyes fell upon his nicely tailored white shirt, which was neatly tucked into the leather belt on his jeans.

'No great sacrifice, 'cos the chips were real tasty.' Finally, Trudi had given in and told him Lulu's surname. Then he'd put two and two together and here he was now.

'Very good detective work!'

His puppyish enthusiasm was ringing all her alarm bells. As was the name Trudi, but she couldn't remember in what context.

'If you want to bin me, then I'll put a lid on myself!' Bruno mimed an extravagant gesture of putting a lid on his head, all the while looking at her with exaggerated puppy dog eyes. 'But it'd break my heart.'

Was that a smile flitting across her face? Since when did she react so predictably to these silly little compliments?

The phone saved her, although it was nothing more than Frau Niemöller wanting to know what progress they'd made. With Bruno sitting in front of her, Carla stated that her employee was following a promising trail and they'd contact her tomorrow.

'Lyin' ain't your thing.' Bruno tried to look serious, but seemed to find his own comment very amusing. He seemed to find everything a laugh and a half. Horrible optimist.

'Oh, why, are you an expert in lying?' Carla snapped at him.

'Not when it comes to matters of the heart. There, I'm always honest.'

'Of course you are.' She'd wanted to make this sound even more sarcastic. In an effort not to drown in his eyes, she kept staring at Wallie's note. The letters blurred and instead of 'urgent' she now saw 'Trudi' and suddenly she had a brainwave, a plan which surprised even her. Obviously, Wallie had had more of an influence on her than she'd expected.

'Would you accompany me to an appointment?' she asked

'Anywhere you want!' He paused. 'Although there's one exception...'

'Hell?'

'Nah, the devil don't scare me...'

'So what does?'

'Your so-called Grandma's hat shop, I'll give that a miss!'

'I'd have expected a little more bravery from you!' He'd nearly made her laugh out loud, but she didn't want to give him the satisfaction. 'But I could really do with an escort tonight, for professional reasons. No hat shops.'

'Sure. I'll pick you up in my cab.' He nodded and saluted in a military manner.

'No, let's meet there in two hours, at the Eden Bar.'

He raised one very disapproving eyebrow and drew in his breath, as if he wanted to protest, but then he nodded. 'I could pick you up from here?'

'Not necessary.' Carla stood up and went to the door. 'See you later.'

After he left, she sat down at her desk again. Even if she wasn't entirely won over by his charm, his visit had come at an opportune time. She now realised where she knew Trudi from: Lulu had mentioned her in connection to the German–American Folk Fair. She must have been the chip seller who'd been praised so highly by Jackov, so perhaps Trudi would know something about this Bobbs. She tried to call Lulu, but nobody picked up.

Then she asked Directory Enquiries for the numbers for Alma's doctors. She called Dr Schollwitz first, who was still at his surgery. At first he was delighted when she mentioned Hochbrück but when she asked about possible violence against Alma, he set off on a long tirade about women who have too little excitement in their lives and therefore have to make up such malicious gossip about their husbands. He was ready to swear under oath that at no point had Hochbrück lifted a finger against his wife. Then he hung up without even saying goodbye. His indignation sounded so genuine that Carla's heart grew heavy. Even if the two men had been Freemasons together, or Hochbrück had built him a villa at a discount price, there's no way such a pillar of society would risk perjury – would he?

She reached Dr Jahn at home, but she was in a hurry, because she had been called in to assist a breech birth. She was waiting for the ambulance to pick her up, so she asked Carla to be as succinct as possible. When Alma was mentioned, she quickly invoked patient–doctor confidentiality. After all, Alma was still alive, and she had nothing to say about her husband, because he'd not been her patient. When Carla refused to be palmed off with such an explanation and asked directly for any signs of violence, the doctor sighed and was silent for so long, that Carla had to force herself not to jump in and say anything to frighten her off. At last Dr Jahn rewarded her patience. 'Let me put it like this. A glass half-full is also half-empty at the same time. But half a lie is not quite the same as a half-truth. I have to go now.'

Great, what was that supposed to mean? Carla locked up the office deep in thought and headed upstairs to get changed and check on her mother.

On the third landing, just below her apartment, little Katrin had curled herself up like a hedgehog and fallen asleep. Carla bent over her with a little sigh and gently touched her arm. Katrin woke up instantly and sat up.

'Your mother will be worried sick!' Carla shook her head. 'You can't do this. You can't be a good detective if you go against what people say and don't respect the rules.'

'Nobody misses me anyway,' Katrin yawned.

'No ifs and buts. So, what did you have to tell me?'

Katrin told her that she'd followed the blonde and discovered two things. First of all, that she worked in a disreputable nightclub. Carla kept a blank face and asked about the second thing. Secondly, she'd seen the blonde meeting up with the strange man who'd been hanging around outside without the Pallutzke woman noticing him.

'Was that the man who was waiting for me upstairs earlier?'

Katrin said it was another one, the one with the worn-out shoes, not such a handsome fella, more of a nondescript one, wearing a hat. The blonde had given him a small package.

Probably the Scottish boyfriend, Sir James Cunningham. She asked what was so unusual about the meeting. Katrin chewed her pigtails thoughtfully and then admitted she wasn't quite sure what process of de-duck-shun had led her to this con-clue-shun, but she'd have a good think about it again and be very logical.

Carla didn't bother to correct her, thanked her and sent her off home. Then she opened the door to the apartment, arming herself mentally. She'd gone against all of the unwritten rules that day – she'd not shown up for either lunch or supper. The far too familiar 'I'll never forgive you' smell of lavender, dust and empty chocolate wrappers hit her as soon she stepped in.

'No, no, Carla, don't worry, my dear!' The forced cheeriness came all the way into the hall from the living room. 'Pallutzke told me you were still alive.'

Carla shuddered, then thought of Bruno. What did he know of hell!

22

Wallie rolled up the third keg of beer at the bar and tried to connect it to the tap. But it seemed stuck. She kept fiddling around with the hose until the sweat poured down her chin. She'd tilted it too much, damn! This should've been Edgar's job but he'd obviously lost his mind tonight, he was dancing on the countertop pretending to be Marlene Dietrich, while Irina and Jutta could hardly keep up with the orders. Although there was so much to do, she couldn't stop thinking about what Paula had told her. She had to admit reluctantly that her sister was not quite the sheeple she'd imagined.

You could cut through the fug with a knife. The whole joint was heaving as Ingrid van Bergen belted out the Criminal Tango on the bar counter. She was dancing with Angel and had started to take off her clothes a couple of minutes ago. How could Edgar keep up with that?

Wallie stood up and searched for something to take the lid off the keg, just as Ingrid was flinging her black turtleneck at the screaming onlookers. Angel took off one black glove, which didn't have quite the same effect.

Wallie bent back down again. After all that pointless running around today, she'd been hoping for a quiet evening in the Eden. Because of the private party, the regulars and students would normally have gone somewhere else and stayed away. But that hadn't happened today.

Rolf Eden had left with Barbara Valentin after the private party and Wallie had started clearing up, while the other guests were also getting ready to leave. Edgar had drunk too much, mostly because he was concerned about not being able to get hold of anyone at the institute where his sister was placed.

Shortly before closing time the actress Ingrid van Bergen showed up and began to liven up the atmosphere. At first she'd danced between the tables, but then she jumped up on the counter and challenged Edgar, who was never normally drunk at work, to a dance contest, sort of like *West Side Story*. 'Berliners of the West, let's dance and search for the best in the West,' she improvised in her approximation of English with her smoky voice. At least that had cheered Edgar up, because he'd been giving Wallie stick the whole evening not just because of Adele, but also because of Hochbrück. The police had been to the hotel, but only to ask if Hochbrück had been drinking excessively during the gala dinner. No one had bothered to check the service roster or the room bookings. Edgar should've relaxed, but instead he kept repeating that he'd been licking boots for ten years to become Head Concierge and how much Adele needed him and his money. Although everyone knew that Edgar was so good at his job that nobody would kick him out, all the guests loved him and any other hotel would've taken him in a heartbeat.

Finally! The beer started running as it should. Wallie wiped the sweat from her forehead, straightened her sequin top and walked up to the sink, where there was another mound of dirty glasses. Everyone had started drinking faster since Ingrid had shown up.

Sometimes she hated her job.

She grabbed a glass in each hand and put them upside down on the black vertical brushes in the sink, moving them up and down to clean them. Angel and Ingrid, meanwhile, were snaking past each other on the narrow counter. Through their dancing legs, someone was waving at her. James? He was on nightshift today.

What? She had to look twice to be sure. Now that was a surprise! She carefully rinsed the glasses and put them to one side. What was Carla doing here? Absurdly kitted out in a little black dress, as if she was going to the opera!

'Wrong address?' she yelled at her. 'What's up?'

'Talk!' Carla yelled back, barely avoiding a collision with Edgar's shins. 'Urgent my foot!'

'You mean here?'

Ingrid van Bergen had just taken off her skirt and was standing in her transparent little red knickers. Edgar froze for a second, then strained all of his muscles. What on earth was he planning? What would be the escalation of that? The idiot made a leap in the air in an attempt at the splits. The crowd oohed.

Except that on the way down he missed the counter, slipped and crashed onto the floor.

'Stop!' shouted Wallie. 'Everyone stop right now!'

But nobody paid any attention, Ingrid hadn't even noticed the fall, because she was too busy taking off her black bra and waving it like a propeller above her head.

There was an ecstatic roar from the crowd.

Wallie ran around the bar to see about Edgar, who was on the floor, in danger of being trampled to death by the crowds. His Angel wig had slipped when he landed, and the rhythm of the stamping feet was turning it into a rag.

She knelt down beside him; he was trying to say something that she couldn't hear. Blood was streaming from a wound above his eyebrows, emphasising how pale he was beneath his make-up.

'It'll be all right, Edgar,' she said, although he almost certainly couldn't hear her. He closed his eyes – oh, goodness, he wasn't going to faint, was he?

At that moment another man crouched down beside her, put his hand under Edgar's back and lifted him up.

'Where?' he shouted. Wallie beckoned that he should follow her and made her way to the dressing room. She did her best to put everything soft she could find on the floor, because there was no place to lie down in that room. 'For reasons,' as the boss liked to say with a wink.

Carla followed the man and was now standing next to him, as he carefully laid Edgar down on the improvised bed.

'We should take him to the hospital,' Carla said to the man, as if Wallie wasn't present. The man nodded.

Edgar touched his face. 'No way! Nothing happened.'

Irina and Jutta stormed in. 'What happened to him?'

'We don't know yet,' said Wallie. 'Please look after the guests.'

'They're going crazy in there,' said Irina, 'We can't cope just the two of us.'

'Give Ingrid the boss's megaphone and tell her Edgar has hurt himself. She loves him and will make a statement that everyone should move on to Chez Nous or somewhere else.'

Wallie picked up the old megaphone from one of the lockers and gave it to Jutta. As soon as the other two girls left the room, Edgar moaned so loudly that they all crouched around him once more.

'This... man?... should be in hospital,' said Carla.

'Just a headache,' Edgar panted.

Wallie didn't believe him.

'You never know, could be summat serious when it comes to the old noggin,' said the man who'd carried him. Wallie examined him. Tall and well-built, with gorgeous eyes and mouth. Who was this guy and what did he have in common with Carla? His eyes met hers and made it through the razor-wire surrounding her heart, as if he'd known her all his life. For one moment she thought he might look like someone to fall in love with, but she instantly pushed the thought right out of her mind. There was no room for that in her plans. Naturally, she was worried about Edgar, that had probably lowered her defences. She knew all too well from her own mother and her friend Frieda just how bad love could be. Nothing but occupational therapy for inmates, young girls and mothers.

She stole another look, just to understand what was going on, to nip things in the bud. She'd always been able to do it before, and it had saved her life. This man was very attractive, but it wasn't just that. There was something emanating from him – like a glow? Nonsense, the leather jacket had nothing mystical about it. There, he was looking at her again, quizzically, intensely, and she had the sudden desire to come out of her bunker and tell him everything. She'd be safe with him, he'd never laugh at her or betray her.

'Bring him to the hospital,' said the man, turning once more to her sister. Ah, so he liked Carla, he wanted to be liked by her. But that one of course hadn't even noticed.

'Nope, bring me home and nowt else,' said Edgar, 'Gotta work tomorrow.'

Her sister bent over him. 'It's best to have this kind of wound stitched up, that's what they told me when I did my first aid course.'

The young man stared at Carla in surprise, even admiration. Clearly they didn't know each other very well.

Wallie stood between them and examined Edgar's face. 'I hate to say it, but Carla is right. Or would you like to resemble Captain Ahab afterwards? No more Lucky Angel!'

Edgar kept complaining, even when they helped him up and realised he could barely walk, because he'd either twisted or broken his ankle. He was stubborn and would only agree to see a doctor that Wallie knew.

Bruno, that was the name of Carla's escort, carried Edgar to his taxi and drove off in the direction of Joachimsthalerstraße.

'About my news about Alma,' Wallie began, because it was so quiet in the taxi, and she wanted to appear smarter than she felt at that moment.

'We'll talk later,' said Carla with a warning tone, 'It was such a bad idea for me to come to Eden.'

'Many ideas seem stupid at first,' said this Bruno chap. His voice was deep and soft, like biting into the glazing of a Punschtorte. 'But then later on you realise they're quite clever...'

'Turn left.' Wallie couldn't bear to hear him consoling Carla. 'Then right and then we're here.'

'This doesn't look like a doctor's clinic,' said the man with the Punschberg voice, as he carried Edgar as easily as if he were a small child through the back door of Joachimsthalerstra⊠e to a shabby annex.

'Who said anything about a clinic?' Wallie avoided Carla's surprised look, she had to get rid of both of them. 'You're not allowed to come inside. This doctor lost his licence because of a thing, so he doesn't like strangers, but he can help Edgar for sure.'

'But...' Carla began protesting, when Bruno chimed in with, 'That's fine, we'll wait outside.'

'No need, I'll call a friend and we'll take Edgar home.'

'Thanks,' groaned Edgar, 'And tomorrow drinks on me at the Eden.'

'Fine, if that's what you want, let's go then.' Carla agreed at last and left with Bruno.

Wallie rang the doorbell and was pleased that she had no time for overthinking things. Carla's friend was wrong. Some ideas were simply stupid through and through.

23

The flickering neon lights were driving her insane. Carla stared balefully at them as she paced up and down the peeling lino in the holding cell. Otto Stratmann had been gone for ten minutes, supposedly to the toilet, and Alma still hadn't shown up.

Carla had waited all night for Wallie, who came back at dawn, after taking that Edgar fellow home and looking after him. He had a slight concussion, but luckily had only sprained his ankle rather than broken it. Carla had made a strong coffee, and finally got to hear what Paula had told her sister.

She had then moved heaven and earth to get an appointment with Alma and her lawyer as soon as possible, but she'd had to wait pretty much all day. She looked at the clock over the door. Eleven minutes.

Alma had to get out as soon as possible, to be with her children.

Heavy footsteps, accompanied by the sound of numerous keys – finally... she sat down.

A woman guard brought Alma in. She looked even worse than last time. Her red hair was now sticking to her scalp like scabs refusing to heal. Her white suit was by now charcoal coloured. Nobody had brought her a change of clothes, obviously. Alma seemed apathetic, as if none of this was her concern.

'Where's the lawyer?' asked the guard, ready to take

Alma back if required.

'He's gone to the toilet. As his assistant, I'm allowed to talk to her.'

The guard seemed uncertain.

'In confidence.'

Carla stood up and repeated the phrase. At just that moment, Otto Stratmann returned. He was much paler than last time, quite jittery, but at least he was holding two hot drinks and handed one of them to Alma. 'The approved coffee,' he said to the guard, who left the room at last.

They all sat down. Alma was staring at the coffee with such astonishment, there might as well have been a goldfish swimming in her plastic cup. Stratmann pushed the other cup towards Carla. She picked it up and took a sip. Much hotter than she'd expected.

'So, what is so urgent?' asked Stratmann.

'Lots. First of all, regardless of what Alma's brother says, he's not a credible witness, because he's a Pervitin addict,' said Carla.

Alma made an indistinguishable sound and then drank all the coffee in one gulp.

Stratman frowned. 'You mean the tank chocolate?'

Carla nodded. 'Aka the Hermann Göring pills, or uppers.'

'They might still let his statement stand. He claims that Hochbrück had often told him that his wife refused to have sex with him, because she didn't want to destroy her figure by having any more children. From their point of view, that's an excellent motive.'

'I don't understand. That surely would've been sufficient reason for Hochbrück to ask for a divorce?' said Carla.

'That's exactly what the police says. But they think that Alma tried to prevent a divorce by killing him off, because it's more convenient to be a widow than to give up on all the money and the prestige.'

'My brother hates me, because I've tried on several occasions to get him clean.' Alma seemed to wake up a little. 'The last time I had to declare him legally incompetent, because he'd spent all his inheritance during his manic phases.'

'And whom did you appoint as his legal guardian?'

'It couldn't be me, of course, despite being his closest relative,' Alma laughed bitterly. 'It had to be a man. And since Alexander thought that we should spare him a stranger, he offered to do it himself. Klaus did not just accept it, he was delighted. His admiration for Alexander became even stronger and he was proud to call himself his friend. Almost as if they'd gone to war together. But Alexander always had a talent for getting out of things he didn't want to do. In contrast to my brother, he never saw any of the action on the front.' Her lips curled in disdain.

'We have to talk about Paula,' Carla told Alma encouragingly.

Alma shook her head. 'I don't see how that's supposed to help.'

Carla turned to Stratmann. 'Paula Becker is the choir mistress at the orphanage. The Hochbrücks are part of the committee there, just like I am, and they're very active. Paula noticed on the most recent summer trip that Alexander Hochbrück was molesting one of the girls.'

'Nonsense, Alexander had found out that Paula was a lesbian. He wanted her fired and she took her revenge,' Alma intervened quickly.

'Ah, interesting, so Paula might have a motive for murder too!' Stratmann hastily wrote something in his notebook.

Carla said softly to Alma, 'We both know that's not quite true.'

Stratmann put away his pen and sat staring at the exchange between the two women.

'I've no idea what you're talking about.'

'Paula's accusation was justified. Your husband liked little girls.'

'That's rubbish!' Alma's voice broke.

'I couldn't understand for the longest time why you put on such a show for us, but when Paula finally explained what she'd observed, it all became clear to me. You did all that to protect Mathilda from him.'

Alma sat there still as a stone, tears pouring down her cheeks. Carla bent over and put her hand on her arm, but Alma shook her off and leant away from her.

'You had to make sure your daughter would be safe and you knew that nobody would believe you. So you put on this charade. You were afraid that if you opened up that can of worms, Mathilda would end up paying for it. It would lead to an epic mud-slinging scandal and the outcome was already decided.' Carla turned to Stratmann to explain. 'Hochbrück was going to get the Order of Merit and he had friends in all the high places.'

Stratmann cleared his throat and swallowed a couple of times. 'Is this true?'

Alma did not stir.

'I'm sure it is,' said Carla, regretting that she'd not spotted it earlier.

'But how is that supposed to help us?' The lawyer took off his glasses and rubbed his nose. 'We can't make that public, because that would give Alma even more of a motive!'

'Exactly,' agreed Alma. 'Carla's theory is a load of rubbish, because it wasn't murder but self-defence, because he was being really violent that evening.'

'Why didn't you stay that evening with your injured son in hospital?' asked Carla. 'I can tell you why not!'

'Is that really relevant?' asked Stratmann.

'For heaven's sake, man!' Carla wanted to shake him. 'It was your duty to check the whole timeline again, this is really a basic skill for a defence lawyer.'

'The nurses sent me home, they didn't want me there,' said Alma.

'No, *you* wanted to go home. You had to, because far worse than your son's flesh wound was the thought of what Alexander might do to your daughter, if you didn't get there before him!'

Alma hit the table with her fists, sending Carla's half-empty coffee cup flying. The liquid spilled over Stratmann's files. He took a handkerchief out of his pocket and frantically tried to stem the flood.

'Yes, fine, yes!' Alma continued hammering on the metal table, tears flowing down her cheeks, looking as manic as her brother the night before. At least it was all coming out now.

The female guard came in and wanted to know what was going on.

'It's all fine,' Stratmann reassured her, jumping up and almost manhandling her out of the door, 'Just a little crisis.'

Alma began laughing hysterically, her shoulders shaking.

'Fine, yes, I killed that damn pig and I don't regret it for a minute! Nobody wanted to help us. My own brother thought I was crazy. And do you know what the doctor said, when I begged for help? Not Schollwitz, of course, no. I thought I was being smart, looking up a foreign doctor in Kreuzberg, because I thought he wouldn't know Alex. But no, he considered it his duty as a man to call Alexander and tell him about my neurotic jealousy of my pretty young daughter. He recommended I be locked up in a psychiatric institute.'

Carla side-eyed Stratmann. Good thing he was bound by client confidentiality and would stick to that, unlike the doctor. Because everything that Alma was telling them sounded like plausible motives for murder.

'So, if I understand correctly, you rushed home to protect your daughter. But didn't you say that your daughter only got home after your husband was already dead?' Stratmann tried to clarify.

'Exactly.' Alma wiped her face with the sleeves of her suit and pushed back a stray lock. 'Because I got there quickly enough. I'd never have stayed away overnight. I always watched like a hawk, to make sure my husband was never alone with the children.'

Had she really got back before Mathilda? Carla remembered something that the admittedly rather loony neighbour had told Wallie. That Mathilda had to take the keys out of the birdhouse because no one was home. She'd dismissed that because of all the other crazy things he believed in, but what if that part of his witness statement was accurate? Although it might be equally true that he'd murdered Hochbrück himself, because he was blocking his path to Walhalla. No, she mustn't get carried away. But the worst thing was that none of this helped to provide further evidence of acting in self-defence.

'Have the police spoken to any other suspects?'

'They claim there are no other suspects. That Hochbrück only had friends and admirers.'

'What did I tell you?' Alma sighed.

'Anything dodgy going on in his accounts?'

Stratmann checked his files. Why on earth did he not have that kind of information at his fingertips?

'No, everything's fine.'

'Was the house searched?'

'Of course. No sign of forced entry. In his office there were fingerprints from his students, they could all be identified and all have an alibi for that evening. The only other fingerprints were from family members, the cleaner and the nanny.' He hesitated a moment and checked his file again. 'On the ground floor there were multiple different children's fingerprints.'

'The hockey team probably,' said Alma in a hoarse voice. 'When can I see my children?'

'Here? Like this?' asked Stratmann, raising his eyebrows.

Alma looked around her. 'You're right, it's not suitable. Can't you arrange something? Carla, after all the help you *didn't* provide, could you at least bring me some clothes?' Her eyes were glittering with anger. Fine, anger was much better than abject misery.

Stratmann promised he'd try to arrange a visit and called for the uniformed guard to escort Alma back.

'That was your last visit with Alma,' Stratmann said in a dangerously quiet voice, as they left the police station.

'Why on earth? You can see she needs me.'

'We're pleading self-defence and don't need any of your disgusting revelations. Please desist from any further investigation.' He left her in the middle of the road and walked to his car.

She looked after him in bewilderment. It was her mistake, she shouldn't have cast any doubts on his professional qualities in front of Alma. But there was definitely something foul about this whole case.

24

Carla wearily locked Alma's and Ingrid's files in the filing cabinet and, after a quick glance at the clock, went to fetch a dram of Asbach Uralt and a cognac glass. Six pm, even Father would have allowed himself a little pick-me-up. What a day! She hadn't even had the time to pick up the clothes for Alma, there'd simply been too much to do. While she poured the cognac, she wondered why she couldn't shake off the feeling that she'd missed something important.

After the conversation with Alma and Stratmann, she'd left the Lehrter police station and gone straight to Youth Services to ask about Mathilda and Gregor. Were they under the observation of a psychologist?

No, sadly not.

Had they identified any suitable foster families?

No, sadly not.

They wanted to wait for the outcome of the proceedings, which in reality meant that nobody was looking after them. Carla had to restrain herself from shouting at them. Alma's children clearly needed help quite urgently – their father was dead, their mother arrested, and their uncle was a drug addict. They needed to be under the supervision of someone who really cared about their wellbeing. After some tough negotiations, she managed to convince them to transfer the siblings into the care of the Berlin Fledglings pending the outcome of the investigation.

Mathilda and Gregor knew some of the children there and at least they'd be able to take part in their activities.

She wanted to tell the children the happy news herself, but was told curtly that they were in school. They'd been forced to go – life had to go on. *Yes, exactly, let's just sweep everything under the rug – something the Germans are so good at.* She took another big sip of cognac. What the children must be going through at school, the gossip, the teasing, the newspaper headlines! She decided to call Vera Hubermann, although she hated asking the psychologist for any favours after the conflict they'd had about appointing Paula. She rather expected that Vera would use the situation to humiliate her, make her beg, but as soon as the psychologist heard about the siblings' situation, she agreed to see them right away.

Somewhat mollified, Carla then visited Lulu at her villa near Lietzen lake, to ask for more information about Trudi. But when Lulu opened the door, she realised that she'd come at a bad time. Her aunt was kitted out like a general about to go on parade: wearing her authentic Chanel suit, with a totally inappropriate hat that would have made Coco cry, garnished as it was with endless feathers, rhinestones and flowers. She remembered Bruno, who had been adamant about not wanting to follow Lulu into a hat shop. Speaking of Bruno, he'd handled the accident and the crazies in the Eden Bar with such aplomb. He must've imagined a very different kind of evening out with her.

Lulu had greeted her with smacking-loud kisses and offered to give her a lift. She was on her way to the exhibition halls by the Radio Tower. An old friend had invited her to the 22nd annual exhibition of the German Broadcasting Company, where the Trade Minister Ludwig Erhard would give a speech. She was hoping to meet important people there. It wouldn't hurt if Carla too mingled with people and tried to acquire new clients. Lulu would love to help, but she had to speak to her old friend

Ladislas Fodor, who was the scriptwriter for the new *Dr Mabuse* series.

When they were in the car, Carla finally managed to squeeze a word in edgewise and ask about Trudi. Lulu's reaction was surprisingly prickly as soon as she heard the name. She peppered Carla with questions. Was it that miserable Ida putting her up to it? Would this never end?

It took Carla nearly the whole journey to the Radio Tower to figure out what was going on. Mother blamed Trudi that Aunt Lulu loved not only men but also women. Father couldn't care less, but Mother considered Trudi the devil's spawn, who'd seduced Lulu on set and sent her second husband to the grave. Utter nonsense. No one could seduce her aunt if she didn't want to be seduced.

It took all of Carla's patience to put an end to Lulu's verbal diarrhoea and explain that she only wanted to ask about Trudi in relation to a case. When her aunt discovered it was to do with a great love affair, she decided to help. She raced past the exhibition halls for Thuringia, Saxony and Pomerania until they got to Western Silesia, where Trudi had opened her chip stand at a strategic distance between the Free Berlin radio station and the police.

'So empty!' Lulu complained as she got out of the car. 'All because of that bloody wall. No one's gonna bother coming to an amputated Berlin.'

Looking around, Carla had to admit that her aunt was right.

'No time to explore,' said Lulu, traipsing over to Trudi and introducing her to Carla, then rushing off to her important networking event in one of the other halls.

'Mad cow!' Trudi said in a tenderly chiding tone. She gave Carla a bag of chips on the house. Her real name was Gertrud Heilbringer and she knew a lot of GIs and Jacks, she even knew a certain Bobbs, an attractive fellow if you happened to like 'em tall and blond. But she couldn't say what his real name was, or which unit he belonged to. She thought it might be Air Force, but that was just a guess. She'd taken pictures with her new Polaroid 900 at Lulu's birthday party but mostly of Lulu. She gave a mischievous grin as she mentioned Lulu's name. She was an amateur photographer and Lulu was one of her favourite models. In fact, Trudi had wanted to become a cinematographer. She rattled her frying equipment, as if it was to blame for her shattered dreams.

'We think we're dealing the cards, but actually it's fate mixing 'em,' she said, without a trace of pity in her voice.

Carla finished her glass of cognac, thought about Mother's leg and Wallie's sudden appearance, and wished she had even half of Trudi's wisdom.

25

'Isn't this illegal? Breaking and entering or something?' asked Wallie pointedly the following day, as they picked up the keys to the Hochbrück villa from the birdhouse.

'It would be a criminal offence if the place were still sealed off with police tape. But there's no sign of that here, which unfortunately means that the police are being remarkably careless. Also, entering the property would be illegal if Alma hadn't asked me to bring her some clean clothes.'

The house stank of overfilled rubbish bins. It was noticeably cooler inside. They looked at each other awkwardly, then Carla entered the living room. Everything looked remarkably untouched, and the rather uncomfortable-looking designer furniture gave the impression of a doll's house that hadn't been played with in a long time.

Towards the far end of the gigantic living room there was a narrow, freestanding iron staircase with no bannisters, spiralling up towards the attic studio. A beautiful but impractical architectural dream. At the foot of the stairs there was still the outline of the body on the marble floor, as drawn by the police team. To Carla it seemed unreal, like an art installation.

'Just look around! Does this look like the police have searched it with a fine-tooth comb? They consider this case to be over.'

'Well, depends who was here,' said Wallie with a grin, 'If it were the Stasi, then you wouldn't spot a trace of 'em....'

'How do you know how the State Police operate?' she couldn't resist asking.

'From Mum. They had their eyes on her because of her photos. Not sufficiently aligned to the system. Mushka showed me how to protect yourself from being spied upon.'

'Mushka?'

'Yes, from Mamushka.'

Carla didn't want to think about the woman her father had loved. She was here to help Alma, she had to keep a clear head. She focused on the staircase, where there was indeed a faint impression of fingerprint powder.

'We could be mistaken, maybe they cleaned up so thoroughly because Hochbrück is getting the Order of Merit posthumously. We should get Alma's clothes as quickly as we can and get out.'

'Are you kiddin' me?' Wallie rolled her eyes. 'Is that the only reason you dragged me along, so you can claim afterwards that you didn't do anything wrong?'

Bull's-eye. Carla could feel herself blushing.

'Couldn't give a monkey's! We're both far smarter than the police and I think Daddy would agree with that.' Wallie was circling around slowly, then went to the wall unit. 'I bet you anything that a guy like Hochbrück kept his smutty pictures somewhere nearby, so he could wank to them when he pleased. I know our dad wouldn't appreciate my turn of phrase, but we've got to call a spade a spade, right?'

Wallie was dead wrong. They had nothing in common, other than some stray genes. And she had to look after Alma, who needed her support, otherwise her children would end up orphans.

'Hello, anyone home?' Wallie pierced Carla's thoughts. 'While you're daydreaming over there, I've started doing a search.'

'And?'

'Other than a well-stocked bar, there's nothing in the living room.' She waved a vodka bottle. 'Polish, it's really good, you should try it.'

'Have you lost your mind? You can't do that!'

'Y' think someone measured the spirit level? Might as well take the opportunity when it comes.'

'Only drunks see that as an opportunity.'

Wallie stopped short. 'You are so... do you even hear yourself?' She took a long slug, as if to demonstrate something, then put the bottle back in the bar. With a triumphant chuckle, she then freed up two cookies in a glass container next to the fruit bowl.

'It would be great if we could find any evidence.' Carla started climbing up the iron staircase. 'Maybe we'll find something in his study.'

'I'll start with Mathilda's room,' said Wallie from below and headed for the hallway.

'Why on earth?' Carla rushed back down and nearly slipped. She heard something hard falling on the floor. She swayed and tried to grab the bannister, which of course didn't exist, and only just managed to regain her balance. 'We have to leave Mathilda out of this, otherwise the whole self-defence theory won't hold. Let's focus on finding proof for our legal argument.' She climbed down the stairs more cautiously and searched on the floor for whatever had fallen there but couldn't discover anything.

'What are you doing? If you're looking for fine hairs on the staircase, please yourself, but I'll start where I think best.' Wallie went to the main staircase and ran upstairs.

Carla was forced to follow her. You couldn't trust Wallie, she might even take the children's piggy banks. When she got to the first floor, she stopped to look at each room more closely. Right by the staircase was Gregor's room. Refreshingly untidy, as if someone actually lived here. There were Lego pieces scattered on the blue rug, there were tin soldiers strewn among the constructions, lying among the ruins of an earthquake. There was something else too. Carla stooped to examine it more closely. Cherry stones. What a mess! She could hardly imagine Alma allowing him to eat cherries like that in his room. There were also much-read *Fix und Foxi* comics scattered on the floor, toy guns and hockey sticks mounted on the walls.

Next to Gregor's room was the children's bathroom, judging by the cheery coloured balloons decorating one wall. Then the main bathroom, very spacious, white marble from floor to ceiling. Two washbasins, a shower and a bathtub, the size of which made Carla sigh with longing.

On the other side was the parental suite, which could be separated into two rooms thanks to a sliding door. Each side of the room featured a wide single bed, with a satin coverlet, a night table with a lamp and a framed picture of both children. Everything here was as tidy as if in a catalogue.

Mathilda's room was at the end of the corridor. Carla had always dreamt of having wallpaper like that when she was a girl: tiny yellow rosebuds growing amid leaves on a white background. There was a serene, tender atmosphere in that room. There was a sky blue flokati rug making the room feel even cosier, providing a nice contrast to the four-poster bed made of dark oak. The pink satin eiderdown housed an entire family of teddy bears. The teddy bears seemed a bit old and shabby.

'All inherited from Mama, no doubt, that's how it goes in aristocratic families,' murmured Wallie, who was standing in front of the white chest of drawers next to the door, examining the bright red suitcase vinyl record player with headsets. 'The record player is the newest model though. Guilty conscience makes for expensive gifts. Even the headset is top of the range!'

Carla stepped up to her and looked at the record

collection: The Story of Little Muck, Sinbad the Sailor, Grimm's Fairy-tale Collection.

Wallie crouched on all fours and tapped the legs of the chest of drawers. Carla stared at her ample upturned bottom. 'What are you doing?'

'Searching for evidence.'

While Wallie searched the floor, Carla took over the floating bookshelves. The *Trotzkopf* series, *Pucki* by Magda Trott, *Black Beauty*. A half-full jar of marbles was acting as a bookend. Carla used to love collecting marbles. She leafed through some of the books. Some of the pages hadn't even been cut properly – they'd almost certainly not been read. There was no note, no dried flower nor any other clue in there.

'Aha!' Wallie waved a loose piece from the leg of the chest of drawers.

'Well?' asked Carla.

Wallie tried to tap the piece of wood against the corners of the carpet, the wall, pulled on it, but revealed nothing more than a few dust bunnies. She turned around and sat down on the floor on her bottom, pulling the skirt below her knees. 'Nothing!' She sounded disappointed.

'What did you expect to find here?' asked Carla. 'A diary describing everything, or better still, a confession from Alexander?'

'Some compromising pictures, perverted photos, that's what I'd hide in her room, nobody'd bother to look here.'

Carla shook her head. She thought of Katrin and what she'd found out about Wallie. 'All the children I know are inquisitive and unpredictable. This would be the worst place to keep a secret.'

'You might be right...' began Wallie, but then she stopped, went back on all fours and crawled to the chest of drawers next to the door, looking steadily at the carpet. 'The poor girl, look here!'

Carla crouched down next to her. Wallie pointed at four

small impressions of the legs of the chest of drawers in the carpet, which were now halfway beneath the piece of furniture, then pointed further along by the door, where there were similar impressions.

'The little girl pushed the chest of drawers in front of the door.' Wallie stood up and pulled the piece of furniture a little away from the wall to try to move it against the door. 'No, too heavy!' she groaned.

'The rug is stopping it, let's take it away, then it will slide better.' Carla kneeled and turned over the corner of the rug.

'Oh!'

They stared in horror at the red–brown outline of a small hand on the back of the flokati.

'She was here, the banshee, the death fairy,' Carla said.

26

'This is definitely blood.' Wallie wasn't quite sure why she'd started whispering. 'Not from long ago either. Mathilda killed him and your Alma was well aware of it.'

'She's not my Alma.' Carla was nearly the same colour as the flokati rug. One might almost feel sorry for her.

'So it's crystal clear now. The crazy neighbour was not that crazy after all, and one of his observations was correct. Mathilda did get home before her mother that evening. Her father comes home. Mathilda tries to defend herself. He's drunk and tumbles down the stairs. If Alma could've told the truth for once in her life, we'd have solved this more quickly and been able to help her.'

'Could've, would've, should've. That's of no use to anyone right now!' Carla stood up. 'Now I understand why Alma wiped the prints off the hockey stick before she put her own prints on it. She wanted to make sure there were none from Mathilda. She reported it as an accident, probably because he stank of alcohol and she thought nobody would doubt that story. She only came up with the self-defence excuse when she was accused of murder, because she certainly doesn't want to go to prison and leave her children behind.'

'It was stupid, she should've pleaded self-defence from the start.' Wallie stood up with a groan, her shins and feet had gone to sleep. She marched in place to restore her circulation and tucked her blouse back into her skirt.

'There's something important that we're not seeing here,' Carla went to the doorway and searched up and down the corridor. Not that there was going to be a sign there, saying: pick your clues up right here.

'Let's face the unpalatable truth here, we need to speak to Mathilda.'

'By no means.' Carla turned towards her like an Amazon warrior spoiling for battle. 'That child is completely traumatised.'

'So our questioning can't make things worse, right?'

'You're full of empathy, aren't you?' Carla's face wrinkled in disapproval. She looked years older all of a sudden, and incredibly fragile. Wallie took a step closer.

'Our father was never as hard and callous as you!' Carla sneered.

Fragile like a bulldozer.

'You clearly take after your mother.'

The way Carla spat out 'your mother' made it sound as welcome as stepping in dog turd. Wallie hastily swallowed down the comforting words she'd been about to say.

'Let's leave this emotional palaver out of it, it's not about us,' said Wallie, feeling she'd got a handle on how to get Carla to cooperate. Of course, it would always be about the two of them too, but Carla would never admit that, because she was so proud of her professionalism. 'We can solve our personal problems later, this tit-for-tat won't help anyone, and Mathilda can probably tell us something important.'

'The women in this family have suffered a trauma,' Carla nodded, as if she'd just realised something. 'Alma said that her husband was in his study when she got home...'

But that woman lies whenever she opens her mouth, Wallie wanted to say, but she forced herself to hear her out.

'...which doesn't make sense. Gregor was his favourite. As soon as Alexander heard the car stopping in front of the garage, he'd have run downstairs to find out what had happened to his son. It only makes sense if he was already dead and Alma invented more or less this story.'

'See how easily you fall for Alma's tales!'

'Says the barmaid who is so experienced in private investigations,' hissed Carla, galloping downstairs, 'Who took those ridiculous pictures.'

'What do you mean? This ridiculous barmaid found the print on the flokati rug, after all.'

'This isn't helping!' Carla yelled over her shoulder, as she marched through the living room and started climbing up the stairs to the study.

'And this barmaid would like to point out that it's a mistake to search only for evidence to prove your point, you have to remain open-minded!' Carla would never know that this was a fairly recent lesson that Wallie had learnt for herself. 'We need to find all the evidence to get the full picture. Let's try and find proof of Alma's guilt – no point in closing our eyes to anything.' She panted a little as she followed Carla into the light, airy studio.

Her sister was striding purposefully to the two large tables placed under the skylights. When Wallie got nearer, she saw miniature trees, which reminded her of endless evenings playing model railways with her cousins in Prötzel. 'Hard to believe that these designs can become real buildings.'

'So let's examine them.' Carla bent over the table and circled it slowly. 'If I'm not mistaken...'

'Which of course Professor Dr Koslowsky cannot possibly be...'

'...then this is the exact same model as the one in Klaus's apartment.'

'That's why the man was his assistant.'

Carla stood up and looked at Wallie as if she'd just woken up from a dream. 'You're absolutely right, I went about it in completely the wrong way.'

'Would you mind kindly repeating that admission?'

Carla merely looked at her, nodding. For one second it looked like she might smile, but then she continued. 'Klaus stamped on his model before my very eyes. I thought it was grief, but was that really the case? We have to show the police that there are other suspects with a plausible motive. Father always said that no one is so holy that they have no enemies – especially those people whom everyone declares to be saintly. I'd nearly forgotten that.'

'Well, we already know that Hochbrück wasn't saintly at all. Maybe we should look at his accounts, find something dicey there.'

'The police say they found nothing suspicious.'

'We're not the police,' said Wallie, smiling at Carla, 'We're better!'

After half an hour Wallie discovered a locked box behind a fourteen-volume Brockhaus dictionary. As she strove to open the box, her sister disappeared. Where had she gone? This box surely must contain the fellow's dodgy pictures. Carla came back with her handbag, rather out of breath and taking out her Minox camera.

'We need to take pictures,' she said, sitting down at the table and asking Wallie to come closer.

'Are you ready?' asked Wallie, as she lifted the lid. Carla seemed to thrive on surprises.

'Ready!'

But the only thing she found there was one boring sales contract after another, which she handed to Carla, who dutifully took pictures of them. They hadn't yet taken a picture of the bloody print, and Wallie wondered if she should remind her of that.

'These are all properties in the two neighbouring streets, Fasanen and Joachimsthaler,' said Carla, 'If I'd known how cheap the properties there were, I'd have bought one long ago.'

'Let me see.' Wallie sat so close to Carla that she nearly doused her in face-powder. 'In Eden we were joking that so many people sold their properties for a song, before leaving for the West, because of the Wall. But these contracts date from last year. Two thousand marks for Fasanenstraße and only 800 for a bigger piece of land in Joachimsthalerstraße, that can't be right, surely?'

'Maybe they paid the remainder in cash, to avoid tax,' said Carla, continuing to take pictures with her camera. 'Have you noticed who the owner of all these properties is?'

'No, can't say I did.' Wallie checked the box once more.

'Klaus Carl-Ferdinand Baron von Stellmark, Alma's brother.'

'There's something else in here, a little vial.' Wallie took it out and held it high. 'Pervitin. What's this supposed to mean? Did Hochbrück also take this stuff? That would be good for our case, right?'

'But Alma would've known about it and used it as a reason for divorce. No, I think Klaus sold the properties to him and received the rest of the payment in drugs. Or else Hochbrück might have defrauded him. That area is going to be built up very soon.'

'I really don't think so. Klaus genuinely admired and worshipped Hochbrück. He wasn't faking it when I spoke to him and the other students in the cafeteria. And he's not stupid, Klaus, even drugged up he wouldn't have allowed himself to be tricked like that.'

Carla laid the contracts down thoughtfully. 'You may be right, there might be something else behind all this. We have to ask Alma about it, of course. Unfortunately, it doesn't help our case all that much, because of course it's an excellent motive for murder for Alma as well, because the properties become hers as the lawful wife. Even if she gets convicted, the inheritance will go to the children. They might even inherit the properties her brother got instead of her, as the male heir.'

'But wouldn't they have inherited them anyway?'

'Only if Klaus mentioned them in his will.'

'I suggest that I speak to Klaus, and you with Mathilda.' Wallie paused. 'Or better still, let's both talk to both. Otherwise we won't make any progress.'

'But first I have to bring Alma some clothes. Then I can ask her about the properties and also if we can talk to Mathilda.'

'No point in doing that,' said Wallie, 'She'll flat-out refuse as her mother.'

'We can't do it without her permission.'

'You can't but I can. I'm sick and tired of fishing in troubled waters.'

'Don't you dare...' Carla packed her camera away, put the contracts back in the box and pushed it back behind the dictionaries.

'We should take a picture of the bloody print.'

'It was a mistake allowing you to come along.'

'And we should search Alma's room while we pack her clothes.'

'You should leave now.'

Nothing for it but for Wallie to take the picture – she had, as always, a camera with her, but didn't want to be so blatant in front of Carla. 'What are you afraid of? If Alma is innocent, we won't find anything, and if she isn't, it's better if we find the evidence. Then maybe the lawyer can prevent the police from using it.'

'Fine, let's pack Alma's things and do a quick search. But you're not speaking to Mathilda, no way.'

'Understood.' It was much harder to lie to Carla than she'd expected. 'I have to go to the toilet, let's meet upstairs in Alma's room.' She climbed down the metal staircase. What a complicated floral design, pretty but pointless. She went to the guest cloakroom next to the entrance and waited until Carla went upstairs. Then she crept into Mathilda's room and took a picture of the bloody print with her camera. She'd confront Mathilda with that.

Yes, she might be a child still, but that didn't make her completely innocent!

27

Carla took out the Polaroids she'd picked up from Trudi and spread them out on her desk. She'd show them to Ingrid Niemöller alongside the pictures taken by the press photographer. Unfortunately, Trudi's photos seemed to show Lulu left, right and centre. There were only two pictures in which you could spot other people in the background. The search for Jack had turned out to be much harder than she could've imagined. Even more unfortunate, because Ingrid needed a man quite urgently now, someone she could present to her boss as her husband. Maybe Wallie was right and they'd have to dig up someone who could play the part for that occasion.

Bruno, she suddenly thought. He proved quite useful in the Eden Bar, without asking too many questions. Besides, he was good-looking and a good talker, he could certainly come across as a salesman. He'd called twice since the Eden evening; he wanted to bring Wallie's light summer coat, which she'd left behind in his taxi. Carla suggested he leave the coat with Frau Pallutzke, but he refused and insisted that he'd return it in person. He was calling her by her first name now, and she rather liked the way he pronounced her name, clearly enunciating both 'A's, rather than the more guttural emphasis on the 'K' sound, which most people did.

She hadn't told Wallie about this, of course, especially since she didn't seem to miss her coat, probably because it was warm every day. Besides, Wallie had not spent the night in the office.

Bright sunrays danced on the desk, lighting up the photos and nearly blinding Carla. She stood up and went to the window to draw the curtains a little. She looked down on Grolmanstraße, where summer was in full swing. Frau Pallutzke was peacefully leaning on her broom and sunning her face. The neighbours opposite had set up their folding chairs and were drinking coffee. Katrin and two other girls were trying to play skipping between the freshly planted linden trees, but it wasn't easy with her terrible brothers constantly running around yowling to annoy them. Carla had to laugh. Despite the brothers and their silly antics, everything seemed so peaceful, just a typical summer day. There seemed to be no crisis in Berlin. They could have gone swimming and eaten ice cream.

The summery picture that Wallie had shown her had stuck in her mind. Where had Carla been on that day? Was it after Mother's accident? Before the accident, Mother had gone swimming every day until winter set in, even during the war. But after she lost her leg, she'd stopped swimming altogether, even though the Charlottenburg Public Pool wasn't far away and offered special sessions solely for disabled people. Father had offered to take her there – but without success.

Carla went back to her desk, and, after a quick glance at the clock, shuffled all the pictures into the Niemöller file. Then she checked her hair in the hallway mirror. It seemed immaculate, but her face was paler than usual and the rings under her eyes were nearly purple. Small wonder, since she'd been ruminating over Alma's case all night, as if the solution were a particularly nasty Minotaur hiding in an endless labyrinth.

Her hope that she might be able to hand over the clothes personally to Alma and talk to her a little had been in vain. The inmates were in weekend lockdown from Friday afternoon onwards. It was horrible that even those on remand were locked away for the whole weekend, simply because of understaffing. They were merely allowed one hour in the courtyard in the morning, and then total isolation in their cells. Even the Sunday service that the inmates were usually allowed to attend would not take place tomorrow, because the chapel was being renovated.

At least she'd remembered to pack a picture of Mathilda and Gregor in the suitcase. But would Alma even get her suitcase?

A ring at the door announced Bruno's arrival. She opened the door. Despite the heat, he was wearing his black leather jacket. He was holding Wallie's coat over his left arm, in his right hand a bouquet of wildflowers.

'For you!'

Using the informal *Du* had been easier on the phone.

'Thanks, I'll look for a vase,' she said, rushing into the kitchen to hide how flustered she was. The flowers must have been picked by him. Frothy white wild carrot, poppies with their tissue-paper flowers, bright buttercups and highly scented pink vetch. A little summer meadow in the middle of her office. It smelled of grass and earth and happiness. The bouquet fitted perfectly in one of her water glasses.

When she came back with it into the office, Bruno had laid Wallie's coat on one of the rattan chairs, but was waiting in front of her desk. When she got nearer, he examined her carefully.

'You need some fresh air.'

She put the flowers down and invited him to sit.

'They're lovely, thank you.'

'Glad you like them, because I want to take you to the place where there's lots more of those!'

'But I have work to do.' It seemed a satisfactory thing to say, easier than driving anywhere with him.

'Poppycock! Everyone needs a break. I should be

studying anatomy today, because tomorrow I'll be on taxi duty, but just look outside!' He gestured dramatically at the windows. 'You lock yourself indoors too much. Just think of the Wall. You never know what will happen, but any minute now it might be too late. Today they closed off access even for those with a work permit for offices on the other side, who knows what they might do next.' His carefree laughter belied the seriousness of his words. 'A spin on my bike helps combat pale skin and can work wonders!'

He seemed to truly believe what he was saying, but Carla knew better than to expect any miracles.

'Would you be prepared to help us in one of our cases?' she asked.

'If you're prepared to go for a spin with me...'

'Some other time, I really can't today.'

'Not even for an hour?'

Carla shook her head and pointed at the files. 'Sorry.'

His shoulders hunched forwards, the sunny smile on his face disappeared.

'I really would love to,' she added, trying to sound as if she meant it.

'Of course you would.' He stood up. 'Well then, I won't get under your feet any longer.'

She bent over the bouquet, taking it all in. 'Every time I look at these flowers, I'll regret my decision but enjoy them nevertheless.'

'Just like in real life, eh?' He seemed mollified with that. He took off his leather jacket and sat back down with a grin.

'Well then, what kind of help do you need? If it involves going to a topless bar again, I'm your man!' His white T shirt was slightly damp, the sleeves rolled up. Carla couldn't help noticing his strong forearms, his golden-brown skin.

She cleared her throat and explained her plan to help out

Frau Niemöller with a fake husband. He thought about it, then asked what this Frau Niemöller looked like. She opened the file and held out the picture of Ingrid in the Marilyn Monroe wig. She was curious as to how he'd react.

He gave a whistle of admiration, which drew her attention to the irritating little gap between his front teeth. He declared it would be an honour for him to help a lady in distress. He was even prepared to refresh his mighty knowledge of door handles, so as to be fully prepared for his role as a husband and salesman.

The phone interrupted him. Carla excused herself and answered. It was Vera Huberman, the child psychologist at the orphanage, and she was irate.

'Are Alma's children OK?' asked Carla in alarm.

'I'm not sure yet just how OK they are, but I'd really like to know why you felt the need to get them additionally examined by an external psychotherapist. Do you think I'm incompetent or something?'

'I don't know what...' She tried to think it through: had Stratmann arranged for something like that, or that slimy Grieser? Whoever it was, this was a bad moment to do it, the last thing she needed was a conflict with Vera.

'There's a woman here who says you sent her on Alma's behalf to talk to Mathilda.'

'Did she produce any identification?' It took a while for the penny to drop but of course, that must be Wallie.

'She must have shown something at the main gate, we don't let just anyone waltz in.'

'Does she look serious?' Wallie could barely pass for a sex therapist, let alone anything else.

'What's going on here?' Vera sounded furious. 'I don't have time for your little games.'

'There're no games. I'll come right away. Please keep that woman there, I'll come and explain as soon as I can.'

'So we are going for a little spin after all!' Bruno was already on his feet, had put on his leather jacket and was closing the windows. She'd forgotten all about him.

'I can't get on a motorbike like this! And I don't think you have a sidecar like Buchholz had in that film.'

'So what? If you hold your skirt a little higher, you can do it!'

She looked out the window. Katrin's brothers were admiring a motorbike down there. 'Is that yours?'

He came next to her and nodded proudly.

'But it only has one seat.'

'Yeah, but it's a big 'un, and, if I may say so, your bottom is tiny! I've often had passengers with me.'

He grinned broadly. He seemed to be making a genuine offer and she was in a hurry to get to the orphanage. It would take far too long to go there on foot. She couldn't keep Vera waiting, and Wallie was not to be trusted. She agreed reluctantly.

'So where are we going?'

'Schaperstraβe, the Berlin Fledglings Orphanage.'

A few minutes later, Carla was sitting on the back of Bruno's motorcycle, her skirt hiked up nearly to her garters, giving rise to cheeky remarks from Katrin's brothers and sly looks from Frau Pallutzke.

'Go as fast as you can!' Carla whispered in his ear, all the while trying not to get too close to him. As they roared off, however, they slid closer together. The scent of summer arose from the back of his neck, a mix of Wannsee water and lemon ice cream. She had to fight the impulse to simply bury her face in the bewitching scent of his skin. This was not the time for such nonsense!

Bruno rode fast, relaxed and confident. If she'd been dressed for it, and not concerned about Mathilda, she might even have enjoyed it. Suddenly the thought of a little spin sounded more seductive. Somewhere far, far away from all her problems.

28

Vera was waiting at the gate for Carla and took her immediately to the arts and crafts room, which always reminded Carla of a cellar, because the windows were really high up. Even the children's artwork pinned all around the walls couldn't alter that impression.

She only recognized Wallie after a second glance. She was standing with her back to Carla, apparently engrossed in examining a drawing. She was wearing a conservative beige suit, brown orthopaedic shoes and the wig with a short grey bob that Carla had previously found in her suitcase. Wallie turned around and nodded briefly at Carla, as if they had an appointment there. Carla tried to hide her surprise in front of Vera, acting as if it was the most ordinary thing in the world for Wallie to run around looking like a granny, with no make-up and an oversized pair of spectacles on her nose.

Wallie turned back to the collage made of screwed-up pieces of coloured tissue-paper, pointing at it thoughtfully. 'You might notice here, Miss Koslowsky, a fascinating piece of art. An eletoise or torephant, wouldn't you say? We paediatric psychologists would call this infant chimerization.'

Carla could feel Vera tensing. Was that complete nonsense or was there really such a term in child psychology? Vera was clearly impatient to find out what was going on here. The psychologist had been fond of

Father, which was probably the reason why she'd even bothered to call Carla. After the debacle with Paula, Vera's bad opinion of Carla had worsened. If she wanted to keep her position on the orphanage committee, she'd better keep Vera onside during this latest crisis.

'Vera, I'm so sorry. There was a misunderstanding here between Miss von Tilling and myself.'

'Miss von Tilling?' Vera opened her eyes wide. 'She introduced herself to me as Gerda Brinkmann.'

'A misunderstanding,' Wallie jumped in. 'I'm here on behalf of Mrs Brinkmann, who works for the Prosecutor's office. I'm here to have an initial interview with Mathilda.'

'And you are a psychotherapist?'

'Of course.' Wallie sounded impatient, as if Vera must know what an expert she was in the field.

Vera stared at Carla in confusion. 'So what now?'

'I'm so sorry, I completely misunderstood you just now on the phone. This is fine. We will interview Mathilda together,' Carla chimed in.

'When interviewing a minor in matters pertaining to a crime, at least one responsible adult has to be present.'

'And Alma agreed that it should be me.' Carla hoped no one would notice the beads of sweat on her forehead. 'Mathilda knows me from the trip to Wannsee.'

'I should be there too. After all, the poor child is quite traumatized!' said Vera.

'I don't think that's a good idea,' Wallie interrupted. 'Three grown-ups interrogating a child? This could trigger a response bias and the poor girl might start making up stories – so as not to disappoint us three adults. Wouldn't you say?' She looked accusingly at Vera.

'Indeed.' Vera chewed on her lower lip. 'That's a possibility. Fine, I'll talk to her afterwards.'

Vera went out and returned shortly afterwards with Mathilda and Gregor.

Gregor was a head taller than Mathilda and had his arm

over her shoulder. He looked daggers at Carla and Wallie from under his oddly misshapen fringe. They must have cut it in haste at the hospital to deal with the wound. His fierce gaze under the crooked fringe and the bandage on the left side of his head made him look both rakish and vulnerable at the same time. His collarless white shirt had come untucked from his oversized Lederhosen, and the white knitted knee-socks had fallen to his ankles, leaving his childish yet muscular calves bare. Next to him, Mathilda seemed even slighter.

What now? Carla looked at Wallie and Vera with questioning eyes. They needed to speak to Mathilda alone.

Vera shrugged. 'Mathilda started crying when I tried to separate them.'

Carla thought of the little tin soldiers in Gregor's untidy room and squatted down in front of his chair. 'Hello, Gregor, we know each other already. I'm Carla, from the Wannsee trip.'

Gregor's face broke into a smile, reminding Carla of Alexander. He nodded earnestly and held Mathilda's upper arm even tighter. 'Mama said I should look after Mathilda. I'll never leave her on her own.'

'Of course not. You'd never let each other down, like Fix and Foxi.'

Gregor looked sceptically from Carla to Wallie and Vera. 'Hmmm.'

'That's perfect, because we need a good soldier like you right now.'

'Hmmm.'

'We have to speak to Mathilda undisturbed. Could you and Mrs Hubermann keep watch at the door to make sure no one disturbs us? There's only one entrance, as you can see.'

Gregor whispered something to his sister behind his hand, so softly that Carla couldn't hear anything. Mathilda nodded hesitantly, upon which he blew her a kiss and let go of her arm.

'I'm ready,' Gregor said and walked up to Vera, who in turn looked furiously at Carla. She'd certainly not counted on wasting her time guarding the door.

Wallie stood up. 'Thank you, my esteemed colleague, how nice of you to help Gregor in this important duty.' She showed them to the door, and Vera and Gregor had to leave.

They'd have to hurry so as not to abuse Vera's hospitality. Carla went up to Mathilda and shook her hand.

'Hello, Auntie Carla,' said Mathilda and curtseyed. Carla got goose bumps every time she heard herself addressed as 'auntie', but her suggestion that the children at the orphanage should stop addressing the personnel as 'auntie' and 'uncle' had fallen on deaf ears.

Wallie gave Mathilda coloured pens and paper and asked her to draw something for them while the aunties were having a conversation with her.

Carla sat down at the table, allowing Wallie to take the initiative for the time being. Maybe Wallie really did know more about children than she did. That infant chimerization thing seemed to have had an effect on Vera at any rate.

'Can you remember the night when your brother had to go to hospital? When they cut him that crooked fringe?'

Mathilda giggled softly. 'It looks so silly!'

Wallie nodded and held out the pens encouragingly. 'Please, help yourself.'

Mathilda looked at Carla and gave her a pink pen. 'Will you draw with me, Auntie Carla?'

Carla took the pen and a sheet of paper. 'With pleasure.'

She'd loved to draw as a child and hoarded any piece of paper that she could find. Lulu had been so delighted by her drawings that she'd framed some of them and hung them up in her kitchen.

'I'll join in too then!' said Wallie. 'And I've got a fun idea.' She took a sheet of paper and drew around the contour of her palm. 'There, now you!'

What a transparent manoeuvre! It was so obvious that the bloody handprint could only have come from Mathilda. Still, Carla went along with it and drew the outline of her own hand. Mathilda was faster than her and looked eagerly at all three. It obviously caused her no distress whatsoever.

'Yours is ginormous,' she laughed, pointing at Wallie.

'That's right, and yours is the prettiest! Now let's draw something for real,' said Wallie, gathering all the outlines together into the green file. She started drawing circles. 'Come on, you two!'

Drawing for real... Carla drew a few tentative lines. She'd stopped giving free rein to her imagination at the age of ten. It had seemed easier to copy things in great detail. Leaves, textile patterns, chocolate bars, intersections. She became really good at copying things, could even draw banknotes with perfect recall. She also began to draw rooms from memory, rooms which seemed to appear complete in all their intricate details, as if by magic.

Mathilda took a light blue pen and started drawing clouds.

'Were you sad when your brother hurt himself?' asked Wallie.

'Hmmm,' said Mathilda, drawing a blue sun.

'Do you always take the keys from the birdhouse when there's no one else at home?' continued Wallie.

Mathilda nodded.

'Does that often happen?' Carla added.

Mathilda looked up at and somehow past her. 'No,' she smiled somewhat unconvincingly, and twirled her hair around the blue pen. 'What are you drawing?'

'An apple factory!' Wallie's answer was instantaneous.

'A fence,' said Carla, surprised to recognise the fence at the Hochbrück villa. 'Surrounding a magic garden,' she added quickly, to distract attention.

'Are there any unicorns there?' asked Mathilda with interest.

'Only one,' answered Carla.

Mathilda nodded, satisfied. 'An evil wizard imprisoned the unicorn there, because...' she giggled enthusiastically, 'because the unicorn drank all his beer.'

'Do unicorns like beer?' asked Carla.

'Of course they do,' replied Wallie, winking at Mathilda.

'And cookies!' Mathilda took the pen out of her hair and laid it back on the table.

'So what do you do when you're alone at home?' asked Carla, as the unicorn made its appearance on her paper.

'I listen to fairy-tales. But I prefer it when Mama is with me. Or Gregor.'

'Naturally!' said Wallie, drawing purple apples.

'When I'm on my own, I'm not allowed to do anything.'

'Ah?' said Carla, adding yellow rosebuds to her surprisingly lifelike unicorn. 'What do you mean, anything?'

Mathilda picked up the red pen, turned the paper over and drew something, concealing it with her other hand. Then she turned the paper over again, threw the red pen away and picked up a green one to draw flowers in one of her clouds.

Carla swallowed hard. What was that all about? Was that how children behaved?

'Was someone really cross that night, when your brother went to hospital?' asked Wallie. 'Your mama, your papa, or maybe someone else?'

What on earth... she was putting ideas into Mathilda's head.

'I was... I don't know if Papa was cross, because he's dead.' Mathilda started drawing black pencil marks all over her picture. 'Do people go to heaven even if they are often cross?'

Carla was silent; she could sense they were skating over very thin ice here.

'Was your father already dead when you got home?'

asked Wallie. Carla gulped and whacked Wallie on her arm.

'Mathilda,' she began, but the girl began to answer.

'I just wanted to get a cookie.'

Carla remembered the cookie jar in the living room.

'Of course!' Wallie smiled encouragingly.

'When no one's home, I get myself a cookie first, then go upstairs and close my door.' Mathilda took out the dark blue and dark green pens and started shading in the area she'd marked with pencil. 'Do unicorns also have to close their door?' she asked, looking at Carla's picture.

'It's essential!' Wallie answered, giving Carla a meaningful look. She was probably thinking of what Mathilda did after she closed the door, namely moving the chest of drawers in front of it.

'Was the cookie tasty?'

'I didn't eat it... because Papa called me, but he was tired.'

'Why do you think he was tired?' asked Wallie.

'Because he was lying down on the floor.'

'Does he lay himself down on the floor to sleep then?' Wallie insisted.

'*Nooo*!' Mathilda rolled her eyes, obviously considering Wallie to be a bit thick. 'Of course not, that's what dogs do. I like dachshunds, but Gregor thinks they're silly. He'd like a sheepdog. But we're not allowed to keep dogs, because Papa says they're dirty.'

'So if your father was lying on the floor, was he dirty too?'

'No!' Mathilda shook her head. 'Papa wasn't really on the floor, he was half on his staircase. Gregor and I are not allowed to go on it. Never. If we get caught, Papa gets furious and hits us.' She stopped for a moment, a smile flitting across her face, as if she'd just thought of something forbidden. 'That's why I didn't take a cookie after all and went straight to my room.'

'And what did you do there?'

'I put on my headphones. Gregor doesn't have any, which makes him angry, but he doesn't punish me for that. Sometimes we listen to something together, we each take one of the headphones.'

'What's your favourite fairy-tale?' asked Carla.

Wallie groaned.

'Little Muck!' Mathilda stopped shading in and laughed. 'I especially like his prank with the magic figs, that give you giant donkey ears, because that means that the Princess Amarza can then marry the right prince. Papa says Gregor has donkey's ears too, he's full of ears.'

What could she be talking about? Did she mean the idiom 'to give someone an earful'? Carla remembered that Gregor's room, though untidy, also seemed to be the only one that was fully lived in.

'And what does Gregor like?' asked Carla.

'Mama also likes Little Muck best.' Mathilda picked up the red pen. 'I know Mama is in prison. In school the other children said that Mama is a criminal, but she's not done anything bad.'

'Have you done anything bad?' asked Wallie.

'No!' Mathilda shook her curls. 'Nobody did, nobody.' Something felt odd here, she was lying, but what about?

'Did someone else do something naughty?' Wallie insisted.

'No, everything that Papa does is good for me and good for all of us.'

'Can you remember what cookies were in the jar that evening?' asked Carla.

Mathilda's eyes shone. 'The cinnamon ones. Mama only bakes them when I've been very good.'

'So you did pick up one after all,' said Wallie.

Mathilda bowed her head, nodding.

'That's OK. Now that you remembered, you probably also remember what exactly your papa said when he called you, right?' continued Wallie. Carla held her breath.

Mathilda nodded. 'Yes,' she said firmly.

Wallie gave Carla a hopeful glance.

'So what did he say?'

Mathilda frowned and shook her head. 'Everything that Papa tells me is our secret. For ever and ever.' She laid her finger over her mouth and said, 'Shhh'. Then she smiled at them, as if expecting applause. Carla felt her hair stand on end.

'Can I have a cookie now?' Mathilda asked, tearing up the picture she'd drawn into many small pieces, then ordering them into three neat stacks. 'Can I keep Auntie Carla's unicorn?' She took Carla's picture and held it to her chest. 'It's so much cuter than mine.'

29

'God, we deserve this,' said Wallie half an hour later, stuffing a huge piece of Black Forest gateau into her mouth.

Carla took a sip of her black coffee. 'I simply don't understand how you can eat right now!' She looked so reproachfully at Wallie over the rim of her coffee cup, as if she'd been engaging in cannibalistic practices.

'I don't think I'll ever be able to eat cinnamon cookies again without thinking of Mathilda,' Carla sighed.

'Don't be daft! What sort of self-deceit is that, then! Making me out to be a monster, simply because I'm hungry. Who'm I helping by not eating?' Wallie took another bite. The sweet cream and chocolate combination, with a sour cherry inside: she closed her eyes and sighed with pleasure. She felt sorry for Carla. She'd obviously closed off everything that might give her physical pleasure. Quite different from Frieda, whom she missed a lot. The sweetness in her mouth turned stale all of sudden. She'd not shown any sign of life, hadn't sent a parcel, not even a card, to her friend.

When she opened her eyes again, she looked straight into Carla's eyes. Full of bittersweet curiosity, just like Dad when he wanted to know how she'd liked his latest present.

'Human misery just makes me hungry,' she mumbled with her mouth full. 'No use to anyone if I punish myself.' And Frieda would get a postcard today, she swore. 'Did you know that Tucholsky also liked to eat cake here in Café Kranzler?'

Carla set the coffee down so abruptly that it spilled onto the saucer. 'We shouldn't be sitting here, filling our faces, while Alma is locked up in prison, despite being innocent.'

Maybe I should order something more, simply to spite Carla, thought Wallie. *She should be grateful that I even got her to speak to Mathilda.* She hadn't a good word to say about that, about her dressing up and introducing herself as a child psychologist to Vera. Only complaints.

'We have to rethink everything!' Carla was talking herself into a rage. 'Obviously Mathilda had nothing to do with his death, because he was already lying on the stairs when she got home.'

'Yes, Miss Marple, we've already chewed this over on our way here. That would explain why he didn't open the door. So the neighbour was telling the truth in this regard...' Wallie was thinking out loud, while laying waste to the cake in front of her. 'Mathilda wasn't lying about that, otherwise she wouldn't have had to pick up the key from the birdhouse.'

'Why was he so drunk?' asked Carla.

'Why didn't his daughter call for help?' countered Wallie, simply to annoy Carla.

'Are you really asking that?' Carla stared stonily at her.

Images of Hochbrück's doughy naked body in the hotel room appeared in front of Wallie's eyes, interspersed with images of his daughter's delicate face, the little girl's room and the small bloody handprint, all blurring together in a kaleidoscope of new, disturbing images. Suddenly, she could feel the cherries rising up her gullet, and she pushed the plate to one side. Maybe Carla was right after all.

'Mathilda must have touched the open wound on Hochbrück's head, otherwise how can we explain the bloody print on the flokati rug?' she said out loud.

'He probably had such influence over her that she really

did go up to him when he called out.' Carla's eyes seemed suspiciously damp. 'And then she did what Alma had taught her. Went to safety. But what I'm wondering is why was he already so drunk?'

'Was he celebrating something?'

'Alone? Did none of the neighbours see anything that might help? Maybe around the time he came home?'

'I spoke to all of them, but they either didn't want to talk to me or noticed nothing out of order... with the exception of the madman, who also mentioned UFOs.'

'According to Stratmann, Hochbrück's secretary had no more appointments for him after twelve noon. Once a week he had his so-called creative space.'

'With any other man, that would be a euphemism for a lover or for going to a brothel.' Wallie wiped her mouth with a napkin. Shame to leave the cake unfinished, but her appetite had gone now.

'In any case, we must make sure that the whole thing can be classified as an accident. There was no cold-blooded murder and Alma can't have done it anyway. If only she'd kept her mouth shut! But when it concerns her daughter, she loses her rationality.'

'We can only prove it was an accident if Mathilda testifies, and you can be sure that your Alma will prevent that.'

'It could be that Mathilda's credibility might be put in doubt.' Carla sighed, and finally decided to peck a little at the tiny cookie that had been served with her coffee. 'I find her decidedly odd.'

'To be expected, with all she's been through.'

'You misunderstand me. I thought that those experiences would have made her grow up faster, but she seems to be far more childish than my neighbour Katrin, for example.'

'Are there any rules as to how you must behave if you've been abused?'

Carla spluttered and blushed. 'Of course not,' she said in a small voice. 'That was not only uncalled-for, but also stupid.'

Wallie suppressed her impulse to lay a comforting hand on Carla's arm, but adroitly changed the topic. 'Is Katrin the little skinny one with plaits, who's always spying on me?'

'Yes, she just wants to help. Her dream is to become a detective, and Aunt Lulu sadly encourages her.'

'Well, the little brat has some work to do finessing her shadowing techniques. She shouldn't jump wildly behind trees or advert-pillars when I turn around. She should just continue walking casually, maybe bend down to tie her shoelaces. You should tell her.'

Carla grinned. 'I will. She's really keen to learn.'

Trees... Something pinged in Wallie's head, but what could it be? She was completely indifferent to nature. 'Not see the forest for the trees...' she muttered. What was she supposed to be noticing?

'What on earth are you on about?' asked Carla, dumbfounded.

'Trees. That rings a bell. Quick, tell me, what do you think of when you hear the word tree?'

'Oak, birch, spruce, poplar, linden tree, beech, pine, promenade, park, forest...' Carla rattled them off.

Wallie shook her head. 'No, I don't mean types of tree, but keep going, I might have it soon.'

'Leaves, bark, bloom, sap, fruit, wild boars...'

'Wild boars?'

'They eat everything.'

'No, no animals, keep going.'

'Resin, crown, branches, trunk, roots, earth...'

'Yes!' Wallie grabbed Carla's arm and pressed it enthusiastically. 'That's it! The tree trunk, where dogs pee. How could I have forgotten! We have to go!'

'Where and why?'

'I'll explain on the way. We have to go to Dahlem.'

On the way there, Wallie explained that the crazy neighbour had observed something else, something she'd forgotten in all the subsequent discussion of UFOs. The gardener who was looking after the house next door to the Hochbrücks had peed on the compost pile. They had to speak to the man, maybe he'd seen something.

It took an age to get to Dahlem and the crazy neighbour was not at home. Or at least, there was no one answering and so they couldn't ask him about the gardener.

'What now?' Wallie looked around in vain for a bench. What a shitty, pretentious neighbourhood!

'Two important points about gardeners...' said Carla, putting up two fingers of her right hand. As if she'd employed hundreds of gardeners in her lifetime. 'First, they usually get paid cash. Secondly, they often also work for the neighbours. Just like cleaners and babysitters.'

'What do you mean?' Her sister seemed to be enjoying herself, while here she was, running around in her itchy, far too warm healthcare worker outfit, which made her look older than her own granny. High time to get changed, obviously it was having a negative effect on her brain. Then again, maybe the housekeepers wouldn't slam the door on her so much in this get-up.

'I think you were very wise to eat, because now we have to rely on good old-fashioned wearing out the soles of the shoes type of detecting. You take this side, I'll take the other.'

'And then what?' She could foresee that they'd just be getting fallen arches for nothing in this snobby neighbourhood.

'You watch out for any gardeners. We'll ring the bell and say we live on the next street along and we've heard about their wonderful gardener.'

'And if it's not the same one?'

'Have you a better idea?'

Wallie shook her head. Carla crossed the road and started with the house of the crazy man. This was such a waste of time. She'd already experienced how unforthcoming the people around here were.

An hour later, she hadn't found out anything and was now working down the far end of the road. Her orthopaedic shoes hurt her far more than her usual heels, and she admired Carla's effortless gliding up and down the road. She was tough, she had to give her that. She was ringing and chatting, ringing and chatting, but on Wallie's side of the road no one seemed to be at home. A crackpot idea, that was all.

All of a sudden, Carla waved to her.

'So, our man lives in Kreuzberg. He's not a trained gardener, but they all swear by his skills, because he's so talented. He's probably a foreigner, because one man described him as a gypsy and two women said he looked so wonderfully romantic. But, although they all swear by him, I suspect few of them would let him into their houses. So, if you ask me, that's the reason he was caught peeing in the garden.' Carla laughed out loud. 'I reckon he's very good-looking, and his talents have more to do with that than with his ability to weed the garden. All the women I spoke to had a gleam in their eyes when they spoke about him, while the men seemed less enthusiastic.'

Wallie looked at her sister. That would teach her never to underestimate her again. 'Is that all?'

Carla gave a triumphant smile. 'Nope! His name is Laszlo, no one knows his surname. But one of the women knew that he can be reached at the weekend in Piroschka, she's often left messages for him there.'

'How on earth did you do all that?'

'I'm good at that: ringing timidly, apologising and acting myself humble. Admiring their house and garden, telling them a heart-breaking story about my poor old mum, who's going to move in shortly into the house round the corner. I told them that my friend Alma Hochbrück had told me how helpful they were and hinted that my husband is a pilot or a professor, depending on what I thought they might like to hear. And then I retreated full of gratitude.'

'Ah. But how can we be sure he's our man?'

Carla laughed out loud. 'Your crazy guy is the only one on the street who doesn't employ him. He obviously has something against gypsies.'

'And why did the police not find Laszlo?'

'Who's going to talk to the police about a black-market gardener, especially if no one thinks to ask about him?'

'So off to Kreuzberg!'

'I have to go back to the office, because Ingrid Niemöller is coming to look at the pictures I found for her. But we can go afterwards. He'll be at the Piroschka on Saturday evening. What do you think he does there?' Carla's light brown eyes were sparkling like wet sand in the sunlight.

'Cooking?'

'He plays violin. Father said clichés can be helpful on occasion because they're often surprisingly accurate. But he warned me not to trust in them too much.'

Wallie couldn't remember such pearls of wall-calendar wisdom from their father. But then she hadn't known him as well as Carla. At first it hadn't mattered so much, but when her mother got ill, she did wonder why he was never around when they needed him.

'Well, we should go and have a listen then. I'll get changed and go to Piroschka, I feel I could handle a goulash from Szeged right now. I only start work at ten tonight in Eden.'

'We should talk to him together.'

'Why? Do you think I might mess things up?'

'No, no,' Carla said hurriedly, 'I'm just curious and if it's both of us, we can be witnesses to what he has to tell us.'

'Fine, then join me there as soon as you're done with Niemöller.'

Carla nodded solemnly. 'Promise me that you'll wait for me and not do your own thing, like you did with Mathilda.'

But they'd have made no progress at all if she hadn't had the initiative to talk to Mathilda. 'Uh-um,' said Wallie, swallowing hard. There was no point in rubbing it in now.

'Thank you.' Carla chewed her lip. What now?

'Mother will be furious that we're not there on Saturday for the evening meal, but we have to do it, we have to crack this case.' She was obviously giving herself a pep talk, for she nodded heartily at the end of it. 'Let's hurry. Frau Niemöller is already losing her patience, we can't risk her going to another agency.'

At least she'd said 'we'.

30

Half an hour later they turned into Grolmanstraße.

'Somebody's missed you!' Wallie pointed at Katrin, who came running up to Carla so quickly that her red-checked apron was fluttering.

'You can tell her that I spotted her shadowing me.' Wallie gave a nod. 'If she's serious about it, I'm sure she'd like to know.' She headed to the entrance of the building, but just before going in, she turned round to say, 'I'll go up and tell Ida that you've fallen in love with a fiddler!' She laughed brashly at the joke, obviously thinking it was a good one.

Carla looked around stealthily – half of Grolmanstraße would believe that. Wallie was like a winning lottery number for Frau Pallutzke.

Katrin stood transfixed, staring after Wallie full of admiration. 'You're kidding me! That's the blonde that you...' Breathing heavily, she turned her big eyes onto Carla. 'Was this a secret mission?'

'It's called going undercover,' she explained, sure that Katrin would try out disguises over the next few days. 'But I'm afraid the blonde noticed you were after her. You have to be more careful when you're shadowing someone. The person being followed notices from the corner of their eye if someone suddenly scampers to one side when they turn round.'

Katrin nodded earnestly and took out a pencil stump to take notes on a used paper sandwich bag. 'Of course. I have to ask you...' she said, looking all of a sudden much younger.

Carla nodded encouragingly.

'For the Abominables, they said they'd beat me up if I don't do it.'

'Go ahead.'

'They wanna ask what kinda bobber that was and if your friend would give 'em a ride some time. All four of 'em. Just a short one.'

Katrin had spoken so fast, just to get the awkward question out of the way, that Carla wasn't sure she'd understood.

'What do you mean "bobber"?'

'The motorbike, that's a Bobber.'

'Bobber?' repeated Carla, her mind racing.

'Yes, a Bobber. It's a bike without front and back. All the metal bits you don't need have been stripped off. It's like a racing bike, just saddle on the wheels, kinda!' Katrin rattled off all the information, as if she was being paid for it.

'So that's a Bobber!' Carla bent over to give Katrin a hug, then lifted her up and twirled her around in a circle.

'What's the matter?'

'You've solved the riddle! Bobbs! Bobbs is a Bobber!'

She carefully set Katrin down again.

'What?' Katrin's eyes were nearly falling out of her head.

'You've solved my case – well, nearly! I'll tell you later, now I must dash. Tell your brothers, I'll buy them an ice cream tomorrow at the Ice Henning on Henriette Place.'

'Why them?' scowled Katrin. 'That's not fair!'

'Life isn't always fair, but of course you can come along too! See you tomorrow, I'm going upstairs.'

As Carla mounted the stairs to the office, she remembered Sally Montana, who'd definitely know something about the motorbike clubs of the GIs. She was sure that with her help, she'd find the elusive Jack who'd courted a pretty blonde lady at the German–American Folk Fair.

The office still held the scent of the meadow flowers from Bruno's bouquet. A quick glance at the clock showed her that Frau Niemöller would be there imminently. She grabbed Wallie's coat, still lying on the back of the chair, to hang it in the wardrobe. Her moves were too quick, the coat slid from the hanger and fell to the floor.

Clank.

That didn't sound like a piece of cloth, more like something heavy or metallic. Maybe the belt buckle. Or a set of keys. Suddenly, she realised that she hadn't really stopped to consider Wallie's fate. Everyone had a key to their home, but Wallie could no longer go there. Carla had never given a damn about that. What about all the precious things Wallie had to leave behind? What about the people who were important to her? How could she remain so optimistic despite all that? She must have inherited that from Father, who always tried to make the best of everything.

She picked up the coat thoughtfully and felt in the pockets, to see where Wallie's key rings were. Left, right, nothing.

So where did that sound come from? She felt around in the coat and discovered a hidden pocket, so craftily added on the inside of the left breast, that you couldn't see any seams. She carefully opened the little buttons and took out everything from the pocket. She didn't have much time, because Frau Niemöller was always super-punctual. Wallie might be in Mother's claws at the moment, but she might also come downstairs sooner than expected.

Carla examined her find. It was indeed something metallic, wrapped in a few sheets of tissue paper. A gold coin on a brooch, with the initials FDJ. Freie Deutsche Jugend. Free German Youth, as Carla knew, although she'd never seen the medal before. On the one side there was a man's head and the name Artur Becker, a name that didn't mean anything to her, but she'd soon find out. Alongside the medal there were three strange coins, with the letters LAG on the one side, and then numbers underneath. The square coin with rounded edges said '.05', the octagonal one '.10' and the hexagonal one '1'. These light grey metal coins reminded Carla of GDR camping gear.

She hurriedly took out one of her pencils and drew the medal and coins. Then she looked at the thin, tissue-like papers. Stamped and signed passes for West Berliners who wanted to visit East Berlin. How did Wallie have so many blank passes, where you merely had to fill in the name and date?

Had she bought some of them on the black market for friends to come and visit her? For the Scotsman? How tragic that these passes were now just wastepaper. Just the previous day the head of the Berlin police had closed the offices that handed out such passes. For political reasons, because that would have meant that they accepted the legality of the building of the Wall on the 13th of August. So since yesterday, it was impossible for West Berliners to visit the East, while the East Berliners were no longer allowed to go anywhere. From a purely human perspective, of course, this politically motivated decision was a catastrophe. Carla felt her lack of empathy keenly. She should really show more consideration for Wallie and her plight.

The bell rang. 'Wait a sec!' said Carla, stuffing her notebook away and wrapping the coins up carefully in the tissue paper, and shoving them back into the secret pocket. Then she hung up the coat properly and opened the door to let Ingrid Niemöller in. No sooner had Carla laid the pictures in front of her on the table, than Wallie came down to pick up her coat.

'See you soon and bring an umbrella,' said Wallie, who'd changed and no longer looked like an old maid. On the contrary, she looked as sexy as if she was off to seduce half a regiment. 'Your mother said she can feel it in her bones that it'll rain later.'

'Yeah, I heard that on the radio,' said Frau Niemöller, without raising her eyes from the photos.

Carla closed the door behind Wallie and sat down next to her client, of whom she was growing a little too fond. She was starting to think of her by her first name only. Although her father had always warned her to keep an inner distance towards their clients.

Ten minutes later, her client pushed the photos away in disappointment. 'I can't believe it, so many men and not a single glimpse of Jack on any of these pictures!'

'But we've made some progress,' said Carla, hoping that she might be able to reach Sally that day.

Ingrid looked at her sceptically. 'Because you can now exclude all those men?'

'No, but after exhaustive searching', she hoped that sounded like extensive hard work, 'We were able to discover the truth about his name. So it won't take long before we find Jack. I'll call you.' She stood up to end the conversation, for she wanted to get to Piroschka as soon as possible. Goodness knows what Wallie might do there without her.

'I'm getting scared,' Ingrid muttered, still sitting there, 'What if I was wrong about his feelings?'

'Well at least you tried.' Carla suppressed a sigh, as she remembered Richard, to whom she'd never confessed her feelings. 'Of course, it's easier and safer to only dream about love. That way, there can be no disappointments. Because even if there's love on both sides, no one knows how long it will last.'

She thought about Alma, who at some point must have loved Alexander. After all, her aristocratic family can't have been too delighted for her to marry a man with no money and, at the time, no career prospects. It was indeed far better not to know what the future might hold, because your dreams so seldom came true.

'You're right, the only constant love is the one you have for a child, or at least the only one with no expiry date.' Ingrid looked Carla in the eyes. 'Maybe all these difficulties about finding Bobbs are merely a sign that I should stop selling those unnatural tablets.'

'Don't be silly.' Carla couldn't stop herself. 'It's a misguided, extravagant notion that all women love their children. What about all the unwanted children that mothers had to have during the war? That was surely more duty than love.'

Ingrid looked at her with huge eyes and Carla was afraid she might've gone too far. It was never a good idea to give clients advice: that was the second most important lesson, right after checking for solvency and getting payment in advance. Lesson number three was never to fall in love with a client, and number four was to never take on a case for a relative.

Ingrid shrugged, took out a cigarette from the elephant box and lit up. She obviously didn't want to leave just yet. 'You're really good, maybe you should take over my job.' She inhaled deeply. 'If I marry Jack...'

'Would you follow him to the US?' Carla had never heard of a GI choosing to remain in Germany for the sake of a Fräulein. She remembered that Ingrid would have preferred to be called Niki, after the artist she so admired. What might she expect in the United States? Did she think she could be the Niki there that she could only be in secret here?

'Of course, it must be heaven on earth.'

'Do you speak English?'

Ingrid put out her cigarette, only half-smoked and smiled wryly. 'Since the day I met Jack, I've been practising an hour a day.' She snapped her fingers, hummed and then began to sing quietly:

Tonight, you're mine completely...

Carla shuffled awkwardly in her chair. 'You have real talent,' she finally said, trying not to stand up to push Ingrid out.

'The Shirelles,' said Ingrid. 'Surely a country that produces such great music can't be too bad, right?'

Carla thought of the country that produced Handel, Beethoven and Wagner and bit her tongue.

'So what does his name mean then?' asked Ingrid.

'Probably that he's crazy about motorbikes and a member of a Bobber Club. What happens after we find him? Where do you want to meet him?'

'Here of course!' That sounded very firm. 'I'll pay you for the disruption, of course.'

'I could recommend a lovely café.'

'No, I'd rather have it here.'

'But why?'

Ingrid took another cigarette but didn't light it this time. 'If I was wrong and he lied to me, then I don't need to suffer through an endless coffee date, force myself to eat cake and make polite small talk. If it's indeed what I hope it might be, then we can of course go off together to a nicer place afterwards.' She lifted her shoulders, as if trying to convince herself.

'Fine, then we'll arrange an appointment here at the agency. I'm sure it'll be very soon indeed.'

'Tell him to come here earlier than I do.' Ingrid stood up reluctantly, 'You prepare him and I'll come a quarter of an hour later, shall we do that?'

'Fine. But now I have to meet an important army contact. I'll tell you as soon as I have news.'

31

The Piroschka restaurant was situated in an insalubrious part of town, where Carla felt so uncomfortable after dark that she picked up the pace. It had started raining and of course she'd forgotten her umbrella at home.

So she was all the more surprised to see Wallie waiting for her outside the venue. She lobbed her umbrella towards Carla, but the water from it hit the pavement with such zest that her legs got splashed.

'We don't have to go inside,' said Wallie instead of a greeting.

'Why not?'

'The fiddler is taking a break soon and will get something to eat in the kitchen.'

'Will we be allowed in the kitchen?'

'Nope, but Laszlo takes his food to his room. Nobody knows why he prefers to eat there. The kitchen porter said she'd rather sleep on a park bench then go into his miserable hidey-hole in the coal cellar.'

'Let's go in anyway, my shoes are completely soaked. And it smells wonderfully of roast and stuffed peppers.'

'I'm not hungry, I'll wait here for you.'

Strange, her half-sister was not one for skipping meals usually. She was constantly stuffing herself, like a bear getting ready for hibernation. 'I don't want to go in on my own.'

'There he is!' Wallie pointed towards a narrow staircase,

where a broad-shouldered, not very tall man was descending, carefully balancing a small tray in front of him. As they stepped up towards him, he turned. Even in the dim streetlight, Carla could see at once how attractive Lazlo was. High cheekbones, big dark eyes and sensual lips worthy of a girl. But he didn't want to speak to them, no matter how much Wallie flirted with him. His German had no trace of an accent, but he used rather old-fashioned expressions such as 'most honoured ladies' and 'would you please accept my apologies for not being able to respond to your request'.

'How much would a conversation with you cost then?' asked Carla quickly, just as he was about to close the door in their faces.

'For this immeasurable pleasure, I think fifty marks might be appropriate,' he replied instantly.

'Twenty!' said Wallie before Carla could recover her voice.

They finally agreed upon thirty-five marks and Laszlo invited them into his 'home ground' only after they paid up. It was dry and warm but with a musty smell. The crooked walls were grey with coal dust and the barred shaft-like window offered little ventilation. A single lightbulb was suspended from the ceiling, barely illuminating the spartan room. A cupboard, a chair, a bed. On the narrow metal bed was a beautifully embroidered flowery bedspread, glowing even in the dim light. He invited them to sit down on it. When Carla showed some concern, he explained that this kind of embroidery from his home region of Szentistván was very resilient. His esteemed grandmother, a doyenne of Matyo embroidery, had made it over sixty years ago for her bridal chamber.

He sat down on the only chair, balanced the tray on his knees and began to eat slowly, with visible pleasure, while telling them the legends associated with this art of embroidery, as if they were his guests. Carla didn't want to be rude and interrupt him.

'The devil stole a bridegroom from his bride in the depths of winter. The desperate bride begged the devil to release him...'

Wallie tried to interrupt at this point, but Carla gave her a prod to stop her. The man wanted to enjoy his moment of fame, and if they really wanted to get something out of him, it would be wiser to be patient. Besides, Carla was curious to hear the story.

'The devil ridiculed the bride but promised her that if she'd bring him an apron full of flowers, she'd get her groom back. But it was midwinter, hard to fulfil that request. The clever bride did not give up, so she embroidered an apron full of flowers. The devil was irate but had to keep his word and return the man.' That's why this type of embroidery was considered a good protection against the devil in Laszlo's home country.

Lazlo laughed cynically. 'But my most honoured ladies, even if the whole of Hungary had wrapped itself up in this embroidery in 1956, the Russian tanks would nevertheless have shredded it. Who knows if we'll ever be able to ban the red devil from there? Forgive me, I forget myself. You're obviously not here to hear my life story!'

Carla explained what they were interested in.

Laszlo put the last bite of stuffed pepper in his mouth, mopped the plate clean with a hunk of bread, wiped his mouth with an embroidered napkin and nodded thoughtfully.

'I'm delighted to be of service because I do indeed remember it clearly. That evening it was at first quite noisy, which is quite common with the hockey boys, but then there was even more commotion because of the Hochbrück boy's injury. Little Gregor is a funny, precocious little creature, who likes to play pranks. Sometimes quite dangerous ones. I struggled with my conscience but finally considered it my duty to share my concerns with his father.'

He paused, to make sure that they were following him. Carla looked at him with interest and he continued. 'Mr

Hochbrück merely smiled and said that a gypsy should be happy that he wasn't being treated as a cockroach, that he gets to do the weeding.'

Wallie mumbled, 'I think the killer of Alexander Hochbrück more than deserves his Order of Merit.'

'But first we have to clear Alma,' Carla whispered back and focused once more on what Laszlo was saying.

'I was tempted to stop working for the Hochbrücks, but there are many like them. Mrs Hochbrück was well suited to her husband, both of them were, if I might use that expression, begging your pardon, honourable ladies, highly condescending. Considered themselves to be far superior and yet were the least civilised people in the neighbourhood. She'd observe me working from the window, without ever talking to me or even waving. She'd leave instructions and money on the table in the garden and even when it was boiling outside, she never offered me a glass of water.' He shrugged. 'But I need to send money to my mother and sister in Pest, and I'm saving to be able to afford something better than here.' He waved at the barred window.

'Did you notice anything else that day?' asked Wallie.

'Yes, a little later. I'd just finished with the apple trees in the Meyerbrincks' garden. They're such friendly people, the Hochbrücks' neighbours, so much more respectful. They have a rare autumn russet variety, which bore a great amount of fruit this summer. Although the harvest this year seems to be far worse than the record harvest of last year, even in my home country. In Frankfurt they say cider is more expensive than usual – that's what my brother told me, who's there in the Sachsenhausen camp...'

Wallie sighed impatiently. They weren't here to discuss embroidery and apple harvests, Carla was aware of that, but he had to tell the story in his own way, so she pressed Wallie's thigh as a warning, just as she was about to interrupt Laszlo.

'At around that time, Mr Hochbrück came back in his Porsche. I know it was his, it's as blue as a bellflower.' He nodded at that particular flower on the embroidered bedspread.

Carla's pulse quickened. At this point she too could have done with getting to the point more rapidly, but all she could do was stare at him encouragingly.

'I assumed that Hochbrück had come back early because he was worried about his precocious prankster, but I was wrong. He was obviously in a celebratory mood and he was not alone.'

'Who was with him, and why do you think he was celebrating?'

'The friend was waving a magnum-sized bottle of Veuve Clicquot, as if it were a trophy.'

The bottle should have been there, but it hadn't appeared in the police report.

'His friend?' asked Wallie.

'Excuse me, honourable ladies, my words may have been confusing. I meant the red-haired brother of his wife, the two look quite similar.'

Klaus! Carla felt hope surging through her veins like a drug. So Hochbrück had not been drinking on his own. Why had the police not discovered that, and why had Klaus not told them anything about it?

'Did you notice anything else?' Wallie interrupted. 'You're wonderfully observant.'

'You flatter me. That is not necessary.' He drew himself up and cleared his throat before reciting:

'If you are a man, be a man,
Guard your independence,
Don't ever sell it for
All the world's abundance.'

Well, he'd already accepted their money, Carla was about to point out.

'Did he put the car in the garage?' asked Wallie, and Carla

was grateful to her for persisting.

'Yes, as soon as the red-haired man got out of the car with the champagne bottle.'

'What happened next?'

'Nothing. He closed the door to the garage and took the outdoor staircase to his attic office. I think...' he nodded knowingly '... they wanted to be alone.'

'Did you see the two of them later on?'

'Yes, well, no, only one of them. About an hour later, when I went to the compost bin to get rid of the grass cuttings and deadheaded roses.'

He paused and Carla wasn't sure how to interpret his expression. Disgust or gloating?

'And?' prompted Wallie.

'The red-haired man was standing there with the empty bottle and was – if you will pardon me, honourable ladies, for mentioning such a matter, but there really is no other way of describing it – vomiting his guts out. He looked so sick that it would have been ignominious of me not to offer my help. So I went up to him, but when he saw me coming, he disappeared through the garden gate as if the devil were after him. He left the bottle behind and I threw it in the bin.'

Carla stood up. 'Are you prepared to repeat all that for the police?'

'Of course not.' He smiled indulgently, as if he was talking to a particularly slow child.

'Even if that might stop an innocent person from going to prison?'

He shook his head and stood up. 'Most honourable ladies...' He showed them the door.

'Wouldn't it be honourable to help two innocent children get their mother back?' Wallie tried once more.

'A dirty gypsy like me doesn't owe those fine folks anything. Excuse me, my dear ladies, but I have to go back to work now.'

32

In the bright Sunday morning light, the back yard of Klaus's apartment looked even more forlorn than when Carla had last visited on Tuesday evening. This time round there were some threadbare shirts and worn-out pillowcases dangling pitifully on a washing line above the muddy ground. The red dahlia in a tin can in the hallway lay bleeding on the windowsill.

'Are you sure it's here?' asked Wallie.

'Let's hope he's at home.' Carla pointed at the collapsed roof. 'Up there is where we have to go.'

Wallie cursed as her heels got stuck in the mud. Although they'd both agreed the previous evening after their conversation with Laszlo that they had to come and speak to Klaus, the sooner the better, Wallie seemed to have woken up in a bad mood.

Carla had cancelled her Sunday visit to the pathology lab and could barely eat any breakfast. As she mounted the stairs ahead of Wallie, she wondered how Klaus would react to the eyewitness account. Would he deny it? Laugh it off as a figment of imagination and kick them out?

She hadn't had much time to think things over last night, because there'd been several missed calls from Lulu and Bruno, who both urgently wanted to speak to her. Mother had behaved as thought it was quite an imposition to have to answer phone calls, so Carla had gone to the office to call them back. She was certain that Mother was actually just curious to know who Bruno was and what Lulu was up to.

In the office, she'd first changed the water for the little wildflower bouquet, because it was starting to smell and look a little stale. The flowers were drooping by now, but although they seemed to call out Bruno's name, she decided to call Lulu first. Her aunt told her that Wallie and her mother had lived in Bern in the 1940s and had returned to the German Democratic Republic in the 1950s – she wasn't sure exactly when. She'd found that out through Trudi, who knew somebody who lived on Tucholskystraße. Henny, one of the Shakefield Girls, had proved useful as well, because her cousin had emigrated first to Switzerland, and then the US.

'Why Switzerland? The von Tillings were not Jewish and the mother was merely a salon Communist. If she'd been a real Communist, she'd not have been allowed into Switzerland, let alone been able to send her daughter to an exclusive boarding school. Nah, she just ran away like a coward and led a good life there.'

'Don't you think any mother would rather her daughter grew up among green pastures and full-fat cheese, than with mouldy bread in coal cellars?' asked Carla.

'If it was Karl-Otto's child, then she stole her away, and made sure that he wasn't able to see her.'

He wasn't home anyway, he was a medic in a field camp, as far as Carla could remember. 'I'm sure Father would've wanted his daughter to have something to eat too.' She paused. 'Wait a second, so you do think that Wallie was indeed his daughter?'

'On the contrary, only an unnatural mother would remove a child from her father. That's why I think that Wallie's father was the director of this boarding-school. A certain Sylvester Pfyffer, what a ridiculous pretentious name! He was married and belonged to the clan of the Pfyffers of Altishofen, very Catholic, upper echelons of

Swiss society, not a chance of a divorce, and of course no bastards allowed in those circles.'

'Sounds like a bad pulp fiction novel.'

'Believe me, child, life is often more pulpy than fiction.'

'And why do you think they'd have moved from comfortable Switzerland back to the misery of post-war Berlin?'

'Cos their golden goose, Director Pfyffer, died!' Lulu snorted triumphantly. 'That's why she got your father to pay up once more. What I don't understand is why they didn't return to the western part of the country? But fear not, I'm on the case. One of my Shakefield Girls knows someone in Lucerne who knows someone in Bern. Don't you get too close to that swindler! I just know in my bones that there's something wrong with her!'

Lulu was often keen to believe what she wanted to believe. She'd once been with Fritzi to see a medium, because the dog groomer she'd had before Alberto the punctuality freak had declared at some point that he was convinced that the poodle was the reincarnation of Magda Madeleine. Carla had of course never heard of her, but Lulu explained that Magda was an actress who'd appeared around 1915 in various films as a high society matron and later, under the name Magda Mohr, she'd performed in the premiere of Arthur Schnitzler's play *La Ronde*. Lulu had obviously been delighted to be the owner of a poodle with the spirit of someone involved in such a scandalous play. Censored for immorality, the author himself withdrew the play from any theatre production, a ban that wouldn't expire until 1982.

Sadly, to Lulu's disappointment, the medium was unable to find any essence of Magda in the poodle's soul. Since then, however, her usually smart aunt had regarded her dog with slightly intimidated eyes and had changed dog groomers.

Before calling Bruno – she was not quite sure why she

kept postponing this – Carla tried calling Sally Montana. She worked in the entertainment unit of the army, responsible for all the social clubs, and could be usually found on a Saturday in the casino bar Silverwings at the officers' club at Tempelhof Airport. Two years earlier Sally'd asked Father to investigate something she didn't want the army to know about, and she'd been so pleased with the results, and the confidentiality, that the Nachtigalls could count on her. Sally was a hopeless romantic and loved motorbikes. She dreamt of being gone with the wind, on a bike through the Sahara with her very own Rhett Butler. She'd been searching for the right man ever since Carla first met her, but no one dared approach her. Sally was tall and built like a tank, bursting with energy, always ready to air her opinions, and most people were too scared of her. So had Carla been at first, but during the course of the investigation she began to realise how pleasant it was to work with a woman who was not shy about openly stating what she did or didn't want. It was a relief not to have to second-guess things. Carla felt very free in her presence, so she had no problem asking Sally for a favour. Sally must know where to find Jack the Bobber-fan.

But it was the wrong time for a phone call because Sally was dealing with an emergency at the club. A couple of officers had smuggled their blonde German girlfriends past the doorkeeper, which happened often and wasn't that much of a problem, except that this time they'd been followed by the girls' German boyfriends, who were causing a ruckus at the door and threatening to beat up the doorman if they weren't allowed in. But she agreed to meet Carla the following afternoon for a slice of Berliner heaven cake at Café Schilling.

When she looked at the clock, she decided it was too late to call Bruno. He was a sub-tenant after all and would surely get into trouble if someone called him at ten o'clock at night.

'Here we are at last, heaven help us!' Wallie's loud groan brought Carla back to the present. 'Finally made it! And boy, is it disgusting up here!' Her half-sister pointed at the pigeons, who were fluttering between the damaged roof trusses. 'They're like rats, but worse. Their shit is pure poison.' She shuddered, then turned towards Klaus's door. 'Crazy to think that only half the roof got damaged. But I guess he knows what he's doing as an architect. I for one wouldn't live here. Horrible.' She knocked.

No answer.

'Maybe he's upped sticks and fled?'

Carla wondered. Would he have been able to plan an escape? 'Don't think so.'

Wallie hammered at the door, but only succeeded in scaring off a couple of pigeons, who fluttered above them and then settled down again cooing.

What if Klaus was on his bed, drunk or coming down from a dose of Pervitin? Maybe they should just go in? The lock shouldn't be a problem.

'Dammit!' said Wallie, hammering even more angrily on the door.

This time the pigeons weren't scared away, but a woman from downstairs yelled out some choice curses on the sinners who couldn't live in peace even on a Sunday morning.

While Carla wondered whether she should take out her Dietrich key again, Wallie rattled at the door. 'Oh!' she said in surprise, as it opened a bit. The door was not locked.

They called for Klaus and went in. The apartment was empty. The models that had been lying on the tables under the skylight had also disappeared.

'This bird has flown!' said Wallie, looking around inquisitively. 'In spite of all the old stuff, this is all clean, you can spot ancient nobility.' She pointed at the chest of drawers with the KvS monogram, which Carla had also noticed the previous time she was there.

'Well, you should know, Miss Waltraud von Tilling!' Carla couldn't resist the sarcasm.

'And you obviously don't,' Wallie grinned. 'The Tillings are the lowest ranks of nobility. Besides, Mushka couldn't care less about all that, she was of the opinion that all people are created equal.'

'Created equal...' Carla repeated. This was not the way Wallie usually spoke.

'Exactly. That's how she raised me and that's why my second name is Rozalia. Waltraud Rozalia von Tilling. Mum worshipped Rosa Luxemburg.' Wallie gave herself a little shake, then stood with her legs spread wide and recited with practised ease: 'This is our greatest misfortune, and these are our true enemies: the exploitation of the people by capitalists and aristocrats, and a government policy that is completely in the service of capitalists and aristocrats and only orders people to pay taxes, do their military service and keep their mouths shut!'

'And how did you get on with such views in Switzerland?'

'It's a republic with direct democracy.'

'And quite a bit of Nazi gold in their vaults.'

'Let's just agree that there's no such thing as the perfect state.'

'I couldn't care less about a perfect state. What would be perfect for me would be to rehabilitate Alma and have her released.' Carla took one last look around Klaus's apartment. 'And for that we need to find Klaus. Question is: where?'

'Given that he seems to be in a permanent state of stupor, I'd bet the nearest bar!'

'This area's full of bars.' Carla would rather dissect corpses than go on a pub crawl. She normally liked talking to people, but to go into a smoke-filled bar full of men and start asking questions seemed to her to be the waiting room to hell. Naturally, Wallie was more familiar with that environment because of her work at the Eden.

'If we divide the pubs between us, it'll be quicker,' said Wallie.

'We should both talk to him, so we can both be witnesses to what he says,' argued Carla.

'You're probably right. Fine, let's do it.'

They left the apartment and went down the stairs amidst the aroma of Sunday roasts, wet toilet paper and coffee substitute. The only living creature they met along the way was a skinny grey cat, who followed them for two floors meowing with hunger.

33

After two hours of fruitless trawling through all the bars in the area, Wallie decided to put a stop to it. 'Not a step further! My feet are raw mince.'

She leant against an old linden tree which had been planted outside the Green Corner pub. What a waste of time! Her sister had done the whole 'Miss Touch-me-not' routine and so it had been left up to her to do that delicate balance between smiling, asking questions, flirting, drinking and turning down advances. All under the ironic gaze of Carla, who'd been watching her as if she were a performing ape.

Wallie put her weight on one leg, lifted the other and took off her shoe. She grimaced when she saw the caked mud on it, then shrugged and nestled it in her armpit, while massaging her foot. She gave a sigh of relief.

'You planning to take off your undies as well?' Carla shook her head disapprovingly.

'Fine one to talk you are! With such rude words, no less!' Wallie had to fight the impulse to throw the shoe at Carla, but she put it back on. 'A miracle that you're not talking about my private parts!'

Carla's face remained unchanged. The woman had no sense of humour.

'We can't give up now,' said Carla, with a bitter undertone, as if Wallie was too frivolous.

'Who said anything about giving up? We've been through

all the pubs in the area, thanks to my efforts. He's got no girlfriend, otherwise the students would've been gossiping about it. He might be at the university preparing his courses for next week. Hochbrück's death must have mucked up their timetable.'

'The university, that's a great idea!' Carla's face lit up. 'That's where we should go.'

'But first we gotta leave someone on guard here, to tell us in case he comes back home.'

'We can't afford that.'

'Ask your mate Bruno.' Wallie couldn't resist adding, 'I'm sure he'll do it for free for you.'

Carla's cheeks flamed bright red, as if Wallie had slapped her. 'Why on earth are you bringing him up?'

'He offered to help us, he likes driving you around, brings you flowers, and we have him to thank for a big clue about the mysterious Jackov.' She wouldn't mind seeing him again either, but that was beside the point.

'Ah, Katrin!' Carla hit her forehead with the palm of her hand. 'I promised to take her and her brothers out for ice cream this afternoon. They were the ones who alerted me to the Bobber thing.'

'Sounds good. I love ice cream.'

'But I've also got an appointment with Sally in Café Schilling.'

'No idea who Sally is, but it doesn't take long to have an ice cream, they can get a cone and we can ask Katrin if she wouldn't mind keeping watch here for the rest of the day.'

'I'm sure she'd love that, but don't you think it's irresponsible?'

'Why? Everyone's a winner here: Katrin learns something about being a detective and doesn't waste her time jumping elastics. It doesn't cost us anything, she's reliable. You meet Sally and we talk to Stratmann.'

'But the neighbourhood here is so dodgy.'

'Katrin will be fine, she could bring her brothers with

her. But if you're really against it, and don't want to ask Bruno, then one of us has to stay here and wait.'

Carla nodded. 'Yes, you stay here, I have to go to the ice cream parlour and café.'

'Not at all, let's draw straws. Or rather Jan Ken Pon.'

'What?'

'Rock, paper, scissors!' Wallie showed the gesture for each as she said the words.

'That's childish!'

'Forget it then!' Wallie walked away. Hard to believe they could be related.

'Fine then,' Carla gave in. 'Let's do it, but without the well.'

Dad had also hated the well, which he claimed destroyed the balance. With rock, paper, scissors you had a chance to win or to lose, but with the well, there were two chances to win, which he felt was unfair. He was always a great one for talking about what was fair and decent.

'Spoilsport,' said Wallie, although she reckoned she'd win even without a well.

She always won in this game – this had nothing to do with training, but with psychology. Most men started with rock. With women it was less homogenous, but very few started with scissors. So paper was a good choice in any case. It was good to think things through rather than leave them to random fate.

Wallie counted to three and beat Carla, who started with a rock. Then Carla chose paper and Wallie won again with scissors. Then Carla insisted on a third round, which Wallie won again with paper.

'Fine, I'll stay here, but you have to free me up in two hours, so I can go and meet Sally. She thinks it's rude to be late and never waits. Please ring at Katrin's door and tell her I haven't forgotten but won't be able to invite her and the Abominables out for ice cream until this evening.'

Wallie nodded and headed off to the nearest U-Bahn

station. Even if Carla was useless at games of chance and small talk in pubs, it wasn't wise to underestimate her. After all, she'd found out about Switzerland. However, she seemed to think that she and Mum had led an easy life there, with afternoon tea, cucumber sandwiches and whatnot. How absurd! Life with Mamushka had been exciting and often completely crazy and tiring. Mushka had a talent for transforming herself into the kind of woman that best suited her current lover: for Karl-Otto she was Luischen, for Alain she was Lisette, for Miranda she became Lisi, and for others she was simply L. Shortly before her death, she was even Luna for her doctor. That possibly suited her best. Not just because she was so pale towards the end, but because she'd circled all her life around men like a moon around a planet. She allowed herself to be absorbed into their orbit, adapting completely to their requirements, being exactly the person they wanted her to be. Regardless of what that planet might turn out to be. She was always delighted to do this, never in any doubt about her feelings, full of joy and love. Until that particular planet lost its shine, and that would spell the end of her satellite status. Her mother hated routine, everyday life, habit. After two years at most the fun was over and Mushka was keen to go back into space and find a new planet to orbit around. The only two constants in her life were her daughter and photography.

Wallie had decided long ago that she'd never be the satellite, but the sun around whom others would circle. Klaus had clearly been circling in orbit around Hochbrück. As she descended the stairs to the underground station, her eyes fell on the clock hanging on the dirty yellow tiled wall.

Just then she realised that she and Carla had made a major miscalculation. What if Klaus had arrived home during those two hours when they'd been searching for him through the pubs? Then Carla would be standing there for nothing.

Wallie hastened back. She wasn't surprised to find her

sister was no longer waiting outside. Maybe she'd had the same idea, or maybe Klaus had just appeared. She rushed through the muddy courtyard, giving up worrying about her ruined shoes. No Carla. She dragged herself up the stairs again and was completely breathless by the time she reached the fifth floor. Just as she got there, she saw her sister coming out of Klaus's apartment.

'What are you doing here?' asked Carla.

'I see we had the same idea.'

'Seems like it. But he's not inside.'

'What if he ran away to West Germany?' asked Wallie as they went back down the stairs.

'Or to the East?'

'Nonsense. He'd be interned and checked out.' Wallie nearly groaned out loud. Her sister really didn't know anything about life on the other side.

'Why, you think they'll send him back?'

'What do you reckon? They don't want any criminals over there.'

'You think East and West Berlin are still swapping information? When they won't even allow day tickets for crossing the border?' Carla sniggered, which drove Wallie wild. 'I bet they're happy to welcome anyone willing to stay in the East.'

'Druggie criminals are not welcome in any country in the world.'

'Nonsense, if they've got money, they're welcome anywhere.'

'Typical capitalist thinking.'

'And you showed up here because you find everything in the West so despicable?'

Wallie stopped in front of a door on the second floor and decided to change the subject. 'Hmm, smells of Thuringian marinated beef with dumplings. I'm starving.'

'Switzerland is not famous for being indifferent to the power of money either!'

Wallie's shoulders twitched. No change of subject, then. She continued downstairs past Carla.

'Why did your mother take you to Switzerland anyway?' Carla called after her.

Wallie stopped and turned slowly around. How much should she tell her?

'Did my father even know about you? And if he did, why would she go away with a baby? Did she ever love...' Carla stopped suddenly mid-sentence.

Wallie turned round and saw Klaus coming up the stairs, in a very sorry state. He looked as if he'd slept in his clothes, and the dark shadows under his eyes were visible even from a distance.

'Nelly? What are you doing here?' he said when he saw her.

'We wanted to speak to you.' Wallie reached her hand out to include Carla.

'Nelly, what might you want from me on a holy Sunday?' He seemed to be more awake now, examining her more closely. 'Architecture tutoring?'

'It has to do with your professor.'

Klaus took a step back.

'I didn't expect you to be such a vulture.'

Wallie went up to him and put a hand on his arm. 'You're mistaken. I know that his death is very painful for you. I remember how warmly you spoke of him at the canteen. We just have to ask a couple of questions...'

'Have to ask? I've already spoken to the police, and you're not the police, are you, Nelly?' He extracted his arm from Wallie's hand and continued up the stairs.

'We want to protect Alexander's reputation.' Wallie hoped that might do the trick.

Klaus stopped and looked at them reluctantly. 'His reputation?'

'I'm afraid he's in danger of being accused of something.' Carla caught on.

Klaus's eyes narrowed; he seemed to be thinking hard. 'I bet my sister's behind this. Did Alma send you?'

'No,' lied Wallie. 'But as his best friend, I'm sure you want to help. It appears no one knew him better than you.'

'What do they want to accuse him of?'

'We shouldn't be discussing this on the staircase,' intervened Carla.

Klaus straightened his shoulders and invited them up the stairs. Five minutes later they were sitting in the two baroque chairs in his apartment, while he paced up and down the room, which drove Wallie mad. Withdrawal symptoms, she suspected.

'What exactly are they accusing him of?' he asked, and without waiting for a reply, he continued, 'In any case, it must come from that witch who happens to be my sister. She can't bear it when other people are happy.'

'What makes you think that?' Carla asked. Wallie poked her in the ribs with her elbow. No need to use the formal 'you', Klaus and she had long ago switched to the informal one.

'Carla means why are you so sure your sister wants to hurt him?'

'Because she's so unsatisfied with her life. Although she had the best husband you could hope for. He loved her and the children above all, he was faithful to her. Never even looked at another woman. I really never saw a man so little given to flirting when he has the opportunity.' He corrected himself with a sigh, 'Had, I mean.'

'So why do you think she was so unsatisfied?' asked Carla, before Wallie could step in.

'Maybe because according to our parents she'd thrown herself away and married beneath her. She had a good dowry and was not exactly bad-looking.' He paused and pushed a chestnut curl behind his ear. 'The von Stellmarks are all rather good-looking.'

Wallie nodded. 'And?'

'I never completely understood my sister, but when she brought Alexander round, I realised she was smarter than I thought. He's had such a good career, who cared that he doesn't come from a good family? His father was a shoemaker and his mother worked as a maid. I think Alma really loved him to start with. Then he suddenly wasn't good enough for her anymore. She wanted to send the children to boarding school, so that they could get to meet the right people. She started producing that silly art stuff. And Alexander was so patient with her, I miss him so!' He fell back on the iron bed, which squeaked in protest.

'What happened the day he died?' asked Carla.

He sat up again with a sudden jolt. 'Why? What has that got to do with what Alma wants to accuse him of?'

The question had come too quickly, too out of nowhere. They clearly had to give him more time, make him feel safe. 'Yes...' Wallie began, but Carla jumped in again: 'There's a rumour that he stole your ideas?'

How on earth had she come up with that? Because he destroyed the models while under the influence?

'Rubbish!' But Klaus sounded all of a sudden less convincing than when he'd spoken about Hochbrück's fidelity.

'You can tell us everything, get it off your chest.' Carla's voice was not just gentle, but had almost a hypnotic quality. 'Most people feel better afterwards.'

Klaus took one of the water bottles standing near his bedside and emptied it greedily, without offering them any. Carla glanced at Wallie and nodded – they seemed to be in agreement for once.

'Who'll be your conservator now?' asked Wallie.

He threw the empty bottle behind him on the bed and shrugged. 'I owe that to Alma too, she can rot in jail for all I care.'

'And what will happen to Mathilda and Gregor?' asked Carla.

'How should I know? But do you think that a man who's under conservatorship will be allowed to be a guardian to children? Besides, the two of them take after their mother, arrogant brats who think they're better than everyone else. Mathilda is the delicate princess and Gregor is full of mischief, nothing that a little thrashing every now and then wouldn't resolve.'

Klaus was repeatedly crushing the woollen blanket on his bed and then straightening it as he was talking, without looking at it. He was obviously upset, now might be a good time to fire their shots.

'Alexander tricked you,' said Wallie, looking at Carla invitingly.

'Alexander used you,' Carla chimed in.

'Alexander used everyone to get ahead. But he turned you into a figure of fun!' Wallie continued.

'I wouldn't say that...' Carla contradicted her, which puzzled Wallie. 'Not a figure of fun, you were nothing to him. Merely someone he could easily manipulate.'

'He really enjoyed having power over other people,' said Wallie, while Klaus shrank back as if he was being dealt blows.

'But he'll get the Order of Merit.' This seemed to cheer him up a little.

'So obviously he must be one of the good guys.' Wallie could barely contain her disdain for this idiot. 'Obviously, just like those others who got one: Peron, Vargas, Battista or Trujillo Molina. Or even Nazis like Karl Ritter von Halt or race expert Hans Globke. The Federal Republic is very open to giving Order of Merits to everyone.'

Carla gave her a curious look, obviously surprised.

'You seem to know your medals,' she muttered in such a low voice that Wallie wasn't sure if she'd heard her correctly. But her sister turned towards Klaus once more.

'You were in love with him,' she said gently. Ah, so she was pretending to be so understanding, to break down his guard.

'I'm not a homo,' Klaus protested sotto voce.

'Of course not,' Carla hastened to agree with him. 'It was a real friendship between men, a platonic love, a real camaraderie, like Goethe and Schiller, Hegel and Hölderlin, like...' Carla looked at Wallie for help.

'Stan Laurel and Oliver Hardy.'

Carla's eyebrows shot up, so Wallie hastened to add, 'Kandinsky and Klee, Marx and Engels, Winnetou and Old Shatterhand.'

'Exactly.' Klaus seemed relieved.

'Exactly, a rare, noble connection,' said Wallie and then fired her deadly arrow. 'A friendship between equals, full of respect, in which one takes over conservatorship for the other and then tricks the drug addict under his tutelage out of his land, so as to build on it with ideas he's stolen from him.'

'That's not what happened.'

'No?' Wallie looked at Klaus's brimming eyes and added, 'Maybe it wasn't like that to start off with, but at some point it got out of hand.'

'You didn't notice, because you loved him,' said Carla.

Klaus began sobbing with a flurry of tears. He was dying to let it all out, perhaps he was looking for absolution. In the end, that was all that anyone wanted: forgiveness. And to be loved. Which made everyone predictable. Wallie took out the notebook she'd brought from the office and started jotting down Klaus's confession in shorthand.

Carla seemed pleased she was doing that but tried to hide it with her hands on her lap, gesturing with her head towards Klaus. She was right, it was best if he wasn't aware of her note-taking. She hid the notebook behind her big handbag.

He told them that their friendship had blossomed after Alexander got married to Alma. Alexander had encouraged him to draw out even his craziest architectural ideas and got him a position as his assistant at the university. He'd offered him a place on his design team, so that Klaus could use Alexander's connections. Then, when Klaus had relapsed, and Alma wanted to get him hospitalised, Alexander offered to become his conservator if he underwent treatment. What a stroke of luck, he'd thought then, there was no better person in the world than his fatherly friend. Then they won another competition, in which Klaus alone had been responsible for the design. They went out to celebrate and Alexander had made sure that there was enough alcohol and Pervitin to tempt him. Klaus relapsed and started accumulating debts. Alexander generously offered to buy land off him, they even joked that they were keeping things in the family. Then they took part in the competition for the design for Breitscheid Square and got a bonus. On the day that Alexander died, they celebrated extensively over a lengthy lunch. They wanted to continue celebrating with a giant champagne bottle and went up to Alexander's studio. While Alexander was bringing out the glasses, Klaus looked at the title page credits for the drawings that had been sent in and discovered he'd only been put down as an assistant, although they'd discussed that he should be made equal partner. It really hurt him, but he thought there must be a logical explanation and so he asked Alexander about it.

Klaus stopped, exhausted, and reached for another bottle of water.

Wallie didn't dare to look at Carla or make any sound, for fear he might not continue.

'I asked him why my name was not down as a partner on the submission and he just laughed, as if I'd made a stupid joke. When I didn't laugh with him, he asked me if I'd lost my senses? Did I seriously expect him to put down the name of a drug-addled, impotent little faggot on his prize-winning plans?'

Wallie could barely write fast enough and was pleased when he took a deep breath. She looked up at Carla, who was very pale and muttering sympathetically, 'That must have been so hurtful...'

Klaus laughed bitterly. 'He pulled the rug from under my feet. It was as if a switch went on in my head and I wanted to hit him. Beat the laughter out of him. At first Alexander continued laughing. He was so much stronger than me. He wanted to throw me out, but I picked up the champagne bottle and hit him with that. He ran to the iron staircase leading down to the living room. I ran after him, but just as I wanted to hit him over the head, Alexander slipped and fell down the stairs. His head was bleeding and he lay there, as if dead.' Klaus rubbed his red eyes, trying to wipe away the unbearable images. 'It felt like war all over again, as if I'd shot him. It all got blurry, I panicked. I was drunk, full of drugs, and I didn't know what to do.'

'Naturally, it could have happened to anyone,' said Carla, and he looked at her gratefully.

So it really was an accident, thought Wallie. But he hadn't stopped to check if Alexander was still alive, nor had he called the emergency services. Carla was right. Alma was innocent. Mathilda was even more innocent.

'What happened next?' asked Carla.

'I washed up the glasses in a trance, then I heard the door opening and suddenly my nerves were shot to pieces. I just wanted out of there. I could not have borne the sight of Alma finding his body. I took the bottle and ran down the outer staircase to the garden. It's all so fuzzy after that, I can't really remember how I got home.'

He covered his face with his hands, rocked back onto the bed, fell to one side, lifted up his knees and sobbed bitterly. Carla stood up, sat next to him on the bed and held his hand. He clung to her like a drowning man to a lifeboat. Carla seemed just about ready to burst into tears herself.

How touching, how pointless. Wallie packed up her notebook. Self-pity was entirely uncalled for here, as was Carla's empathy. Wallie knew that Carla would think she was heartless, but whom was this helping?

Carla was telling Klaus he was not alone in feeling like this, but Wallie knew it *was* his fault for being an addict, it had been his choice to continue taking drugs. The war was over. Many had experienced far worse things. Yes, it was hard, but when was anything ever easy? Why show so much empathy when Clara knew just as well as she did, that they would have to use what he just confessed in order to free Alma, for the children's sake?

Wallie stood up. She needed some fresh air.

'You have to let it all out,' Carla was whispering to Klaus. 'You'll feel so much better.'

'I was such a coward,' Klaus was mumbling, 'I should've gone up to him, taken him to hospital, done mouth-to-mouth...'

Pitiful. Of course he'd only thought of himself in such a situation, that's what everyone did, and anyone who claimed otherwise was lying. Of course, some had a thin layer of something, which Wallie called humanity and decency on a good day, but on bad days thought was only fear of punishment.

'You can't change what happened, but you can prove yourself honourable from now on,' said Carla.

Klaus scoffed in disbelief.

'You can save what was most important for Alexander.'

Impossible, thought Wallie cynically. Alexander's giant ego was dead. But she had to admit that Carla was playing a good game.

'The Breitscheid Place design?' Klaus seemed to perk up.

'No, his children.'

'I don't have any connection to them.'

'But it would be a last act of love for him. Would Alexander want them to grow up in an orphanage?'

'No,' he admitted, looking from one to the other. 'How can I do that?'

'We'll go to the police and you tell them that it was an

accident,' said Wallie.

'Do you believe me?'

'Of course!' said Wallie immediately, then realised that Carla had answered at the same time as she did.

'I'll think about it.'

Of course he would, and he'd consult no doubt with his dear friends alcohol and Pervitin.

'I want to be alone now.' Klaus pointed at the door. 'Ask me again tomorrow, after I've had a think about it.'

They left the apartment in silence. In the hallway, Carla checked the time on her watch and blanched. 'Damn!' She began to run so fast down the stairs that Wallie could barely keep up.

'We have to talk about Klaus,' she called after Carla, frightening a mustard-coloured cat. 'What we do with his confession.'

Without turning round, Carla replied, 'Yes, we will, best you type it all up, if you know how to type.'

She could type super-fast actually, but she had no intention of being Carla's secretary.

'We'll talk later,' Carla rushed, 'go and have ice cream with the kids. I have to see Sally, she hates waiting.'

When Wallie finally reached the bottom of the stairs, she could see her sister racing down Köslinerstraße. Cursing inwardly, she hurried after her.

'Wait a second! Why should I type it out?'

Carla, who was looking for a taxi, seemed surprised at her question. 'Obviously, because we're going to take it to him tomorrow and get him to sign it.'

A taxi stopped on the other side of the road and turned to pick up Carla. Her sister got into it and drove off without another word. Well, she was ready to bet that Klaus would never sign such a thing.

34

When Carla got out of the taxi in front of Café Schilling on the Ku'damm, she spotted Sally leaving the place and heading north. She ran to her and apologised profusely.

'I can't bear being set up!' said Sally.

Stood up, Carla was about to interject, but bit her tongue and praised Sally instead for her progress in learning German. She explained her delay, saying that something unexpected had come up in the course of one of her investigations and reminded Sally that she too had benefited from that once upon a time. Sally finally relented and agreed to at least listen to Carla's questions over a slice of heaven cake. They'd sit inside, of course, not on the terrace. Sally hated insects even more than she hated Communists.

Once Sally had got a slice of cake and a cup of coffee inside her, she was prepared to listen. Of course, there were several motorbike clubs for the soldiers, she didn't belong to any herself, because although women were supposedly equal members, in practice they weren't viewed kindly. However, Sally had an idea how to find this Bobbs.

In the Turner Barracks in Grunewald, where the armoured unit were housed, there was a man who might be able to help Carla. She'd put her in touch with Jackov.

Carla's pulse quickened. 'Did you just say Jacob or did I hear correctly – Jackov?' she insisted. Maybe Sally had spoken unclearly – after all, every third American seemed to be called Jim or Jack.

'Yes, Jackov. Every Bobber knows him. That's what they call the best mechanic in the army. The man you call when you've got problems with your equipment, when no one else can help you, when you need a spare part that can't be ordered anywhere. He can do anything and get hold of anything, it's a near miracle. Only recently he built a replacement valve cover gasket for Major Bixby that was so clever, he should've had it patented.'

'Is Jackov a Russian name?'

Sally laughed out loud. 'Not at all! You're way off the mark! No, it's a nickname, a sign of respect, it comes from Jack of all trades.'

Carla stared at her puzzled. Her English wasn't bad, but she had no idea what this might mean.

'That's what you call an all-rounder,' Sally explained. 'He's the kind of genius who only has to look at a bike and figure out which screw is loose.'

'So you know him personally?'

Sally shook her head. 'Not yet, but if one of my three machines were to start making odd noises, he'd be the first person I'd consult.'

'What else do you know about him?'

'As far as I know, he's never deceived anyone, even though he could easily do so. Seems to be one of the good guys.'

'Do you know any others in the army who might be called Bobbs or Jackov?'

'No, there aren't that many who have such a gift! It's really something special.'

It must be the right guy – the burn mark on his wrist might be the result of a repair he'd done.

'Do you happen to know where Jackov is from?'

'I happen to know exactly where he's from.' Sally picked up her coffee cup and pretended to be surprised. 'Oh, no, it's empty!'

'Don't keep me hanging...'

Sally set the cup down very deliberately.

'OK, order anything you like. Are you playing games with me?'

'Champagne!' Sally grinned and, when Carla nodded, she called the waitress. Carla ordered a Piccolo Henkell Dry, but Sally frowned in disapproval. She wasn't going to drink on her own! So Carla had to act delighted and order a regular-sized bottle, despite the cost.

Sally seemed satisfied and finally put Carla out of her misery. 'He's from Atlanta, Georgia.'

Atlanta! Bullseye. Just as Ingrid had remembered. No wonder Sally could remember it so clearly, because Atlanta was the city of Scarlett O'Hara, her favourite heroine. Sally was convinced that if Scarlett were living in the present day, she'd be riding her bike through the Sahara Desert, leaving a trail of broken hearts behind her.

'Does Jackov look like Rhett Butler?' asked Carla. This must be the right Bobbs, everything seemed to fit.

'I've never met him, unfortunately, he doesn't seem to be a club-goer. But I don't think he's bad-looking or tiny, otherwise I'd have heard jokes of the type "Jackyshortov" or "Shrimpov" or "Nastyjackov"!' Sally seemed to be on a roll.

Carla interrupted her. 'Do you know his real name?'

'Jack Johnson.'

'You're joking!' Johnson must be as common as Meier or Schmidt in Germany. Even if Ingrid had known his full name, Carla would still have had trouble identifying him. Thank goodness she'd managed to find him with the Bobbs clue. It would be surprising if this Johnson turned out not to be Ingrid's GI, everything was pointing towards it.

The waitress came and opened the champagne bottle with a flourish, which Carla found embarrassing, while Sally was in the mood for the cork to hit the ceiling. They toasted and Sally poured half the glass down her throat, licking her lips, while Carla barely took a sip. She had to keep a clear head.

'Has Johnson got a family?'

'Not that I know of.'

'Could you arrange an appointment for him to come to my office, and pretend that you want to meet him there?'

'What's it all in aid of?' Sally poured out another glass and leaned back. 'I can't afford to upset such a leading light, especially since I might need him in future. And the other guys would soon hear about that.'

'You might be saving his life. He told my client that they were made for each other.'

Sally sighed, either because she was overcome with romantic feelings or because she was getting impatient, Carla couldn't quite tell.

'Made for each other,' she repeated, looking Sally firmly in the eyes. 'And my client is no sentimental fool, she's an intelligent working woman like you, who's got a grip on her life.'

Sally shrugged and gave a strange smile. Carla couldn't quite figure out what it meant, unless it was the champagne.

'Is there something wrong with him?'

'If Jackov said that to her, I'm sure he meant it. Especially given what I heard about him.' Sally looked thoughtfully out the window. 'We women turn into fools when it comes to men.'

'What are you hinting at? He says that to everyone, that's his patter?'

'No, he's not that kind of guy.' Sally turned to her and replied honestly, without hesitation.

'Are there any rumours?' asked Carla carefully. 'That he might not be interested in women?'

'No swishy men in the US army!' Sally shook her head indignantly.

Carla swallowed down a retort. In Sally's world, only men and women could kiss, and only if they happened to be of the same race. They'd had a fight about this during the previous case, which had escalated badly, and Father had had to intervene.

'If you could arrange a meeting, I'd be eternally grateful!' she said quickly, to cover her faux pas.

'Fine, good detective work is expensive. And you never know when I might need you again.'

'And you'd be helping a great love affair along.' Carla pretended to be Cupid shooting an arrow.

'But what if it all goes wrong?' Sally emptied her glass in one go, with a shudder, and poured herself another one.

'Impossible. If they're both mistaken, they're free to fall in love with someone else, and if they really are made for each other, then you were their fairy godmother.'

'Happy ending.'

'Exactly!'

'Speaking of happy, I think I might need another slice of cake while I mull it over.'

Carla hastily ordered whatever Sally wanted.

An hour later, Sally was full and the champagne bottle was empty. Carla was mildly annoyed, but they did have a game plan. Sally would call Jack Johnson and ask for his help, letting drop that he might be doing one of his commanders a favour. But for that, he had to come to Carla's office. Sally at first insisted that she should witness the meeting from a neighbouring room. Clearly she was expecting some kind of kick out of it, and seemed mightily amused. Carla couldn't figure out exactly what the deal was, but managed to talk her out of it, after mustering all her persuasive skills and ordering two glasses of Schnapps. They agreed to make the appointment for the coming Wednesday, at 5 p.m. Sally thought that at that time there was a film viewing at the Turner Barracks. *The Magnificent Seven*. Maybe Jackov already knew that film and wouldn't mind giving it a miss. Sally would give him an exit permit for two hours. Of course, Carla had to promise to give a blow-by-blow account of the love story over dinner at Ritchies.

'Want to bet on it?' asked Sally as she got up to leave.

'Bet on what?'

'That the two get together and get married.'

'That's unethical.'

'Coward!' Sally held out her hand to shake on it, but Carla refused. Her clients were not racehorses to bet on.

'You Germans are funny! Our little joke won't harm anyone.'

Wallie would almost certainly have agreed to a bet, and so would Lulu. The latter would probably have betted on it all going wrong. Love was nothing but a temporary hormonal rush according to her aunt, entirely unsuitable for lasting attachments.

'Not all Germans are like that, you simply picked the wrong one,' retorted Carla – and her boring answer made even her cringe.

After they parted, Carla stopped to wonder why it was so hard for her to be more open. She'd never been easy-going, not even before Mother's accident. Sometimes she felt like a bird in a cage. Nothing was missing, she could eat, sing, see, hear and smell, but she could never fly freely. The awful thing was that no one else had built this fence around her, she was the one who had to dismantle the cage she'd created for herself. She just didn't know how. She envied Ingrid and Wallie, because it seemed to her that the two of them were free to fly anywhere.

Goodness, what a strange train of thought. It must be the drink.

She did hope that Ingrid and Jackov would get together in the end. If they did, that would make anything seem possible, maybe even for her. But she knew deep inside that Sally had withheld some crucial detail about Jack 'Bobbs' Johnson. It had to be a delicate matter, because Sally usually had no problem blurting things out. Had Johnson perhaps been wounded in the Korean War and was now impotent? Was that the reason he didn't have a family and had seemed so reserved with Ingrid?

35

The following morning, Carla slammed the phone down and glared at Wallie, who was sitting on the rattan chair in front of her and placing the giant ashtray in position. She still hadn't got rid of that monstrosity, which made her even more furious.

'This Stratmann must have got his law licence in a lottery. How else can we explain the fact that our news doesn't make him happy? We offer him Klaus's confession on a plate and he doesn't want to know.'

'He's only worried about his fee.' Wallie lit a cigarette. 'What d'you expect?'

'I expect him to call Klaus in to make a statement under oath and free Alma.' Carla stood up, smoothing out her skirt, and started pacing up and down. 'Crystal clear!'

'It's just hearsay as far as he's concerned though. He isn't sure you're tellin' him the truth. After all, he's a lawyer!' Wallie blew smoke circles so carefully, as if they were the most important things in the world.

'Yes, I know.' She stopped in front of Wallie. 'Give me a cigarette too.'

Her half-sister took a cigarette out of the elephant box and handed it to her. Carla inhaled hungrily.

'Thanks. If Alma were my legal client, I'd clutch at any straw to free her. I'd have called Grieser personally and hastened proceedings.' She exhaled slowly. 'Right, that's where we need to act. With Grieser. Let me call Lulu!'

Carla sat down and dialled her aunt's number.

'Wouldn't it be better to get Klaus to sign the pages I typed and then take them to Grieser and Stratmann?' Wallie pushed a small pile of papers in her direction. 'Couldn't sleep last night after Eden, so I typed it all up.'

Carla stuck the receiver under her chin and examined the first page. Wallie had indeed written down Klaus's statement word for word and typed it all up with no mistakes. A signed confession would not only impress Grieser, but he'd also have to act. She hung up, even though it had started ringing. First things first.

'How come you know shorthand and typing? Didn't you tell Mother you'd been a hairdresser and a singer? Then you told me and Lulu about the bright plastic phones and you're now a barmaid...'

'I'm multi-talented, what can I say? Shorthand was a subject in school, just like Russian.'

The phone rang. Carla picked up. It was Lulu, who wanted to know if it had been her calling, because she was about to call her. She wouldn't be surprised if that were the case, because they'd always been close and had a certain telepathy.

No time for theoretical discussions right now, so she interrupted Lulu. 'I need your help quite urgently, with Grieser. Could you arrange for another appointment with him?'

Lulu was somewhat put out that Carla was so abrupt, but she promised to try. Before saying goodbye, however, she said in her best drama queen voice that Pandora's box had been opened now, and each person would see what their heart wanted to see. Her dear niece was renowned for being so kind-hearted. When Carla looked up, she could see Wallie's blue eyes sparkling with mischief, as if she'd just heard a good joke and was trying not to burst out laughing.

'Let's go see Klaus,' she said hurriedly. 'But first let's call

Ingrid and tell her about the most important appointment of her life on Wednesday evening.'

Wallie cocked her perfectly arched eyebrows. By the time Carla had returned home after her champagne-fuelled meal with Sally, Wallie had already left for Eden. Meanwhile, over breakfast, Mother had been full of indignation about the closing of the border-pass offices and had decided to write a letter to the *Berliner* newspaper to complain that poor cousin Wallie was now unable to visit her friends and family in the East. Wallie had offered to write down whatever Mother dictated, which brought a squeal of delight, as sickly-sweet as toffee, that made Carla's teeth ache.

For a split second, it seemed that Mother was about to hug Wallie, and that the only reason she didn't do so was because Carla was there. Mother hadn't even given Father a hug when he returned in 1948 from POW camp in Italy. The accident with her leg happened a short while before that. Would Mother still like Wallie so much if she knew who she really was? Wasn't Wallie at all ashamed of this act she was putting on for Mother?

Carla had to pretend she was in a rush to get to an appointment and had gone downstairs to call Stratmann.

'So the meeting with Sally bore fruit?' asked Wallie.

Was Wallie really not aware of all of these undercurrents or did she merely pretend not to notice? That's what true freedom must feel like.

'Why are you staring at me like that? Something on my nose?' asked Wallie.

'No, no. Yes, my meeting with Sally was very useful.' Carla tried to keep it light, as if it were nothing special. 'We're probably going to be able to arrange a meeting between Ingrid and Bobbs the day after tomorrow.'

'Well, colour me pink! I'm so pleased for Niki, that's such a great thing for her.' Wallie stubbed out her cigarette, jumped up and began singing. 'Won't you buy yourself a big balloon, blue or purple or green...' It sounded a bit discordant, as she danced around her rattan chair, eyes wide open to represent being in love. She blew kisses in all directions, curtsied and sat back down again. Had she imbibed some peppermint liqueur with Mother?

'A really stupid film!' Carla said. 'Bland ice dancing with a ridiculous love story. Singing is clearly not your forte, right?'

'That may be so, but who cares?' Wallie mopped her brow with a cheerful shrug.

Carla did a double-take. Wallie was using one of Father's handkerchiefs. Fine white linen with a little embroidered nightingale and the initials KOK. Nobody had dared to touch these handkerchiefs after Father died.

Wallie folded it neatly and put it back in her pocket. 'You go to the cinema to be educated, obviously, and watch existentialist black-and-white films that decry the terrible sadness and futility of life. Well, to each their own, I guess. Anyway, I'm delighted for Niki. She's a remarkable woman.'

'Niki?'

'That's what Ingrid wants to be called.' Wallie winked at her. 'I never thought you'd be able to identify Bobbs so quickly out of the six thousand or so soldiers stationed here.'

Some compliments sounded almost like insults in disguise.

Without further ado, Carla called Ingrid, who answered so promptly she might as well have been camped right next to the phone. Ingrid was overcome with emotion and kept asking if Carla was serious about this. When she realised that the meeting would take place in just two days, she began worrying whether she'd be able to get a hairdresser appointment so quickly, or find the right dress, or hat, or... – and she had hung up.

'Now, off to see Klaus.' Carla stood up, put the typed

pages in a folder and placed it in her bag. She picked up her gloves. 'Let's go.'

Wallie looked outside: a fine drizzle. She sighed and pulled on her summer trench coat. The one with the secret pockets. With the strange medals and coins and passes. Carla had to find out what that was all about. As they went downstairs, Carla asked how the ice cream rendezvous had gone.

'I thought you'd never ask.'

'Well, you were so keen to write down what Mother dictated, and I had a job to do,' Carla said, nodding at Frau Pallutzke, who was cleaning up a brown mess in the entrance hall with a rather disgusted look. When she saw Wallie, she dropped her mop and came up to them.

'Miss von Tilling, I'd never have thought... Your Elsterglanz recommendation was spot on. Now we'll have the shiniest doorbells in all of Charlottenburg!'

'Pleased to be of help. Any time!' said Wallie.

Carla envied her the nonchalance with which she walked past Frau Pallutzke, as if the conversation was over.

'Elsterglanz?' she asked after they stepped outside. The drizzle had stopped, but the cobblestones still gleamed wetly, and there was a smell of petrichor.

'It's a polishing wax for Trabis, but you can make any metal shine with it.'

'So you were a cleaner as well?' Carla said as they set off in the direction of Ku'damm.

'That too!' Wallie chuckled, as if it were the best joke in the world.

'Ice cream seller?'

'No, not that,' she said, and her face darkened a little. 'Your little Katrin refused to have any ice cream with me. She was deeply offended that you didn't show up. The boys couldn't care less, they had huge quantities of ice cream and tried to behave like gentlemen. Do you know what those pipsqueaks are called?'

'Katrin calls them the Abominables or Terrors. Or uses the initials, T and B, AB1 and AB2.'

'And you never thought to ask?'

'Of course I did,' Carla had to laugh, 'According to Katrin, it's T for Tyrant and B for Bastard, while AB1 is for Absolute Bonkers and AB2 is for Asshole Beast.'

'How on earth did you remember all of those insults?' Wallie seemed genuinely surprised.

'Practice. Let's take a taxi. The sooner we see Klaus, the better.'

'As you wish. But you should know that the boys are actually called Abdiel and Abraham, Timon and Barnaby. And your Katrin is actually a Bathsheba.'

'But I heard her mother calling her Katrin.'

Wallie shrugged, 'Because she's a stubborn little brat and won't answer to anything else. How come you don't know all this? I thought you and Katrin were friends.'

'The family only moved here a year ago.'

'So long already? And you never discussed her brothers with her? Or what the parents do or all that?'

'As far as I know, it's just the mum, and she's got more than enough on her plate.'

Mother, Frau Pallutzke, Niki, and now Katrin's family – was Wallie sucking up to all of the people in Carla's world or did it only seem so?

'Anyway, anyone is free to call their children whatever they wish. This isn't a police state, you're free to practise your religion.'

'Poor kids!' said Wallie drily.

'Maybe,' Carla shrugged. 'No one wants to be Bathsheba at school. I remember there was a Lioba in my class, everyone called her Lio-bum, because she had a rather large bottom. Everyone teased her. Children hate anyone who is different.'

'All the more reason to watch out for one's neighbours. Nothing to do with a police state.'

'Think what you like, I like Katrin. I rescued her doll, and when I noticed how she gets bullied by her brothers, and that no one really looks after her, I befriended her. I give her books, I listen to her. I don't want to interrogate her about her family – that's just not done.' They reached the taxi stand and got into the first one.

Five minutes later, they were turning into Klaus's street and it started drizzling once more.

'Tears of joy,' said the taxi driver. 'A police guard from Treptow managed to cross over the border today. I tell you that wall won't last another week. They can't just lock up a whole population.'

Lock up... Carla couldn't help thinking of Alma and the children. Tears of joy. Not if Klaus refused to sign the statement.

36

Wallie got out of the taxi, while Carla paid. She stretched, her face turned up into the falling rain, and gave a mighty yawn. Heavens, her sister was full of energy today! Of course, she hadn't been the one typing up Klaus's report for two hours after a shift at the Eden. Amazing how rusty her fingers had become, she'd barely been able to keep up with Klaus's confession and initially kept making mistakes while typing. That's what happens when you only have to make oral reports. But it was like riding a bike, once learnt, never forgotten. Ida's dictation earlier went much more smoothly. Carla's mother was quite capable of expressing her thoughts clearly. Just like Frieda. The two of them having a cup of coffee... Wallie could feel a smile blossoming on her lips. Ida would be making polite small talk, while Frieda would start congratulating her on the missing leg. It's a goldmine, she'd say, just what is missing in my esta-bleesh-mun. Frieda liked to talk about her establishment. Then she'd tell an astonished Ida about customers who found women's missing body parts a real turn-on. She called them 'cripple fetishists', although she didn't judge them. Frieda didn't consider any kind of lust to be despicable, as long as no one was being forced into it.

Nonsense, the lack of sleep was leading to her imagining things. Although the two women were so similar, they'd never get to have such a conversation, obviously. Ida would slip on her bitter smile and put on an offended silent front.

Wallie was quite impressed with how well Ida managed to dominate her daughter out of her wheelchair, but she did wonder when and why this had all started.

Carla put her wallet away and held her large handbag over her head to protect herself from the rain. 'It was a good idea to type it up so quickly. But we need a Plan B – if Klaus refuses to sign, if he's changed his mind? How can we put pressure on him?'

Putting pressure on someone... Had Carla just looked at her when she said that, or was it her imagination? Putting pressure... Carla had no idea just how many possibilities there were.

They went through the front building, where some youths wearing Lederhosen were playing marbles. All five of them stopped suddenly and stared. Wallie winked at them conspiratorially and swung her hips; she loved to get the brats a little hot under the collar. Two of them blushed, and the others giggled and whispered among themselves, swinging their bags of marbles somewhat awkwardly. Then one of them got a bit braver and they all ran shouting after the two women through the empty inner courtyard.

Her sister stopped and shook her head. 'Wallie, stop it! And you boys should be in school. The holidays are over. Those who skip school stay stupid!' When the rascals still didn't show any signs of leaving, she stuffed her handbag under her left arm and waved the other arm in their direction, saying 'Shoo, shoo, shoo!' until they finally gave in and ran out onto the road.

'Let them have a bit of fun. Do you really think they'll go to school now?'

'I hope so.'

'Dream on.'

'You're so irresponsible and cynical.' Carla rolled her eyes, as if waiting for help from above. 'Oh, God!' she exclaimed as she looked up. 'Quick, we have to hurry!'

Wallie looked upwards in surprise. 'Damn!' She bolted

after Carla.

Damn, damn, damn! As they bounded up the stairs, she kept hoping that the man who was standing so close to the edge of the damaged roof wasn't Klaus but some other ginger-haired man in a suit. Unlikely. Klaus wouldn't normally have the guts to jump, but maybe he was pumped full of drugs? Carla was right. He mustn't jump before signing the confession. Images shot through her head. Klaus circling as he fell upon layer after layer of flokati rugs, all with a cheery pattern of bloody handprints. Even if Alma had lied to them, the children deserved better than that.

When she finally reached the fifth floor, panting heavily, she saw that Carla was already out on the roof, edging her way towards Klaus among the piles of rubble, broken tiles and roof beams sticking out at odd angles. He was so close to the edge that Wallie's heart nearly stopped beating. She stepped out onto the roof as well, and was instantly cooled by the rain shower, which was turning the rubble and dust into mud. Wallie had to be careful not to slip.

'Klaus!' Carla called out when she was within arm's length of him.

'Don't come any closer!' he said, backing dangerously away from them.

They had to find an alternative. Carla stood still. 'You didn't survive the war just to throw your life away now!'

'And you know that, because you were at the front and are now in my position?' Klaus slipped and staggered so close to the edge that Wallie held her breath.

Carla heard her behind her, turned round and gave her a meaningful look. Except she couldn't figure out what it meant. That she should do the talking? Not a good idea. According to Wallie's experience, it was impossible to stop those determined to kill themselves. It was their right to do so, after all. Death is the wish of some, the relief of many and the end of all. Wallie found this quote by Seneca oddly comforting. But standing here now with a man on the very edge of the roof, her whole being was shrieking: *forget about Seneca, save this guy*! Klaus had to live. She had to rescue him, if it was the last thing she did.

'I understand that you feel terrible...' said Carla softly.

'Oh, do you? What can you possibly understand?' His voice dripped irony.

'I understand that you're suffering, and that you feel this is the only way you can get rid of the pain.'

Carla sounded really sincere. *That's good,* thought Wallie, *just keep him talking and I'll try to grab him from the other side.*

'Stop with the whining drivel!' Klaus laughed bitterly. 'One should die proudly when it is no longer possible to live proudly, death of one's own free choice, death at the proper time...'

'And you think Nietzsche would consider this the proper time?' asked Carla, still inching her way forward towards him.

Stop droning on about that syphilitic Nietzsche, don't be an idiot, don't throw your life away, thought Wallie. *Help us to prove Alma's innocence.*

Just then, she got stuck on a nail or piece of wood. She managed not to cry out, but could feel something liquid dripping down her calf. Never mind, just a few more centimetres to go, then she could grab him while he was listening to Carla. Wallie mimed a duck's bill with her hand, hoping that she'd get it and continue talking.

Carla nodded, barely perceptibly.

'Klaus, you have to do something honourable first, before you die,' said Carla. 'You can build the Breitscheid Place project, after all, it was your idea, your design that got the go-ahead.'

Good point, thought Wallie, but Klaus didn't react. A sudden movement seemed to course through his body, and he stepped forward.

Wallie grabbed him and pulled him back, but he shook himself free, staggered backwards, slipped sideways two steps, broke through the roof and disappeared.

Wallie ran to the hole he'd fallen through, ignoring the pulsating pain in her calf, and looked down. Luckily, Klaus had only fallen a metre or so and had landed between the washing lines in a sort of attic. She could hear him groaning and cursing, so he'd definitely survived the fall. He'd not even been stunned, because she heard him clearly say, 'Damn nuisance, womenfolk!'

'How are we going to get him out of there?' Wallie said, standing up gingerly. Carla was on the other side of the hole, her face as white as a sheet, her eyes dark cut-outs, trembling. 'This, this...' she said to Wallie, her eyes spinning.

'No!' Wallie jumped towards her, not caring a jot about the beams or nails, sliding rather than running. 'Carla, pull yourself together, please!'

Her sister was no longer taking in what she was saying. Carla had closed her eyes and was swaying, holding her arms spreadeagled, as if she was being crucified. Tears were pouring down her face and she fell backwards. Wallie was able to leap forward and stop her from following Klaus into the hole, but as she pulled her back, she lost her own balance. They both fell hard on their backs. Something sharp was poking in Wallie's right shoulder, while the smell of mould and rusty iron choked her. Add to that the powdery smell of Carla's hair, which had come loose and was hanging around her head in heavy strands.

Wallie gasped for air and contemplated her pale, motionless sister. She couldn't hear Klaus anymore either. Were they breathing? It was far too quiet. Not even one of those stupid pigeons. 'Carla?' she ventured, checking to see if she'd hurt her own ears. Obviously not, because she could hear herself speak. Wallie got up carefully; there was something blocking her movements, something stuck in her back, her left shoulder, but as long as she could move her arms and legs, that was OK.

She turned to Carla. Fainted like Sleeping Beauty. Wallie avoided touching her cheek but felt for her pulse. It was racing – over a hundred. Shock? She should maybe raise her legs, but no, that was too dangerous. They had to leave this place and also help Klaus.

'Carla!' she said and shook her gently. Why had her sister suddenly lost it so badly? She was normally so resilient. In her conversation with Klaus just now she'd seemed so cool and collected. Could she be pregnant, maybe by this Bruno chap?

'Carla!' She shook her a little more vigorously. Still no reaction, so Wallie slapped her cheek. Perhaps a little harder than warranted.

Carla's eyelids fluttered, then she opened her eyes and stared straight at Wallie, as if she were an alien species.

'What?' she asked, swallowing hard, as if her mouth was full of dust. 'Where?' Her cheeks suddenly turned red, so she must have remembered.

'I'm so sorry!' she whimpered, tears pouring down her face. 'So very sorry!' She pulled her legs up to her chest, curling up small.

Wallie's throat constricted. What on earth was going on here? What should she do? Maybe look after Klaus first. She dragged herself painfully towards the hole and looked down. One of his arms was twisted in an unnatural way, his eyes were closed and he wasn't answering. Chrissakes! What if he'd ruptured some internal organs? There was no blood to be seen externally, so his head must be fine.

She called him once, twice, but the only ones to react were a pair of pigeons who flew up and settled on the edge of the gap.

Wallie crept back to Carla. Each time she pushed herself forward with her right arm, she could feel a burning pain in her back. As if someone was plunging a knife into it. Her sister was still lying there, rolled up like a hedgehog, not visibly harmed.

'Carla, please recover! We don't have any time to lose.'

Carla slowly released her legs and sat up. She wiped her tear-stained face with her palms and sniffled. 'Sorry, please forgive me.'

'We'll talk later, but now we need to get help and take Klaus to the hospital. Can you stand?'

'Yes,' said Carla, bending down and trying to get up. But she went pale again and fell back. Not another fainting fit!

'Pull yourself...' Wallie started to say, but Carla said something, first in a whisper, then louder. She was clearly desperate to get the word out, that much was clear, so Wallie bent over to catch it. 'Signature' and 'Save Alma'. Then she finally stood in front of Wallie, slightly crouching, like an Amazon ready to fight, but still trembling.

Tough girl, thought Wallie, who was starting to feel weak herself. Whatever was in her shoulder was starting to throb.

'My handbag?' asked Carla, looking once more through the gap where Klaus had fallen. She quickly looked away, shuddering.

'You're on top of it.' Wallie pointed at her feet. Carla picked up her bag and relaxed a little.

'And what happened to you?' she asked her sister. 'I can't remember a thing. Did you fall too?'

'You pulled me on top of you. It's OK, but...' Wallie turned her back towards her. 'What's on my shoulder?'

Carla made a noise that Wallie wasn't able to decipher. Was it a snort or a giggle? Was the woman getting hysterical, had she hit her head so hard? She must be in shock, tears were pouring down her face again and she was laughing like a crazy woman.

'What?' yelled Wallie, 'Just calm down, will you?'

'Maybe...' she said, finally quietening down. 'It really is a sign from God.'

'Feels more like hell to me.'

'You won't believe it,' Carla bit her lip, 'but it's a crucifix that's stuck in your shoulder. You must have fallen on the nail that was keeping it hung to the wall.'

'Where's this from?'

'No idea. Although Lulu did warn me about this neighbourhood – not only that it's insalubrious, but also that once upon a time there was a dodgy Catholic sect in this area.'

'Are you having me on?'

She shook her head. 'It wouldn't occur to me, it's so ridiculous...'

'As ridiculous as a detective who just falls into a dead faint.'

'Let's take Klaus to hospital,' said Carla, ignoring Wallie's dig. 'And a doctor will have to remove your Jesus as well, it may have damaged a blood vessel. You stay with Klaus and try to talk to him, don't move, and I'll go find a telephone and call for help.'

Wallie could barely nod, the pain in her back was getting worse, as if someone had shot a whole quiver of arrows there. Jesus on a cross, well, hopefully it wouldn't lead to any ugly scars. Who wanted to have such a reminder of eternity on their back?

37

It took an hour for Carla to find a doctor in the neighbourhood, with the help of the little truants, and get Klaus off the roof. The doctor called an ambulance for Klaus and took Wallie with him, because the object embedded in her shoulder needed to be removed with a scalpel under a microscope. Wallie was by now very pale and too weak to protest.

Klaus had not recovered consciousness by the time the ambulance set off, but the doctor thought that might be caused more by his drug consumption rather than any internal injuries.

Once the ambulance departed, Carla tried to get rid of the boys, so that she could go back into Klaus's apartment without any witnesses. She gave each of them one mark as she shook their hands, and suggested they might like to spend it right away on an ice cream.

'*Naaah!*' said the eldest, rolling his eyes at Carla's obvious stupidity, 'That'd be dumb!' He waved the net full of marbles at her. 'We're gonna put all the money together and buy the best shooters and beat those Kösliner nitwits!'

'Sounds good to me!' Carla said, eager to get rid of the boys. 'In fact, I think your plan is so clever, that I'll give each of you an extra two pfennigs for ice cream, but only if you promise to go to school tomorrow.'

The five of them gathered in a circle and whispered frenetically, then the eldest came up to her. 'Deal!' He held out his hand.

'Word of honour?'

'Cross our hearts and hope to die!' he said earnestly and held his hand up in the air as if swearing an oath, while all his little mates nodded vigorously.

Carla was glad she had enough cash on her. Rule No. 7: carry sufficient cigarettes and cash on you at all times. You never know when a little tip might be helpful. She waited until the boys disappeared around the corner, then ran back upstairs to Klaus's apartment, determined not to think about what had happened on the roof.

She gave herself a quick once-over: torn tights, dirty hands, tangled hair and a few bruises on her back. Nothing major wrong with her. She'd recovered her calm after that embarrassing breakdown. A shame that Wallie had witnessed it, but she didn't owe her any explanations. They had to focus on getting Alma out of custody. Her clients paid her for results, not for feelings, after all.

She was hoping for a farewell note as she went back upstairs. Most suicides left a letter explaining their reasons. Maybe Klaus would have had the decency to try to explain things to Alexander's children. So that they wouldn't grow up believing that their mother had killed their father. Of course, it was entirely possible that he'd merely followed an impulse by going out on the roof, that his drug-addled mind had conjured up a voice summoning him up there, promising that he'd be reunited with Alexander if he flew off the roof.

The door to the apartment was unlocked and everything seemed untouched. Incredibly tidy. That seemed to speak of a planned deed. If he'd acted on sudden impulse, he wouldn't have taken the bedsheets off the bed and folded everything neatly with military precision. There was a suitcase next to the bed, and nothing strewn on the floor. Nothing on the two tables either. But there was something on the old-fashioned cherrywood chest of drawers under the window. Carla's heartbeat quickened as she approached, her hunch seemed to be correct. There was an envelope, thick cream stationery, printed with the golden initials KvS.

There was a handwritten address on it: *To be handed to Frau Hannika.* Who was that? Why a letter to a woman? Was she his lawyer, was this his will?

The envelope was well sealed. She felt the contents: quite bulky, there must be more than one piece of paper in there. Did wills run to several pages? There must be some other explanation. But why was this addressed not to Alma but to a Frau Hannika?

There was no running water or stove in Klaus's apartment, so no chance of opening the envelope by steaming it. She had to take it with her. Nobody would miss it for the time being.

She hurried back to Grolmanstraße, trying to ignore her aching back and using all her willpower to banish those images from the roof. She had to think of Alma, who'd begged for her help. The image of Mathilda's drawing rose up, mixed with the Hungarian floral embroidery belonging to the gardener and then the cross on Wallie's shoulder. Aunt Lulu would consider that a sign, of course, that Wallie was being crucified for her life choices. It would serve the con artist right, she who wanted to ruin Lulu's brother's reputation and destroy Carla's life.

Carla didn't believe in signs, but she couldn't help thinking of the secret pocket in Wallie's trench coat. That coat was now ruined too.

Once she got back to the office, she washed her hands and face, and combed her hair without looking in the mirror. She put on a fresh pair of tights and a clean blouse, which she always kept handy in the office. Then she put water on to boil and picked up the thick envelope, waiting next to the cooker. She watched the bubbles starting to form on the grey metal base of the pot, she heard the bubbling, but could not look away. Water fizzing, sparkling, bubbling up, bigger and brighter, until the memories came flooding back...

***

Crowing with joy, she ran ahead of everyone! She'd done it! She held the little parachute to her scrawny chest for protection, stuffing it under her far too large blouse, which Mother had sewn for her eighth birthday. Her short legs carried her onwards, faster than ever before in her life, joy was giving her wings! Nobody could take it away from her.

She'd done it, done it, done it!

She found a jogging rhythm that she could keep up all the way from Tempelhof to Charlottenburg. Two hours there and two hours back. But it was worth it. Tomorrow Mother would have a really happy birthday, because at last Carla had something to give her. Something much more precious than any of her drawings – a sensible present. She would wrap it up, of course, in one of her flower drawings, she'd sacrifice the prettiest one, the one with campanulas, to make it even more of a surprise.

Mother would be astonished. Then, for the first time in her life, she'd say, 'Well done, Carla!' She'd give her a kiss on the neatly combed parting. OK, maybe she wouldn't go as far as a kiss, but she'd certainly beam with delight. Even if Carla was a disappointment otherwise, this time Mother would approve.

Carla had been twice already to Tempelhof Airport, because she'd heard about the Raisin Bombers, but couldn't believe it was true. It sounded like a fairy-tale. But it was indeed true that some of the pilots would throw little parachutes full of sweets out of their planes before landing. Specially for the children. The pilot that had started it all with chocolates wrapped in handkerchiefs had such wiggly wings on his plane that they could never quite guess where the wind would bear the sweet burden.

Carla had studied the matter in detail, because she was determined to catch one of those parachutes that day. So that for Mother's birthday they could have some chocolate instead of just nettle soup. But Carla wasn't the only child there. Even after she managed to catch one of the parachutes, the others jumped on her, asking her to share, but she needed it all, she wasn't prepared to give anything up. Which was why she was running so fast.

Her plaits slapped against her shoulders, her feet burning in the oversized sandals, she could feel blisters forming on her heels, but it was a good pain, keeping her alert. Sweat was pouring out of all her pores, her scratchy blouse was ruined, her heart was hammering, but she was laughing all the way home, imagining Mother's contented face. She had to navigate two dangerous corners where the big boys hung out, and stopped to draw her breath on the Pestalozzi Street.

Big mistake.

Only then did she notice the two braindead fellows. Blond Huns with hands like shovels, the twins were no longer 'all there' since they'd been buried in the rubble with their entire family. They were pulled out of the ruins, the sole survivors, after a whole day and night. The Müller twins had the habit of demanding a toll from anyone smaller in size than they were – so virtually everyone, even the adults – and would mercilessly hit anyone who didn't comply, as if all their human emotions had been buried in the rubble too.

Carla panicked and fled into the nearest cellar on Pestalozzi Street. But too late, she was trapped now. She might be safe in the cellar, for the deadbeats would never go inside one, but they'd just wait outside, propped against some junk, until thirst or fear would force her to come out. She could only hope that some other, more valuable victim would pass by.

It took forever, but she finally heard Mother calling her.

With that long drawn-out, angry 'Caaar-la' which made her shiver. It meant no food, no more going out, no mercy. Still, she climbed up the cellar steps and peeked outside. Mother would punish her, but it was out of love. She was better than the braindeads.

'Here I am!' she called. Mother stopped in front of the two fellows in the twilight, swinging a lamp in front of them and threatening to call the police, which didn't upset them in the slightest. They gave a nasty chuckle and pushed Mother. The lamp fell to the ground and broke, and Mother stumbled into the junk pile just outside the entrance. Carla ran out towards her, but there was a dull thud and her mother vanished into thin air. Even the twins were stunned.

Carla screwed up her eyes, but it was as if Mother had been swallowed up by the ground. The flame from the lamp lit the pieces of paper lying around, they caught fire and the deadbeats ran off. Carla approached the area where her mother had been standing and discovered that under the junk there was a bomb crater. 'Mum?' she called.

'All your fault!' her mother yelled, apparently unharmed. 'Dirty good-for-nothing, God's punishment for all my sins, but dear God, have I not paid enough? See to it that you get me out of here!'

The neighbours were alarmed by the fire and some of them came running to stamp it out and help Mother out of the crater.

Once they got home, Mother forced Carla to look closely at the damage she'd caused. Mother's left leg was badly grazed, and there was a corner of green oven tile stuck in her left foot. It had been a hot day and Mother had gone out in her slippers.

'We have no money for a doctor, because I've got this useless daughter, who runs around all day instead of helping me. Just look what a thorn in my side you are!'

Mother took out the tile with a pair of nail scissors. She

gathered the splinters in a big Murano ashtray. She kept flinching, suppressing a moan, beads of sweat running into her eyes, getting paler by the minute. Then she put iodine solution on the wound, which made Carla look away.

'I'm so sorry,' she kept whispering, wondering how she could ever have believed that one of her ideas would lead to something good. Rules were there to be followed.

After Mother had finished cleaning her wound, Carla had to stand in front of her to get her customary clip round the ears.

'Respect!' Mother thundered at her. Slap on the left. 'Gratitude!' Slap on the right. 'Listen to your parents.' Slap on the left. 'Who do you think you are?' Slap on the right.

Then she pulled Carla by the hair towards her and yelled in her face, 'Where were you all day?'

Carla tried to explain and held out the squashed parachute with the sweets that she'd stuffed in her blouse. Hoping. Hoping.

Mother threw the parachute disdainfully on the table. 'All this pain for some old chewing-gum?'

Her voice pierced Carla's chest like an icicle, she froze and could barely breathe. She really should've known better.

Mother unpacked the treasure: a Hershey bar, some bright yellow chewing gum and a little brown bag with a pattern of Ms on it. '*That's* what you were so disobedient for?'

'Sorry,' she whispered, annoyed with herself that her mouth was still aching for the goodies, in spite of everything. 'I'm very, very sorry.'

Of course, neither of them knew then that Mother's foot would become inflamed and sepsis would set in so badly that she'd have the leg amputated above the knee. Neither of them ever forgot that day.

38

The sound of the phone ringing brought Carla back to the present. The water in the pan had nearly evaporated and the envelope was fully open. She switched off the cooker and took the envelope with her while answering the phone. She'd barely lifted the receiver to her ear when she heard her aunt, already in full flow.

Lulu had invited Grieser for a beer after work, although with Grieser it was never just a beer, but women, wine and song. Incidentally, it might be helpful if Carla didn't dress like a sorrowful widow when she came to meet him, she should scrub up a little. Sadly, Lulu wouldn't be able to give her a helping hand on this occasion, because she'd suddenly got an appointment. Trudi had organised a rather promising interview.

Helping hand? It had been Carla's thighs that had suffered Grieser's touch on the previous occasion, not Lulu's hands. Grieser was sceptical but prepared to listen to the shocking revelations that Lulu'd promised. Carla mustn't disappoint him. She hung up with a cheerful, 'Break a leg!'

Not disappoint him. Carla laughed maliciously – she could imagine what that meant.

She pulled herself together and examined the contents of the envelope. There was a watermarked piece of paper wrapped around a bundle of twenty-mark notes. Two hundred marks' worth. You could tell at once that the writing on the paper was too brief to be an explanation, and she read, to her disappointment:

Berlin, 28.08.1961

Dear Mrs Hannika,

Please find enclosed the rent for September plus a little extra for any inconvenience. You are welcome to keep the furniture in my apartment, or to sell it. The chest of drawers and the two chairs have some value.

A final farewell,

Klaus von Stellmark

That was it?

Carla turned the paper over. Nothing. She'd have liked to tear it up but managed to control herself. What sort of a man plans his death, nobly covers his rent but doesn't stop to consider the other people he might have wronged?

What a mess! The actual evildoer was dead and had caused further victims even after his death. Mathilda, Alma... The children needed their mother, but she'd only be released if Klaus made a statement. And he obviously did not want to state publicly what he'd told them. He'd rather die than talk openly about his humiliation.

Carla went to the wardrobe and took Klaus's confession out of her handbag. It was in a remarkably good state, bar a couple of wrinkles.

This was the truth, both she and Wallie were witnesses to it. Alexander's death was an accident. Accidents happened all the time, without anyone getting punished for it. She sat down at her desk and stared at Klaus's note. Grieser was expecting new revelations. Something based on evidence.

Almost instinctively, her right hand reached for a soft pencil, while her left hand took out the sketchbook, where she'd drawn Wallie's coins and medal.

She opened to a fresh new page and examined the few lines written by Klaus very carefully. Signature, place and date. She traced the letters with her finger. Clear, nicely swirling, big loops at the top, harmonious proportions to the S.

Simple story. He'd signed right up there on the roof, for Mathilda's sake, before losing consciousness. If he came to and denied it, who'd be more believable, a drug addict with a dead mentor, or a former law student with a clear head? Even if he denied it, at least his statement would be out there in the open. Wallie could testify that that was what he'd said, she'd been there and written it all down.

If Grieser tried to sweep this under the carpet and Stratmann thought it was useless, then Carla could take the signed statement to the press via Nepomuk. Alma would then be released and the children's suffering would end.

But for that, she'd have to do something illegal. Something bad. It was time to take a risk.

What could go wrong? No one was going to lose a leg! But if they did find out, that would be the end of Nightingale & Co.

Carla put pen to paper and started tracing the K. It was surprisingly easy.

39

'Nelly, what mischief are you up to now?' Edgar limped into the ward with an enormous bouquet of red and white lilies, greeting the other four ladies staring at him with a nod and a sparkling smile.

Wallie felt better instantly. She'd been downcast: not only was she not allowed to move her left arm, but she also had to put up all morning with unappetizing details about bladder problems, kidney stones and gallstones. Urology had been the only free ward in the Westend Clinic.

'You came just in time. Thanks for the flowers, we can take 'em home right away. Help me get dressed, I need to get outta here.'

'Seems like we've had a run of bad luck!' Edgar said, shaking his head as he came up to Wallie's bed to kiss her on her forehead, while examining her tightly bandaged arms and shoulder brace. 'You should stay lying down. I'll go and fetch a nurse to ask about the greenery, don't run away!' He limped out of the room, with a gallant little bow towards the other sickbeds.

'Lookee here, your fella, is he?' asked the kidney stone.

'*Naah*, he looks too short,' intervened the gallstone.

'I still would...' said the bladder, laughing, but she instantly screwed up her face with pain.

Just then Edgar came back with a vase and a rather stern-looking nurse in tow.

'You're not allowed to go yet! The first drip will be

attached shortly, or do you want to have septicaemia when you get home?'

'I'm fine, I want to leave. The doctor said I had a lucky escape and that the shoulder will heal.'

'The Lord obviously held you in His protection,' said the nurse and the whole ward started giggling, much to Edgar's surprise.

The nurse grabbed Wallie's sick notes at the end of her bed. 'After all, you saved a soul for Him.'

Protection? If that were the case, he shouldn't have let her fall in that pit, nor brought her to this university hospital. They didn't operate on her when she came in with Klaus, but kept her waiting for ages, giving her painkillers, so that she could present a strange case study for students. They were supposed to suggest next steps or treatment. Yes, of course she'd been asked for permission, but it was clear that they were expecting her to give it. She had the choice to refuse and be kept waiting even longer, or to keep her mouth shut and let it all wash over her.

The nurse got closer, frowning as she felt Wallie's forehead. 'I don't like this, we'll have to take your temperature. We might have a case of cryptococcosis here,' she said, highly satisfied to be the bearer of catastrophic news. 'From the pigeon shit.'

Wallie moaned out loud.

Edgar gently touched the nurse's arm. 'Would you be so kind as to allow me to speak to the patient for just five minutes? I'll be gone after that.'

Not even he could disarm the militant nurse and get her to smile, but at least she nodded. 'Three minutes.'

'Obviously, I'll die if you go over that by even half a minute.' Wallie took the newspapers with her healthy arm and looked at the headlines. 'Why are they sending General Clay to Berlin, why now?'

Edgar took the papers away from her, which made the other patients stare even more.

'Edgar, I was reading that...'

'Wait, let me show you this. We're off the hook!' he whispered, showing her the page three headline. *Order of Merit awarded posthumously to Hochbrück.*

Wallie skimmed the article. What now? Police were now satisfied, thanks to the statement made by Hochbrück's brother-in-law, that his death had been an accident. When did that happen? As far as she knew, Klaus was still downstairs in the Psychiatry Department, where visitors were not allowed. Did they make an exception for the police?

She continued reading. Alma von Hochbrück had been released with an apology and would go to Bonn next week together with her children to receive the Order of Merit on behalf of her deceased husband, directly from the hands of President Lübke. Typical bureaucratic pussyfooting, Lübke was due to come to Berlin the following day, he could've handed it over then.

Edgar passed his hand over his bald head. 'Happy now?'

'We were never in any danger, we didn't do anything bad.'

'And here's a little something from Irina and Jutta.' He gave her a bag. Wallie felt inside, a soft textile. She pulled it out: a delicate pink lacy baby-doll top, with a matching pair of knickers.

Gallstone gave an enthusiastic whoop, while the others started giggling again.

Wallie had to laugh despite her bad mood. 'Well, colour me pink!' She draped the chiffon over her bandaged shoulder. 'I'm sure the nurses will help me get changed. Or...' she waved it at the other women in the ward, 'maybe the doctor would like to get involved?'

They were all laughing now.

'Irina sewed it all by herself, she wanted me to tell you. The boss sends his greetings. He said there'll always be a spot for you at the Eden, 'cos it looks like it'll be a while till you can serve drinks again. Your Scottish friend also asked about you. I didn't tell him anything, because I wasn't sure if you wanted him to show up here?'

'Well done. James is more bothered about his own welfare, so just tell 'im I'm travelling. Otherwise he'll feel bad for not yakking up any excuses for not being able to visit. Anyway, I don't wanna stay here a day longer. I'll take responsibility and discharge myself.'

She stopped, remembering that she no longer had a place of her own, nor a Frieda to pep her up with her stoic talk. She'd have to crawl back to Nightingale & Co. How would Ida react to her accident? Would she be allowed to move to the guestroom? After all, she'd saved both Klaus and Carla. Although Carla might not be aware of that – she'd seemed pretty out of things up there on the roof.

'Better stay here as long as necessary. Adele damaged her shoulder once when she tried to run away from the nursing home and got stuck in the fence.' Edgar shuddered, remembering. 'Since then she gets bad pains whenever the weather changes.'

'Sorry to hear that. Thanks for everything, but you really should go now, or the nurse'll be on my case.' She raised the hand holding the baby-doll outfit and pointed behind Edgar, where the nurse was standing with a thermometer in her hand, shaking her head in disapproval.

He turned around to nod at the nurse, then turned back to Wallie and bent over with a twinkle in his eye to whisper in her ear, 'Fine, I'm off, let me know if you need anything.'

Half an hour later it became obvious that she was running a temperature and wouldn't be discharged just in case she had something contagious, which Wallie thought was absolute nonsense. But she couldn't risk becoming a nuisance, and at least she'd be allowed to make a phone call. She was even taken off the drip so that she could use the public phone next to the cafeteria.

She called Carla, who promised to visit tomorrow. She couldn't make it today because she was about to go with Bruno to pick up Alma from the police station. They might even be able to pick up the children from the orphanage and take them all back to the villa. And then, that evening, there'd be the meeting between Ingrid and Bobbs.

'Shame I can't be there. I read in the papers that Klaus did make a statement after all.'

'Yes,' said Carla curtly. 'Anything else?'

'This U-turn is a bit of a miracle.'

'A miracle, as you say.'

'You know that people can tell when a signature is forged.'

'And?'

'And it's a punishable offence.'

'You don't say. Punishable offences are obviously your area of expertise.'

'What happened up there on the roof?'

'I'll visit you tomorrow.'

'Don't just visit, get me out of here. I can stay with you, can't I?'

'Mother would consider it unchristian to do otherwise.' Carla made a funny sound.

'How funny! I only landed in this place because I saved your butt up there.'

'See you tomorrow.' Carla hung up without a word of thanks.

That wasn't like her. What was going on? Wallie didn't believe in miracles, but she did believe in conducting an investigation.

Ten minutes later and ten marks out of pocket, she was sitting by Klaus's bedside. Potential suicides were clearly allowed to have private rooms. His left leg was in plaster from the knee down, he must have fractured his tibia.

'Nelly?' He stared in astonishment at her bandaged shoulder, then his face darkened as he pointed at the

Berliner Zeitung on his nightstand. 'I'll sue you and your friend.'

'Because we stopped you from flinging yourself down into the backyard, where your body parts could have lain comfortably for ages amongst the washing lines and the children's marbles?'

'Mock me, but when I finish with you, we'll see who laughs last.'

'I've no idea what you're on about.'

'Really? I spoke to you in confidence about that evening, I certainly didn't sign a statement.'

'You weren't quite yourself, can you be sure about all the details?'

'I'll request a handwriting specialist.'

'You're mighty feisty for someone who wanted to give up the ghost earlier.'

'You might have falsified other documents in my name.'

'But it was the truth,' she said. Aha, so Carla had been lying.

'The truth is that people are reading between the lines and consider me a murderer.'

'Did you want to die because in secret you too consider yourself a murderer?'

He looked her straight in the eye. 'I was confused, now I'm clear-headed and I'm not going to let such an accusation sit upon me.'

'The truth is that your soul has become deaf and blind thanks to war and drugs. The Alexander that you look up to so much never existed in the first place.'

'How would you know?'

'He used everyone and laughed at them, just like he did with you. He tricked you and Alma and he even...' She bit her tongue, she had to keep Mathilda's secret. 'He abused everyone who depended on him. No one'll miss him.'

'I will.'

Wallie stroked Klaus's arm. 'You'll only recover when

you forgive yourself for loving that monster. Otherwise, the only thing left in your life will be the ice dagger in your heart.'

40

'Sometimes you have to decide whether you're gonna be a gentleman or a friend,' Bruno said as he got out of the taxi and held the door open for Carla. 'So please forgive me for acting like a friend today and asking you what happened. And I don't mean the misadventure on the roof and the scratches on your arm. In spite of your charming dress and the lipstick, you look like a TB patient on her last legs.'

'Well, thank you very much!' she said, and added, just to stop him, 'Women's matters.' That always seemed to work with men. She'd not been able to sleep a wink the last two nights, although everything had gone according to plan. After a hearty meal, Grieser was prepared to officially recognise Klaus's statement. But Carla had to promise that when Klaus fully recovered, he'd come to the police station to answer some questions. She expressed her deep sorrow that Klaus would first have to go on a detox programme. She reminded Grieser repeatedly that she was sure that he wouldn't want to keep the widow of a recipient of the Order of Merit a day longer in custody. After all, she was the mother of the recipient's children and surely their welfare was of utmost importance to him. Especially now it was clear that it was an accident which had made them half-orphans.

All of those lies had come surprisingly easily when she thought of Mathilda. But night-time had taken its revenge.

She saw herself rotting in jail in the room with the flickering neon light where she'd spoken to Alma together with Stratmann, all because of Paragraph 267 about falsifying a legal document. Who'd take care of Mother in that case? Even if her sentence was a short one – not likely, for it was in connection with a murder case – she'd certainly lose the licence, for Nightingale & Co. Detectives had to be cleaner than clean. And she had no savings at all.

While she paced through the apartment, trying not to wake up Mother, she realised that there were just two solutions to her problem. Either Klaus would remain an addict for the rest of his life, or else his next suicide attempt would be successful. When she realised what she was considering, she reeled. She staggered to the drinks cupboard and poured herself a good measure of Berliner Luft. There had to be some other solution. Maybe she could convince him, with Wallie's help, that he really had signed the statement, which was a truthful account anyway. But for that, she had to tell Wallie everything, and she was reluctant to do that. She didn't want to give Wallie any kind of hold over her.

During the day, she was able to keep those dark thoughts at bay with work, but she winced every time she heard a police siren, expecting them to come and put handcuffs on her under the scandal-hungry eyes of Frau Pallutzke. This fear was repeated every quarter of an hour, because all of Berlin was on high alert thanks to the visit of the Federal President Lübke.

'Women's matters?' Bruno asked with a silky-smooth voice, which nearly made Carla burst into tears. She nodded.

'Sorry to hear that. Should we stop at a pharmacy? Do you need something for your head as well?'

'No, thanks.' She felt terrible about lying to him.

'I have three older sisters, so I know something about women's monthly cycles.'

Carla blushed. She'd never discussed 'women's monthly cycles' with anyone, other than that first time, when Mother had shown her how to handle it and told her to keep away from men from now on.

'Have you got cramps?' Bruno asked.

'No, all good. I just didn't sleep well.'

'I see. Well, just let me know if I can do anything to help. You're allowed to feel weak on occasion.'

Carla swallowed hard and looked out of the window. He was so wrong, but what could he know? She'd always had to be strong. She glanced at his profile, he looked like a big bear in his black leather jacket, and yet he was so gentle. He noticed her looking at him, took his hand off the gearshift and put it carefully on her own hand in its lace glove.

'I know you're a strong woman, but no one needs to be a warrior all the time.'

When she didn't react, he put his hand back on the shift, which looked like a child's toy in his hand. Carla suppressed the desire to put her hand in his and hold tight. She looked out at a police car driving alongside them.

Bruno noticed that Carla didn't want to talk about herself, so he talked instead about his upcoming first practical class in anatomy. What if he felt sick? One of his classmates had fainted.

She was so relieved about this change of subject, that she replied that the worst thing about dissection was the penetrating smell of formaldehyde. She found it helpful to put menthol cream under her nose. He was so stunned that he braked sharply, stopped and asked her what on earth she knew about corpses.

'Father had a friend who's a lawyer and he knows a pathologist, who allows me to assist when he performs autopsies.'

'But why would you?' He looked at her full of wonderment, as if he'd just discovered he'd won the lottery and his day couldn't get any better.

'Because I wanted to understand.'

'Understand what?'

'Connections.'

'As in...'

'Every wound, every bruise, whether resulting from an accident or from a crime, tells a story. The more I know and recognise such stories, the better I can solve cases. I started studying law, but I soon realised I'm more interested in forensic pathology.'

'You could start studying that, you're still young.'

'Mother is handicapped and needs my help, Father was sadly unable to provide sufficiently for her wellbeing.' Possibly, Carla suddenly realised, not just because he was a spendthrift, but because he had two families to provide for.

'We've arrived. Shame. We need to talk about this again. I'll wait for you outside, I don't like going into prisons, they spoil my good mood.'

***

Inside the building, Carla couldn't find Alma anywhere. She searched for an information booth but all she could find was a helpful hunchbacked caretaker, who informed her that there were often delays in discharging prisoners.

Damn. Bruno had to go to his practical anatomy class, and she had the meeting between Ingrid and Jack. Looked like Alma would have to pick the children up on her own.

The caretaker told her to sit down on a wooden bench at the entrance and promised to check how things were progressing.

Carla felt like she was walking on hot coals. Why was it taking so long? Had Grieser found something out and was now punishing Alma for it? She tried to distract herself by taking out her notebook and scribbling in it. After a few minutes, she got lost in her drawing. She drew a room full of Lego bricks and little tin soldiers. Gregor's room.

'Fix and Foxi, what a blast!' said the caretaker cheerfully, tapping on her shoulder. She was so caught up in her drawing that it took her a moment to realise what he was on about. She snapped the notebook shut and put it back in her bag.

'The lady's lawyer hadn't shown up, so we made a few phone calls, but she'll be coming now,' he said, pointing towards the back, where they could hear the sound of doors opening and keyrings rattling.

Soon Alma was shuffling towards her, accompanied by the female guard. Her clothes were dirty, her hair matted, but in her hand she held the elegant Uli Richter bag, looking for all the world like a beggar who'd just been caught stealing.

When she saw Carla, she bucked herself up and hurried towards her. She stopped right in front of her and looked at her suspiciously.

'What did you do? I was told that I can go and that charges will be dropped. Stratmann didn't even show up. Did you...' her voice dropped to a whisper '... reveal Mathilda's secret?'

'Of course not.' *Merely destroyed my integrity*, thought Carla, but it didn't sound so bad now. 'Your daughter is innocent.'

Alma gave a sigh of relief, her blue eyes filling up with tears. She gave Carla a hug. Carla could feel her body trembling. She felt much better all of a sudden about everything she and Wallie had done to move this case along.

'It'll be all right,' said Carla and hoped that Alma would indeed recover.

'Thank you.' Alma squeezed her even tighter. 'I know I don't exactly smell like a bouquet right now, but I had to hug you. How can I ever thank you?'

'By paying my fee,' Carla smiled. As a widow, Alma now had sufficient money.

Alma let go. 'Of course I will. And now tell me how you managed to get me out of here?'

'Your brother Klaus made a statement in a moment of clarity, explaining that Alexander had a fight with him while they were both drunk and that he fell down that clever little architect's staircase in your house.'

'And they believe him?' Alma's eyebrows were raised. 'Of course, because he's a man!'

'I think it's rather because he didn't have such an obvious reason as you. He doesn't inherit anything.' This was something of lie, since Alexander had defrauded him so much that revenge could have been a motive.

'Everyone's convinced he's telling the truth, and it fits with what other witnesses have said. Your husband was already dead when Mathilda got home. She really doesn't have anything to do with it.'

Alma stood taller. 'My goodness, I should've believed her!'

'You just wanted to protect her.'

'And made everything worse!' Alma obviously wanted to be contradicted, but Carla didn't quite feel able to do that.

'Well, you're out now and can go home with your children. I actually was planning to pass by and pick up the children and take you all back to Dahlem, but we're running out of time. We can take you home though.'

'It's better this way. I don't want the children to see me in this state. I want to be freshly washed and perfectly dressed when I pick them up, so that they can see their world is now fine again.'

Carla doubted that the world could be fine again with a mere change of clothes, but at least it was a start.

41

Jack rang the doorbell at 17:00 on the dot. Carla invited the tall, broad-shouldered man in. The impressive uniform fitted his muscular body like a glove. He gave a brief nod and smartly saluted with his hand to his forehead.

Her office suddenly felt too small, filled as it was with male energy and high spirits. He looked around and seemed surprised that there was no one else present. 'So where is your boss?'

His baritone voice vibrated through the entire office. It reminded Carla of Dean Martin, which made her almost forgive his question. She smiled as she told him that he was looking at the boss of Nightingale & Co.

Jack stopped short, his grey eyes turned bluer as they opened wide. 'So sorry,' his face clouded over, 'This war produced so many widows.'

What did he mean by that? It was true Mother considered her an old maid, but surely he must see that she was too young to be a war widow.

She offered him coffee and cigarettes, which he refused with a friendly demeanour. He didn't smoke, but he wouldn't mind a herbal tea, if it weren't too much of a bother. He really didn't look like a health freak. Carla was surprised, but invited him to sit down, and went to the kitchen, hoping she still had some mint tea somewhere.

She was grateful for this brief moment to collect her

thoughts. Ingrid had described him as attractive, but she hadn't mentioned that he was such an exciting mix of Johnny Weissmuller and Burt Lancaster. Hard to believe that this man was unmarried, or that he didn't have a girlfriend in every port.

She brought him his tea, which he received with a German *Danke* as gratefully as if she'd just handed him a Chateau Margaux 1928. He inhaled the steam and then asked why he'd been asked to come here. Was it a secret mission? Something to do with the Wall? Were they going to set up Bobbers around it and use them as booby-traps?

Carla shuddered. Was that what the army had in mind? Sally would not want him to divulge anything, so she gave up on her plan to gradually introduce to the subject. Instead, she showed him the picture of Ingrid with her Marilyn Monroe wig at the prize award and waited for him to react. Would he merely stare, puzzled, because he'd already charmed dozens of other Fräuleins in the meantime?

Just as Carla was pondering the best way to mention Ingrid, she was greeted by a storm. A storm of enthusiasm.

Jack kissed the photo. Really? A man kissing a photo?

Then he called out, 'Praise the Lord!' He jumped up, ran around the desk, prised Carla out of her chair and hugged her enthusiastically, wrapping her in a cloud of woody aftershave and freshly starched shirt, before she could react in any way. Jack couldn't be contained, everything came tumbling out so fast that Carla wasn't quite sure if she understood it all. This wonderful, unique woman was the woman of his dreams, the woman that God had planned for him. A miracle! That was exactly what Billy Graham had told him so often, 'If you entrust your soul to God, you're invited to take part in all the great miracles He has in store for you!'

Billy Graham, at least she caught that name correctly. She knew exactly to whom he was referring: the so-called Elvis Presley of evangelism. She clearly remembered a fight her parents had had about him. Soon after her fifteenth birthday, Father had been assigned to be Graham's personal bodyguard. He was appearing in the sold-out Olympic Stadium in Berlin and the local police couldn't or wouldn't find sufficient personnel to ensure his safety. Mother found this distasteful, as if Father was protecting a Mafia boss. But he'd told Carla that Ida's father and grandfather had started their business at the turn of the century with private security and personal protection. That was how the private detective business had begun in Berlin. Grandfather Nachtigall had earned his money primarily by being the bodyguard to the film stars in Babelsberg Studios. He loved to tell stories of that time, especially when he'd accompanied Josephine Baker through night-time Berlin. That was when he'd decided to anglicise the name of the agency, make it sound more appealing to foreigners.

Jack had finally fallen silent. He looked at Ingrid's picture with reverence.

Billy Graham. So that was what Sally had hidden from her. The reason why Jack hadn't been too pushy with Ingrid at the jolly folk festival. Billy Graham was an arch-conservative minister, sex before marriage was frowned upon, the family was holy and abortion was a deadly sin. How would Jack react when he heard about Ingrid's job? Her lies? She looked at Jack, who was pacing up and down in front of her desk, looking even hotter in his excitement. It was painful for him to slow down and speak clearly, but you could see how important it was to him that she should understand his position.

After the folk festival, he'd tried searching for Niki, but had been unable to find her. There was no Niki Müller in Otto Street. Her personal details must have been incorrect in the registration form for the competition. And where in Berlin should he start searching for her? At first he thought it was a sign that God didn't want them to get closer. But then he prayed and realised that it was wrong, that God was merely testing him. It was his holy duty to be patient and wait. He'd been praying every day that God would show him the way to that wonderful woman and now his prayers had been answered.

Only because Ingrid had moved heaven and earth to find him, and paid for the privilege, instead of praying.

The doorbell rang. Ingrid was too early.

Carla excused herself, hoping to intercept Ingrid outside in the hallway and warn her of what would await her in the office.

'Has he come?' Ingrid whispered, her face rather pale under her perfect make-up. The off-the-shoulder blue dress with white polka dots, a tight corset and wide skirt, accentuated her slender figure, looking both seductive and refined. Only a necklace with a cross could have made her even more perfect for Jack.

'Yes, he's here,' Carla tried to reassure her. 'You look wonderful!'

'Have you told him everything?'

'Not yet.'

'I'm scared,' Ingrid whispered, holding on to Carla's hand as if it were a lifeline. 'Do you think he'll forgive me for lying to him?'

'He's very Christian, at any rate,' Carla said. Ingrid's hand was cold and damp. 'We should go inside, he's very eager to see you. Just talk freely.' She nodded at Ingrid to encourage her and they went in together.

Jack's eyes fell on Ingrid, who stood there stiffly, almost ready to fall over. Carla held her breath.

'Jack,' Ingrid whispered, 'I'm so sorry.'

For a split second, he looked annoyed, then stared at her in disbelief, and ran to her, pressed her to his chest and twirled her round. Yes, she looked a bit different, but it was her, his Niki! Hallelujah, the woman that God had meant for him!

After her initial surprise, Ingrid relaxed and started smiling. It was clear that he didn't care about her hair colour, that he thought the false address had been a mistake and that their reunion was part of God's plan.

He also understood that her real name was Ingrid but she preferred to be called Niki. After all, he preferred to be called Bobbs rather than Jack. He breathed a sigh of relief when he heard that she wasn't an air stewardess, after all it was a dangerous and slightly disreputable job. It must have been the language barrier leading to this misunderstanding.

Ingrid sat down to explain what her real job was. She cleared her throat and told him that she was a pharmaceutical representative. Before she could finish her sentence, he interrupted saying that was yet another sign of God's endless bounty. He congratulated her on a meaningful job, ensuring that people didn't suffer pain, by providing aspirin and the like.

Carla was wondering whether she should intervene, but Ingrid's pleading looks kept her silent. After all, it was Ingrid paying her fees, not Jack.

Jack didn't seem to notice the looks passing between them, he was too busy thanking God that his Niki would be so good at looking after her children, because she'd be so familiar with all the medicines. His wife would never have to work again, and of course he'd leave the army and open up a motorcycle repair shop in Atlanta. He was delighted to hear how much her English had improved.

Ingrid was beaming as much as Jack by now.

He had just one question, an important question which he should've asked earlier. Ingrid exchanged a nervous look with Carla.

Jack took Ingrid's hand and looked in her eyes.

'Do you believe in the Bible?'

While Ingrid hesitated, surprised, he continued, 'Do you believe we humans are born in sin?'

Ingrid was about to reply, but he continued, ever more insistent. 'Do you think that our only chance of redemption is to believe in the resurrection of Christ our Lord? Do you believe that Heaven has streets paved with gold and pearls and trees that bear a different fruit every month? And that the flames of Hell are more fearsome by far than anything we can imagine?'

Carla held her breath. How would the Ingrid she'd come to know react to all that?

'Yes,' said Ingrid with a dazzling smile, 'I believe in all that.'

'Hallelujah!' Jack made a happy clucking sound and kissed her hand.

'I think we'll go out for a drink,' Ingrid said to Carla, without looking her in the eyes. 'Thank you, Miss Koslowsky, for everything. Please send me your final bill.'

Jack clicked his heels together, bowed in Carla's direction and held his arm out for Ingrid. They walked down the staircase together. A beautiful couple.

Carla closed the door behind them and sighed. Could a marriage be successful if you had to give up and deny your entire life before the time you met? Or would this dream evaporate, because it was nothing but a hormonal mirage?

'Nobody's perfect,' as Billy Wilder had said to her. Ingrid was trying to appear to be perfect for her Jack, was giving up her entire life for him, submitting to his rules and beliefs, although she'd wanted to be free. She might get called Niki by him, but she'd certainly not lead the life of an activist artist.

To her surprise, Carla found herself wondering what Wallie would think of the Jack and Ingrid story.

42

An hour later she was telling Sally how the meeting had gone and had sent off the invoice for Ingrid's case. She then picked up the phone to thank Lulu, because without her help the Grieser situation wouldn't have been resolved. But no one was answering. Maybe she'd got a part in a film after all? Just when she was ready to hang up, someone knocked at the door.

It must be Katrin. She opened the door and greeted her. No reply.

Katrin slunk in silently, her head bowed, sat down in one of the rattan chairs and started sucking one of her plaits. Bathsheba really seemed like the wrong name for such a girl!

'Would you like to drink something or have a cookie?' she asked, concerned that the girl seemed so listless. 'What's up with you?'

'Nothing.'

'To what do I owe this honour?'

Silence.

'Come on, dear.'

'You didn't go for an ice cream with us!' Katrin burst out. 'You didn't get the Abominables to go for a spin with the Bobber. They beat me up about that and now that blonde is your new friend. You're *soo* silly!' Katrin's shoulders were sagging as if the whole weight of the world was upon them.

Carla jumped up and walked around the desk, crouching in front of the seated girl and holding her hand. 'You're right, I've been very silly. I should've kept my promises. We'll take care of things right now.' She called Bruno. He'd just come back from his anatomy class and promised that tomorrow evening, after his lecture, he'd take the boys for a spin. Carla reminded him that they were supposed to be picking Wallie up from the hospital the next morning. When Bruno asked her if she was feeling better, she hinted that she was not on her own and hung up.

Katrin didn't seem impressed. 'We'll see if he shows up, maybe he'll send a stand-in with a wooden scooter.'

'I'm really sorry I stood you up, but it was something important. I thought it would be better for Wallie to take you for an ice cream than not to have one at all.'

'Am I as bad as the Abominables?'

'Of course not. But Wallie isn't that bad either, is she?'

'Hmm.'

'I'm so sorry.'

No reaction.

'Honestly.' Carla was starting to get tired of this.

'Want to know what I found out about the blonde?'

'The blonde is lying in a hospital now, because she stopped a man from jumping off the roof.' *And helped me too*, Carla added to herself. 'And whoever saves one life, saves the whole world.'

'So just because she's a heroine now, you don't want to know, do you?'

'No, I do.'

'Well, she went to a meeting.'

'What meeting?'

'The one organised by Mum's new friend, Jehovah's Witnesses.' Katrin rolled her eyes at Carla's slow-wittedness.

'Is that not allowed?'

'No, but it's strange, who goes there of their own free

will? And sometimes she makes signs in chalk on one of the phone booths. Always the same one, by the way.'

'Aha.'

'And in Viktoria Luisa Square, she sat on a park bench, took pictures of the fountain and then left a newspaper there with a small package inside. I thought she'd forgotten it, but someone came and picked it up.'

'Let me guess: that someone wore a hat and trench coat. Sounds like you've been watching too many mediocre spy films.'

Katrin groaned. 'I was sure you wouldn't believe me.'

'Are you sure that Wallie didn't notice you following her? Maybe she wanted to play a trick on you. She always spotted you before.'

'Not this time. I've become an ace at shadowing now.'

'Do you know what was in this small package?'

'It was wrapped up in sandwich paper. Not big, maybe the size of a pack of aspirin tablets.'

'Thank you, that's all very interesting, I'll have to think about it. Would you like to go for an ice cream with me?'

'Nope.'

'So it's not just about me, something's wrong...'

'You just think I'm talking rubbish.'

'No, I don't. But we don't know why Wallie is behaving like this and we shouldn't jump to conclusions.'

'Then what about the fact that she was there where your boyfriend, the one with the Bobber, lives?'

'Bruno? He's not my boyfriend,' said Carla hastily, but the butterflies in her tummy said otherwise. She couldn't help but think of his strong hands with the golden hairs as they rested on the gear shift. She knew so little about Bruno. He lived somewhere near Fehrbelliner Square. Had Katrin really followed Wallie all the way there? And had Wallie gone to visit him? After all, there must be plenty of people living there.

'Did she meet up with him?'

'Don't know. But she gave his caretaker some money, which she didn't need to, he was mighty happy to help her. Just like the Abominables – after an ice cream with her, they were ready to marry her.' She rolled her eyes again. 'They're so stupid. I tell you, that Wallie of yours is a bad sort!'

Katrin waited for a while, but Carla didn't react, so she stood up and seemed even more disappointed.

'I for one would love a banana split with a lot of chocolate sprinkles, but it's no fun on my own, so do come with me,' Carla begged her.

Katrin shrugged.

'Are you just my clever assistant detective, or are we also friends? What else is up?'

'Told you. Mum has a new boyfriend.' Katrin seemed to shrink. 'He wants her to return to the community, but they left it long before Dad's death.'

'And you don't want to go back there.'

'Nope.'

'Do you like him?'

'He likes his wine best, far better than he likes me or the Abominables.'

'Is he strict?'

She stood up. 'I think I'd like an ice cream after all.'

Carla nodded, then explained that she'd try to call Lulu first, but again no answer.

They walked around for a good half-hour in the warm summer evening on their way to Henriette Square at the Ice-Henning, which was open until ten in the evening. Katrin was silent all the way there.

Carla saw Ingrid and Jack from a distance, sitting at one of the tables, holding hands, deep in conversation. Like an advert for a love story.

'D'ya think all Communists are eternally damned?' Katrin asked, after they'd sat down and ordered.

Carla stared at her in astonishment. What was going on

today with all this talk of damnation and sin? Full moon had come and gone, as far as she knew.

'Why would you think that?'

'Why don't grown-ups ever answer a question?'

'Everyone is free to think what they want, no one is damned for it.'

'Mum's new man is from the East. He escaped via the sewers because of the Wall going up. Mum thinks he's a hero, but all he does is berate her for leaving the Witnesses and that we'll all be damned if she doesn't return.' Katrin poked holes listlessly in her banana split, without eating.

'He says that the Communists in the East are devils, because the Witnesses are even more persecuted under them than they were under the Nazis. If that's true, then I should believe him when he says that anyone who's not a Witness is damned for eternity, and I really shouldn't be talking to damned people like you.' She stuck her fork in the banana as if it were to blame for everything. 'And we need to go twice a week after school to Bible classes. So much for being your assistant.'

I can't stand this man either, thought Carla. 'Don't worry, we'll find a way.'

'So do you think you're damned for eternity?'

'No,' she began, trying to push away the image of the green tile embedded in Mother's foot.

'No,' she repeated, more firmly, 'I'm not damned, that's utter nonsense. But I'll get very bad-tempered if you don't eat up your damn ice cream.'

Katrin stared at her in astonishment. Carla had never cursed in her life in front of Katrin. She started giggling, piled up ice cream on her spoon and choked when swallowing it, which made her laugh all the more. Finally, she was starting to behave more like a ten-year-old.

Carla repeated the word damn and winked at Katrin. On the one hand, she was relieved to see her more cheerful, but she didn't feel entirely satisfied. How on earth could she keep her promise to help Katrin? And how was she to interpret what Katrin had told her about Wallie?

43

Carla woke up early the next morning to prepare the guestroom for Wallie, because it was currently used as a storeroom. To her surprise, she discovered that her mother had already cleared it and could barely wait for 'poor, poor Wallie' to move into their apartment. She'd put out the best linen bedsheets, the ones with an embroidered nightingale, and she'd covered Father's boxes with several tablecloths. The boxes had been placed along the wall since his death, like a cardboard screen, because nobody could bear to throw them away.

At breakfast Mother reminded her to buy some painkillers from the pharmacy, because she knew what pain meant, unlike her clueless daughter. Then she set off to bake a cake, humming cheerfully.

Humming!

It was the famous Nachtigall walnut cake, which she hadn't made since Father's death. When Carla asked where she'd got all the ingredients from, Mother explained that Frau Pallutzke had gone shopping for her, she always asked her what she needed and was very helpful.

The phone interrupted the rather indignant retort that Carla was about to make.

It was Alma, who burst forth breathlessly as if the dam had broken. She wanted to invite Carla and Wallie for coffee, to thank them properly. Besides, Mathilda had a little surprise for them. Then Alma hesitated a little, sounding more like she had before her release. Now they were getting to the actual crux of the matter.

There was a reporter from *Constanze*, who wanted to write a story about Alma, a 'home story', she repeated, probably so that Carla could keep up. Carla chuckled inwardly, because she knew from Muki that this was the series about famous people in their homes, and that it was one of those borrowed words that an English speaker would never use. Just like 'old-timer' didn't mean a vintage car in English, but an older person or a veteran.

She tried to focus once more on what Alma was telling her. She was admitting that she was nervous, but her idea was to praise Nightingale & Co. for securing her release. Surely a bit of advertising wouldn't hurt? The reporter seemed delighted and wanted to take pictures of them all. She hoped Carla wouldn't mind, after all, *Constanze* had more readers than all the other women's magazines combined.

Mother's walnut cake would have to wait a while. Carla promised Alma she'd be there. She'd have to ask Wallie, of course, whose health was still fragile.

She said goodbye to Alma, told Mother that she didn't know when she'd be back, and made her way to the bus stop. Bruno had wanted to help, but he had to slog away during the day, so that he'd be free to take the Bobber out in the evening. She was planning to take Wallie back from the hospital in a taxi.

When she arrived at the hospital, Wallie was already waiting in the foyer. She seemed much smaller and very pale, with dark rings under her eyes. Or maybe it was because she'd never seen Wallie without make-up before. She'd worn lipstick even when she'd dressed up as a middle-aged psychologist.

'Are you sure you're well enough?'

'Yep, let's get out of here!' Wallie nodded. 'But first we have to talk about Klaus.'

'Why?' Her pulse started racing. Would this be haunting her until the end of days? She had to learn how to deal with it.

'They're sending him to a sanatorium because he can't live in his apartment with his broken tibia.'

'The man wanted to die, so I'm sure a stay in a sanatorium won't hurt him.'

Wallie looked surprised. 'You're not usually so cold-hearted. But since I saved his life, I feel somehow responsible for his wellbeing. Couldn't we ask Alma to put him up for a few days? After all, his witness statement is what secured her release.'

'That would be irresponsible, he's a drug addict and Alma has to look after her children.'

Wallie grabbed hold of Carla's shoulder and turned her to face her. 'Shouldn't we look after Klaus, before he gets any stupid ideas?'

She might be right about that, but how would that work? 'I thought he hated his sister, doesn't he?'

'I spoke to him and I think that if Alma were to come here and offer to host him, it might work. She owes you that much, after all, you did your best to free her.'

'Fine, then let's go to her right now.' Carla forced herself to smile.

Wallie raised her eyebrows. 'I thought I'd have to spend ages convincing you.'

'Alma invited us to celebrate with her and the children. A reporter will be there, and that might be a good occasion for Alma to prove what a noble creature she is.'

'So now that she's out of jail, she's playing the merry widow?'

'Why not? She has to recover her reputation, and appear in public as the martyr, the victim of an incompetent justice system, for the children's sake as well as her own. And Nightingale & Co. could do with a little publicity. We need new clients.'

They soon reached the villa in Dahlem.

Alma opened the door. What a transformation for the press. The copper green sheath dress paired with a long pearl necklace provided a flattering contrast to the immaculately coiffed hair. She might have been receiving the President and the Order of Merit in that outfit.

'So pleased you could come.' Alma sounded slightly out of breath, but hugged Carla and looked at Wallie's bandaged shoulder with concern. 'I'm so sorry that this happened. My brother's a complete madman. Please do come in.'

Alma led them through the spotlessly tidy living room out onto the terrace, where she'd set a table fit for an English tea party. Gold-rimmed white porcelain, cloth napkins in silver napkin rings, cream cakes, cucumber sandwiches, scones and marmalade.

'Please sit down, what would you like to drink?' she asked.

'Champagne,' Wallie gurgled as she sank down into the trestle chair with a sigh.

'I do have some, but I didn't know if the reporter might misunderstand that. It might be too much of a celebration for a widow?' Alma looked at them both.

Wallie burst out laughing. 'And isn't it the best thing that happened to you?' Alma exchanged a look with Carla, but then she started giggling, and by the time they sat down at the coffee table, they were all laughing. When Wallie moaned softly and put a hand to her shoulder, the laughter finally stopped and they all became serious once more.

'I'm sorry, I shouldn't have...' said Alma, tidying away a lock of hair behind her ear. 'That was inappropriate.'

'Is this going to be a thing like "At home with the charming Kennedys"?' Wallie asked, waving at the extravagant table. She bagged herself a cream cake and polished it off in just two bites. 'Heavenly!' she said with her mouth full.

'Sort of. Alexander of course was no politician and I'm no Jackie. And of course she isn't a widow.' Alma smiled, all cool Irish faerie queen once more.

'But I think she too has problematic siblings. Can we talk about Klaus?' asked Wallie.

'Do we have to?' Alma looked questioningly at Carla, who nodded.

'Well, you want to play happy families with the reporter, don't you?'

'What do you mean?' Alma's smile died. She turned helplessly towards Carla. 'You don't want to tell them what Alexander did to Mathilda, do you?'

'Of course not,' said Carla.

'Which reminds me... here, let me give you this before the reporter arrives.' She went into the living room and came back quickly, with a big sheet of paper in each hand.

'Mathilda drew these for you, as a surprise.' She handed them the drawings. 'They're pretty, aren't they? I'll be right back, I'll bring the coffees.'

Wallie laughed as she showed Carla Mathilda's drawing. 'It looks amusing, but I haven't got a clue what it's supposed to be?'

Carla looked at Wallie's picture. It showed the face of a woman with short hair, who did indeed resemble Wallie, but the woman had giant donkey's ears. Carla thought about it for a moment. 'I think that's supposed to be you after eating the magic figs from Muck, and your ears start growing when you lie.'

'Amazing chimerization...' said Wallie, smiling. Carla still didn't know if that was a real word used in paediatrics. But before she could ask, Wallie pointed at the picture in Carla's hands.

'Well, I'll be damned, what is that?' Wallie studied the drawing carefully. The paper was filled with straight lines, colourful and close together, not drawn with a ruler but free-handed, which made the lines seem to vibrate. 'Looks like a living rug!' said Wallie, while Carla was strangely moved by Mathilda's selection of colours. Alternate flaming colours, red, pink, green, purple, yellow and orange. There were no dark colours there at all.

Alma brought the coffee pot, wrapped in a thick tea cosy, and laid it on the coffee table. She contemplated her arrangement with a satisfied sigh, then turned to Carla and Wallie, who were still holding their pictures.

'Mathilda explained to me that the picture with the ears was Auntie Wallie as the Princess of Liars. And the other was Auntie Carla's secret heart, but I don't know what that means.'

The doorbell rang. 'That must be the reporter. Carla, could you bring the children? They're somewhere in the garden.' Alma paused. 'I can rely on you?'

'Absolutely,' said Carla, standing up and going to the back of the garden where the swing and sandbox were. But there was no one there. She went round the back of the house to the other side.

'Mathilda? Gregor?'

'Auntie Carla! We're here!' Mathilda was sitting with her brother on the outer staircase leading up to Alexander's studio. She jumped up and waved so energetically that her yellow linen dress rippled in the sun. Carla's eyes paused for a while on the little hand fluttering back and forth like a humming-bird.

The handprint on the flokati rug. Carla blinked rapidly, to banish the thought. It was all over. She waved back and wondered what Gregor found so fascinating that he didn't even bother to turn his head to look at her, although he was standing at the top of the staircase and had a better view than Mathilda.

The nearer she came and the longer she looked at them, the more she felt a troubling sensation in her chest.

'What are you doing there?'

She reached the staircase, went up a few steps and sat

next to Mathilda.

'We're playing Chase the Monster.' Mathilda nodded at her brother. 'Go!'

Gregor dropped a big blue marble from the top, it bounced down step by step and stopped just three steps above Mathilda.

Carla felt dizzy. Chase the Monster... Suddenly, it all made sense. Alexander had slipped on the stairs. The thing that had fallen from the stairs when she went to fetch Alma's clothes. The glass of marbles, half-full. The boy who liked to prank his father.

They'd never asked about that.

Not pranks, but self-defence.

Gregor came down the stairs, picked up the blue marble and put it together with the others in the net. In his confirmation suit with a white shirt and black bow-tie, he looked like a miniature version of his father, despite the crooked fringe and arm in a plaster cast.

'It works best with the smaller ones.' He went up to Mathilda. 'Like David and Goliath,' he explained and put a protective arm around his sister.

He smiled at Carla, full of pride. 'And David wins.' He gave Mathilda a boisterous hug, as if to confirm it. When she started giggling, he put his finger over his lips and whispered in her ear, so loudly that Carla could hear it too: 'Our secret for ever and ever!'

'For ever and ever,' Mathilda repeated earnestly. 'Our secret.'

Gregor met Carla's gaze and kept his steady. Strong, collected. She had the sensation that a rug was being pulled from under her feet.

He handed Carla the net full of marbles. 'This is for you!'